P

The Deadly Sins Series

S.L Wisdom and S.J Noble

Copyright Statement

Copyright © 2024 by Sophie Louise Salter (aka S.L Wisdom) and Sarah-Jayne Waldron (aka S.J Noble). All rights reserved.

The right of Sophie Louise Salter and Sarah-Jayne Waldron to be identified as the Authors of the Work has been asserted by them in accordance with The Copyright, Design and Patents Act 1988.

This book or any portion thereof may not be reproduced or used in any form or by any electronic or mechanical means, including information storage and retrieval systems, nor be otherwise circulated in any form of binding or cover other than that in which is it published and without a similar condition being imposed on the subsequent purchaser, without the express written permission of both authors, except for the use of brief quotations in a book review

This is a work of fiction. The events described in this book are fictitious; any similarities to actual events and persons, dead or alive, are entirely coincidental.

Paperback ISBN: 9798325774188
eBook ASIN: B0CZS59GGS

Cover design by Francessca Wingfield
Editing by Ria Hockey at Moon and Bloom Editing

To every woman who ever let her pride get in the way of what she wanted. It'll be ok girl. There's still time to let the hot tattooed guy who wants to kill you, fuck you with his knife on the forest floor.

Trigger Warnings

Pride is the first book in The Deadly Sins series. Please be aware that this book may touch on subjects that the reader might find uncomfortable. Although this story is part of a series, it can be read as a standalone. However, it would be beneficial for the entire series to be read in order, due to character stories intertwining.

This is a slow burn, dark romance with explicit scenes and some graphic depictions that some may struggle reading. Please continue at your own discretion.

Triggers include but are not limited to:

Child trafficking, child slavery, child abuse and the death of children on and off page, murder, torture, knife play, blood play, death, forced proximity, kidnapping, praise kink, primal play, rough sex including choking, spitting and a touch of breath play.

This book is intended for readers 18+.

Enjoy.

111

Intuition

Trust your gut, Listen to your heart.

Pride

We are rarely proud when we are alone.

The Sinclair Legacy

Alexander and George Sinclair, the sole survivors of a traumatic fire that engulfed their family home late one evening in July of 1970.

It was a tragedy that headlined every paper from England to America and left the two small orphan boys with nobody but each other. But the question that plagued the entire nation…Who was to blame?

Born to a family of wealth and power, the two brothers rose from the wreckage of their former lives and forged themselves a new story based on revenge. They set out wholly to avenge the deaths of their family, but in the throes of life, they too, in turn, ended up with more enemies than they could deal with themselves. And so, the youngest brother worked under the guise of a legitimate law firm and the oldest brother built their real empire in the shadows. A team of trained assassins; The Sinclair Legacy was born, and a whole new meaning was given to the word family.

Their world soon became dark, depraved and dangerous, but they refused to back down from their assignments. Honing their skills to every aspect of becoming a merciless killing machine. Word rapidly spread through the city of their expertise, their specific skill set caught the attention of the world's underground and clients were happy to pay handsomely in return for a silent outcome where they would in no way be associated.

With the eldest of the brothers taking on new jobs that included security, intelligence, murder and even the occasional kidnapping, it was left to the youngest to ensure their work went undetected, perfectly camouflaged in order to corrupt those who had sinned and needed to be brought to justice. Their desire to execute each job to their own high standards became of the utmost importance. There was no room for failure.

As the brothers grew older, their need for an heir became blinding and so they focused their abilities on finding one of their own, an orphan who needed a guiding hand to navigate through life. A child to mould into the business, to become a legacy.

With any empire, there is an expectation that an heir or two would finally take over the business when the brothers were no longer able. However, in this case, the Sinclair Empire grew by seven.

Seven children, all rescued from a life they didn't deserve to be left in, and each given a new life in exchange for an execution of their talents.

The eldest Sinclair brother was no fool when it came to choosing the heirs of their legacy. He travelled far and wide to find those who would be the greatest asset to his business. Each one provided a talent that made up a ruthless team of soldiers. They rose from their own depictions of hell and with the brothers' guidance, were soon ready to rain down their own hell, burning a trail of retribution everywhere they went.

The seven children soon became a loud whisper amongst the underground and were given their very own name to be feared. The Deadly Sins. Another masterpiece of Sinclair production.

However, scars had been burnt into the very fibres of these children, from years of hatred and anger that were not so easily healed, igniting them in the very sins they represent. And so, each has their story to tell, their own revenge and justice to seek, and their own paths to follow.

As the lives of children of the Sinclair Legacy begin to unfold, the need for survival and success brings each to a crisis that none of them can avoid.

Will they eventually learn to overcome their sins or will they become them? Using them as the very weapons they have become. Only one thing is for certain, and whether they are ready or not, their lives are about to change and there's nothing they can do to stop it.

PROLOGUE
17 YEARS EARLIER
AGED 10

Adanna

Ding! Ding! Ding!

Like clockwork, the sound of the morning bell echoes throughout the room, painfully wrenching me from the darkest depths of slumber, the only real escape I have in this place. I lie still for a moment, squeezing my eyes tightly shut, wishing that when I open them again, I'd no longer be here in the pits of this hell. But like every other morning since I arrived here, I have no such luck. I find myself staring up at the offensively beige ceiling, at the same spot of peeling paintwork that I always stare at when I wake. I rub my eyes to clear the sleep from my vision and inhale deeply, engulfing my nostrils with the overwhelming smell of damp, causing my stomach to roll. I swear if I'd have eaten anything recently, I'd throw up. After months of being held captive in this place you would think I would be used to the stench, but still it suffocates me.

The beds, if you can call them beds, are nothing more than grubby thin mattresses on the cold stone floor. Each of them is covered with old brown stains that have long embedded into the thin fabric, making me wonder how long they've been here and what happened to the last child that slept upon them. Were they wishing for a better place every time they closed their eyes too?

There are four of us in this small windowless room and many others in the rest of the rooms that occupy the building. I am the youngest in our chamber at ten. Jane is twelve, Ivan is thirteen and the other boy who doesn't speak, looks to be around fifteen. He's taller than the rest of us with a noticeable shadow of stubble on his chin and sapphire eyes that mirror the bluest ocean waters. We know he's been here the longest out of the four of us, but he never answers our questions when we ask. He simply fixes us with straight lipped stares before turning away without a word. I've given up bothering to get any answers, but I do often find myself comforted by his presence which is strange, because in this place we are never safe.

Reluctantly, I pull myself from what little warmth my bed provides and grab my shirt and trousers, ignoring the worn out holes in the material as I pull them on quickly, trying to lessen the chill that creeps through to my bones. This place has no heating, or if it does, they don't waste it on us. Pulling my socks on and grabbing my boots, I tie them quickly as my hands begin to shake from the cold bite in the morning air. My fingers already feel stiff and numb from the bitter cold throughout the night so I rub them together, frantically trying to get the circulation to flow through them. My hands are the only useful thing I have here. I need them to work. I need them to survive.

    I glance around the room, the others are dressing too, and they all look as cold as I am. We all know to get ready quickly before the guards come in and beat us for making them wait. It's the first instruction we learnt here, it was quite literally beaten into us, along with the direct order not to ask questions about going home. I learnt that one the hard way.

    Like clockwork, the guards barge through the door within five minutes of the bells ringing, and order us into single-file as they escort us to the main hall. In an ideal situation, one where I wasn't taken from my family and being held hostage, forced to do a horrible Russian man's work, I would be amazed at the sheer size of the room we're marched to. Its floor to ceiling windows span the length of one wall giving an extensive view to the outside world, a world we're now forbidden from entering. The deep walnut floors are harsh and heavy against the stark white snow that covers as far as the eye can see, blanketing the ground outside in the most beautiful way. Further in, opposite the wall of glass, there's a metal staircase leading to a large balcony that overlooks the entirety of the room, and from there is another smaller room. That is the boss man's office. He often comes out and watches, smirking at us as we work. I hate it, the way his eyes roam over us all, it's like a snake slithering over my skin as his eyes burn into us from above.

We all move silently to our assigned spaces along the length of the table on the right hand side of the hall. There are a further two tables that match ours, one in the middle and one on the left hand side. All three of them are large and ominous in their presence, I can barely reach the middle of the table being so small. As we wait, I catch a glimpse of the boss man on the higher level, slinking back into his office before my attention is caught by the sound of footfall coming towards us. The children from the adjoining rooms are being brought in to fill up the spaces on other tables. I pretend not to notice how low on numbers we seem at the moment, forcing myself to stare directly into a knot fused into the grain of the wooden table. Once they are all positioned, we are given boxes of arsenal to put together. Endless, overflowing boxes. It's only once we have built thirty pieces of ammunition each, that we are allowed to have food and water. The work is tedious and repetitive, but I've become one of the quickest at the mundane task. The only one in the room to beat me is the boy who refuses to speak, he smirks at me everytime he finishes ahead of me. I suppose he has to find some enjoyment in it, even if I can't.

"Listen up," a loud voice booms through the air. The thick Russian accent sends an overwhelming feeling of dread straight through to me as heavy footsteps descend the iron staircase. This is the man who brought me here, the man who runs this place. He once told me that I was sold to him when my parents could no longer keep up with their debt repayments. I refused to believe him, but the last time I argued, I ended up with a black eye. Lesson learnt: keep my mouth shut. My eyes snap to him as he speaks, though I'm careful not to make direct eye contact as he slowly makes his way to the door. I stare after him, hatefully wishing every awful thing that could ever happen to a person would befall this man. He's of medium height, with what my mother would have called, a drinker's belly, with dark hair and a thick dark shadow of stubble covering his chin and neck. He looks like any regular man, until you come face to face with him. His eyes hold an emptiness that makes my stomach curl every time I've had the misfortune of looking into them. They're soulless, pitchblack and are the very thing that fill my nightmares as I sleep. A voice I don't recognise filters through the room and I notice the boss man is no longer alone, he has another man with him, a stranger. It's odd, the new man doesn't fit in here at all. He looks the complete opposite to the boss man, with light sandy brown hair and light coloured eyes, they look kind even, and he's noticeably taller than our captor with less weight piled around his middle. The strange man almost looks friendly, but I've learnt that looks can be deceiving.

    A loud clap cracks through the room, summoning our attention. "We have a visitor today, he is interested in our stock. I expect you all to show him the quality and care that we put into each piece of ammunition." Nobody dares speak a word. He claps his hands again, ordering us back to work. "As you were, slaves." Slaves. Yes, that's exactly what we are. I'm sure some slaves have it worse than us. But still, this existence isn't one I would have ever imagined for myself. I'm stuck in a whirlwind of memories today and it isn't until my eyes meet those of the man with light hair and kind features, that I realise I haven't started working again. The stranger smiles at me and my stomach knots with fear that I have been caught. I immediately cast my eyes down and focus on the task at hand. He's friends with the devil, he is not a good man, I repeat to myself. Our captor leads the new man around the room and I look at Jane who is mindlessly connecting each piece of the gun she is working on together. She doesn't look up as they pass her. I force myself to pick up the pace, clicking together the weapons, just like I have been shown, and I continue until I feel a hand on my shoulder.

"You are very good at this, little one." A soft voice speaks from behind me. I know without looking that it's the fair-haired man. The hairs on my arms prickle as he speaks to me but I freeze, unsure how to respond for fear of punishment and I'm unable to will my fingers to keep on fitting the pieces of my gun together. I slowly lower the ammunition to the table, careful not to draw any unwanted attention.

"You don't have to be afraid," he assures me as I slowly turn my head towards him and look up into his eyes. I want to believe there's nothing but kindness there, but something sinister gnaws at my stomach warning me to be careful. He smiles, sensing my hesitation before he draws his shoulders back, standing tall and turning to follow the devil himself out of the room. I look around to see if the others noticed the interaction, the only person to be watching me is the boy who refuses to speak, he glares at me, his eyes narrowing before he looks down, continuing his task. He is too far ahead of me today. The visitor has distracted me.

As the morning draws on and we all eventually make up our equal amount of ammunition, we're given porridge. It's luke-warm, painfully bland and has the consistency of wallpaper paste but still, it eases away the hunger pains. As I force down another mouthful, the thick gloopy slop sticking to the roof of my mouth, I allow myself to think back to the interaction with the stranger today. I wonder if he'll come back and set us all free one day. I almost laugh at myself and my silly thoughts, I still have hope. Even if that hope is pointless.

The morning break ends quickly, some of the others haven't even finished their breakfast as the guards take their bowls from them, but they are faced with no dispute. We all know what happens when you break the rules here. I used to plan how I would escape this place until one day a boy named Byron tried his luck. He had a bullet straight through his head before he even made it to the doors at the end of the corridor. I screamed at the sound of the bullet piercing straight through his skull. I remember hands covering my mouth, hushing me as they held their palms firmly against my lips. I looked up, and my eyes clashed with shocking blue ones. I wonder if that's why he doesn't speak, if he had seen this happen many times before and learnt better from it. The memory of Byron lying there dead still churns my stomach. The way his blood pooled around his lifeless body etched itself into my eyelids for a long while after that day and even now, it still haunts me while I sleep. My eyes subconsciously hover to the spot where he was executed. I can still see a tinge of where the blood soaked the wooden floor. The guards carted him off like he was nothing. I suppose to them we are nothing. After that I don't even contemplate trying to leave anymore, I would rather eat porridge slop for the rest of my life than become a stain on the woodwork.

The rest of the day goes on as normal, continuous and boring as we build and build until we're escorted out of the ammunition hall to the food hall where we all gather for dinner.

In the line, waiting my turn to pick up my dinner tray, his voice cuts through the hall. I look up along with everybody else in the direction of the boss man who's stomping his way across the room. Oh no, he's angry.

"You!" he snarls, pointing his finger at me, narrowing his black eyes into slits. "Come with me, now."

No. No this isn't happening. I freeze as he closes the distance. My heart beating rapidly behind my rib cage causes my breath to catch in my throat. I can't move. I can't even breathe. He's going to kill me for what happened earlier, I just know it. I will my legs to move but they won't. They know I'm about to be led to my death.

As I war with myself whether to oblige or to run and try to give myself more time, I feel a strange yet familiar presence behind me that immediately ceases my inner turmoil. I glance up into those beautiful blue eyes. He squeezes my shoulders, encouraging me to move before leaning in and whispering so close to my ear that a trail of goosebumps spreads across my skin. "Go, find a way out of here."

    I gasp, suddenly caught off guard at finally hearing him speak, annoyed that I can feel my cheeks turning a hot crimson red as I blush under his striking gaze. I try, but fail to respond, only biting my bottom lip as I nod and my feet begin to move of their own accord in the direction of the man who has had me living in hell for as long as I can remember. Casting my eyes back one last time to the boy with bright eyes, I smile, hoping one day I'll see him again. He nods before the guards move him along.

    As I follow the boss man to a room I have never been to before, he stops me before we enter, grabbing onto my arm, crouching low and close to my face, spitting his words at me. "For some reason, the man I brought here earlier showed an interest in you. If you want to make it out of this room alive, I advise you to stay quiet and do as you are told. Do not embarrass me." He pushes the door open to reveal the fair-haired stranger standing in the centre of what looks like an old and long forgotten library. His face immediately relaxes as soon as he sees me and he smiles, his eyes softening around the edges. I look down, not understanding what is happening. Is this some sort of test? I don't know what I'm supposed to do. The hand on my arm tightens as the devil himself digs his nails into my bicep so tight I'm sure there'll be marks under my shirt. The vice-like grip causes me to wince as I attempt to pull free. I look around the room, my eyes are immediately drawn to a sparkling ring. My mind races, that ring, it's my mother's diamond ring. I thrash forward, finally freeing myself from his grip as I leap towards the desk. I get so close, my heart leaps into my throat before I'm suddenly forced backwards.

"Ahhh not so fast slave, that is not your property anymore. Mr. Sinclair and I have struck a bargain, haven't we Alexander?" the words fall from his mouth like a slithering snake.

"We have an agreement, Vladimir, the girl is mine and you get to keep running this little *business*." The stranger barks at my captor, Vladimir, that's his name. I snap my eyes to the stranger, confused by his words but he isn't looking at me, his stare is glued to Vladimir's tightening hold on my arm. In a split second the atmosphere changes and the stranger morphs into a completely different man. His features darken as he steps towards Vladimir, who only stares straight back at him, daring him to make his move. I hold my breath, waiting for what's to come. But it doesn't happen.

Vladimir releases his hold on me and pushes me forward. "Take her," he snaps as I stumble forward to the safety of this kind man who seems to have come to my rescue or worse, my end.

The stranger crouches in front of me and smiles at me as Vladimir leaves the room, slamming the door behind him. "Hello, little one. You might not believe me but I won't hurt you. My name is Alexander Sinclair and I'm here to take you away from this place," he explains. Before I can respond, I feel a sharp sting in my neck and the room instantly swims around me, blackness bleeding into my vision. I can feel my head becoming weightless and my eyelids grow heavy before I collapse into darkness, somewhere I am unusually familiar with. Only this time, my sleep isn't plagued with nightmares of black lifeless eyes, it's filled with dreams of hope.

That was the first time I met Alexander Sinclair, the person who rescued me from a fate worse than death. In the days that followed, he explained what would've happened if I'd stayed there. How I would have been sold like a cow at the cattle market or worse, slaughtered like one. Instead, he offered me a life of freedom. One that I intended to grab with both hands and be proud to call my own. That day I left my old life behind and I was reborn as Adanna Sinclair.

CHAPTER ONE
7 YEARS EARLIER
AGED 25

Nikolai

    The view of the busy street below calms the inner havoc that's expanding so viciously within my body that I have to stop my hands from shaking as I shove them into the pockets of my jeans. I'm not sure why I'm anxious, call it intuition or irrationality but something doesn't feel right. It hasn't felt right from the moment we set foot in this country. The air is different than it is back home in Russia, and the weather is too unpredictable. Even now, I watch as the sky turns black before my eyes, whereas moments ago the sun cast its heated gaze across the city, leaving obscure shadows scattered across the ground. Something is brewing, and I long to rid the taste of it from the back of my throat, but I daren't speak up and ask what business has made us travel so far. I know he'll tell me when it's necessary.

We've been in London for almost three days now, holed up in the Peninsula Suite of an overly priced and overly lavish hotel. The cream carpets and silk curtains are a stark difference to the thick dark furnishing of The Manor back home and it only makes me even more desperate to get back on home soil. The private terrace and 24-hour gym access have been my saving grace when I needed to clear my head. I'm not used to sitting around and waiting, I'm usually elbows deep in enemy blood, grinding bodies into the dirt and burning the flesh from their bones. This dormant state of waiting is nothing short of torture for me.

For the last ten years, I have learned to survive off of very little, to do what is expected of me and to keep my head down. I do what I do to avoid being on the other end of my own brutality. It's not what I had planned for my life, but those dreams were shattered the day I turned fifteen and my family was slaughtered right before my eyes. I can still feel the ghost of my mother's scolding blood as they sliced her carotid and the spray covered my face. I used to shy from the memory, until I learned to let it fuel the darkness that was born the day I wished I'd died alongside them.

A low buzz probes my memories, clearing the daydream and focusing my vision as rain tracks its way down the length of the window, and the busy streets below become a mirage of blurred lights and moving vehicles. I close my eyes and listen intently to the one-sided conversation, already sensing the change of atmosphere in the room before I turn to face him.

His neck has turned a deep shade of red, matching the stitched edging of the cushions that line the sofa and chairs as he throws the phone across the room, cursing loudly. As the small device smashes against the wall above the coffee bar he stands, knocking his chair backwards and flipping the glass desk over in a fit of rage, sending an explosion of shattered glass across the floor.

"Sinclair!" he bellows, his entire face now a matching shade of red. What follows next is a long drawn out slur of Russian obscenities, some I can decipher, others obscured by the sound of breaking furniture as he typhoons his way through the suite's living area. I furrow my brow, questioning who this Sinclair person is and what they've done to insight this amount of anger. The name seems somewhat familiar, but I can't place it. A few moments pass before he finally calms enough to catch his breath and gingerly lowers himself on an untouched chair near the fireplace. He beckons me over with a silent wave of his hand. I comply immediately, taking the chair opposite him as I wait for him to explain. "That was Damien, our British contact. He has been working alongside Dimitri to finally land the largest gun import we've had our hands on in the last 30 years," he says, with a burning fire raging behind the blackness of his eyes. He stares directly into my eyes and even without the burst of anger, I can tell from his tone that something has gone horribly wrong. I've never met Damien, only heard of him when discussing transportation of stock between the UK and Russia. But Dimitri, he has been a prominent part of my life for the last ten years, moulding me into the very evil I've become. He became somewhat of a second father to me over the years, second to the piece of shit I'm now forced to call father. Dimitri showed me kindness in an unkind place, so the mention of his name has me on high alert though I sit stoic, my face completely void of emotion, just like I was taught. "They're dead. Dimitri and the new vendor. Both shot dead by that fucking Sinclair bitch," he seethes, spitting into the crackling fire. That name again. Sinclair. "I want her dead, Nikolai. Dead. Do you hear me?" he demands, leaning forward on his chair, his nostrils flaring.

"Who is she? Who are the Sinclairs?" I ask, noticing the bare of his teeth as I say their name.

"Don't you remember, my boy? That silly little brat who took her chance at a new life without a second thought for who she was leaving behind. What was her name? Kath? Kat? KATE. That's it, Kate. That arrogant fool Alexander offered her a new life and she left you all to rot. And at only twenty-years-old, she killed my fucking men with a bullet between their eyes and snatched our chance of a new partnership from right under our fucking noses." he hisses, spitting as he curses her and her family again.

I grind my teeth, cracking my jaw as I process what's just been said. Dimitri, dead. I refuse to let the unfamiliar emotion that's encompassing my senses consume me as I shake my head, a little disbelieving. The man who taught me to fight, to survive, to take the life of another - killed by a so-called treacherous little bitch who deserves to suffer. I flex my fingers, feeling a desperate need to release the tension crippling my body as I rise to my feet. "Ya ub'yu yeye. Ya ub'yu ikh vsekh." *I'll kill her. I'll kill them all.* I vow, narrowing my eyes at the man staring back at me. His face hardens, but a sinister smirk creeps across his lips.

"You will get your revenge, my boy. But first, you wait and you watch. You learn everything there is to know about the Sinclair girl and her family. That fool Alexander will regret the day he took what was mine. I want you to know the ins and the outs of the Sinclair organisation, every-single-thing there is to know, and report it back to me. Then and only then do you get your revenge and take back everything that she snatched away from you." He stands, slapping my cheek in a reassuring gesture before heading for the door leading to the adjoining rooms. "I've got some calls to make. Get your shit packed, we fly home before nightfall." he calls over his shoulder before stopping at the frame, turning on his heel and cocking his brow. "Oh, and Nikolai, with Dimitri gone, you're my second now, son. You'll do well not to disappoint me."

"Yes, Father." I nod, pressing my lips into a firm line. I knew this day would come, it's everything I've been training for for the last ten years, but I didn't think it would come so fast, or that Dimitri would lose his life in order for it to happen.

I inhale deeply at the cool, crisp, Russian air as soon as we step off the plane, revelling in the feeling of being back home. I can't wait to have a proper drink, the vodka tastes as good as fucking toilet water in London and the beer is no better. Vlad grunts beside me, seemingly unimpressed with the harsh cold while throwing his fur coat over his shoulder and pulling it under his chin as he makes his way to the car that's waiting on the opposite side of the runway.

    I sit in silence on the drive home, processing the sudden but huge change that is about to take over my life. I am ready for this, I know I am, but I never wanted any of it and I sure as shit don't want the responsibility that's about to befall me. I crack my knuckles and rest back into the leather seat, closing my eyes.

    Tonight will be chaos once we arrive back at The Manor. Word will no doubt have spread already about the death of Dimitri and the accompanying death of our business deal. The usual celebration of life will be contaminated with anger and the need for retribution. My cock twitches at the thought of release with one of the house girls and as the car slows to a stop outside the gates of the compound I smile. One last night of freedom, then I can make good on my promise.

    The earlier tension shrinks as I enter The Manor, until I look at the familiar faces of our fellow brothers who rise to their feet upon our return. Their sombre expressions only reignite the fire for justice at the loss of my friend as I walk further into the drawing room, followed closely by my father.

    "Wipe that look off your fucking faces before I put a bullet through each and every one of you. He's dead, we all know the risks in this life. Now somebody get me a fucking drink," he scolds, slumping onto one of the empty sofa's and laying his arm out across the back.

The room stays quiet and still and I can't help but smile to myself and shake my head at their stupidity. He really will shoot them, and given his current mood, I don't think he would need much more of a reason. I head for the bar, the room of men moving sideways to allow me through. Some offer me their sympathy as I pass by, others wisely keep their gazes locked down. They know my new position and they daren't try to question it. Not in front of Vladimir. I sigh, resigning myself to the fact that this was the first of many tests that will be thrown my way, though I hadn't thought about it at the time. Dimitri always poured the first drinks, now I take on his role in more ways than one. Reaching for the bottle of Stoli Vodka from the top shelf, I forgo the shot glasses, laying two crystal cut tumblers onto the bar instead and pour them half full before returning the bottle to the shelf. I can feel the heat from the room's gaze as I make my way back through the group, standing tall and determined in front of my father as I hand him his glass.

His eyes bore into mine, silently assessing me as I hold the drink steady for him to take. A moment passes before his lips stretch wide into a devilish grin, flashing his teeth as he stands, taking the glass from me and raising it above his head. "Do smerti," *Till death*, he salutes, receiving an echoing hail from the room as they call out our family law. The only way out of this life once you're in it, is death. His eyes snap back to mine as he holds his glass towards me.

"Do smerti," I nod, clinking my glass to his before throwing the harsh liquor to the back of my throat, swallowing the fire it leaves behind.

He smiles darkly, following suit and emptying his glass, hissing as the liquid burns his throat. "Tomorrow my boy, you get to work. But tonight, we will drink!" He laughs, smacking my shoulder as he calls for another drink and walks towards the bar. The room is louder now as the tension has melted away and the celebration of sorts can begin. Although it seems tame right now, I know within the hour there will have already been two fights and by morning at least one man will have come close to losing his life, if they haven't already become one with the dirt. I care very little for sticking around to watch that happen so I silently remove myself from the mass of bodies, going in search of my own celebration in the form of a busty blonde who's a pro at giving head.

It doesn't take me long to find her dusting one of the spare rooms, completely unaware of the chaos that's ensuing downstairs. I always hated this house. Its walls are covered in stoic photos of leaders before us, watching over me with their dead soulless eyes that are blacker than the depths of hell. Each photo only serves to remind me how little I look like them all with my piercing blue eyes that I gained from my mother. I shake the thought away as I close the door to the room, making Anya jump as the lock clicks into place.

"Nikolai," she gasps, spinning round to face me, her rounded cheeks blushing instantly.
I can't ignore the way her ill fitting dress pushes her breasts together, causing them to spill out over the fabric and my cock throbs in response, begging for release. I don't usually make it my business to get involved with the staff. I have strict rules, but I'm still a

man with needs, and a handjob can only suffice for so long. One drunken night, I became acutely aware of the way Anya could work her lips around my cock and since that night she's willingly sunk to her knees for me every time I've sought her out. I stalk forwards, covering the short distance between us within a few strides. She already knows what's coming as she sinks to the floor, her lips curving into a sly smile as I unfasten my belt, watching her with piercing eyes as she eagerly takes over, pulling my solid erection from my briefs.

   Anya wastes no time, parting her lips and running her tongue over the tip of my cock. Her eyes flick up to meet mine as she swallows me to the back of her throat, flattening her tongue on the underside of my cock to allow me further in. "Oy churt," *Oh fuck.* I groan, throwing my head back. It's been at least a month since I last fucked her mouth and I almost forgot how fucking good it feels. I plunge my fingers into her hair, twisting at the root, uncaring of the pain it's undoubtedly causing across her scalp. I hold her firm, unable to hold myself back, thrusting my hips vigorously against her face, releasing the tension that plagues my mind and body. Anya's hands fly to my thighs to keep herself balanced and I can't help the sick grin that comes over me as I glance down. Her face is a fucking mess already, thick tracks of black mascara stain her crimson cheeks. I release her hair with my right hand, pinching her nose and cutting off what little oxygen she has left. Her eyes immediately snap open, she tries to protest but every attempt she makes is muffled by my cock as I fuck her throat. It's fucked up, I know, but the panic in her eyes as she struggles against me has my balls hitching, I'm almost there. Only when her fingernails dig into the flesh of my thighs and her strangled scream vibrates its way through my dick do I release her nose while I shoot my load to the back of her throat. I tighten my fingers in my hair, thrusting myself deeper, keeping her steady, leaving her no choice but to swallow my cum instead of breathing. Her throat bobs as she empties me, hollowing her cheeks with a final suck before I release her, gasping for air as she falls back onto her ass, with a trail of saliva mixed with my release dripping from her chin. I smirk at the way she gazes up at me, a confusing look of panic mixed with pure fucking lust plastered on her face. I needed that. Fuck, did I need that.

I redress silently, noticing Anya carefully wiping away the makeup tracks from her cheeks and smoothing out her dress. This arrangement between us is always easy, there are no questions, no strings and certainly no feelings, but tonight I hesitate only for a moment before leaving her to return to her duties.

Feeling clear headed for the first time in too long, I make my way out of The Manor, leaving the party in full swing behind me as I make my way across the deserted walkway to my own house, just a few minutes walk away. Vladimir's instructions were clear, learn everything there is to know about the Sinclairs and what better time to start than now.

CHAPTER TWO
PRESENT TIME

Adanna

Thick blood trickles down my hands, running down my finger tips before dripping on the concrete floor. I bring my bone saw to my shirt to wipe it clean of any remaining residue from my latest target. Looking down at remnants of the man I had been paid to take out, I smile at the sight of his innards gathered at my feet. Sometimes I wonder how I don't vomit at the sight of the oozing fluid that's pooling on the floor, but I find it calming, almost comforting me with the fact that another evil has been eradicated from the world.

As time ticks on, the dark liquid begins to congeal on the white kitchen tiles of this unoccupied house on the outskirts of London. The target I'd been ordered to take out was a cruel man, a known rapist among the back streets of London and a high level prostitution ring organiser. Known for forcing drugs into his 'girls' before leaving them without protection at the hands of their clients. I took pride in making him suffer before I made my final blow. I wipe my hands over my shirt to get rid of the excess blood before reaching into my back pocket. I pull out my phone, my fingers and nails are stained red with filthy blood, but I wear it like a badge of honour as I call my sister. The phone rings out for a good few minutes before Narcissa finally picks up, but I can't say I expected anything less from her.

"Uhh, what do you want Adanna? You woke me up," Narcissa yawns down the phone. I roll my eyes. It's 10:00 AM, how is she still sleeping? Although, knowing her and her extra curricular activities, she was most likely up half the night endlessly scrolling for information.

"Narcissa, how nice of you to answer your phone. I need you to get a clean up arranged for me. I'll ping my location over to you." I huff at her. If Father finds out she's lazing about in bed, he's going to be furious with her for not pulling her weight.

"Fine, but then…" Narcissa begins to whine in a high pitched voice, but I cut her off before she has a chance to continue.

"I wouldn't even think of going back to sleep, I can tell Father you helped me on this job, but we both know he'll be home soon and expect you to have the information that he's asked for." I snap at her. I hate it when she's on the receiving end of one of his torrents, she's the youngest of the seven of us and for that reason I have always felt slightly more protective of her. Sometimes tough love can be positive, especially when I know she needs it.

Silence. She's silent. For fucks sake, she hasn't done the job he asked of her. Why can't she just get her shit together? I feel the panic rise in my chest. I have, on many occasions, gone to face Father when I have failed and it never has the best outcome. He is kind but he is ruthless, he didn't get to his position for being a gentle push over. But I hate to fail him, it's completely unnatural for me to fail and the disappointment on my father's face chips away a part of me each time I do. It's why the others tease me for being daddy's pride and joy.

"Narcissa, please tell me you have his information. I can't keep covering for you. Father already knows I do it, but he won't let this one pass." I plead with her as I run my hand over my hair. Although it's short, barely brushing my shoulders, I keep it pinned up in a neat ponytail when I'm on a job. Nobody likes having blood in their hair, even me. I close my eyes counting to ten while I try patiently to wait for her to respond. As I open my eyes, a glimmer of my reflection catches my attention from the kitchen window. My outfit is made up of tight black leather trousers, paired with black combat boots and a black long sleeved t-shirt that is tucked in. Black is definitely a good colour for me, not only does it show off my lithe, toned figure, but it matches my hair and hides the blood stains better than anything else. My blue boot covers clash but at least I won't have to throw my boots away this time. Narcissa sighs bringing me back to the conversation.

"I have the information sis, you don't need to cover for me. It's just…" she begins but falls silent again. She's hiding something from me.

"Narcissa, what's wrong?" I demand. What could she possibly be worried about?

"It's nothing, it's just your next job. Father will explain when you're home." She says, her voice lets on that there's much more to this than she's telling me but I'm not worried, Father only sends me on jobs I can handle. So it's something else. I don't have time to probe her about it right now, I really need to get out of here.

"Right ok, Cissa. Get me a clean up and then at least make an effort to move from your pit would you?" I snap at her before hanging up and sending her my location.

I begin to bag up the body parts in preparation for the collection crew, the dissected flesh is dripping through my hands as I toss it into the bags, leaving me completely coated with blood and innards. Fuck! I'm going to have to throw these leathers out, and I liked how they clung to my curves, but the smell will stick around, and no amount of washing will get rid of it. The collection crew are always efficient and never take more than twenty minutes to arrive at any given location. Narcissa has some kind of deal with them that gets us priority. As lazy and lax as she is, when she puts her mind to something, she is invaluable. My adopted siblings and I all have qualities that are vital to our father's organisation. To the underworld we are known as the Deadly Sins, and for the right price, we cater to everyone.

Once I've finished moving the bags to the door, the crew arrive. I hear their van pull up outside and the doors open and close as they make their way to the house. They may think I'm crazy doing this so early in broad daylight but I've staked this place out for the last few months, the building site has been left unguarded and empty due to improper health and safety documents preventing the continuation of work and so, this house has been left unoccupied, making it the ideal place to torture my victims without being seen. It's like a ghost town of mostly completed houses. I'm surprised squatters haven't made it in. The kitchen and bathrooms are all completed, plaster on the walls too. Something must've really gone wrong for them to walk away and leave so much.

The guy in charge has shaggy light-brown hair, brown eyes and a slim figure. He's quite good looking, but I don't involve myself with my father's associates. No doubt he would kill them without a second thought. The man looks at me for a moment, trying to decide if he should say what he's thinking. I smirk at him and raise my eyebrows, giving him the green light to go ahead.

He nods at me, straightening his shoulders as he fully takes in the sight of my blood covered body. "We would've bagged him up, it's part of the service."

I frown at him for a second and see the colour drain from his face as he averts his gaze away from me, after all, I'm a highly skilled assassin, it's best not to piss me off.

"I know that, but I take satisfaction in my work. I like to do it well and make sure it's done properly. Will his remains go to the pig farm or the vat of acid today?" I inquire, so I know if anything goes wrong who to come for.

"Pigs, they'll enjoy this one." He replies as he signals for the two men to start getting rid of the body bags.

"OK, make sure the teeth are ground down before they're disposed of, I don't want any evidence." I snap at him, giving him my sternest look. He audibly gulps and nods, not saying another word before joining his colleagues to help them with the bags. I wait, watching each and every move they make as they begin the clean up operation. I know I'm making them uncomfortable, but I enjoy it. I enjoy watching them squirm while they clean the blood stains that have splattered up the walls and I enjoy the side-eye looks they give me when they think I'm not looking. I take my boot covers off and tuck them in my bag to take care of later. I'm happy to see that my boots fared better than my trousers.

As soon as they finish, they all mutter a quick goodbye before rushing back to the van, leaving me alone once again. I watch until their vehicle has made its way down the unfinished road and is out of sight before returning to the kitchen to check their work, because if it isn't up to scratch, they'll be out of a job. There isn't a speck of blood or stain in sight and the tiles look cleaner than before I started. Smiling to myself, I thank my sister for having good connections. Careful not to touch anything in the kitchen, I slip my boots off and make my way to the bathroom on the first floor. The tiles are white up here too and everything is pristine. It really would make a lovely home if they were to carry on building, but for now, I'm taking it as my own. I remove my clothes and place them into a black bin liner that I plan to burn before I leave. Hoping my weeks of watching the place out have paid off, I switch the shower on, letting out a sigh of relief when the water immediately begins to pour. Who leaves a building site and doesn't switch off the water? Idiots. I step into the shower and close my eyes, letting the steam engulf me as the water flows down my body. The warmth of the water trickles down my back and soothes my muscles as I lean against the tiles and take in the events of the morning. I executed my plan with ease, staying out of sight and taking down another piece of scum. It took a lot to ensure it went perfectly, ensuring the building site would remain empty and nobody would interrupt my work, hours of endless watching and waiting, but in all, it's nothing compared to the horrific acts of the man that has now become nothing more than pig slop. Breathing in, I finally open my eyes, watching as the blood is washed away, rinsing me of my sins. Once I'm certain all visual evidence is gone, I grab a towel from my bag and quickly get dressed in clean jeans and a shirt. I forego underwear, my boobs are perky enough to be able to miss out on a bra. I turn to the mirror and wipe away the steam, I take in my own reflection, my dark brown, almond shaped eyes, sharp cheekbones and full pink lips. With my thick black hair making my skin look even paler, I'm sure some would liken me to a vampire. I suppose my reputation would say I am blood thirsty.

I quickly wipe down the shower, making sure it doesn't look like an assassin took a shower and take one last look around the room before grabbing the black bag of clothes and my small duffel. I exit to the back garden where a small fire pit sits, perfect for disposing of my soiled clothes. Sitting in the corner of the garden, I empty the blood soaked clothes into the pit and douse them with a small can of lighter fluid before striking a match and throwing it on the pile. The flames ignite immediately, raging over the contents, burning away every piece of evidence there is. I stare at the inferno, watching it dance around, not letting a single thing remain. I wait patiently until the blaze has died down before spraying water over the ashes to ensure it is extinguished and then empty the remains into a box, packing it into my bag to take it with me. We have all had the important lesson drilled into us, that we must never, ever, leave behind evidence that could connect us to any of our missions.

    After I've conducted a final sweep of the house, I'm happy to leave and slip my boots back onto my feet. Making my way to my bike, my phone rings. I look down at the caller ID and smile, it's Niamh, she must have finished her rehearsals at the club already. I bring the phone to my ear as I lean back on my bike.

    "Hey you," I say with a smile. Niamh has always been the most carefree of my siblings, she's always had that flirty yet cunning nature being the epitome of lust. Plus, with her blonde hair and blue eyes, she is a knockout. Most men fail to resist her, making her the perfect honey trap.

"Hey love, fancy swinging by to collect me from the club? I am worn out already and I'm back later tonight." She says, and from the soft tone of her voice, I can just envision her fluttering her long lashes at me to get what she wants.

I roll my eyes and snort, "Sure, but you'll have to come with me to the shooting range for an hour. I need to get some practice in today." That should please her.

"Uhhh fine, I'll catch you up on the latest club gossip, I promise I won't leave out any details of size, including girth," she giggles at me. Her crude remarks make me smile.

"Looking forward to it, I'll be with you in ten." I tell her and hang up.

Opening the compartment behind my seat, I shove the duffel bag inside and reach for my gloves. I definitely need another manicure, my nails are fucked. I slip on my black leather gloves and swing my leg over my motorcycle, bringing my black boots to the pedal and gripping the handle bars tightly. Leaning back, I take in my surroundings, the trees swaying in the wind, the sky's are blue with liquorice coloured clouds, a warning sign that the heavens will open soon. Niamh isn't going to be pleased that she has to ride on the back of my bike when that downpour arrives, the thought of it makes me laugh. I pull my matte black helmet on. I'm going to regret the damp hair when I get home. Revving the engine to life, the loose gravel and dirt kicks up behind me as I release the clutch and head out of the estate. I quickly make my way back to the main road, the feel of the wind whipping against my body intoxicates me, mixing with the adrenaline already surging through my veins.

The closer I get to the club, the more eager I feel to get to the shooting range. Gaining more speed I take the last corner, skidding slightly before gaining traction as I pull up to the curb that Niamh is waiting at. I grin at her even though she can't see through my visor. She's already raising her eyebrows at me and I can tell she is about to throw a hissy fit for not mentioning I had my bike today.

"*Really* Adanna, you failed to mention you had this monstrosity of transport today?" she sulks.

"Oops, my bad. Will your hair be able to fit into my spare helmet? It looks like you've used an entire can of hairspray on that thing." I tease as I hand her my spare.

She stares down at the helmet, her eyes are blue and bold but the disgusted look on her face shows how much she hates the fact that she's going to have to put it on and ruin her hair and makeup. "Do I really have to put it on? The shooting range isn't too far from here. I should have called Gulliver. He wouldn't be seen dead driving this." She gestures at my beautiful bike, stomping her foot like a stroppy child.

"Firstly, yes you do need to put it on because as skilled as I am, one wrong turn and it won't be just your hair that will be messed up, your face will be a pretty little mess, too. Secondly, that is because the fucker wouldn't drive himself anywhere, he would send a limo to come and get you. He spends every penny he has, the frivolous idiot." Sighing, I push the helmet into her hands and restart the engine. I hear Niamh tut loudly before she jumps on the back of the bike. Once I'm sure she has a firm grip behind me, I pull away from the curb, going slower than I would on my own just to keep the peace. It takes no longer than ten minutes to ride from the club to the range and Niamh has been clinging onto me for dear life for the entire journey. I park close to the entrance and Niamh jumps off the bike as quickly as she can, dropping the helmet on the seat before checking her hair in the reflection of the building's window. Rolling my eyes, I fight the urge to tease her and tell her that her hair looks awful, but that would be a lie, she looks stunning as always. Looking up at the building, it looks like any old brick warehouse on the outskirts of London. It has plenty of space out back for target practice and is out of the way from nosey and irrational neighbours. I can shoot here until my heart's content without anyone watching or encroaching on my space. This is my safe space, and the place I usually go after a kill to wind down.

"Okay, it's not so bad, is it?" Niamh says, smiling at me and gesturing to her hair that looks no different than when she first took the helmet off.

"It looks fine, Niamh, you always look great. Come on, I don't know how much time I've got here until Father calls me back for debriefing." I state, linking her arm with mine as I guide her to the brown oak door. Pushing it open, I see the receptionist, a brown-haired mousy looking girl. Her eyes snap up to mine as the bell dings on the door and she smiles immediately. She's used to me coming here, getting to know me as much as I'd let her over the last seven years. She's always been friendly, sometimes too friendly, but hey its service with a smile so who am I to complain? She's a lot nicer than the other receptionist who works here, Deborah. She's got a face like a slapped fucking ass and looks like she would rather be anywhere else than here when she's on shift.

"Hi, Miss Sinclair, usual booth? Do you want me to clear the area?" she asks as her eyes flit between Niamh and me. Out of all of my siblings, excluding Narcissa because she has never set foot in here, Niamh has been here the least and let's face it, she looks like she just stepped off a runway, not like she's experienced with guns.

"Yes please, Emily. Book it out on my account for the next hour." I advise as she begins to book me in on her computer. Emily reaches over to pull the keys from the drawer.

"Row 1 - 4 is all yours, here are your ear defenders and eye protection," she says, passing over our ear defenders and goggles, making Niamh sigh at having to wear them.

"Thanks, Emily." I nod at her before making my way down the corridor to the door at the end. I can hear Niamh's heels clicking on the floor as she follows me into the booth area.

"I reckon she fancies you." Niamh comments, turning to look back at Emily.

"No she doesn't, she's just being nice." I say and follow her gaze over to the receptionist. Sadly for Emily, we catch her staring and she darts behind the desk quickly.

"Yeah, sure, keep telling yourself that." Niamh sighs as we walk into the range.

Four booths occupy the room, each with dividers to separate them and facing targets for practice. Moving towards the cupboard at the end where the ammunition and firearms are located, I key in the code that Emily supplied me with. Opening the metal door, I assess the armoury in front of me. Everything is top of the range and neatly organised. I opt for the Glock 17, it's a firm favourite for me. Its precise accuracy is impressive and like most guns, it gets the job done. Turning, I see Niamh making herself comfortable on the seat next to the booth I plan to shoot from. She's already on her phone messaging away. I roll my eyes making my way over to the booth and without any warning I fire at the target.

"Jesus Christ!" Niamh shouts. I can't help but giggle at her as she gapes at me with wide eyes. "Give me a warning before you do that, Adanna!" she shrieks at me.

"So, come on, what's the club gossip you promised me? And don't leave out the fine details." I smile, wiggling my eyebrows at her.

"Fine details, like the size of Marcus's cock, damn that man is packing!" she giggles, gesturing with her hands how big he is.

"Nice length, but girth? He's not a pencil dick, right?" I question her. There is nothing worse than a cock that prods you but doesn't make you cry out as it stretches you open.

"Well, he's a decent circumference I would say. I mean, I haven't tried him but Hannah said she was quite sore after her rodeo with him." Niamh says, picking at her immaculate manicured nails.

"So wait, Marcus is the new male stripper right? How has Hannah already ridden his cock?" I ask as I take aim again at the target, focusing on the bullseye. I fire, hitting the target in the middle. Smirking, I turn to Niamh who has her hands over her ears. "You might want to put the ear defenders on, it's what they're for."

"No shit," she grumbles, rolling her eyes as she manages to wedge the defenders over her hair. "Well, Hannah is a quick mover and have you seen her tits? They are massive. He had no chance resisting those things." She laughs and pushes the protective eyewear on too. "Anyway tell me, do I need to hook you up with him? Or is Tony still available for hookups?"

"Me and Tony called it time." I admit, loud enough so she can hear me as I take aim again, this time going for where the heart would be on the target. I pull the trigger and the bullet precisely hits the intended spot.

"You mean he asked for more?" Niamh smirks, raising a brow at me as she takes a selfie on her phone.

I shake my head. "Yes, exactly. More isn't an option with me, with any of us. Look at Gulliver and Leviah. It's a disaster. And it's a pointless waste of energy." I sigh as I line up my next shot and squeeze the trigger.

"Maybe, but don't you wonder what it would be like to have someone to love you? Like, really love you? And not the way we love each other as siblings." She says, her eyes boring into me until I start to become uncomfortable with the niggling feeling in the pit of my stomach. Before I can respond to her, her phone rings out her Rihanna's S&M ringtone. Niamh's eyes drop to the caller ID and she immediately removes the ear defenders and answers. "Daddy!" She beams. Fuck sake she's always the most charming person. "I'm ok, I'm with Adanna at the shooting range," she explains. I turn once again and take my aim, my gut feeling tells me it's my last for today. I steady myself and pull the trigger, watching the bullet soar through the air and hit the centre of the bullseye. "Oh, you've been trying to call her? Do you want to speak with her now?" Niamh asks. I'd turned my phone off after picking Niamh up. I wanted to practise with little distractions. Niamh looks at me and holds the phone out to me, mouthing an apology as I take the phone. Taking a deep breath, I place the gun down and remove my ear defenders.

"Father, is everything ok?" I ask, bracing myself for whatever comes next.

"Why is your phone off? Narcissa told me you finished the job," he snaps.

"Yes, she arranged the clean up. She was very efficient, you should praise her." I state, deflecting the question about turning off my phone.

"Don't avoid the question, Adanna, I don't need to know the reason. But you know I worry about you all. Have you got it out of your system? The range always helps, doesn't it?" He asks. This man is the most ruthless person I know, but in moments like this, he's my father, the man who only wants the best for me and the man who sometimes I think knows me better than I know myself.

"Yes, it helped." I say quietly.

"OK, I need to talk to you about your next job. It's imminent. So make your way home with Niamh on the death trap of yours." he instructs.

"It's not a death trap, Dad, but we'll leave now. See you soon." I assure him.

"Drive safe," he adds before hanging up. I take a breath and pass the phone back to Niamh. "Looks like I have been summoned, sis. Time to go home." I sigh. Niamh gives me a reassuring smile but it doesn't reach her eyes. I know the reason she came here with me. The reason she always checks in with me after a job. Underneath the flirty exterior is the kindest soul you'll ever meet, she wanted to make sure I wasn't alone. She wanted to make sure I was ok.

"Good. I'm hungry. I wonder if I can convince Lyssa to make me some lunch." She grins as she jumps from her seat, leaving her ear defenders and goggles behind.

I guess it's time to find out exactly what this urgent job is, the one Narcissa seemed to be worried about, the one Father is eager for me to complete and the one that will inevitably be my biggest test yet.

CHAPTER THREE

Adanna

The ride home gave me time to lose myself in all the possibilities of what this next mission will entail. Something feels off about this already, so I have no idea what I'm going to be walking into once we get back home. Niamh has been almost silent since leaving the shooting range, if it wasn't for her nails digging into my back the whole ride here, I would've forgotten she was there. The cool breeze whips around us as we approach the gates of the Sinclair estate. The estate is large, and is situated a few miles outside of London. I still remember the first time I saw it, driving through the gates I had to pinch myself to make sure I wasn't dreaming. Everything looks huge to a ten year old child, but I had never seen a house look so grand that I could ever dream of calling my own. But that was what Alexander had given me, a home. And although it's large and imposing, it quickly became my safe space. It is a stark reminder of what could have been. All well as

Father and Uncle George, the estate is big enough to house all seven of us Sinclair children, though Uncle George hardly ever leaves his flat in the city except for the holidays when we're all together to celebrate. The rest of us have other residences in and out of the city too but most of us choose to spend the majority of our time here. I think we've been together for so long now and grown so close that it has become hard for us to be alone. The entire property is surrounded by a wrought iron fence, seven foot high and daunting to anybody who visits. There is a large garage to the side, housing the majority of our cars, and where I keep my bike and a small but generously sized cottage housed at the back of the garden that Uncle George tends to use more often than his actual room, though nobody ever questions it.

      The gates click as my bike nears them, automatically registering my number plate and opening. I drive up the half a mile long block paved drive slowly, taking the extra minutes to settle myself. As soon as the bike comes to a stop, Niamh jumps off, handing me her helmet before giving me a weak smile. "It'll be OK, whatever this job is. You know you're the one Daddy has the most faith in. Don't tell the others I said that, but it's true. You never let him down, why would this time be any different Ada?" Niamh says softly before turning to head inside the house.

      I look up at the brick building, fully taking in its beauty. I never get tired of looking at the intricate details. White panels frame the windows, and the front door is painted a deep shade of navy blue with white pillars surrounding it. It really is somewhere most people would dream of growing up. I follow Niamh to the kitchen, I need a drink, something strong before I seek Father out. As I enter the kitchen, I see Lyssa frying up an omelette with Niamh already begging at her side to make her one too.

"Can I have one, sis?" Niamh pleads, batting her eyelids at Lyssa. Lyssa takes a deep breath, I can see she's annoyed at Niamh but Lyssa, for all the pent up rage she has, can be very patient with the rest of us.

"Sure, have this one, but you have to do my hair for the next fight night, you know, those braids you do?" she smirks at Niamh as she slides the omelette onto the plate for her.

"Fine, you have yourself a deal, I love making you look fierce." Niamh sticks her tongue out before grabbing the plate and making her way to the table to join Narcissa who is having some Cheerios.

Lyssa rolls her eyes and begins to whip up more eggs as I stride over to the counter and grab a mug to pour myself a coffee. I nod at her and she smiles. The relationship with each of my siblings is different, Lyssa is someone who just gets me and I her, we don't need words to communicate, we both understand the drive to succeed.

"Adanna," a voice booms from the doorway, and all three of us fall silent. I turn and see my father, Alexander Sinclair. He's tall and broad, and other than the few stray grey hairs, he has barely changed since the first day I saw him.

I smile warmly at him, "Hey Dad, have you had breakfast yet?"

His gaze roams over me and I know he's checking to see if I'm injured. "Yes Adanna, Lyssa kindly made me something earlier, before she went training." He moves closer to Lyssa, pulling her in and kissing the top of her head. She doesn't say anything but smiles at him before serving her food and taking it to join the others at the table. I watch her take her seat, the others glance our way before continuing their chatter. I can feel their apprehension as they each side-eye us. It's like each of them already knows my fate and they aren't sure how I'm going to react when I hear it for myself.

Father clears his throat, drawing my attention back to him. "My office Adanna. We need to talk. This next job is a personal one and one that cannot wait." he states, squeezing my shoulder and gesturing to the door. Bringing the mug to my lips, I take the first and final gulp of my coffee, savouring the smooth rich taste before I place the mug down on the counter and follow my father out of the room, refusing to look back at my sisters.

My father's office is on the same floor as the kitchen, just a few doors down. I approach the door, noticing that it is left a jar for me to enter. Freezing before I take the last few steps, I take a deep breath in and slowly out, readying myself. I'm ready. Standing tall and drawing back my shoulders, I push open the door and step inside. My father's eyes meet mine from behind the desk. He has a file placed in front of him.

"Take a seat," His tone isn't harsh as he gestures toward the chair opposite him, but I can tell he isn't happy about what he's about to say...I do as I'm told and reach for the folder he has on the desk but his hand stops me before I get there, making me to gasp as I make eye contact with him.

"Before you look at this, you need to know, this job is one you cannot fail. If you do, they will come for all of us. Do you understand? You're my pride and joy, Adanna. I know you'll do your job." A shiver runs down my spine at the praise he gives me and I nod and he gives my hand a reassuring squeeze before letting go. I take the file, stroking my fingers gingerly over the bold lettering on the front that spell the word 'CONFIDENTIAL' before I open the file, taken off guard at what I read. The name at the top of the file is a name that I've had burnt into my memory for over seventeen years. The name that still haunts the darkest of my dreams. Someone who I will more than enjoy watching life fade from his eyes. Vladimir Sidorova. The man who stole me from my family when I was only ten years old. But even worse, he murdered them in cold blood all as an act of reprisal. I vowed ever since my father broke the news of their deaths, that I'd have my revenge for what he'd done, not only to me, but to all of those innocent children who he cruelly starved, enslaved and slaughtered. I can feel the rage, sadness and burning desire rush through me all in an overwhelming mixture of emotions, taking my breath away until I'm lost to the whirlwind of it all coursing through my veins as I imagine all of the ways I could end his life. How he'll beg as I gouge his eyes from their sockets, plead for his life before I grant him mercy, but not before I show him who his grim reaper is.

"Adanna, do you know what this means?" My father snaps. I blink out of the trance. A single tear rolls down my face and I look up to meet my father's eyes. He smiles, he knows exactly what this means to me.

"It means I finally get my retribution for not only myself, but all those he has heinously wronged. It means I'm going to enjoy this job very much." I say darkly with a smirk on my face.

"Yes, but failure is not an option. You will need to move through Russia with great care, you mustn't be noticed. This has to be a clean kill, Adanna. We can't afford theatrics. The person who has paid for this kill wants a quiet and immaculate job," my father explains. Nodding my head as he continues, I take great gratification and delight in my work. I can sometimes get carried away with making a show of it but I understand the delicacies required with this one.

"Can I at least take a souvenir of my kill, if I can't make an example of him?" I question. I like to keep trophies. I have several boxes of the ashes of my victims under my bed, but for this, it requires much more than a box of ashes. I want his damn head hung on my wall. My father chuckles and smiles at me.

"As it is you, yes. Just don't hang, draw and quarter him. You really can't afford to mess around with this one," he states pointedly.

"Just hang, draw and slaughter?" I joke.

"Adanna, I mean it." He says sternly. "I have a

contact in Russia who will meet you when you arrive and brief you on all Vladimir's movements. He's been keeping a close eye on him for the last few weeks. He will be your main link to us. He will provide you with weapons and inventory while you're there. I've asked Narcissa to keep a track on your devices and be available should you need anything that Lev cannot provide."

"You asked Narcissa, or you told her?" I quiz. I know full well he would have demanded she get her act together.

"I asked. She would do anything for you, you know that. Anything to keep you safe, as all of you would for every member of this family. It's our legacy. It's what makes us the most feared and efficient mercenary firm in Europe," he says, letting me know that I am not to question his tactics when it comes to handling us. "Our love as a family comes before all else. We protect our own, Adanna."

"I wasn't questioning your devotion to us or the devotion we have to each other, Dad. I just worry about her. I know the lengths this family will go to protect one another." I smile at him but I know what Narcissa is like. Her sin sloth. She's lazy, and that scares me. Not for myself but for what Father would do if she were to fail him.

"Good, now go and pack, say your goodbyes to your siblings, your flight leaves this evening." He says dismissing me.

This evening? He really does want this done ASAP. "Yes, sir." I stand and salute him before I head for the door.

I hear him chuckle. "Don't be cheeky, I need you to come back in one piece, the alternative is not an option, Adanna." He says, affection filling his words but as I turn to face him, I note the worry in his eyes.

"I'll come back in one piece Dad, don't worry. Your pride and joy hasn't let you down yet, and I don't intend to start now." I nod as I leave the room. Nothing else needs to be said. I have a job to do, and damn I'm going to enjoy doing it, but first I need to round up all of my fellow sins for my goodbyes.

As I enter my room, Niamh is lounging on my bed with her phone glued to her hand as usual. I close the door behind me and lean back against it with a smile on my face, basking in the excitement and prospect of what is to come.

"So, is it dangerous?" Niamh asks.

"Isn't everything we do dangerous, Niamh?" I smirk. "This just happens to be more enjoyable than any other job I have been given." I say, unable to wipe the smile off my face. I'm finally getting what I have wanted for the last seventeen years. A chance of retribution.

"Yes, but you could be killed on this one, I overheard Dad booking flights to Russia last night." She says with worry in her voice. Reaching out to her, I place my hands in hers before grinning.

"It's OK, this job is the one I have been dreaming of for seventeen years. But before I say more, can you get everyone in here, get Leviah and Ottie on video call. I don't want to repeat any of this again."

"On it, as long as you promise me, right now, that you'll be safe, and you won't take risks. I need my big sister, we all do," she says and as I stop to really look at her, I notice the tears pooling in her eyes.

"I'll make sure I am extra safe. Narcissa will have eyes and ears on me at all times. Don't worry." I reassure her, giving her my most sincere smile. She smiles back at me while giving my hands a reassuring squeeze before she leaves to round up the others. Once she leaves, I turn to my wardrobe and pull out my suitcase and grab an assortment of clothes to take with me. I don't need weapons or ammunition as Father explained Lev will be providing those but I chuck a pair of leather gloves into the case anyway. I heard Russia is cold and they have a good grip. As I add the last few items to the case, my siblings, my fellow sins, pile into the room.

"Looks like you have everything, I'd suggest a dress or two but I know that would be pointless." Niamh sighs as she scrutinises the contents of my case. It's almost as if it pains her that I won't be dressing up. I roll my eyes as Lyssa props herself against the wall near the window and the others make themselves comfortable.

"So what job has Daddy's pride and joy been granted now?" Gulliver sneers at me from the armchair in the corner, he has a glass of what I can only assume is whiskey in his hand, sipping on it as though it's going to solve all of his problems. I take a deep breath trying not to rise to his attitude.

"Can you get Leviah and Ottie on the phone please Niamh?" I ask.

"Already on it," she says, turning the phone to face me as she group-calls them. The phone rings out and Leviah doesn't answer, only Ottie picks up. It frustrates me. She's currently in America studying to become a surgeon. I understand the time difference would make this difficult and that it would be very early hours there, but still, I can't ignore that little pang of sadness that she won't be able to comfort me with her rational thinking. She's always got such a level head, it's why she's so good at what she does.

"Hey guys," Ottie chirps from the phone. "Which one of you is on a near death mission then? Adanna, Niamh, Leviah?" she asks. Making me smile, too smart for her own good.

"It's me, Ottie. I want to talk to you all about the job. I had hoped Leviah would have picked up too." I say, disappointed that one of the others will have to relay this to her later on. For this particular mission, I need all of their support. I know I'll have no problem getting the job done, but I just need us to be a complete unit before I head off to get revenge.

"She's probably fucking that new boyfriend of hers, isn't he like a dentist or something? Who has time to answer the phone when you're a hot college girl having fun." Ottie blurts out. Before I can ask how she knows this, an explosion of glass and whiskey bursts across the room.

"What the fuck, Gulliver!?" I yell.

"I've heard enough, get the point Ada." He snaps, his anger is palpable, his knuckles turn white with his grip on the chair.

"You're paying to get that cleaned up!" I demand. How dare he make a fucking mess of my room.

"Whatever, get to the fucking point or I'm leaving. I don't need to hear about my sister fucking other men." He snarls.

I blanch for a second, other men…what does he mean by that? But the darkening look in his eyes tells me not to question it. "Alright, fine. I'm going to Russia to take out Vladimir Sidorova. It will be a quick in and out job, but Father has said I can take a souvenir." I say suddenly exhilarated at the prospect of this assassination, the one I've been waiting for.

"Adanna…" Niamh gasps as her perfectly manicured hands cover her mouth.

"I'll be tracking you, I know what this job means for you but can you try to come back in one piece, no risks, please. I need you here to keep Father off my back." Narcissa pleads with worry in her voice.

"Yes, you had better fucking come back, we can't be the Deadly Sins without Pride." Lyssa states with a deadly serious expression.

"Right, well if that's everything?" Gulliver asks, unfazed and standing to leave. As he gets to the door he turns, fixing me with sympathetic eyes, "Just make sure you come back, OK? We do need you," and with that, he leaves the room without another word.

Rushing to the door after him, I can't help myself as I shout down the hallway, "I'll send you the bill for my carpet, Gulliver!"

"Shit, I have to get back to this meeting, but Adanna, please be safe. We all know what this means to you, but don't let it distract you. Make sure you give me a call when you're back, we need to catch up." Ottie says before hanging up the phone, not giving me a chance to reply.

I turn to Niamh who opens her mouth to say something but her eyes quickly snap to the door and her mouth closes again. Father steps into the room, eyeing the stain on the carpet. "He's drinking again?"

"It looks that way. What time is the flight?" I ask.

"It leaves in three hours, so we need to get a move on to get you to the airport in time. I'll meet you in the car, Adanna, say your goodbyes," he instructs.

I nod, silently hugging my siblings goodbye before they leave my room muttering their encouraging words of good luck, not that I'll need them. Once I'm alone again I quickly double check my case before I leave, using it as a calming distraction as I try to think of anything but what I'm about to do and everything that's about to be thrown my way. This mission is going to test my limits, but I've never felt more ready. I only hope I can make my father proud in the process.

CHAPTER FOUR
Nikolai

"Go, find a way out of here." I urge, squeezing her shoulders, pushing her towards the boss. I can tell by the look in her eyes that she's petrified, we all know that if you're called out like this, it never ends well. But I can't pretend to have ignored the exchange between her and the posh man that was here earlier this afternoon. Something's happening, something different, and if she can get us out of here, she fucking needs to do it now. If this gives her the encouragement she needs to get a move on, then I hope she remembers us when she's on the outside to send help. I watch as she bites down on her bottom lip as a deep blush spreads across her face before she nods and turns away. The feeling that rushes through me is unfamiliar but nice. Can I put my hope in this child or will she end up like the last one who tried to leave?

I watch her walk away, catching her gaze as she turns back to me one last time with a reassuring smile softening her face. But it's one I cannot return, for the apprehension of what this could mean, it constricts every one of my emotions. I nod, unable to offer her anymore before I turn away, putting my faith in a girl I know nothing about.

A distant banging clears my mind. Shit, I did it again. I scrunch my eyes, leaning forwards with my hands resting on either side of the bathroom vanity as the banging grows louder. Can I hear somebody calling my name? I shake my head, clearing the memory that festers deep within the vessels of my brain. Every time it's the same flashback, to the day Kate left us, and everytime I grow angrier; at myself for telling her to go, and at her for not coming back to help the rest of us.

Bang...Bang...Bang.

The next second, my fist connects with the mirror. The loud crack brings a resounding silence in its wake before I peel back my knuckles that are embedded into the reflective shards. I tilt my hand, focussing on the blood now trailing its way across my wrist and winding a path around my forearm. I can't feel the pain, just the slow trickle and warmth of the blood. My knuckles are too marred with scarring from my past to feel another split in the skin. Just as the blood reaches the crook of my elbow the bathroom door bursts open.

"Finally grown so tired of looking at your reflection that you had to take it out on the mirror, huh?" Ivan smirks.

"Otvyan," *Fuck off,* I counter, carefully pulling a piece of glass from my knuckle and throwing it into the sink. "What's the news?"

Ivan grins at me and laughs, "What makes you think I have news?"

I shoulder him lightly, pushing him aside and making him laugh again as I make my way back into the bedroom and glance toward the clock. "It's not even seven, you definitely have news." I grab a piece of cloth from the top drawer of my dresser and wrap it tightly across my knuckles, something I find myself doing ever more frequently these last few months.

"The shipment is ready. I've already contacted the buyer and they'll be ready to exchange within the hour."

"Location?"

"Just outside the city. It's almost an hour drive though so you better get dressed and get out to the yard. The guys are already loading the truck. Oh and before you ask, because I know you will. The new litter arrives this evening."

I smile to myself. "This is why you're my man, Ivan." I grin at him, slapping his shoulder with my unwrapped hand then proceed to pull on some clean clothes.

"I'll meet you down there, Ubiytsa." *Killer.* Ivan chirps before leaving the room.

Stepping out into the early morning mist, the sun is barely breaching the treeline, dripping the compound in a beautiful sepia hue. I breathe deep, filling my lungs, taking a quiet moment to myself and enjoying the simplicity in it before I walk into havoc. The day that Dimitri died changed the hierarchy within the business and although Dimitri had always told me I was destined to lead, I never thought I'd be here long enough for it to actually happen.

  I gaze around the compound, at the limited number of houses it holds, all evenly spaced around the larger building in the middle. The Manor. A place where I now hold a room, being Vladimir's second in command. I shudder at the thought of living under the same roof as that man, a man who calls himself my father, but is anything of the kind. To the annoyance of *my father,* I refused to give up my own refuge in the compound and move in under his watchful eye. I need my privacy, there's no way I was going to give that up without a fight.

  "Nikolai!" I hear from a distance, turning in the direction of the gruff voice.

  "Vladimir," I nod, showing the respect that is expected of me.

  "I need you at the meeting tonight, there's a new litter arriving and I want to go over the arrangements beforehand," he states. It's not unusual to see him out of The Manor this early in the morning, especially when he's bringing in a new group of children to The Facility. It always gets him a little on edge until they're finally in their holding cells. But today, I have a suspicious niggle in the back of my mind that he's making sure I'm doing my job properly. The last few years haven't been the easiest, with law enforcement breathing down Vladimir's neck every chance they get. They almost caught a runner last year, and if it wasn't for my quick thinking and relentless ability to fuck the Police General's daughter into submission, I'm sure we would have been caught and be serving out our life sentences behind bars.

"I'll be there," I agree, flexing my jaw and biting back what I'd really like to say and do to the man before me.

I arrived here seventeen years ago after being ripped away from my mother's arms. The sight of her clawing at her own throat after it was slashed and she struggled to breath, drowning in her own blood, used to be the worst thing I ever thought I would live through. That was until the day Vladimir used it against me in order to 'get me in-line'. He threatened to do the same to me right there and then, but I swallowed that anger, buried it deep inside of me. I did it to allow myself to grow and to learn everything this man wanted me to know so that I could eventually use it against him and when the time is right, I'll end his life, just like he did mine. His smirk as he retold the story of my family's murder made my blood boil. It was him who instructed it, for reasons I'm still unsure of.

Vlad grunts his approval before nodding his head and making his way back to The Manor, where I don't doubt he'll drown his misery in strong liquor and obsessively keep track of his incoming delivery until the meeting later tonight.

If there's one thing I'm glad of, it's that I'll be out of the way for a few hours, taking pleasure in something as mundane as a business deal. I don't usually make the effort of attending, unless necessary, but considering this is a new client and Ivan has taken it upon himself to source them and make all of the arrangements without me, I'm merely there to step in if they refuse to pay. I trust Ivan, and in doing so, I trust that this will go well and I'll be able to grant him permission to continue without my say on any more of the transactions.

Right on cue "Ubiytsa," *Killer*, I hear Ivan shout from the perimeter gates, pushing me to move myself forwards.

"Where have you been?" he asks when I make it to the now fully loaded and waiting van.

"Vlad caught me outside The Manor and I got lost in thoughts of all the different ways I'd like to murder him." I state with a sly smile. Ivan shares my hate for Vladimir. After Kate left, everything changed and Vlad became a man possessed with revenge and even though I was chosen to become the new son of Sidorova, a name I never knew would carry so much weight, Ivan and I became close, making a silent vow to each other that we would one day get our own revenge.

Ivan shakes his head and chuckles. "Please tell me you thought of something better than just slitting his throat," he says quietly as we climb into the two remaining seats of the van. There are two others joining us today, another two men I have grown and fought with over the last seventeen years; Aleksei and Maksim. Behind the wheel, Maksim pulls out from the compound gates as soon as we pull the van door closed, aware that we're going to be cutting it extremely close for time. Aleksei sits next to him in the passenger seat as they converse in Russian. Both strong, hard working, brutal men, who just like Ivan and I, were torn from reality and thrown into this life with no other way out than death. Only, they didn't start here as kids, they were thrust into it by their own families, for honour and to withstand the hand that would be dealt to them if they refused.

"What's so wrong with that?" I smirk.

"He deserves something long and painful, not that quick." Ivan states with a harshness in his tone he doesn't even try to hide. I stay silent for a moment but nod my head, agreeing that he does indeed deserve some torture before I take his last breath. But, there is a time and a place for everything, and right now, it is neither of those so I swiftly change the topic of conversation.

"So you're sure this new customer is legit? I don't want another fucking reason for General Kozlov to come snooping around the compound again."

Ivan throws his head back with a loud laugh and slaps my shoulder. "Yes and I'm sure he doesn't want to find you railing his daughter again. I checked their credentials several times, went through their affiliates and held surveillance on their shipment yard for 48 hours, everything looked good."

"Right, well just so you're aware, if it does go wrong, and you've not already been killed in the crossfire, I will be slitting your throat for your incompetence." I chuckle, returning his slap to the shoulder in a brotherly manner.

Ivan smirks, "Seems fair," he says through a long yawn, leaning back in his seat and closing his eyes.

"Tired, are we?" I mock.

Without opening his eyes Ivan chuckles. "It was worth it," and I know that's code for; 'I spent the night fucking Jane'. Jane and I grew close over the years, not as close as her and Ivan though. Since the three of us formed our friendship through a shared trauma, our bond is that of a real family, one I would happily kill to protect. Jane is like a little sister to me, three years younger, so when Ivan first showed an interest in her, I beat the shit out of him and threatened to gouge his eyes out. It's clear to say it never deterred him, and their relationship blossomed from there, and I was happy to see it happen. Over the last few years I've seen less and less of her though, with my jobs becoming more demanding, with more time being outside of the compound and her jobs being based inside with the rest of the women, our paths barely crossed unless I went out of my way to find her. I had to rely on Ivan's word that she was doing alright, because deep down, none of us wanted to be here.

The hour-long journey passes quickly with Maksim behind the wheel. I'm not sure where he acquired his driving skills but he's definitely teetering on the edge of 'fast and furious' with a hint of suicidal. Although, on the very rare occasion that our best laid plans have gone to shit, he's proven himself to be a great getaway driver whenever we needed one, and much to Vladimir's annoyance, he's bloody brilliant at hotwiring vehicles.

"This one is all you Ivan." I state as Maksim creeps the van into an empty parking lot at the back of an abandoned toy factory. Ivan huffs out a laugh but doesn't argue. He knows this will be a test for him, and that I'll make good on my promise to slit his throat if this goes to shit.

A minute after we arrive a large black van pulls around the building and comes to a stop beside us.

"You're up." I grin, slapping Ivan on his shoulder before getting out of the van. Ivan follows me out, but as I head to the back of the van to open the doors and unload the guns, Ivan walks straight towards the black van and the two large men who're now making their way to us. I glance over to Aleksei who hangs back between Ivan and our van, we share a look and with my eyes I tell him to be ready. We're not new to this but sometimes situations can change drastically within seconds. We all need to be on our mark. Maksim decides not to exit the van at all, and is still behind the wheel, intently watching our new arrivals in case we need a quick getaway.

It doesn't take long for the deal to wrap up, a few handshakes, a quick check of our ammunition and a handover of cash and we're making our way back to the compound. It was smooth, the way these things should be and as I look over at Ivan, I know I won't be hearing the last of it anytime soon as he sits humming to himself with a shit eating grin plastered on his face.

"Well, I'm glad I didn't have to kill you. I don't think I could survive this meeting at The Manor on my own tonight," I laugh, causing Ivan to hold his face in his hands.

"Radi blady," *For fuck sake,* he mutters, eliciting a chorus of laughter from the rest of us. "I think I'd rather be dead," he whines mockingly, sticking his tongue out and closing his eyes.

"Oh, it can still be arranged my friend, don't worry about that." I chuckle before my phone diverts my attention. It's T, my Russian contact in the UK.

"Nikolai." I say as I answer the call. I've never had time for hello.

"Mr Sidorova…" I cringe at the use of my father's surname… "I'm calling to alert you of a flight that's been booked, leaving late this evening from Farnborough, UK and scheduled to arrive early tomorrow morning in Moscow."

I inhale sharply, I already know the answer before I ask, but I need to hear him say it. "Who is it?"

"Adanna Sinclair, sir," he says so smoothly, like he hasn't just expelled the air from my lungs.

"You're sure?"

"Positive, sir. I've been keeping close tabs on their accounts like you asked and at twelve-thirty this afternoon; a return flight was scheduled on their private plane, flying out from Farnborough airport, UK to land at Vnukovo airport in Moscow at around one tomorrow morning."

I can feel my heart racing in my chest, the blood pumping fiercely in my ears as I ask my next question. "Skolko celevek na bortu?" *How many on board?*

"Ona edinstvennaya, sare." *She's the only one, sir.* he states.

"Otprav'te mne dokazatel'stvo." *Send me proof.* I snap, ending the call and allowing myself to breathe before I can feel that familiar frustration beginning to build, that overbearing need to release myself from my own darkness. Christ, maybe I will kill Vlad tonight if he pushes me hard enough. My phone pings a moment later and I can't open the attachment quick enough. There it is, in black and white, a single passenger flight plan scheduled to land in Moscow tomorrow morning with her name the sole entry on the boarding log.

"Ebat!" *Fuck!* I spit, disliking the sour taste at the back of my throat as my mind wanders all the way back to when I was a fifteen year old boy being pushed and threatened into taking the life of another by my now so called father. A life I never would have been forced into if it wasn't for her. But why is she coming here? And why now?

"Niko?" I hear the question in Ivan's voice and as I open my eyes, I notice that the van has stopped and all three of them, Ivan, Maksim and Aleksei are watching me, waiting for me to fill them in on what just happened. But can I? No. They would never understand, not the way I do. I've carried this with me for so many years. I've obsessed over this woman, watched her grow, watched her kill, watched her live and breathe a life I was owed and envisioned every way I would kill her given the chance. Now as it all becomes a reality, I want to be selfish with it, to take every piece of her that I'm owed, but to do that, I must keep her little secret for a little bit longer.

"There's a private plane landing at Vnukovo, early hours of tomorrow morning with a single passenger on board. I don't know why they're coming but for whatever reason it's going to be trouble for us." They all share a quizzical look between them.

"What kind of trouble?" Maksim asks.

"The kind that we don't want boys." I glance outside, recognising the strip of land we've pulled into and knowing we're only a few miles from the compound. "Not a word of this to anybody until I have assessed the situation wholly and given word to Vladimir myself." I order, opening the door to the van and pulling off my jacket. "Am I understood?"

"Da," *Yes,* they all sound in unison. I strip my shirt off next and shake out my arms as the fresh air bites into my skin. "I'll meet you back at the compound." I state before pushing off from the van and starting on my run back home.

I usually run during the night, when sleep is my enemy. To be alone in the world before anybody else wakes up provides such a comforting sense of solitude while the savage burn in my lungs reminds me that I'm still alive. I've trained hard for my body. Dimitri pushed me for years; day in, day out, from morning till night and when I would break he would only work me harder. Making me run, making me fight, making me lift. At the time I despised him for it, even wished for his death on too many occasions. But now I thank him for what he taught me while I push my body harder on the solid terrain.

    I clear my mind and run for what feels like hours, focusing intently on the parts of my body that are screaming at me to stop. I take note of the pain, the shake of my legs as each foot hits the ground in turn. The fire burning a rampage through my chest, threatening to split me open with the intensity of it and the piercing numbness that coats my upper body as the temperature continues to drop with the falling sun. Each foot forward is torturous, but I can't ignore the way I welcome it, so I drive onwards until I've finally made my way through the dense forest of trees that surround the southern side of the compound. Not many people wander through the thickness of the trees for fear of becoming lost, but over the last ten years, I've become accustomed to the winding tracks within its roots and enjoy the freedom the darkness brings from the canopy above.

    I break from the tree line and head straight home without slowing to a walk. I'm in desperate need of a shower and a drink before I'm dragged through the mental torture of Vladimir's meeting tonight and I'm not in the mood to speak to anybody else on my way.

    I make it through the compound to my front door without interruption. Feeling a heavy sigh of relief when I close the door behind me and take note of the deafening silence of my home. It's not huge like The Manor, but I've never been one for luxury. I have what I need, a roof over my head. And although I hate him, I do find myself extremely grateful to Vladimir for this one small kindness in letting me live here, when he could so easily force me under his roof.

    I smile to myself for a second, a brief moment where I take in all that I have around me while trying to calm my breathing. A decent sized living space with an open log fire that acts as the centre point of the room, surrounded by dark wooden furniture with brass accents and dark lights fashioning the walls. A large fur rug covers the majority of the wooden floor in this room. A large mahogany bar topped with bottles of vodka, gin and rum stands opposite an even larger bookcase, its shelves filled with stacks of first edition books that have been passed down within my fathers family. I make my way through to the kitchen, quickly grabbing a bottle of water from the fridge and gulping it down. This room is much the same with deep, dark wooden accents surrounding the built-in appliances and a large hand carved dining table that takes up an entire half of the room. I don't spend much time in this room, usually grabbing food elsewhere but I've always liked the open view of the forest from the windows on this side of the house. I make quick work of the stairs leading to the second floor of the house, ascending them in three long strides, quickly removing my boots, cargo pants, socks and briefs before scolding myself under a quick shower.

    The dark aesthetic continues upstairs, my bedroom houses a large four poster bed, draped generously with blood red sheets, a large mahogany wardrobe, chest of drawers and bedside table to match and a sizeable wingback chair positioned in front of the window that gazes out across the vast expanse of wooded area. The bathroom hosts a beautiful clawfoot bathtub which in my opinion is wasted on me, I've never used it, I don't see the point. A wall of mottled glass separates the shower, as well as the dark vanity unit and toilet. There's a spare room up here too which has never been occupied, other than by Ivan when he's been too pissed up to make it back to his own house, scared of what Jane will do to him once she sees him in such a state.

  I scrub my skin, letting the searing temperature of the water slowly resuscitate my frozen body back to life and as I do, with a much clearer head than before, I can't help but wonder why the girl who ruined my entire life is coming here to Russia seventeen years later. Why now? Could it be a coincidence? Is she coming for Vladimir? Does she know I'm still here? I scold myself quickly at the thought. Why the fuck would that even matter? The bitch is as good as dead as soon as she gets here anyway. And I can't wait to deliver her her just reward.

  A few hours have passed since I returned home, and I have stayed in my dark solitude, contemplating the best and most satisfying way to end the life of Adanna Sinclair the entire time, letting it consume my every thought that I was almost late for Vladimir's meeting. Slipping through the front door of The Manor and into Vlad's office to find him sitting behind his desk.

  "Vy opazdivaete, Nikolai." *You're late, Nikolai.* He voices without looking up from his paperwork. Shit.

"Prosty, Otetz." *Sorry, Father.* Honestly, I'm anything but, I'd rather have my fucking eyeballs eaten by ants than be here to listen to this fucked up shit. But appearance is key and I must play the willing son, the next in-line to take over the business.

He places his paperwork down and looks up at me over the rim of his black-framed glasses, narrowing his eyes every so slightly.

"Let's go. Everybody else has already gathered in the library." He grunts, piercing me with a disapproving glance before he exits the room. I follow, wishing painfully that I could stab my knife into the base of his skull to feel the snap of his spinal cord and take his life. It would be so easy. I stretch out my fingers, resisting the urge. It's not the right time.

I follow Vladimir into the library. He was right, everybody else is already here, and as our presence becomes known, the room falls silent as we walk through, taking the two remaining seats at the front of the room. I quickly scan the faces of the men before me. Dipping my chin to Ivan who sits on the far right of the room. Everybody else is a regular, a ranking soldier in Vladimir's sick little army. When I was first brought here, I never understood the severity of the situation and at only fifteen-years old, I learnt quickly to keep my mouth shut and my eyes wide open, to listen to instructions and to never try to escape. Little did I know how huge the operation I was now a part of was.

Once the dynamic changed and Vladimir took me under his wing, I was thrown into the lion's den, the viper's pit, the depths of hell. Whatever I call it, it was shit. I was one child out of the hundreds that had been stolen over the years and forced to work for Sidorova's slavery unit and that was only just the beginning. At first I was just forced to fight, to keep the other kids in line, they soon learned that my presence was a threat, and my name became a way to blackmail them into staying in line. Fighting turned to torture, and over the years it eventually turned to murder. The first time Vladimir ordered me to take the life of another, I refused. It almost cost me my life, I still bear the scars to prove it. He whipped my body raw, until I physically couldn't feel the pain, but mentally, I broke. My body could only endure so much until blackness took over and I woke up two days later, the deep cuts from the thick leather straps, embedded with small rough cut stones, blazing across my body. I did what I had to do to survive from there on out, even when I wished for death myself.

"Do it, boy. Fucking kill her or I will make her death long and painful and force you to watch every god forsaken second of it. Then I'll start with another until you're man enough to fucking kill them all!" Vladimir spits in my face.

My body shakes with adrenaline and pain, I'm not sure which is worse. Sweat and blood cover my naked torso and my back feels as if it's on fire from the lashing's I've already received for disobeying his orders but I can't fucking do it. I grit my teeth, refusing to look the petrified girl in the eyes. How am I going to do this? I can't fucking do it. The barrel of the gun cracks against my temple, causing my vision to blur and my legs to give way. I crash to the floor, retching up the contents of my stomach as I try but fail to compose myself.

"You waste of fucking air. I chose you because you had the most potential, don't fucking disappoint me now boy. Kill her or I will end your pathetic excuse of a life right now."

I shake my head, wiping the back of my hand across my mouth as I look up at Polina. Her bones protrude from her shoulders, and the sickly pale complexion of her skin is only worsened by the dark black circles around her eyes and the bruises mottling her skin. "Please!" she chokes, barely able to lift herself from the floor. "Please!" I know what she's asking of me, but if I do this, I'll never be able to forgive myself. I can't blame her for wanting a quick way out of this nightmare, but I don't know if I can be the one who gives it to her.

Vladimir's sadistic laugh causes us both to flinch and he stalks behind Polina, shoving her body with his heavy black boot before ripping her head back by her hair making her scream.

"Stop!" I shout, the word flying out before I have a chance to think about it. "Stop!" I say again, slowly standing. "I'll do it." I snap, forcing down the bile that threatens to take me to my knees again. Polina's eyes widen as they lock onto mine but she mouths a 'thank you' that hits me so hard I have to look away.

"That's my boy." Vladimir smirks, shoving Polina's fragile body back to the floor before he forces the gun into my hand.

I take one last look, my eyes pleading with hers to let her know how fucking sorry I am, for what I'm about to do, but the serene smile that she gives me is something I'll never forget as I squeeze the trigger. Brain matter covers the wall as Polina's body hits the ground, a pool of blood immediately forming from the gaping hole in her head. I can't hold back as I throw the gun to the floor, doubling over and retching until my throat is raw and my eyes sting with tears. What the fuck have I done?

"I knew you wouldn't let me down, Ubiytsa." Killer. *Vladimir laughs before he leaves, leaving me wishing more than anything that I'd turned the gun on him instead.*

"We have a litter arriving in three hours," Vlad begins, his voice loud and clear to the room, reminding me I'm no longer in that dark place, I'm no longer that weak fifteen-year-old boy.

I glance at my watch, it's just turned eight, they should be arriving by eleven. "They're being transported via the usual route, straight to The Facility where Bogdan will take the lead." I glance at Bogdan who nods, his face completely impassive. He's a brute of a man, Vlad always has him lead on the arrival days because with his huge frame, thick Russian accent and intolerance level of zero. He scares the absolute shit out of the kids, resulting in them following his instructions, petrified of what he may do to them if they don't.

"How many?" I ask, not wanting to hear the answer.

Vladimir smirks as his gaze falls on me. "Sixteen." Fuck. I hold his stare, refusing to be the first to break eye contact. "Agata will meet you at the gates, Bogdan. She will do an inventory and quick health check on the litter, clearing them for work." I scoff to myself. It isn't work. It's fucking torture, and Agata is a cruel woman. If Bogdan doesn't give the children nightmares, she sure will. Agata is our version of a doctor, though I'm not sure where she trained, if at all. The only person she's nice around is Vlad, and that's because it's no secret that they've been fucking for the last ten years, between his whores at the stripclub, Agata will always open her legs for him in the hopes that he doesn't get sick of her and kill her.

The rest of the meeting continues with Vlad going over the room assignments for the newcomers, a new supply schedule and a threatening note to the room to keep an eye out for anything suspicious. I narrow my eyes at him while the rest of the room files out, retreating to their homes or to security duty for the night but I don't move from my seat.

"Anything I need to know?" I ask through gritted teeth. He smiles a one-sided grin and sucks his teeth.

"General Kozlov has been asking questions again. Trying to get through to our buyers."

An internal groan reverberates its way through my chest. I know exactly where this is going and before he can even say the words I cut him off. His open mouth closes with a snap.

"Ya sdelayu eto." *I'll get it done.* I snarl, already making my way out the door before I hear his promising threat behind me.

"Make sure you do, boy, or it'll be you I send to the noose."

CHAPTER FIVE
Nikolai

Kira's mascara stained face stares back at me through the bathroom mirror of the club, her mouth gaping open as I pound my cock into her. It didn't take much to track her down. Being the daughter of a stuck up piece of shit who thinks he owns the city is sure to make you want to revolt. And as soon as I texted her to meet me, that's exactly what she did. Kira has no idea of the impact her need for attention can bring upon her father, and as I pull my phone from my jacket pocket, fisting her hair with the other hand, I make sure the flash is on and my face is cropped from the photo before collecting what I need.

"Ulybnis pape." *Smile for daddy*. I grunt as I yank her head back, eliciting a guttural scream from her throat as she arches her back, pushing her ass into my crotch while looking directly into the camera. She has no idea the true meaning of my words as she moans around me and I take the prize shot. I only need one but snap two for extra reassurance.

    I continue my movement, the thumping bass from the club fights to drown Kira's enthusiastic moaning as she grinds herself back into me. I slip my phone back into my pocket, only to feel it vibrate a moment later. I would usually finish first but something in me needs to know who it is. Glancing at the screen I feel my throat become thick. T has sent me a photo. I open the attachment and my rhythm falters. Fuck. I blink repeatedly as I stare at the photo, her face, her body. Fuck. What I could do to that body. I feel my cock twitch at the thought, still deep inside of Kira's pussy. She moans loudly, flicking her hair as she glances over her shoulder at me. My mind races with the need to have her underneath me, to be writhing against my body as I fuck her. What's wrong with me? I tighten my fist into Kira's hair once more, looking intently at the photo on my phone while I fuck her faster, feeling myself drawing closer to the precipice.

    Kira wails, her knees buckling. "Fuck, Nikolai! I'm going to come."

    "Zakroy roth," *Shut your mouth.* I snap, my eyes narrowing in on the woman, the woman I'm going to track down and kill. The woman I want to sink my teeth and cock into at the same time, tasting her beauty while she rides me. Adanna Sinclair. One final thrust and I unload myself into the condom. My cock throbbing painfully at the force of my orgasm as Kira comes down from her own. What the fuck was that? I need to get out of here. I make quick work of removing the condom, ensuring I flush it down the nearest toilet before I leave.

"Wait, please stay," Kira pleads as I reach for the door handle and she smooths her dress back down across her thighs, the scrap piece of material barely covering her ass cheeks from behind.

"I've got business." I snap. I owe her no explanation. I leave the room without a second's hesitation and call Ivan on my way back to my car.

"Ivan," I snap before giving him a chance to speak. "I need you to get over to Vnukovo airport and tail the incoming threat I spoke to you about earlier. I'll send you a photo. Don't let them know you're following. And let me know when you've got eyes on." I hear hushed tones through the line but they're too muffled to make out the conversation.

"Leaving in two, Ubiytsa," he confirms.

"Say goodnight to Jane for me, won't you?" I smile, knowing he's probably getting an earful from her as I hang up the phone. I take one last look at the photograph of Adanna, trying to ignore the way my cock has already begun to harden again against my jeans. I grind my teeth, growing rapidly frustrated at my own body for betraying me as I open the message T had sent along with it.

Taken at Farnborough Airport before boarding her flight. - T

Oh Adanna, what a silly little thing you are coming to play over here in my territory. Do you not know what devils lay in the darkness over here? I guess there's only one way we'll find out.

    I minimise the photo, forwarding it to Ivan. Then type a quick message and attach the photo, to General Kozlov, using the encrypted link I use for such purposes, threatening him to back off or everybody in the northern hemisphere will learn what his precious daughter's face looks like while she's being railed in the bathroom of a nightclub. I fire a text to Vladimir too to let him know the job is done and that Kozlov will not be continuing with his interrogations.

    My palms sting with nervous anxiety as the silence in my car swallows me whole. I can't shake the feelings brewing inside of me and as I make the drive back to the compound, I irrationally check my phone every two minutes to see if there's been any update from Ivan, knowing he wouldn't even have made it to the airport yet. I groan, rubbing a hand across my face and into my hair. It's going to be a long night. I have dreamt of the day I would see her again, to make good on my promise and make her pay for all of the damage she caused me. But I had a plan, a plan I'd gone over and perfected for the last seven years, methodically plotting out the best way to torture her, ensuring she endures every bit of pain I thrust upon her before I finally take her life.

    I barely register the drive home, my subconscious taking the correct turns for me to bring me all the way back in one piece. It isn't until I pull past the security guards on the perimeter gates, that I realise where I am. Both men dip their heads to me as I crawl past, their AK machine guns hanging lazily over their shoulders. I drive slowly between the row of houses through the middle of the compound, the stones crunching beneath the tyres as I pull into a large gravel opening and switch off the engine. My body is still thrumming with something I refuse to fully acknowledge, an uneasy jittering running rampant through my limbs as I practically sprint the short distance back to my place of solitude.

    I head for the bar, pulling out a bottle of half empty vodka, popping the top and swallowing enough to choke on the burn it leaves in its wake. "Ebat!" *Fuck!* I cough, slamming the bottle onto the bartop. What is wrong with me? I check the time, flicking my eyes towards the large metal rimmed clock that sits above the fire. It hasn't been long enough, I need a distraction before I go out of my fucking mind. I take another large drink of vodka before stripping off my jacket and shirt and heading back out the door to run. To clear my thoughts and to escape the vivid images of Adanna Sinclair that are running rampant through my mind.

    It's close to an hour before I notice my phone vibrating in the pocket of my trousers. Deep in the middle of the woods, accompanied only by the silver slithers of moonlight through the trees, I answer, already fighting the urge to put my fist through the nearest trunk.

    "Niko," I snap.

    "You didn't tell me she was going to be this hot, Ubiytsa. What is this, some sort of joke? How is this woman a threat?" Ivan laughs down the phone, his playful tone irritating the fuck out of me as I push my thumb and forefinger into my eyes, massaging away the tension that I can already feel building between my temples.

"Where is she?" I snarl, already losing my patience with the conversation. I should have just gone myself and killed her as soon as she stepped foot off the plane, ensuring the job was done.

"She's walking through...Wait, there's a guy here." He says, his voice cutting off at the end.

My eyes snap open immediately. "Kakogo parnya?" *What guy?*

"He's taking her luggage, looks like they know each other." I don't understand, T said she was alone.

"Did he get off the plane with her?" I ask, almost too impatient to wait for his response, I find myself bouncing from foot to foot to keep myself moving, to distract myself just enough to keep my head straight.

"No. Looks like he was waiting for her. They're making their way out. Do you want me to follow?"

"YES!" I shout, loud enough for my voice to echo through the woods, travelling between the trees. "Follow them and get me every piece of information there is on that man. I want to know who he is and how they know each other. And I want it yesterday, Ivan." I order through gritted teeth.

His reply is serious as he regards my orders but he doesn't dispute them, he would be a deadman walking if he did. "Understood, I'll call you when I have something." I hang up, feeling more frustrated than before as I pocket my phone and pick up my pace again to head back home.

I hadn't felt the vibration of the photo message Ivan sent me as I started the run back to the house, but as I stripped from my trousers, my phone screen lit up as I placed it onto the table beside my bed. I showed no restraint, quickly opening the photograph, my fist curling around the device so hard that the screen cracked across the corner from the force of it. I found myself staring directly into the eyes of the temptress and already as hard as steel beneath my boxers at the sight of her. There was no denying Adanna Sinclair was hot, her tight black jeans curved across her ass and highlighted the strength of her legs. I knew she worked out, I've followed her routine, day and night, for the last seven years. But somehow this feels different. She looks so much more beautiful compared to the usual CCTV images I've seen of her through the years. Her cropped black hair is settled perfectly above her shoulders, intensifying the ivory of her skin with such stark difference. I roam my eyes down her body, wishing to see what lies beneath the leather jacket wrapped tightly across her chest.

This feels wrong, but my body disagrees with my mind's reservations as I wrap my hand around my cock and begin to pump. Wild images of Adanna's full lips in place of my hand and her mascara stained face flashes in front of me as I throw my head back and a loud groan rips through my lips. I swear I will make this woman pay. I lose whatever control I thought I had on my own body and commit to my own selfish pleasure. I tighten my fingers around my cock and fuck my hand until I explode with her name a silent cry against my lips.

I wake the following morning not remembering falling asleep. The empty bottle of vodka on the side table probably being the reason for my thumping headache and loss of time. But it was the hardest sleep I've had for weeks. Reluctantly, I roll from my bed and head for the shower, hoping the cold shock of water will expel the impending hangover before it fully takes hold.

The moment I step from the shower my phone brings me right back to reality with a text from Vladimir.

Get to the Manor. We have business to deal with. - Vladimir

I groan. What the fuck is it now? If this is anything to do with the new litter, I don't want any part of it. I hate seeing those kids in a place I know all too well. I was labelled as lucky to have been hand chosen to become Vladimir's protégé. But in reality it turned into my own living hell. None of the other children ever made it back to the compound, either being discarded out into the streets to fend for themselves, or killed, and if it wasn't for me, Ivan and Jane never would have made it either.

I dry myself quickly, pulling on a fresh t-shirt, a thick black jacket and a pair of fitted black cargo pants before lacing up my boots. I pull my holster belt across my shoulder and chest ensuring my set of custom-made throwing knives are secure before placing a blade at my hip, thigh and ankle should I need them. Here we go.

"Otetz." *Father.* I call as I saunter through the front doors of The Manor, already heading through to his office on the ground floor. I refuse to knock, taking a quick controlling breath as I push the door open to reveal the room empty.

"Otetz," I shout again, louder this time, ensuring my voice travels the length of the hallways.

I hold my breath as my name faintly reaches my ears, barely distinguishable through the size of the house. I know where he is. Spinning on my heel I head for the kitchen. None of the morning staff have started work yet so the room is silent as I pass through, making my way toward the basement door that is situated in a well hidden alcove behind the pantry.

"Chto proishodite?" *What's going on?* I snap, as my boots hit the last step down to the basement. Vladimir doesn't stop what he's doing as he grabs an AK out of a large black container, quickly examines it and throws it into a large open duffel bag on the table beside him. The space opens out down here, expanding out below the expanse of the entire house. It's where we keep our own personal supply of weapons, especially ones that Vladimir refuses to let our main competitors know we have. I glance around the wide open room, taking a moment to quell the annoyance I feel that's already threatening to rip from my chest. Each wall is perfectly lined with weapons, each one in its place. Heavy artillery, guns, knives, grenades, flame throwers.

Whatever it is, we have it. There's a large stainless steel table to the side of the room, Vladimir's very own torture device. There haven't been many men deserving of that wrack, but those that end up down here, never make it back out again. The drain in the floor, faultlessly positioned to allow the blood and water to drain away once cleanup commences.

"We're making a run to The Dell." Vladimir grunts, throwing a belt of bullets into the bag before tossing it to me and making his way out of the room. I catch the bag without trying, my senses now on high alert at the mention of our main rivals' ammunition post. "They're taking liberties, trying to sell their shit over our borders. We had rules, we agreed! If Balakin cannot abide by those rules, then he will suffer the consequences." Vladimir reels off, his eyebrows scrunched together tightly as he spits Pasha Balakins name like it burns his tongue.

"Has anybody shifted?" I ask, knowing there's no way out of this ending in anything but bloodshed. There are rules in this world, and you either follow them, or you die.

Vlad smirks, the devil dancing in his eyes as he turns to face me. "Nikto nay nastolko gulp." *Nobody is that stupid.* And he is right. Too many people have seen his ruthlessness first hand. Vladimir Sidorova is a name feared through our country, for he has no acceptions, he will maim, torture and kill whoever he sees fit. I have seen it firsthand, he doesn't discriminate when it comes to serving his own fucked-up sense of justice. "Get a couple of men, Nikolai. Vyyezzhayem cherez pyat." *We move out in five.* I stifle the protest on the tip of my tongue and nod, already pulling my phone from my jacket.

"Maksim!" I bark as he answers on the second ring. "Find Aleksei and bring the van over to The Manor, we're heading out."

"Are we going anywhere nice boss or shall I bring something to keep me busy?" Maksim chuckles down the phone. The mad man loves a fight as much as the rest of us, but he is much more useful behind the wheel.

I grit my teeth. "The Dell." I hear his intake of breath at the mention of the ammunition post that's on the eastern side of the city.

"I'm on my way," is all he says before ending the call.

I step outside The Manor to a light drizzle of rain from a miserably dark grey sky and take a moment for myself, slipping into the cold, emotionless killer I'm known to be. I close my eyes and face up to the sky. Just one moment, I breathe in. That's all I need. Just one moment to take my blade across Vladimir's neck and this will all be over. I breathe out. "Scoro." *Soon.*

The loud crunching of gravel pulls me back. Maksim understood the urgency, skidding the van to a sudden stop two inches in front of my boots. I glance down through the upkick of dust and shake my head.

"How close?" he holler's through the open window with a disgustingly smug grin on his face. Prick.

"Just flatten me next time, yeah?" I laugh. "Where's Aleksei?"

"He's coming, don't worry. Where's Ivan?"

I glance over my shoulder, ensuring Vlad is out of earshot. "He's busy with something." My answer is short but I fix it with a look so that he knows not to push it any further.

"What did I miss?" Aleksei calls from behind the van, his breathing slightly rapid as he catches himself, throwing his gun over his shoulder.

"Nothing, get in the van." I nod turning to face the front door of The Manor as Vladimir steps out, a cold hard look etched into the age lines of his face. I notice how much older he looks as the grey flashes amongst his scruffy black hair. He's not alone as he strides towards us, his two regular guards, the twins, Dodge and Tolya, falling in step behind him. Their faces are completely void of any emotion other than the need to kill. They've been with the family for longer than I have and have shown no mercy when it comes to following Vladimir's orders, I've suffered their brutality too. They will rip out the throat of a man at the snap of his fingers and not think twice about it. I follow their movements carefully as they approach the van, taking in their identical appearance. The only thing that makes it easy to differentiate who is who is the fact that Dodge doesn't speak. A punishment for once lying to Vladimir about where he had been when he didn't attend for duty on the gates one evening. They've both proven themselves worthy of his trust over the years and earned their place at his back.

Beside's Vladimir's repetitive curses towards Pasha Balakin and his stupidity to try and sneak under our noses to steal our customers, we travel in silence. Maksim rolls his eyes each time Dodge grunts in his own way of agreement with Vlads outrage. I'm trying desperately hard not to check my phone every two minutes for an update from Ivan. If Vladimir finds out she's in the country, he'll kill her himself, and this kill is much too sweet to share.

Vladimir's voice lowers an octave and our attention is back on him. "I don't care for explanations. Nobody undermines me, and if they do, they certainly don't survive it." Another resounding grunt from Dodge. "Shoot to kill. Let them know who they've crossed, and let my name die on their lips as they take their last breaths. This will keep Balakin in his place." He snarls. "Do smerti." *Till death.*

The four of us echo his promise. "Do smerti." with Dodge raising a closed fist to his chest and beating it twice before nodding.

"Two minutes out," Maksim calls, his knuckles whitening as his grip on the steering wheel tightens.

"Prigotovitsya!" *Get ready*! I shout, throwing the duffel bag into the middle of the van, allowing them to take their piece.

"Maksim, keep the van hot. This won't take long. Aleksei, bring up the rear. Dodge, Tolya, you two split and meet in the middle." I begin to reel off my orders before narrowing my eyes on Vlad. "And you…nay daite sebya rasstrelyat." *Don't get shot.*

Vladimir smirks at me, misplacing my worry from a place of protection, father-son type love, but in reality it's anything but. His death is only allowed by my hands, and in order for that to happen, until I decide it's time, I will kill anybody who tries to take that pleasure away from me. "Stay close." I order.

The van jolts as Maksim slams his foot on the accelerator and smashes through the security gates heading straight towards a large steel framed building. "Here we go," he sings, enjoying his position behind the wheel. Gunshots have already started ringing out as we speed closer to the entrance of the building and before Maksim even slams to a halt, Tolya thrusts open the side door to the van and we fall out, one by one, covered from the onslaught of bullets by the van as Maksim allows us time to get to cover. Vladimir stays right on my back as we take down their first wave of defence, laying them out in easy succession before we take our chance to move towards the large metal crates in the middle of their warehouse floor.

"Spustitsa." *Get down.* I shout, spinning on my heel to push Vladimir closer to the crates as a group of men barrel through a back doorway, their guns raised and ready as they narrow their eyes in our direction and begin to open fire.

I move quickly, crouching low to roll behind a discarded oil drum. I scan my surroundings, noticing Aleksei twenty-feet in front, peering out from behind a stack of broken pallets. We lock eyes immediately, a silent communication passing between us as he holds up four fingers. I nod before silently mouthing for him to cover me. He nods his understanding and as I internally countdown from three, I remove three knives from their holsters across my chest and swipe my thumb across the blade, digging the tip into the pad of my thumb hard enough to draw a bead of blood. A calming tick I've become accustomed to before I unleash them. I open my eyes, Aleksei nods and as I break cover, Aleksei delivers a clean headshot to the first of the group. I widen my stance and with the first blade gripped, I draw back and release. It hits its target, taking the second man down instantly while he chokes on his own blood, the blade lodged deep through his neck.

I am certain when I say that in many ways I am nothing like my father, but the thrill of adrenaline coursing through my body as I release my last two blades in quick succession, taking out the remaining two men, is overwhelming, powerful and dangerous. And each time I sink my blade into the flesh of another human being, I get dragged deeper and deeper into something I'm afraid I can never return from.

A high-pitched whistle echoes behind me. "Khoroshiy brosok, Ubiytsa," *Nice throw, Killer,* Aleksei commends as he slaps my shoulder before Tolya and Dodge jog over to us, eyeing up the bodies on the floor.

"I think that's all of them," Tolya huffs as he tries to regain his breath. The familiar sound of tyres on gravel fills the area as Maksim drives through the entryway in the direction of the metal crates. Vladimir slowly emerges from behind the crates and nods in my direction.

I raise my eyebrows. "You think?"

"Don't worry, I'm sure you can throw your pretty little knives if anybody else decides to pop out on us, *Killer*." Tolya smirks, rolling my nickname around on his tongue to a deep throaty laugh from Dodge. Vladimir made the name stick, torturing me with it every day after I shot Polina.

"Idi na khuy, Tolya." *Fuck you, Tolya.* I snarl, lunging forwards, only to be caught across the chest by Aleksei. His large tattooed arm holds me tight across my waist, and in that moment he was the only thing holding me back from putting my blade, hilt deep, between Tolya's eyes.

"What are you going to do, Killer? Kill me?" he howls, shoving into his brother's shoulder as they fall over one another laughing.

"If I was going to kill you, you fucking waste, I would've done it already. I'd have driven my blade so deep into your thick fucking skull that your mute twin here would be the one screaming in pain."

Dodge's face tightens momentarily before he lunges. Aleksei throws me to the side, taking the hit before I can straighten myself to land my own fist into Dodge's face. I feel the crunch beneath my knuckles before I hear it, and as he rounds his face back to me, I smile as the blood pours down from his nose and drips from his chin.

"Got nothing to say?" I mock, noticing Aleksei and Tolya throwing fists at each other from the corner of my eye. I remove my switchblade from its sheath at my hip, giving it a quick flick, the blade snapping into place. Dodge steps back and carefully assess the blade.

"Vozvrashchaites vie fourgon!" *Get back to the van!* I snap, fully aware that more of Balakin's men could already be on their way here and Vladimir won't stand for petty fighting. "We don't have fucking time for this."

Dodge snarls, baring his teeth as he grunts an unintelligible slur before spitting blood at my feet and walking back towards the van. "That means you, too." I raise my voice to ensure Tolya and Alexsei can hear me as they continue with their fight. "Teper!" *Now!* I shout, moving forward to grab Aleksei by the collar of his shirt, ripping him back before his fist lands another hit on Tolya's face. "Get back to the fucking van. I won't ask again."

Tolya narrows his eyes, one already turning purple with swelling and forcing itself shut. His breathing is laboured and heavy and there's an open gash slicing through his right eyebrow. I squeeze Aleksei's shoulder, knowing he didn't hold back on the cunt, even for fear of Vladimir's repercussions and I thank him for it with unspoken gratitude.

I pull Aleksei to face me as Tolya stalks off. "Don't ever do that again. Do you hear me?" I won't let any man take a hit that is meant for me.

"Oh don't flatter yourself boss. That was like being hit by a four year old girl with oven mitts on."

I cock my eyebrow and hold his face between my hands, angling it to one side to take a look at the split in his upper lip and reddening bruise on his cheek. "You'd let a four-year-old girl punch you in the face?"

"Only for you," he chuckles, shoving me in the chest and jogging back towards the van.

I shake my head and laugh at his idiocy, feeling grateful to have a friend like him in my corner. Moving quickly, I remove my knives from the three men that I killed and make my way around the building to do a quick perimeter check, slashing the blades through the throat of each body I find to ensure there's no chance that we leave anybody alive. With each body and every new splattering of blood that covers me, I make sure to build that internal wall higher and higher until all of my human emotions are shut away and I am nothing more than an empty shell, as dead on the inside as the ones who lie motionless in a growing pool of blood.

I stand from the last body, wiping the blood from my blade across my thigh before slipping it back into place against my chest as I break into a run back to the van. Maksim and Aleksei are loading in the last crate of ammunition while Tolya and Dodge stand watch from the front and back of the van.

"Vy luchshe, cham kto-libo, dolzny ponimat posledstvia neposlushania, Nikolai." *You better than anybody should understand the consequences of disobedience, Nikolai.* Vlad shoves his finger into my chest, ignoring the blood stains that cover my body as he moves his face to within an inch from my own. "Nay doposhchu!" *I won't allow it!* I equal his stare with my own, refusing to back down or even blink before he does. I am not scared of this man, but his power makes me furious. His eyes narrow when he realises I refuse to dispute him and his signature smirk pulls his lips to one side. "Sadites vie fourgon," *Get in the van,* is all he says before turning on his heel and leaving me to swallow my anger.

CHAPTER SIX
Adanna

I step off the aeroplane with my luggage in one hand and my phone in the other. The icy wind nipped at my face and the shock of it took my breath away. I was expecting it to be harsh compared to the weather back in London, but it still takes me a moment to compose myself. I stiffen my shoulders, reminding myself that I'm in enemy territory now and thinking it's best not to stay out in the open for longer than I need to. Scanning the area as I make my way inside the airport, I look for a dark blonde Russian guy from the photograph Father showed me before I left.

As I enter the building, I hear someone shouting my name. "Syuda, Adanna!" *Over here, Adanna!*

I look up and see a guy sitting on one of the leather sofas waving at me. Lev, I smile, quickly making my way over to him. As I open my mouth to greet him, he cuts me off first.

"Vau, the vyglyadish thick ze, kak ona," *Wow, you look just like her,* he blurts out.

My eyebrows pinch together, not understanding who he's referring to. "Kto?" *Who?* I snap, making Lev suck a breath in as his eyes flicker between mine.

"Vasha mat." *Your mother.* Lev replies, leaving me reeling. Wait…what? He knew my mother? Why didn't my father tell me that? Before I can question him further he interrupts the whirlwind of questions, leaving me speechless and completely dumbfounded. "My mozem pogovorit ob ethom vie drugoi raz, Adanna. U nas yest missia, kotoruyu my dolzny vypolnit. Poyekhali." *We can discuss this another time, Adanna. We have a mission to complete. Let's go.* Lev grabs my luggage, gesturing to the exit. I follow, silently trying not to let my mind unravel, but it's too late, I have so many questions and I want them answered. But I know Lev is right, now isn't the time, we have a mission to complete. Anything I wish to know about my birth family can wait until this is done, until I have my revenge on the man who took me away from them.

Passing through the sliding doors as we leave the airport, the cold wind hits my face, once again, taking my breath away as I pull my leather jacket across my body to shield myself from the harsh bite of it. I don't know what I expected in terms of a car but the small navy Kia parked between two of the most expensive cars in Europe definitely wasn't it. I guess Lev likes to be as inconspicuous as possible out here, and I'm happy for it. I slide into the passenger's seat as Ivan puts my luggage into the boot and I rub my hands together to keep them warm. As soon as we pull away, Ivan reaches for the radio, turning it up as a heavy techno band begins thumping through the car.

"Lev…how far is it to your place?" I ask over the music. All of my instincts scream at me to ask about my mother, to find out how he knows her and what he knows of her but I bite my tongue and hold myself back. I pride myself in keeping up appearances in every situation, and especially now, I can't let on how much it's affecting me.

"Not far, twenty minutes, maybe thirty if we hit anything problematic," he grunts as he reaches over to the glove compartment and pulls out a handgun, throwing it into my lap. It's small but a weapon is a weapon. I release the magazine and check that it's full before reloading, throwing him a questioning look. "Incase of trouble. I tried my best to make sure the flight plans weren't traced but even the best of us can miss things." he states.

"What do you mean? Who actually gave us this job? I never did ask my father, and he wasn't exactly forthcoming with the information himself. He just said they were to remain anonymous." My chin raises as I hold his gaze.

"It doesn't matter who ordered it, Adanna, the job needs to be done. Vladimir is dangerous and deadly, even in his old age. Many want him dead but this place is corrupt and only works to benefit those who have money, not who is just," he says, turning the music up louder. I guess that is the end of the conversation. I stare at the road in front of me taking in the long stretch of tarmac and the snow gathered at the sides.

I'm definitely pleased with my choice of thick leather coat and boots but that doesn't keep the cold from my bones, even in the car. I can see my breath steaming in front of me, my nose feels frozen and I shiver thinking how absolutely crazy people must be to enjoy living in a place like this. I thought the UK was bad, but this is a frozen hell I can't wait to get out of. Lev's eyes snap to me as I shudder, trying to keep my teeth from chattering from the cold and he turns the heating up giving me a sympathetic smile. The rest of the journey is made in silence, I don't want to probe Lev anymore, he seems nice enough but if he's out here alone and my father has him as a contact, it means one thing. He is not someone you make angry.

After what feels like the longest and most bitterly cold ride of my life, we turn down a street that I otherwise would have guessed was abandoned, pulling up to a large block of flats. Lev is quick to get out of the car and retrieve my case before hurrying inside, leaving me behind. I wait a few minutes bracing myself for the arctic weather outside before I push the gun into the back of my trousers and exit the car. As soon as I am out, I hastily run in the direction that Lev went and follow him up six flights of stairs. He eventually stops in front of a green painted door, the paint is chipped and like the rest of the building, it looks like it's seen better days. Lev fumbles unsuccessfully with the key in the lock before he shoulder barges the door open, muttering under his breath. "Dolbany klyuch." *Fucking key.*

We enter into a narrow hallway with three rooms on the right, one on the left and one at the end of the corridor. "Close the door, Adanna." Lev orders as he opens the second door on the right and leaves my case next to it. As I pass the first room I notice it's a bedroom, it must be Lev's as he didn't offer it and I quickly pass by. The room to the left is the bathroom. The third door is closed and as I approach it Lev fixes me with a serious stare. "Weapon and computer room, leave it for tonight, we can make a plan in the morning. But first you need to eat. Come sit." I nod, knowing I don't stand a chance at winning the argument and I follow him through to the room at the end of the corridor into an open plan kitchen and living space. One side of the room houses a worn down sofa, a small TV and a sad looking bookcase. The city lights illuminate the large windows covering the side of the room with a warm hue that leads to a beautiful display of the night sky. I glance around, noticing Lev is already making himself busy in the kitchen and I take a seat at the small wooden dining table, removing the gun from my trousers and placing it on the table in front of me. I pull my phone from my pocket, staring at it for a moment before I decide to call Narcissa. As soon as it begins to ring I contemplate hanging up, I'm only calling to give them confirmation I have arrived and that I'm safe and Narcissa will already be well aware of that.

"Adanna! You got there okay?" Narcissa asks immediately.

Frowning, I wonder why she seems so on edge, but then I hear Father. "Adanna, is that you? I was just asking your sister for an update. As agreed, Narcissa is going to keep close contact with you and track the target's movements while you're over there." This explains why Narcissa is on tender hooks, he's pressuring her to do her job. And although he won't openly say it to her, he knows she is the best at this, he's just a control freak, something we have in common.

"It's okay, I'm alright. Lev is just making me some food before we start making a plan. Keep me updated on Vladimir's movements. I want this job done as quickly as I can. I won't lie, Russia is not the climate for me." I chuckle, trying to lighten the mood between them both.

"Okay, I'll ping you his location as it changes. If you need anything, call me sis, we want you home quickly, too." Narcissa sighs. I can tell she's finding father overbearing and it makes me smile, I'm usually the buffer between them. I miss them both already and their strange dynamic

"Okay, speak to you soon," I say, hanging up. All of a sudden I realise how tired I am from travelling and the mental load that this job brings with it. I need to plan this job efficiently, and to do that I need Lev to tell me everything he's learnt while he's been surveying Vladimir.

Glancing back to the kitchen I spot Lev muttering to himself as he brings over what I can only assume is an attempt at an omelette. I smile as he places the plate down in front of me and quickly grab his hand as he moves to walk away. "Thank you for this, Lev, it looks great. But can we talk about the plan now?" I ask, meeting his gaze.

Lev's eyes slowly hover over my hand on his wrist and his body tenses. "Let go! That conversation can wait until the morning. Eat, drink, and sleep. We have a long few days ahead," he orders as he snatches his hand away and leaves the room without another word. Great, I've pissed him off already. I eat what looks most edible of Lev's cooking before washing the plate up and heading to my room. I hate to admit it, but Lev is right, I need rest. I opt for a quick shower, letting the warm water lull me before I head to bed.

As I slide into bed, the fresh linen smell of the sheets engulfs my nostrils, comforting me in such an unfamiliar place. The lack of heating makes me shiver and I pull the sheets up under my chin, wishing I was back in the comfort and warmth of my own bed. I keep the gun Lev gave me close by and slowly I let my mind wander about the best way to end Vladimir's life before my eyes close and I drift off to sleep.

A loud bang outside of my window startles me awake and I immediately reach for my gun, jumping out of bed. I stand with my back against the wall, gun ready and listen. It's a hard reaction to control but my brain is hardwired to fight. Hearing nothing but my own heart thumping in my ears, I peer out of the window and sigh as I glance down to the street, realising that it was nothing more than a car exhaust backfiring. Damn my irrational brain. Checking my phone, I see it's 05.34am, I guess now that I'm up, It's time to get started. I don't want to be here any longer than necessary. A rush of excitement floods my body at the thought of finally planning out Vladimirs execution and I practically skip to the bathroom to get ready for the day ahead. It's quiet here compared to what I'm used to and although I can hear Lev in the lounge with the radio on, it's nothing compared to a house full of never ending chatter. After I'm washed and dressed, pulling on a thicker jumper with the hopes that it keeps me warm, I join Lev. He's sitting at the dining table eating something that looks like porridge. He nods towards the pan on the stove as I walk into the room. I spoon a small amount from the pan into a bowl, letting it slip from my spoon. It's thick and unappealing consistency reminds me of the time I spent in that hell hole Vladimir enslaved me in and my stomach churns at the memory. We would eat this sludge twice a day and it was barely enough to fill our stomachs but if we refused, we would starve. I know I made a promise to my father to kill him and get out, to simply do the job and leave, but I'm not sure I can do that. I don't want to just kill him. I want to burn his entire empire to the ground. I want him to look at me as I take his life and I want it to hurt.

    Lev clears his throat, "Best I can offer this morning I'm afraid. It will keep your energy levels up though. Come, sit." he says, tapping the chair next to him at the table. I do as he asks, sitting opposite him and placing my bowl down on the table. "Read this," Lev nods, pushing a brown paper file towards me. Our eyes meet for a split second before my gaze shifts down to the papers in front of me. Nothing I read tells me anything new about Vladimir, other than he's fatter than he was back then.

His picture is also present, although it doesn't look to be recent. I read through every detail of the file twice over, taking it all in. Pages upon pages of information containing all aspects of Vladimir's life, from birth to the present. As I flick over to the last page, I stop, realising I've missed a page, it's a list. A detailed list of his known victims. People he has killed, their names, ages, time and places of death. I take in a steadying breath, searching down the names and I freeze as I read the names Daniel Werth and underneath, Mila Werth. My birth parents. I feel my eyes burn, defying every fibre inside of me but I will not show weakness. I blink, refusing to let the tears fall. He will pay for taking their lives. He will fucking pay.

I am so focused, it startles me when I feel a warm hand touch mine. "I am sorry, Adanna, I didn't wish for this to upset you." Lev apologises, giving my hand a reassuring but gentle squeeze.

"It hasn't upset me, it confirms what I already knew." I smile sadly, meeting his eyes. He doesn't believe me, I can tell, but he nods anyway.

"Your mother was a dear friend of mine. We grew up together. Not far from here actually." He sighs and closes his eyes, taking a deep breath. "Her death was something that pained me greatly. But we will take revenge for her, Adanna. We can stop him taking these kids away from their families. We can make sure no one else goes through what you, and so many others have endured." His voice is powerful and inspiring. I agree, this has gone on for long enough.

"Tell me what I need to know, Lev. This trip down memory lane may fuel the fire but it will not burn him to ashes any quicker." I say, straightening my back and tilting my chin to meet his stare as I slip my mask back into place, falling into my role.

"He will be at his facility this morning where he keeps the children, he always has a cigar outside around 10.30am. That will be your green light. I hear you are an excellent shot, you can take him out quickly and easily, Adanna, and then be on a flight home to your family by lunch time." Lev says with a smile. But it doesn't feel right to me, I don't want to just put a bullet through his head, I want to make sure he suffers. I can't let him get away with everything he's done, not just to me but to every child he's ever forced under his roof. I shake my head, my damn pride is trying to get the better of me. I know what I've been assigned to do, take the target out, not let my emotions, my pride, alter the outcome. Do not let it win. I nod at Lev though I'm unable to say the words, silently agreeing because I don't trust myself not to argue. "Agreed then. Finish your breakfast, Vladimir's facility is a couple of hours away and it's already getting on. We need to make tracks." Lev leaves the room and I quickly finish the so-called porridge, I've got a monster to kill.

CHAPTER SEVEN
Adanna

A little over two hours later, Lev parks his car next to a large field that is covered with frost, not quite snow but still the air feels sharp and bitter. I mentally high five myself for the extra layers this morning and the tight fur lined jacket that acts like a personal radiator. I have various handguns and knives attached to my thighs and a sniper rifle harnessed around my back. "Take this, it's a comms device and will ensure I can communicate with you at all times." Lev hands me the small object and I put it in my ear.

"Thanks Lev." I smile before starting my way across the field to The Facility, it's where Vladimir keeps the children. Lev's voice crackles through comms, interrupting the otherwise silent surroundings. "Adanna, once this is done, anything you want to know about your parents you just have to ask." I glance back at him across the field, meeting his gaze and nod before continuing on my path. I plan on asking him everything I can as soon as this is over. I have so many unanswered questions.

As I hike the rocky, harsh terrain, I reach the top of the peak and veer off the well trodden path, wading my way through the dense foliage. Lev advised me it would be a good idea to stray from the path, making my tracks harder to follow through the thick undergrowth, and I couldn't disagree. Eventually, I come to a clearing. It has some coverage with the overhanging trees and plenty of bushes to hide in. I crouch down, keeping myself hidden and that's when I see it, The Facility. The sight of it makes my blood turn cold. This is where I was taken, where I learned that the devil is a monster in human form. Pulling my binoculars out from my pack, I take my time to survey the area. It's well lit and has several security guards manning the entrance on the gates. Setting my rifle up and adjusting the scope, I can't help the smile that creeps across my face. Now I just have to wait for an opening to either sneak in or for Vladimir to leave.

As the hours go by, I've had several check-ins from Lev. I see a few trucks come and go, dropping off shipments, until a large white van creeps through the security gates and stops before the doors.

My breath catches as I watch a man jump from the van. I know him, but I am not close enough to decipher how or where from. I study him closely, my mind wandering, tracing back through all of the kills I've ever executed to see if anything sticks out. But nothing does, it's almost as if I know him from another life, a dream of sorts, but I'm forced to swallow down the unfamiliar sensation and Vladimir walks into my line of sight. He's laughing with the man that follows him. My blood boils as I see him making a grand gesture with his hands, throwing his head back with a laugh. He looks older than I remember, and his large belly wobbles as he moves. This sight of him makes me feel physically sick. I can't help but think how much satisfaction I would feel to remove his innards and disembowel him with my bare hands. Taking his life as he begged for me to stop, he would finally know how it feels to be helpless but that can't happen. This is it, a clean, quick kill, just like Father wanted. I peer down the scope and take aim, my finger resting on the trigger guard as I line the scope up to his forehead. I take a deep breath and exhale completely, steadying myself as I prepare to take his life, but there's a disturbance behind him. The doors to the building fly open, and a whirlwind of chaos explodes in front of my eyes, rooting me to the spot as two children run out. I try to follow them as best I can through the scope of my rifle. They can't be more than thirteen years old, they look desperate and malnourished, their clothes hanging from their bodies. They both rush to get free, bolting through the group of men they clearly hadn't expected to be there, only to fail at the last hurdle. My heart is in my throat, bile rising through my stomach. I want nothing more than to take every one of these fuckers out so they can get free. Without thinking, I find myself scaling down to the opposite side of the hill and making my way towards the facility gates. I can't let them die. I make it to the edge of the shrubs, crouching low and preparing to make a run for it when everything freezes. I watch as Vladimir pulls a gun from his belt and shoots the smaller child in the head without so much as blinking. His slimy grin makes me want to shove his gun down his throat and make him choke on it. Blood explodes everywhere, coating the other boy. He freezes and falls to the floor. He knows he can't escape his fate now. My mind switches off and as if a higher being is controlling my actions, I take a grenade from my belt and pull the pin, launching it towards the opposite end of the fence around the building. The grenade explodes with a ground shaking boom, the flames bursting as it lands, sending shards of metal fencing, dirt and debris through the air. It worked and they're immediately on high alert, rushing towards the blaze, guns drawn, all of them shouting across the commotion in Russian. The distraction won't last long, I need to hurry the fuck up and get to the boy before they realise whats happening.

    I nearly jump from my skin as I hear Lev in my ear. "Adanna, chto eto bylo?" *Adanna, what was that?* Shit! I forgot he was here too.

    "Just a little hiccup, change of plans, heading back, need to regroup, this plan is a no go." I recall. Lev immediately starts shouting profanities at me in Russian that I can't quite follow, so I rip the device from my ear and pocket it quickly, feeling a surge of adrenaline take over my body. I can't help the smile that cracks my face. Sorry Father, your way didn't work. Now it's my turn to plan the demise of Vladimir Sidorova. But before that, I have a little boy to save.

    I head back to my post and gather my rifle, ensuring the ground behind me doesn't look disturbed, and quickly make my way back down to the boy who's still cowering in the dirt. I spy a broken crate near the entrance and dash for it, perching behind it until I know it's clear.

"What the fuck happened?" I hear one of the guards ask as they walk towards my hiding place.

"I don't have a fucking clue but it better not stop the boss from going to The Loft Club tomorrow night. I can't stand it when he's here." the other replies. I can't help but smile, it appears Vladimir's own men don't like him much either. I can't wait to snatch the breath from his lungs and burn his body into the dirt. I wait as the guards disappear towards the burning aftermath of the explosion and discreetly peer out to see the boy still frozen in place. His tiny body shakes violently with fear, the dead body of his fellow escapee laying next to him, his blood soaking into the earth. My heart breaks for him as I allow the memory of Byron's escape attempt to flood my memory. I can't let the same happen to this boy, I can't let him become another stain, forgotten and trodden into the ground.

In the chaos, they seem to have forgotten about him so I take my chance. I run towards him, on quick, silent feet before grabbing his arm and whisper-hissing for him to get up, "Dvigaysya, malchik, esli khochesh sbezhat!" *Move boy, if you want to escape!* The young boy snaps his head up to look at me and I grip his arm tighter and pull him to his feet. "Ya skazal dvigatsya!" *I said move!* I spit. And he does, scrambling to his feet, as I drag him along behind me into the wooded area. I pull another of my grenades and throw it at one of the vehicles parked behind the van, watching as it explodes with an ear splitting boom. Dark thick plumes of ash and smog begin to creep into the air around The Facility and flames ensnare the wreckage of the vehicle. It's a beautiful sight, and only the beginning of the destruction I intend to cause, but we can't stay here, I need to get this boy to safety or that will all have been for nothing. "Beggy malchik!" *Run boy!* I shout and begin to run myself. As we push our way through the thickness of bushes up the side of the hill, gunshots and shouting ring out behind us and the young boy freezes. I crouch low, forcing him to look at me, needing him to listen to the urgency in my voice. "Sleduy saa mnoy, yi the budes vie bezopasnosti." *Follow me and you will be safe.* The boy nods and does as I tell him as I drag his fragile body behind me through the bushes.

  Putting my comms back in my ear, I can only hope that Lev won't be too angry with me for going silent or for completely going rogue. "Lev, can you hear me? I've got a situation, we are probably three miles west of your location. I'm heading for the barn on the southern side of the trail." The barn was a backup plan, a failsafe if everything went to shit.

  "Adanna, what the hell is going on and who the fuck is we?" Lev screams at me. I can't help but snort a laugh at his annoyance, I'd been on my best behaviour up until now.

  "Look, plans change. I wasn't going to let him kill anyone else. Can you get to us or not?" I ask quickly, not wanting to engage in a full on argument as I run for my life, we need to get out of here.

"Your father is going to kill me, Adanna Sinclair!" Lev exclaims before his tone levels out. "I'll be with you soon, as long as they don't intercept me first. You promised to be discreet, Adanna." He whisper-hisses at me.

"I did, but like I said, plans change and I couldn't stand by and watch him kill another innocent child in front of me. That isn't who I am. It's not all bad though! I have information on Vlad's movements tomorrow night, and this new plan will be so much more enjoyable." I say with a smug smile. I feel a small hand tug against my own and my heart clenches. "We're going to follow this track down to the main road where there's a barn we can wait in. My friend is coming for us. You're safe with me." I explain, not faltering in my stride as I drive us both forwards. He doesn't respond, likely not understanding what I've said but he looks up at me with wide eyes and squeezes my hand and that's good enough for me.

"Adanna, make sure you're not being followed and for God sake, no more grenades," Lev snaps.

I roll my eyes. "Yeah, yeah, I hear you."

We continue to trek towards the main road, the sound of a vehicle travelling at speed catches my attention. Grabbing the boy, I pull us down behind a bush just as Lev calls through my earpiece.

"Adanna, Adanna, I'm at your location but I can't see you."

"We're here Lev, I just didn't want to run out into the road, in case you were one of Vladimir's guys."

"Good point, this place is no doubt crawling with Sidorova members by now. Hurry up, we need to get moving." Lev orders, the anxiety rising in his tone.

"Don't get your knickers in a twist, we're right here," I call as I open the side door and lift my new companion in, slamming the door behind us.

"What the fuck Adanna!? This wasn't a rescue mission!" Lev scolds, staring open mouthed with his eyes racing back and forth between me and the boy.

Ignoring him, I turn to the boy pulling up the blanket that's covering the backseats and throwing it over his body. "Lie down and keep yourself covered, we don't want to risk you being seen." He does as I ask, shaking the entire time.

I look at Lev and sigh, "I couldn't leave him to die. It's not in me. I'll get the job done regardless. I promise you, I swear on all that I love."

"You can explain to your father why you are sending him a stray." He grunts at me without taking his eyes off the road.

"If you can get him to my father then I will gladly explain it all." I state vehemently, my father will understand. After all, he's the one who saved *me* from that place all those years ago.

"Vladimir will be at the Loft tomorrow night. I need a few things to look the part, a dress, heels, that sort of thing. This ends tomorrow night." I state confidently. Lev nods and grumbles in Russian and as I look out the window and watch the billowing smoke bleed into the distant sky, I smile, knowing his end is near.

The journey back to Lev's place is quiet. I'm pretty sure I fell asleep for some of it, jostled awake as Lev ushers the boy from the car and rushes him inside the building. It doesn't take long for Lev to get him comfortable in a fresh pair of clothes and into the bed in his room before he lets exhaustion win and falls asleep. I sit for what feels like hours on the couch and contemplate the events of the day. Maybe I shouldn't have saved the boy but my conscience wouldn't have let me live it down and whether I like it or not, the decision will be one I wear with pride from now on. Memories flood my brain of the children I had seen Vladimir kill during my time in that god forsaken place. Before I realise what's happening, tears spill from my eyes, blurring my vision as I hear their broken cries, begging for him to spare them. Their blood stained the floors and the putrid smell of decay permeated the air, clinging to every surface if they didn't move the bodies the same week. I choke back a sob as a small knock at the apartment door has me reaching for my gun with my heart beating hard against my chest. I wipe the tears from my cheeks and move. My footsteps are silent as I stalk closer to the living room door and an agitated female voice travels down the corridor. "Here as you requested, Lev. But I am not a personal shopper, next time call someone else," the woman snapped in a harsh Russian tone. Lev grunts something I can't quite make out before I hear the front door click and his footsteps come my way. I move quickly, sitting back on the couch, and as Lev re-enters the room carrying multiple bags, I turn my head away, not wanting him to see my blood shot eyes.

"You don't need me to tell you how foolish you were today, Adanna. While you are dealing with Vladimir tomorrow night, I'll make arrangements for the boy to travel back to London."

I nod in agreement. "It was foolish but my only regret is that I didn't save the other boy, too." I stare him directly in the eyes as I raise my chin. I will never regret saving someone from a fate much worse than death.

Lev narrows his eyes at me, he can see I'm upset but doesn't comment on it as he continues to speak. "I have ordered a dress, shoes and makeup for tomorrow night. Your sister Niamh sent me your size so I hope everything fits." He shoves the bags in my direction, and I smile. She will love what I am about to do, it's her area of expertise after all.

"Thank you Lev, I do appreciate all you are doing." I say with my head held high as I leave the room. Now I need to prepare myself.

CHAPTER EIGHT
Adanna

"Make sure you wear that plum lipstick I told Lev to buy for you. I told him the exact shade to purchase to match your bag," Niamh squeals over the video call. The sound of her excited voice makes me realise how much I've missed her, even though it's only been a few days and my heart aches a little in my chest.

"Well he got plum lipstick, Niamh but I don't think it's the one you asked for. And seriously, I'm going to look like a hooker wearing these heels with this dress." I sigh in disdain, the dress itself isn't the problem, it's a tight fitting dress that comes to my mid thigh with thin straps and black ruched material that accentuates my figure. It's the heels that are the problem, they're about 4 inches high, threatening to cripple me with long ribbons that slither like a snake up my ankles. These shoes won't make it easy for me to escape quickly, should I need to. I'm tempted to wear my combat boots, but just as that thought comes to my head…

"Don't even think about wearing those horrible boots, Ada. You catch more bees with honey and this outfit is pure sugar. That is exactly how you're going to lure him in." She winks at me, knowing exactly what I would usually do.

"Well, you would know," I say mockingly.

"Exactly. Look, you've got this. I know how hard this is for you but it's a job, treat it like one and don't let your pride get in the way this time. Kill the bastard and come home to us. Father has been in a foul mood since you left and the only person who he hasn't shouted at is Narcissa for once. He's insufferable," she whines but it only makes me smile.

"I'll be home soon. Don't worry, I'll come back and take the brunt of his mood swings so you all don't have to." I chuckle.

"Good, because he's worried, you know, we all are," Niamh says with a tilted, sympathetic smile.

"I know, look, I've got to finish doing these damn shoes up then I need to head out. Lev is going to be busy tonight so can you make sure Narcissa is doing her job and is available should I need her?" I ask.

"Busy? What with? He's supposed to be watching out for you." Niamh questions.

"I have to make my own way to the club while he sorts something for me, okay?" I say vaguely.

"What do you mean? What have you done, Adanna? Please say it's not something that will make Father even more of a grump." she begs.

"Well, I can't say he'll be happy, but promise me that what Lev is sending to you, you'll take care of it.

Once I am home, I'll explain everything. He will understand, but I don't have time to explain it all now, I need to get to the club." I sigh, trying not to spill blush powder everywhere.

"Uhh fine, I promise but you owe me one, Adanna Sinclair." she relents, clearly not happy with me.

"I know, and don't worry I'll send you a selfie before I leave," I say, smirking as I hang up. I reach down to tie these insanely difficult heels around my ankles, wrapping the long thin ribbons around and around until they feel secure. I wiggle my toes and hips as I stand, making sure it feels comfortable before doing a final check in the mirror. Wow. I very rarely dress up, but the woman staring back at me takes my breath away. I look fucking hot. My jet black hair frames my face perfectly, my eyes are smokey and alluring, and the plum lipstick plumps my lips just the right amount to entice my prey. I really have outdone myself. I trail my eyes down my body, smiling, Niamh picked a beautiful dress. The material clings to my skin, showcasing my hourglass figure, snatching it at my waist and leaving nothing to the imagination. My legs are strong and they shimmer with the tanning moisturiser that Niamh made sure Lev got for me. I know exactly how good I look, and I can't help but pop my hip as I pout and snap a picture of my outfit as promised and text it to Niamh.

My taxi will arrive in five minutes, I need to stop getting so distracted and get my shit together. I grab two knives and two hand guns, checking that they are loaded, before strapping them to my thighs. I pull my dress down as far as it will go to conceal the weapons and do a quick once over in the mirror. A loud horn startles me, I glance out of the window to the street below and see my taxi waiting in front of the entrance to the building. Breathing in deeply, I snatch my black leather jacket from the hanger and briskly make my way to the front door.

    I pull the front door open and freeze as I hear Lev's footsteps approach behind me. I don't turn around, but I wait to hear what he has to say. "Be smart tonight, Adanna, don't let your emotions get the better of you again." I simply nod acknowledging his words. I can hardly dispute what he's implying, seeing as he is taking care of the problem I caused by letting my feelings cloud my judgement. But truth be told I would make the same choice over and over again to save an innocent child's life. It's not that I have a problem with morally taking a life or that I particularly care about the boy, it's more about my desire to do what is right. I am and always will be the best at what I do, even when I take a detour on the plans.

    "Are you all set?" I ask. He is taking the boy, whose name I now know is Stepan, to the airport and sending him to my father. I couldn't tell Niamh earlier that that's the reason Father is in a foul mood. I just needed to make sure someone would be looking out for Stepan when he arrived, to make him feel welcome and let him know he's safe. I know Gulliver won't be the most friendly, Narcissa has enough on her plate already and the others are too busy with their own jobs to babysit Stepan.

"As set as I can be. It shouldn't take me long to get the boy boarded, then I'll be able to pick you up when the job is done." Lev instructs.

"Okay, well, be safe and I'll call you as soon as Vladimir has been taken care of." I say, grasping the front door handle and leaving the apartment. I don't look back as I take the stairs down, the damn heels making it difficult to take more than one step at a time.

Once I am outside, I slide into the taxi. "Nochnoy klub Loft, pojaluista." *The Loft nightclub, please.* I instruct the driver. The journey is about thirty-five minutes long and I spend each painful minute shivering in the backseat of the cab. It's so cold that my nipples scratch against the material of the dress, like a razor blade cutting against my skin. The driver notices my jaw chatter a few times and turns the heating up a little, but he also seems to enjoy watching my nipples harden underneath my dress, trying to sneak a peek when he thinks I'm not looking.

Soon enough the driver parks up next to the busy club entrance. The sign 'The Loft' is lit up in neon green lights and the music is loud, booming through the walls. I turn to the driver giving him cash and muttering my thanks, but he says nothing, just nods as his eyes roam over my body one final time and his tongue darts out between his lips. I know I look hot but fucking hell. I glare in disgust at the creep before exiting the car, glad to be getting away from the perverted fucker.

My heels click the floor as I make my way to the entrance of the club. As I approach, I refuse to wait in line, seductively sashaying my hips as I stroll up to the door that is guarded by two heavily tattooed men. All that stands in my way is a thick velvet rope that dangles between them. Giving them the once over, I notice that they're armed but it makes no difference to me. I'm getting inside this club with them dead or alive. Luckily, I don't have to do much to get their attention, I relish the fact that their eyes immediately land on me. I look up at them, fluttering my eyelashes, taking a leaf out of Niamh's book as I lean into the chest of the closest one.

"Zdravstvuyte, rebyata. Chto dolzna sdelat takaya devushka, kak ya, chtoby popast vie takoye mesto?" *Hello, boys. What's a girl like me got to do to get into a place like this?* I sigh. Their eyes trail my body from head to toe, momentarily stopping at my tits, legs and then back to my face.

"Takaya krasivaya zhenschina, kak the bosse nay budet vozrazhat, esli my vpustim vas kie kachestve VIP." A *beautiful woman like you. The boss won't mind us letting you in as a V.I.P.* The taller of the two unclips the rope, allowing me access to the club and access to my revenge.

"Spasibo, krasivvy." *Thanks, handsome.* I purr, giving them a wink as I saunter past, swaying my hips, revelling in the feeling of their eyes now glued to my ass. Pushing through the door, I'm immediately dazzled by the strobe lights that reflect around the room. A mist of smoke moves throughout the dance floor making the visibility hazy and it takes a moment for my vision to adjust. The dance floor itself is crowded with people moving to the music, moving against each other with gyrating hips and sweaty skin. I make my way over to the bar, clicking my heels and swaying my hips as I move. The bar is equally crowded but it gives me a better view of the room. I prop myself against the counter, watching the male barman as he locks eyes with me, I smile suggestively until he makes his way over. "Vischi vie chistom vide, so idom." *Whiskey neat, with ice.* I order, needing the drink more than I realise. The barman nods and quickly gets my order, pushing it across the bar with a mischievous wink. I giggle, playing the part, and thank him before leaving payment plus a tip on the bar and turning my attention back to the room. Sipping on my drink, I scan the area, looking for my target. Then I see him, Vladimir Sidorva, the man who murdered my mother and father, lounging in a booth along the back wall. He's smart with his choice of seating, in direct line of both exits should he need to escape, but I know I can entice him out of the spotlight. He's sat with two other men and a woman whose face I can't see as she drapes herself over his body. I watch as Vladimir roughly gropes at her tits, pulling them out of her top for all to see. No one bats an eyelid at the nudity or the fact that she doesn't really seem to be all coherent either. Downing the rest of my drink, I decide I need to make my presence known sooner rather than later.

    Placing the glass down on the counter top, I wink at the server before moving to the dancefloor. Sliding through the crowd of people, I position myself directly in front of my prey, swaying my hips to the beat of the music, and using my hands to caress my body as I move. I close my eyes and continue to let the vibrations of the beat flow through me, trailing my fingers across my hips, breasts and up through my hair, zoning out everybody else in the room. Once the song comes to an end, I open my eyes to see Vladimir's hungry gaze burning through me and I smile. Gotcha. He lifts his hand and motions for me to come forward as he shoves the other woman over to his friends. I don't think twice about what I'm doing, my body moves on instinct and I swing my hips side to side as I stalk towards his table.

    Standing in front of him, I place my hand out for him to take and he does, rubbing his thumb over my knuckles and pulling me into his lap. His legs are either side of mine, caging me in. My body is pressed tightly against his large gut, and I can smell the liquor on his breath as he whispers against my skin. "What a pretty little thing you are." I move closer to his face, my lips millimetres away from his and I have to force myself to swallow down the repulsion.

    "And what do you like to do to pretty little things like me, sir?" I whisper against his lips. From the deep throaty groan he elicits, I know he likes that response. Moving my arms up, I trail my fingertips down his shirt, toying with him as I push him back into the seat. I lean in and purr into his ear. "Follow me if you want to see what I do with powerful men like you." I nip his ear before pulling away from him. His eyes trace the length of my body as I leave the table and his sick grin splits his chubby face. I sway my hips across the dance floor and walk into the bathroom knowing he's already on his way after me. I breathe a sigh of relief as I enter the empty restroom, thankfully there won't be any collateral damage tonight.

I perch against the sink, readying myself for the biggest most important moment of my life. A few moments later, the door swings open and like a panting dog in heat, Vladimir practically drools at the sight of me ready and waiting for him. And I guess I am, but not in the way he thinks. "Lock the door, I want you to myself," I say with a flirtatious giggle. He turns the lock without question and I smile as I glide across the room to him. I pull him closer and his arms engulf me before he picks me up, shoving me against the nearest wall. I can feel his large belly grinding against me as he rocks his hips forwards and God do I want to vomit, but I stay in character and cover my disgust with a faux squeal of delight.

"You like that, you slut." He gasps into my ear as he gropes my tits, pinching them so they hurt. God, does he even know how to pleasure a woman, obviously not. I feel around his body, tracing my hands across his back, hips, and stomach, purposefully touching every place I know he'd conceal a weapon and I want to laugh at his stupidity when I realise that he's come in here unarmed.

"Let me take care of you," I whisper.

He smiles, licking his lips before he steps back. "On your knees then whore." He orders and I step forward as I reach for his belt and remove it with one swift swipe. He closes his eyes in anticipation of the pleasure he's about to receive, but he has no idea that the pleasure will be all mine. It almost seems too perfect, too easy. But then I remember what he followed me in for and the thought of his stubby little dick getting anywhere near me makes me cringe. I pull my gun out of its holster and press it firmly against his head. His eyes snap open immediately.

"Turn around and face the wall, arms out behind you, or I pull the trigger, your choice."

"Fuck you, cunt!" He spits at me with his lip turning up into a snarl.

I throw my head back with a laugh, "Now, now Vladimir, do as I say and I promise this won't be as painful as I'd like it to be." He glares at me and I smirk, thoroughly enjoying having the upper hand. Slowly, he complies, and with his arms out in the sign of surrender, he turns around. Using his belt, I secure his hands behind his back and kick the back of his knees so that he falls to the floor with an uncomfortable grunt. I remove his tie and shove it in his mouth so I can muffle his cries before whispering against his ear, "Do you know who I am?" Vladimir narrows his eyes at me and just as I think he's got it, he shakes his head and growls something completely incomprehensible. I tut loudly, tilting my head as I regard him. "Don't tell me you've forgotten all about me! But I guess you've had so many children through your Facility that you don't remember all of your slaves." I taunt him, toying with his hair, twirling it around my fingers. I can feel his body shaking, I am not sure if it's from anger or fear but whichever it is, I am fucking loving it. Walking round to face him, I smirk, maintaining eye contact as I use my gun to tilt his chin to look at me. "Adanna Sinclair, happy to make your acquaintance." His eyes widen and his already large pupils dilate even more as he tries to pull his hands free from his restraint. He knows exactly who I am and what I do to my victims. Vladimir tries desperately to fight his binds only to flail around like a fish out of water and I can't help but laugh at him. The man I once thought was evil, that plagued my nightmares for years, now kneels before me, quivering like the coward he truly is. "Foolish man, aren't you?" I shove the gun further under his chin, enjoying watching him squirm until I hear shouting outside of the door. Vladimir's eyes widen, he hears it too. I'm running out of time. I move behind him, removing my blade from my thigh. This isn't how it was meant to happen. I wanted to torture and maim him, to paint the walls with his blood and bathe in it. But I refuse to let this opportunity slip by me again. "Say hello to my mother for me, she'll be the one torturing you in hell." I hiss, piercing my blade into his neck. Blood sprays over me as my knife punctures his carotid, and I smile like a mad woman as the door opposite flies open with a loud bang.

  My heart falters in my chest and I see nothing else but piercing blue eyes as a man enters the room. If it weren't for Vladimir convulsing on the floor, and his blood pooling at my feet I would be convinced it were just the two of us. I can't take my eyes off the stranger, slowly taking in the rest of his form. He's the most beautiful man I've ever seen, rugged, the ultimate bad boy type, tattooed and wholly fucking dangerous fully decked in a black leather jacket. My body tenses at the filthy images of all the things I'd like to do to him and him to me and slowly, I drag my gaze back to his face to find him staring straight back. For a moment I could swear I see the same lustful longing mirrored in his icy blue stare, but it quickly changes to anger as his eyes flick over Vladimir's body. The stranger moves at the speed of light and I feel his hands tighten around my neck as he barrels me against the wall. His body presses so tight against my own that Vladimir's blood now covers him too and it's hard to focus with the intensity of his hateful stare, but I smile at him, because whatever happens next, I can die happy knowing that I finally got my vengeance.

    Vladimir lays dying on the floor of the club bathroom, like the piss stain he is, and as my head grows fuzzy. I can't help but wonder why this man isn't doing anything to save him. My vision begins to darken around the edges as he continues to strangle me, but he leans in closer as he whispers a threatening promise that sends a shiver through my body. "That's the last thing you'll take from me Kate." It's the last thing I remember before the full shadow of darkness pulls me under.

CHAPTER NINE

Nikolai

It's been two days since I received the phone call informing me of Adanna's flight to Russia. Two long, agonising days that I found myself getting lost in each updated photograph that Ivan sent me as he kept watch on her. And two torturous days of fucking my hand while imagining it was her lips wrapped around my cock, the release barely able to satiate what I was truly craving. I've spent years fucking my hand over photos of this woman, and now that she's within reaching distance, I want to know what it feels like to be inside her.

There's a meeting tonight at the club in town, a new favourite location of Vladimir's to conduct his business. The amount of whores who are ready and willing at the click of his fingers is obviously a factor. There is nothing any ordinary woman would find attractive about him, but money and power are worth more than life and love here. When it comes down to it, these women know that where there's money, there's power and Vladimir oozes it. I've seen the way their eyes glass over when they squeeze their bodies up against his, gyrating their hips across his lap, holding his cigar between his lips while they caress his thighs. It's nauseating but he fucking lavishes in it, groping their bodies with heavy hands and pulling their tits from the pieces of fabric they cover themselves with, only to fondle them until their nipples are raw. He is anything but gentle.

 I shake my head, trying to ignore the overwhelming urge to keep him as far away from Adanna as possible. He still doesn't know she's in the country, and I plan on keeping it that way for as long as possible. I pace the ground floor of my house, tempted to make my way down to my basement, desperate to rid the memory of my father's teeth bearing down on the nipple of a blonde girl earlier today who looked like she'd only just turned sixteen. She barely fought to keep her tears at bay, her wide eyes pleading with me to help. But I couldn't, my only choices were to stay and watch, or walk away, so I took my drink and made my exit, refusing to look back as her cries reached my ears.

 I shake out my hands, cracking my knuckles to help from putting my fist through the wall as tension rolls throughout my body. I would sever his hands from his body if he ever laid a finger on Adanna and not think twice about it while I shoved them down his throat and choked him to death. This sudden urge to make sure he never has the chance to even get close catches me off guard and the thought of Adanna being at the receiving end of Vladimir's sadistic games makes me think things that only make me feel more violent.

My phone vibrates in my pocket and for once, I want nothing more than to throw it at the wall. The vibrations stop only for them to start straight back up and without looking at the caller, I bring the phone to my ear.

"What?" I snap, brushing my hand across my head and down my face.

"Ubiytsa. *Killer.* I have something you're going to want to come take a look at." Ivan says calmly. "Or rather, someone." I hear a muffled protest in the background but can't make out any words.

"What did you do?" I ask, already grabbing my leather jacket and heading for the door. "Where are you?"

"I'm in Ruchey. I caught us a little friend."

My heart suddenly falters. "The woman?" I ask, praying deep down it isn't, because if anyone is capturing her, it will be me. I don't trust Ivan to keep his hands to himself.

"No boss, her male friend from the airport. I lost sight of the woman, but there's a boy here, too. I found some papers on the guy, looks like he was trying to get him out of the country." I crease my brows, momentarily confused. Trying to get him out of the county?... Then it hits me. The explosion at The Facility. That sneaky little bitch. Vladimir was practically on fire yesterday after two explosions at The Facility cost us a run away. I've never seen him so angry and the guards on duty all lost their lives for simply standing too close to his rage by blowing out their brains. I hear muffled grunts again, my thoughts causing havoc as I start my car.

"Don't do anything until I get there, just keep them secure and text me the exact location." I order, not bothering to wait for a reply before throwing my phone onto the passenger seat and flooring it through the compound past the guards at the gates who throw their hands up in annoyance as they're engulfed by a cloud of dust as I pass. Ivan's location comes through before I've cleared the compound from my rearview and I dial it into the GPS on my dashboard then hit the gas.

Anticipation floods my body the closer I get to the little pindrop on the map. I'm barely keeping it together as it is with Adanna's face haunting my every waking moment. But as I get closer to Ivan's location my skin tingles with the need for some violence.

When I arrive, I slam on the brakes, almost snapping the key from the ignition as I hurry from the car towards the empty building on the northwest corner. I quickly scan my surroundings. It's a pretty run-down part of town, most of the windows are smashed or boarded and all but one of the street lights along the road have been smashed, fragments of glass and plastic casing litter the pavements. The last flickering bulb illuminates a secluded alleyway and I slip through towards the door. I slip my knife from my hip, flicking the blade open and ready for the unexpected, sliding my thumb against the sharp edge before I enter the building. I've always favoured my blades over any weapon. Guns are loud and sloppy, but there's nothing as precise and delicate as slicing your blade through somebody's artery, watching as life oozes from their eyes and their blood coats their body. There's an artistry to it, and I've grown used to the peace it gives my mind.

 I slip through the door, the muffled sound of scuffling feet leads me towards the kitchen where I find Ivan standing over a dark haired man with one eye swollen shut and a cloth gag shoved in his mouth. His hands are bound together behind his back and there's a small line of blood running from his bottom lip down to his chin.

 "You got here quick," Ivan laughs as I walk into the middle of the room. I take a quick glance around noticing the way the man's eyes widen as he faces me. I wonder if he knows who I am. He must, considering he's working with the traitor.

 "Gde malchik?" *Where's the boy?* I ask. I need to confirm that she was the one responsible for the attack last night. Ivan opens the nearest door, leading into a small sitting room where a scrawny little boy covered in unmistakable black and blue mottling his skin, cowers in the furthest corner, trying to make himself as small as possible.

 "Eto ego nay khyataet na obyekte, nay thuck lee." *He's the one missing from the facility, isn't he."* Ivan follows me as I enter the room. It's more of a statement than a question. We both know that's exactly where he's from. The telltale signs of starvation, desperation and rough handling screaming at us loud and clear as I narrow in on him. I know my duty to my father would be to eliminate the boy on the spot, he's too much of a threat now he's outside of the walls of The Facility. He could tell anyone and bring Vladimir's whole operation to ruins. But as I stare at his cowering frame, his bones protruding beneath his now too-large clothing, I can't help but feel like he's been given a second chance at life, one I wished I had been given. And at that moment, I decide he is not my main concern, quickly turning back into the kitchen sharing a knowing look with Ivan before he follows suit, shutting the door on the boy and concentrating back on the man before us.

"Where is she?" I ask, keeping my tone calm as I take the seat opposite him at the table. I don't miss the way his lips twitch momentarily but he doesn't give me an answer. I'm not in the mood for games. Usually I would love to draw them out but Adanna's sudden absence fills me with such a sickening need to find out where she is that I almost find myself choking on it. As I ask him again, I lunge across the table, wrapping a hand around the back of his neck and quickly slamming his face onto the table, enjoying the thick crunch of his nose. "It doesn't pay well to ignore me. Now, where is she?" I sit back against my chair as the stranger slowly lifts his face to look at me, his teeth bared and covered in the blood that's now pouring from his broken nose as he smiles at me.

"On her way to end him," is all he says, throwing his head back with a twisted laugh, spraying blood further across himself and the table. I glance at Ivan who looks just as confused as I am, and then everything makes sense. Vladimir.

"Blat, mne nuzcho popast vie klub. Ona idet saa Vlad." *Fuck, I need to get to the club. She's going after*

Vlad. I choke, pushing the chair across the room with the force that I stand. "Otvedi ego vie osobniak, a zathem otpravlyaysya vie klub!" *Get him to The Manor. Then make your way to the club,* I shout over my shoulder, already half way through the door. That fucking bitch. I may already be too late.

I floor it as soon as my car purrs to life, trying to ring Vladimir on my way. He doesn't answer, of course he doesn't, he's fucking useless with his phone. I race through the streets, the bright lights from passing vehicles and buildings all blur into various streams, like shooting stars either side of me as I fly through red lights and stop signs to get to The Loft.

My stomach twists as I throw the car around the final corner, my tyres screeching across the tarmac as I slam on the brakes. Barely giving myself time to shut off the engine before I bolt across the street to the guarded entrance of the club.

Two large, heavily tattooed men guard a thick velvet rope that dangles between them in front of the door, their guns tucked away at the back of their tight fitted trousers. They may aim to be subtle, but when you know what you're looking for it becomes even more obvious when they try to hide it. I scan my eyes through the busy line of guests waiting to get in but come up short. She must be inside. "Dermo!" *Shit!* The two doormen notice my arrival as I approach the velvet rope. Their miniscule glance of recognition towards each other doesn't go unnoticed as their demeanours change and the larger of the two unclips the rope from his end of the barrier.

"Mr Sidorova," they both nod in unison, allowing me entry through the overly decorated club doors. "Have a good evening, sir." I hear the comment before I'm completely out of earshot but still, I smile. Oh you have no idea, I think to myself as I enter the club. Loud techno music bleeds into my ears, forcing me to grind my teeth. Everytime I've been here, I've left with a fucking headache from the shit they call music. One time threatening to slice the DJ's hands off if he didn't put something decent on.

I'm momentarily blinded by strobe lights and smoke but as my eyes adjust to the darkness, I feel a chilling sense of calm envelop me. The need for blood is coursing through me like a raging wildfire. It's smoke spreading rapidly, too anarchic to get under control, almost suffocating me with the thought of her blood on my hands as I concentrate to survey the entire building.

I move forwards, the large area opening as you walk through the club is two steps higher than the rest, giving me a better vantage point as I look down over the floor below. The main source of light emanating through the room comes from the bar. The floor to ceiling walled mirror reflecting the wall sconces as they illuminate the array of bodies pressed into one another while they wait for service. My eyes snap over to Vladimir's regular booth, perfectly positioned along the back wall in view of the entrance, exit, bar and dancefloor. He always likes to be able to watch his surroundings, and takes great pleasure in getting off on the girls sashaying across the floor when his usual lap-bunny isn't cutting it for him. Vladimir's seat is empty. I jump down from the platform, pushing my way through sweaty bodies entwined with lips and limbs and come up to Vladimir's table. Dodge and Tolya both undisturbed by my arrival with a busty blonde girl who has her head thrown back while they suckle on her tits. I lean forwards, yanking Tolya by the ear until his face is a few inches from my own. He throws out his arms in protest, his face still a mix of deep purple and blue bruises from his run in with Aleksei at The Dell. "Gde Vladimir?" *Where is Vladimir?* I snarl, pulling tighter on his ear.

"Blyat, Nikolai, on poschel vie toilette s zhenschinoy. *Fuck Nikolai, he went to the toilet with a woman.* Tolya confesses. The toilets. For fuck sake.

"You fucking delinquent." I spit, shoving Tolya's head towards his brother and the blonde who are oblivious to the altercation as Dodge slides his hand beneath her skirt. I turn quickly, almost frantic as I barge my way back through the web of bodies towards the restrooms.

I go straight for the ladies bathroom, something in my gut telling me that's where she is and that's where I'll find Vladimir. I waste no time pushing into the door, only to be met with resistance from the other side. The door is locked, and my worst nightmare is coming true. I need to get on the other side of this door. I stand back and brace myself, raising my leg as I prepare to kick straight into the wood.

"Ubiytsa." Ivan's voice filters through the music. A moment later his hand hits my shoulder. "What the fuck is going on?" he asks.

"You got here quickly. Where did you leave the man?" I ask, furrowing my brows in confusion as Ivan chuckles.

"What can I say? Maksim is a bad influence. He's detained in the kitchen utility. He'll be asleep for a few hours."

I snort a laugh then focus on the restroom door again. "Vladimir is in there, with her." Is all I say before I raise my foot and smash it through the door, slamming the wood into the wall behind with a loud bang. I know there are people watching but I refuse to acknowledge them as I step into the brightly lit room, the fluorescent bulbs a stark difference to the darkness through the rest of the club. I can feel Ivan on my heels as we walk through and he closes the splintered door behind us.

Instinctively, I slip my hand to the blades strapped to my chest, pricking the tip into the pad of my thumb as I ready it in my hand. I hear Ivan shift his gun from his holster, following my lead, but as we slowly stalk around the white tiled corner, our weapons raised and ready, nothing could have prepared me for the sight staring back at me and for the burning rage that consumed me thereafter.

There she stands, eyes wide and lips parted as her gaze locks onto mine and the air leaves my lungs. A mirage of sin adorned in the tightest black dress I've ever seen, leaving nothing to the imagination, and failing to conceal the holster on her thigh. Her deep brown eyes bore into my own before I narrow in on the blood covering her body. A spreading pool of blood catches my eye and I have to force myself to look away from her, down to the floor where the dying eyes of Vladimir stare vacantly into nothing. There's a single stab wound to his carotid, the gushing blood slowly diminishing as his life slips away. The anger I feel is unprecedented, it's like a white hot poker has been thrust into my body and the only way to subdue that pain is to inflict it on somebody else. Vaguely unaware of the exact moment it happened, something inside of me snaps. How dare she take this from me. I haven't waited all of these years and been subjected to the abuse from this man to have his deserved death be taken from me, and to be done in such a quick and reckless manner.

    My fingers flinch as they come into contact with her throat, constricting her airway until her pupils blow wide with terror. It's the most beautiful sight I've ever laid eyes on, to see her scared for her life by my hands. This woman has a lot to answer for. My lips pull up with a sickening grin as I lean in closer to her, ensuring Ivan is out of earshot as I breathe a whisper across her delicate skin before she becomes a dead weight between my hands. "That's the last thing you'll take from me, Kate."

    "Mne nuzhno, chtoby vy razobralsis s ethym." *I need you to sort this out.* I say in a calm tone that surprises even myself considering the need to rip this entire restroom to pieces. I haven't taken my eyes from Adanna's blood splattered face, her unconscious body now cradled against my chest. Her small frame is athletically sculpted, with curves and muscles in all the right places. She fits so perfectly against my body, hard and rigid with the urge to break her.

"Get his body out of here and call an emergency meeting at The Manor as soon as you get back." I order, finally turning to face Ivan who stares at me with his lips pressed into a firm line.

"What about the woman?" He asks motioning towards Adanna's limp body in my arms.

"I'll deal with her. She's got a lot to answer for." I snarl, tightening my hold on her, for reasons I don't yet understand. It'll be a miracle to get this dealt with without raising suspicion, I lock eyes with Ivan once more and he dips his chin.

"Nachalnik." *Boss.* He vocalises, the title blanketing me in a suffocating layer of conscience.

"Discreet, Ivan. Nobody must know." I add, before taking one last parting look at Vladimir's body then carrying Adanna through the club back towards my car. Nobody bats an eyelid at the unconscious woman and even the doormen know not to ask questions as they move aside to let us through. It wouldn't be the first time a drunken woman had been carried out of the club, and certainly won't be the last.

I drive back to the compound, finding myself regularly checking her breathing as she slumps against the passenger side door. There was no way I was putting her in the backseat. If she's next to me, I'll be able to see if she wakes up easier. At least that's what I told myself the reason was. I could have just thrown her in the trunk.

She remains completely comatose as I carry her through my house and down to the cellar where I place her onto the mattress in the middle of my very own steel-barred cell. Her delicate body looks so out of place in such a harsh environment. I take my time studying her. She's nothing like the photographs. Her porcelain skin glistens where it isn't covered with intricate tattoo's painting their way across her body like a piece of artwork. I follow the path of a snake from head to tail, starting at her collar bone, its forked tongue licking across her neck and its body wrapped around her entire left arm. What a magnificent creature this woman is. I drag my gaze over her ample breasts, resisting the urge to rip them from her pathetic excuse of a dress as I carry on down her body, appreciating her wide hips and supple thighs.

A while later my phone vibrates with a message.

We're ready. - Ivan

Fuck, I've been down here staring at her for the last two fucking hours without realising. I brush my hands across my face, already annoyed with what I have to do next and the pretence I have to continue to live. I ensure to lock the cage door as I leave, taking the key with me as an extra precaution.

I enter The Manor, the atmosphere already stifling with anticipation for the reason behind this emergency meeting. I'm met with a raucous commotion leading me straight to the library, and just as I'm about to enter, Ivan meets me from the other side of the door.

"What happened to the woman?" He asks, closing the door behind him, muffling the sound of impatient men.

I'm momentarily taken back by his question, why should it matter? He should trust in me to have sorted it. Afterall, I am his new Boss and for him to question me like this would be a murderable offence. I decide to offer him a small truth. "She's in the cell."

Ivan immediately fires out another question. "Who is she?"

"Somebody you shouldn't be concerning yourself with."

"Nikolai, she just killed Vladimir. How…"

"That's enough, Ivan." I snap, my frustrations with him becoming unbearable. "You will do well to remember who you're speaking to from now on." I add, the taste of the words are vile on my tongue as I speak them. I never fucking wanted this.

Ivan's eyes grow wide before he casts his gaze down and moves out of the way. "Boss," he yields. I know he won't let this go easily. But for now, I have more worrisome men to face than Ivan Baburin as I inform them of my new role as their leader, and I have a little sinner that I'd like to get back to as soon as it's done.

CHAPTER TEN
Adanna

My eyes snap open and I inhale a deep, dry breath as I try to work out where I am. Breaking out into a cold sweat I remember what that blue eyed monster whispered to me. Kate, he called me Kate. Except he didn't look like a monster, his face had that look that can stop you in your tracks and make you forget everything around you for just a moment, before you realise how much danger you're in.

Shutting my eyes tightly, I try not to remember the way his body felt pushed against mine, hard and rigid and utterly perfect, or how my body betrayed me and reacted in ways that it shouldn't. I bring my fingers to my neck, still feeling the pressure his hands forced on me as they wrapped around my throat and I faded into darkness. Those shocking blue orbs were the last thing I saw before I woke up here, a place that feels too familiar. The mattress instantly reminds me of being held captive as a girl and the smell of damp invades my nostrils, making me retch. My heart begins to hammer against my chest and panic clutches at my lungs, stealing the ability to breathe. I force myself into a sitting position, turning my head frantically to get a better look around the room. Fuck. The bastard put me in a cage. Cautiously, I move to the edge of the mattress, the coldness of the floor beneath sends a violent shiver through me, reminding me that I am still only covered by the thin material of my dress, and to my surprise, my heels are still on too. I rub my eyes, trying to soothe the ache caused by the single fluorescent bulb dangling from the ceiling. Slowly, I rise to my feet, but stumble as I move closer to the bars, these goddamn heels will be the death of me. I try to call out but my throat is sore and as I swallow down the dryness it feels as if I've chugged on a bucket of broken glass. He better not have damaged my vocal cords when he strangled me. I pull at the bars frustrated, rattling them to find any weaknesses, but they don't budge. The anger consumes me, releasing in the only way I can down here and I scream, but it's pitiful and painful, only pissing me off more. Slumping back against the bars I glance around, trying to spot another escape route, one that my captor may have overlooked, but unfortunately, there is only one way in and out.

  Suddenly, the door to the room opens with a loud bang, making me jump and stumble, my ankle twisting painfully as I try to right myself. But I'm unable to stop. I land hard on the concrete floor, hissing out at the pain shooting through my foot. I hadn't heard his descent into the room but as I look up, his body towers over me, large and imposing. My captors eyes burn directly into my soul as I meet his gaze, the deep pools of blue pulling me in and making my stomach flip. He stares at me silently, unmoving until his lips curl and his words bring me straight back to reality. "Just where you belong, at my feet, begging."

"I will never beg you for anything." I sneer at him as I climb to my feet. His gaze roams over my body, and from the way they hover for just a second too long, I can tell he likes what he sees, even if I can feel the hatred rolling off him.

"They all say that at first. Do you like your new home?" He taunts, motioning to bars surrounding me. I look away, not wanting to give him anymore satisfaction. "It's not like your pretty mansion back home, is it Printsessa?" *Princess?*

"And what do you know of my home?" I snap back at him. There's a siren blaring in the back of my mind. How does he know about The Mansion?

"I know a lot about you and your family. How is dearest Daddy Sinclair?" he asks, smirking.

"Get fucked." I spit at him.

"Making an offer already, Printsessa?" *Princess* he laughs.

"I wouldn't touch you if my life depended on it!" I hiss, not entirely knowing if the words are true. Even now, his sharp jaw, large tattooed hands and thick muscular arms send disturbingly vivid images through my head that I have to shake off.

The stranger throws his head back and laughs even more as he replies, "What about the lives of your friends? Or the lives of your beloved siblings? Perhaps your dearest father or uncle?"

How dare he threaten my family and friends. My nostrils flare in anger as I spit at him. "Are you still loyal to the scum I killed? I would do it again and again. I regret nothing. I dare you to come for those I love and you will live to regret it, svoloch." *Bastard.*

His eyes heat at my words and his jaw tenses. "Maybe I should start with your friend, Lev Rogov, is it? He's been helping you hasn't he? He helped you break into the facility and rescue that boy."

Shit, Lev. "Leave him alone. It's me who killed Vladimir Sidorova, not him." I plead.

"No Printsessa, you don't tell me what to do. My revenge is going to be slow and sweet. I'll have you on your knees begging me for forgiveness, but not before I take all those who you care for." he sneers in disgust.

"Vie tvoikh mechtakh." *In your dreams.* I shoot back at him, banging my palms against the bars of my cage.

A dark look passes over his face, "I hope killing him was worth losing your friend."

Anger and panic rise in my chest. I need to get out of here, I need to save Lev, he doesn't deserve to be punished for a murder that I committed. "Who are you? Vladimir took my life from me, he deserved what he got!" I scream at him. He moves so quickly I don't have time to move away from the bars. He reaches into the cage, grabbing my already bruised neck and pulling my body hard against the cage. My hands claw at him as he snarls with his face close enough to my own that I can taste the mint and whiskey on his breath.

"What he took from you is nothing compared to what you took from me. Mark my words, I will make you regret ever leaving us that day, Kate."

As soon as the words leave his lips, he releases me, shoving me back with a bruising force.

"I don't go by that name anymore." I choke out.

The man smirks, his features darkening as he leans in closer, "I know, Printsessa Sinclair." My blood runs cold, I'm completely out of my depth here, I have no idea who this man is or how he knows who I am. I was stupid with my need for revenge and I let it overshadow everything else. I should have completed the job as I was ordered to do. I should have listened to my father and Lev. But now, I watch my captor stalk away, his chilling laughter echoing around the small room as he makes his way back up the stairs and I, for once, don't know what to do.

The door slams and I'm left alone once again. My heart is beating hard and fast as I try to piece together who he is and how he knows me as Kate. I haven't gone by that name for so long. He said I left them, was he like me? Captured and enslaved by Vladimir. If he was, why isn't he thanking me for taking him out? So many questions spiral in my head but I can't think straight. I know I need to find a way out of here, I believe him when he says he will go after everyone I care for. The look in his eyes didn't lie. I worry for Lev, I hope and pray he is okay, and that he managed to get Stepan out of the country. I had so many questions to ask him about my mother. In truth, he had become someone I respected, I don't want to see him hurt because of my own selfish pride.

CHAPTER ELEVEN
Nikolai

Russian. She speaks fucking Russian. I barely managed to keep myself together down there, subconsciously thanking myself for having those bars between us as I squeezed my hands around her throat, feeling her pulse quicken beneath my fingertips. I have never been more turned on and irrationally fucking furious in my entire life. Imagining my solid cock pounding between her plump lips and cutting off her oxygen as she choked on me. Her eyes betrayed her bravado when I called her by her real name, and the sight was almost my undoing.

I slam the door hard enough to hear the wood splinter as I make my way back to the kitchen. Although I now own The Manor and have the right to live there as Bosse, there is no way I would give up this house, especially not when I'm keeping a feral princess locked in my basement. Luckily, everybody was in agreement with me taking over after Vladimir's demise. They were quick to show their support, drinking way into the early hours of the following morning. I ordered Ivan to kick them out before dragging the man we now know as Lev, into the back sitting room until I returned and made sure to secure a swift exit back home to check if my sleeping beauty had finally woken.

    I make my way to the front of the house, the late night sky is still black across the compound, the only sounds coming from the creatures that roam the forest at night, hidden beneath the shadows of the trees. My body feels like a livewire, alert and overstimulated as I step out onto the gravel footpath. I need to get the image of Adanna's mouth swallowing my cock out of my head before I storm back down there and make it happen. I also need to have a chat with Mr Rogov.
    The Manor is deathly quiet at this time of night, the large empty hallways echo with my footfall as I pass through. Tolya and Dodge frequently held rooms here but they were advised never to return to them unless they wanted their eyes removed, so the house is completely empty, bar Ivan and our hostage. Even the house staff had been sent elsewhere for the night given the circumstances.
    Walking into the large open room, hardly ever used by Vladimir due to his personal hate for having more than one sitting room, my eyes immediately narrow in on the shirtless man bound to the chair, his sagging head swaying as Ivan circles him. I watch silently for a moment, acknowledging the large woven

rug and solid oak coffee table that have been shunted off to the side then clear my throat, announcing my arrival.

"Ubiytsa," Ivan smiles as he looks up. "Levy here isn't much of a talker…Are you, friend?" he taunts, yanking on Lev's hair and pulling his head back so he faces me. His already swollen eye is now a deep shade of blue that has spread across his nose and cheekbone.

"You can leave now, Ivan," I say loudly, making myself clear that this isn't a party for three but Ivan begins shaking his head, pulling back harder on Lev's hair as he bares his teeth at me.

"No." He snarls, "Why would you lie?" His anger is getting the better of him. He's asking me why I didn't tell the others who killed Vladimir during the meeting. When asked who it was, I simply denied any knowledge, ignoring the confused look on Ivan's face as conspiracy theories were thrown around regarding retaliation from what happened at The Dell. "Who is that woman and what makes her so fucking important that you would lie to the entire compound about her?"

I realise that Ivan isn't going to let this go, or leave like I asked, so I make sure to focus on Lev, using him as a distraction. At the mention of the kill and Adanna, Lev's demeanour changes subtly and even though he tries to hide it by pretending Ivan is hurting him, I'm already on my way over. My feet take four long strides before my fist connects with his jaw, spraying a satisfying amount of blood across the darkwood floor. "Who are you?" I growl, slamming my fist into his face again when I'm met with no answer. "I asked you a fucking question. Who. Are. You?"

Ivan chuckles as he walks away and throws himself into one of the old mahogany armchairs that surround the fireplace and faces our direction. "I told you he wasn't much of a talker."

I turn my attention back to Lev. "Who do you work for?" Nothing. I throw my fist into his stomach, his body folds in pain as he gasps for air. Time to change it up. "Why were you spotted picking up Kate from Vnukovo airport, three days ago?"

"I don't know anybody called Kate," he voices, stiffening his shoulders as he looks me dead in the eyes, but I can only smile.

"Oh, that's right. You know her as Adanna Sinclair." I smirk, catching the shift in Ivan's body from the corner of my eye. "Now, tell me…"

Ivan interrupts me as he flies to his feet. "Znachit lee etc, chto…" *Does that mean…*

"Prekratit!" *Stop!* I snap, jerking my head to face him quick enough to give me whiplash. Ivan immediately presses his lips together with a frustrated scowl pinned across his face. His outbursts are already pushing boundaries with me today and if he doesn't keep himself in check, I will be checking him into an unmarked grave, permanently.

After a final warning glance at Ivan, I demand more answers. "Tell me why you're here with Adanna Sinclair."

Lev throws his head back, wincing as he laughs, shaking his head. "If I tell you that, my life wouldn't be worth living."

I crouch down to his level, ensuring he can see the severity with which I say, "I find it funny that you think you'll have much life left after I'm finished with you." The beauty of fear in a person's eyes when you promise them death is a delectable truth I will never tire from. "Let's see how Adanna feels when she sees you, shall we?" I don't wait for a reply before pummelling my fists into his stomach and taking a final swing at his face, splintering his nose and rendering him unconscious.

"Privedi eye syuda." *Bring her here.* I order, throwing the cell key to Ivan who merely nods and walks away. He must have a thousand questions he wants answered. And I will answer them, just not right now.

I take solitude in the momentary silence. My bruised fists are throbbing painfully from the impact on Lev's body but I concentrate on it, letting it lull me until muffled protests land on my ears.

Flicking my gaze in the direction of the noise, I see Ivan struggling to keep hold of Adanna as she thrashes wildly in his arms, kicking her legs, trying to break free. Her eyes are wide and dilated, she looks petrified at the sight of Lev's body sagging unconsciously against the restraints in his chair. I'm beginning to enjoy the look of distress on her a little too much. I nod my head at Ivan, giving him the go ahead to remove the cloth gag he'd shoved into her mouth to keep her quiet.

"Let him go!" She barks immediately, almost snapping Ivan's fingers in the process before he moves her arms around her back, keeping her in place.

I feel my lips curve up into a devilish grin as I stalk slowly closer to where they stand. "And why would I do what you ask, Printsessa?" Adanna jerks her shoulders forwards but Ivan is prepared for the move, countering her shift and moving with her before slamming her back into his chest causing her to wince. The pain is ever so fleeting as her face straightens again and she's put her mask back in place. But I can see through her, she's not fooling me.

"He hasn't done anything to you. Let him go. I was the one who killed Vladimir. He had nothing to do with it," she pleads.

I shake my head at her words. She really has no idea, does she? "This isn't about him. He was as good as dead to me anyway. This is about Dimitri Petrov." I snarl, ignoring the glaring eyes from Ivan as he takes in the conversation.

Adanna's face scrunches in confusion as she stares directly into my eyes, like she's searching for some hidden meaning behind all of this. "I was given a job, and I delivered. Like I always do."

"A job?!" I snap, her lack of pity snaps something inside me. I need to make her suffer for what she did that day, and for every day of pain she has caused me since.

I lunge forward, pulling Ivan's gun from his waistband and holding it at her temple, breathing rapidly at the adrenaline coursing through my body. "Give me one good reason why I shouldn't shoot you." I offer, wondering if she's weak enough to beg me for her life.

A sly grin appears on her face as her eyes narrow in on mine, testing me. She was calling my bluff and I was going to fucking win. "Do it." she snaps.

I plunge my free hand into her hair, the thick black locks entangling themselves around my fingers as I wrench her from Ivan's hold. Her fingers splay out across my chest and I know from the gasp that leaves her throat that I caught her off guard. With her body pressed so tight to mine, one hand in her hair, one hand wrapped around the gun nestled at her temple, she remains motionless as I lean forwards and slowly skim my lips along her neck all the way up to her ear, leaving a ghosting of gooseflesh in my wake.

I hear her sudden intake of breath as I gently graze her lobe between my teeth, and it takes everything in me to not make her make the noise again. "Not today, Kate. You deserve to suffer."

I force myself away, holding her at arm's length, firmly gripping her hair as I fire. The bullet hits its target with little effort. Lev's body jerks with the impact, his head snapping sideways as a spray of blood and brain matter burst from his skull. It's fucking beautiful. Only heightened by the piercing scream that rips from Adanna's throat.

I catch her before her knees buckle, throwing her lithe body over my shoulder with such ease that it feels obtuse. I don't stop to hear Ivan's protests as I leave the room. "How does it feel, Printsessa? *Princess?* To have somebody you care for taken away from you?" I snarl, bringing my palm to her ass hard enough for the sting to ripple across my palm.

"You bastard. Let me go! You fucking bastard!" The noise she produces as I connect my palm to her ass a second time makes my cock twitch.

I take the stairs two at a time, not thinking straight about what happens next. Lev no doubt had communication with Adanna's family and if they don't hear from him soon, they'll come looking. And that's something I cannot afford right now. The entire Sinclair family would be a deathwish.

I continue down the corridor all the way to the last room on the second floor, its one of several empty rooms that Vladimir would demand to be kept to as high a standard as the rest of The Manor. Kicking the door open, I take two strides inside before throwing Adanna onto the large double bed, the silk sheets crumpling as her body bounces against the mattress.

"Don't you dare." She hisses, kicking herself from the bed as she lunges at me. I side step her advance, narrowly managing to close the door, as she screams at me from the other side.

"I'll be back, Printsessa." I smirk, turning the key in the door and pocketing it for safekeeping. It turns out it was a good idea for each room to have a lock and key afterall.

CHAPTER TWELVE
Nikolai

I can still hear the Sinclair woman's pounding against the door to her new and improved cell as I make my way back down the stairs. The sounds only lessen as I walk back into the room still housing a deceased Lev. His body is folded limply against itself with a steady drip of blood pooling beneath him from the gunshot hole penetrating his head.

First thing's first. I need to see what's on this guy's phone, and I need to buy us some time with the Sinclairs. That is, if they aren't already on their way. "His phone. Did you take his phone?" I snap, forcing Ivan from his comfortable position in a lounge chair. He pulls the phone from his inside jacket pocket and flips it over in his hand, eyeing me suspiciously.

Ivan lowers his head, his eyes watching me carefully as he continues to fondle the phone between his fingers. I can tell he's contemplating his next choice of words carefully. There's been a significant shift between us in the short time since Vladimir's death and if I didn't know him any better, I'd say that he was jealous, hating me for taking my father's place. Hopefully he isn't so stupid. He knew this would be the plan all along when I took Vladimir's life myself. Although that pleasure was taken from me far too soon by my little sinner upstairs.

"Are you going to tell me what the fuck is going on?" he asks, the irritated tone of his voice causing my fingers to twitch as I resist the urge to throw one of my knives at his head.

I flex my hands, extending it through my wrists and arms until I roll the tension from my shoulders. "The only reason you don't have one of my blades embedded inside of your skull right now is because I know I haven't exactly been forthcoming with you." Ivan lowers his shoulders as his brows knit together in confusion. "I've kept information to myself for no other reason than that of selfishness and a desire for revenge."

I make my way to the small glass cabinet on the wall behind Lev's body and pull out a golden bottle of Russo-Baltique vodka and two glass tumblers. I return, offering a glass to Ivan and keeping one for myself.

"A bottle of the good stuff. This must be big." Ivan snorts at the $1.3 million dollar bottle as I pour us both a generous measure.

"Do you remember the day that the important visitor came to The Facility and Kate, the girl in our room, was called into Vladimir's office but never returned?"

Ivan nods and takes a small sip of his drink and I do the same, the taste is exquisite, smooth yet sharp as it slides down my throat, but the gold and silver bottle topped with a diamond encrusted cap shows the levels of stupidity that Vladimir would go to to keep his appearances up. These bottles were only ever brought out when there was a point to prove, and Vladimir's ego needed boosting. Now, I'll be sure to drink them all and laugh at his idiocy. "Well that man was Alexander Sinclair…and the woman upstairs is Adanna Sinclair, his daughter."

The crease between Ivan's brow becomes prominent. I can see the thoughts whirling around as he puts the pieces together. "She is Kate." It's more of a statement than a question as the information settles.

I nod, taking a long sip from my glass. "Seven years ago, when we were in London and Dimitri was killed…" I take another drink, the anger at everything she's taken from me resurfacing all over again. "It was her. She was the one who took the shot."

I hear the shallow intake of breath before Ivan stands and raises his voice, the anger I felt all those years ago now shared with him. But he simply can not feel the force of it the way I did. He wasn't chosen, he didn't endure the torture that I had to survive to get to where I am now. And he didn't have Dimitri as his only saviour in a time when all I wished for was death.

"The phone call. It was her wasn't it? You knew she was coming here to kill Vladimir."

His insinuation rattles me. "I knew she was coming, but I never thought it was to kill him. If I did, he would still fucking be alive." I snap.

"Why isn't she dead?" Ivan barks as his hands fly up to his head.

I ignore his outburst, allowing him to feel his emotions. "Trust me, I wanted to kill her the moment Vladimir told me. But he gave me my orders, and they were to watch, and to learn about her and her family. He craved his own sick version of justice and instructed that she was to be disposed of only when he saw fit." My eyes glass over at the memory of the first time I followed Adanna through the numerous hacked CCTV screens. I lost almost seventy-two hours that first time, completely sucked in by her and fueled by the need to feel her life drain from beneath my fingertips.

"Ubiytsa." *Killer.* Ivan's voice brings me back. I rub my hand over my face and stand. "You're in charge now. You can give your own orders." He says and now I'm the one who's looking at him in confusion.

"Not yet. She doesn't deserve a quick and easy way out of this." I stand, throwing back the remainder of my drink and walking towards him. "Not after everything that she has taken from me."

Ivan's eyes flick between my own for a long moment before he nods and hands me Lev's mobile phone. "Do smerti." *Until death,* he declares, holding firmly onto the back of my neck and bringing our foreheads together. I return the gesture, his allegiance a promise to fulfil my unspoken wish. I shall be to one to end Adanna Sinclair's life.

"Do smerti." *Until death.* "Now, I need you to get Aleksei. I need to see what's on this phone. And get rid of this." I order, throwing my chin towards Lev's body.

Ivan nods and quickly exits the room, leaving me with my thoughts and the dead man. "What a fucking fuck up," I mutter, foregoing my glass and necking the expensive liquor straight from its golden bedazzled spout.

Thirty minutes have passed and I've drunk too much vodka. Lev's body has been removed and is currently being carted off to the nearby incinerator to be disposed of, and the regular clean up crew are working on destroying any evidence of his body ever being inside The Manor.

Aleksei stares at me from the opposite side of the desk as I slide Lev's mobile across the darkened wood. "I need to see what's on this phone. I need to know who he's been in contact with." After Lev's body was removed, I decided to move into Vladimir's office, my office, to give the clean up crew more room to work.

Aleksei nods and reaches for the phone. He had little to say when I explained the situation to him. He never knew Kate so he was given the need to know version and unlike Ivan, he was happy with simply being privy.

"I need to use your computer." Aleksei states, tipping his chin in the direction of Vladimir's computer. I haven't had the time to transfer his belongings yet so everything in here is still his.

I move aside and motion for him to go ahead. He lays his bag on the desk and pulls out a laptop, some wires and switches on Vladimir's desktop and his own laptop. Ivan and I watch in silence as he connects the phone to his laptop and his laptop to the computer and begins tapping away on both keyboards. "I'm in," he chirps with a smug grin.

I round the desk and stand behind him looking at both screens, neither one I understand.

"Who was he last in contact with?" I ask, needing the answer immediately.

Aleksei scrolls through the phone, inserts codes into his laptop and sits back in the chair. "There's a British number who has been in regular contact with him for the last few weeks. More so over the last three days. They have checked in twice-a-day since then. The last message sent from this phone was yesterday evening, and the last one received was six hours ago."

"Ebat!" *Fuck,* I snap, banging my fist onto the desk. They will know something isn't right, it's been over twenty-four hours since Lev last checked in. "What does the message say?"

"*Requesting an update. Adanna's tracker has now been lost and you have failed your first check in. Can you confirm that everything is going to plan or shall I send reinforcements?* The initials at the end of the message are A.S." Aleksei states, causing my palms to twitch. Alexander Sinclair, Adanna's father.

"Can you send a message?" I bark, spinning Aleksei to face me on the chair.

"Sure. What do you want me to say?" He shrugs, spinning back to face his setup and waits for me to respond.

I glance at Ivan who simply holds his hands up and offers no advice. "Go back through the messages and see how he usually checks in. Imitate it and say there has been a delay with the execution. That Adanna has had to go in blind with no communication and no tracker to reduce the risk of being caught in case they caught onto the signal but everything is going to plan. No need to send reinforcement, everything is under control."

Aleksei has already begun typing as I reel off something to try and placate Alexander via Lev's phone. As he hits send a small shift of weight lifts from my shoulders but I know this is far from over. "Keep the line of contact open. I want to know immediately when he responds." I instruct both men. "And this goes without saying gentlemen, but this is to stay between us. What has been spoken of in this house, stays in this house. Do I make myself clear?" I warn, narrowing my eyes at Ivan, silently ordering him not to speak a word of what we discussed prior to Aleksei joining us. They nod in agreement.

We continue to talk about the ammunition haul being delivered this week but I can't concentrate on the conversation. I vaguely catch on that Aleksei and Ivan are now discussing new transportation methods over to Europe while my mind is off in another direction.

"That will be all for tonight." I say as I stand from my chair. The siren upstairs calls to me and I can't ignore her any longer. Both men stand, their conversation halted immediately. "I'll keep the mobile with me for the time being to wait for a response. I trust that you'll both keep your word. Do not speak of this to anyone. Not even each other." I don't bother to wait for a reply. I'm already out of the door and making my way towards the stairs when I quicken my steps.

  I stand at the bedroom door and slowly turn the key, pushing the door open to reveal her body, highlighted only by the moonlight that slices through the room. Her ethereal beauty steals the air from my lungs as I step forward, quietly inching myself towards the bed. I take her in, the dark silk sheets make her already pale complexion ghostly and the absurd urge to see her naked body covered in blood instantly makes my cock hard. I drag my gaze down her body, her pathetic excuse of a dress has bunched up revealing the tops of her thick thighs and giving me a peek at the bottom of her plump ass as she curls into herself. The entire manor is doused in silence, making the rapid beating of my heart sound even louder than it truly is as it bangs back and forth against my sternum.

  I've watched and waited for years to have this woman in front of me and since she's been here, I haven't been able to get the temptress out of my mind. She's too tempting a treat laying there completely oblivious to my presence. I reach my hand forward, gently caressing my index finger along the curve of her face, ever so slowly whispering across her lips as I lean over her body. I admire the bruising marks left by my hands as I follow the slender length of her neck, rounding her shoulder and drag my finger down her arm. Smiling at the way her skin reacts to my touch, even when she's sleeping, as gooseflesh prickles her skin. I graze across her fingers before my eyes catch on a silvering of scar tissue on her right bicep. I'd almost forgotten she had this scar, not noticing it before when she was in my cell.

    Five years ago, I watched her through a forgotten and overlooked surveillance system on a derelict building site. Adanna and her father had managed to follow their target after weeks of surveillance and although everything seemed to be going to plan at first, I realised before she did that her mistake almost cost not only her life, but that of her father's too. I could have sworn I could taste the pain she felt as the bullet pierced through her arm. The live video at the time had no sound but I could see from the way she bit down on her bottom lip that she was in absolute agony. Her one misstep blew their cover completely. I was surprised they both made it out alive. But here she is now, wearing that scar like a badge of fucking honour. I wonder if she'd admit to her mistake if I asked her?

    Adanna's chest rises as a small whimper escapes her lips. I snap my hand away from her body, the sudden temptation to wrap it around her throat again becoming hard to handle at the chance of her waking up.

    My fucked up mind suddenly darkens, knowing how easily her skin bruises beneath me sends a shiver down the length of my spine and automatically has my hand reaching down my trousers.

    It's irrational, the thought of having her beneath me as I pound into her, breaking her and forcing her to submit to everything I am but as I pull my solid erection from my pants and tighten my hold around my cock, I slowly begin to fuck my hand at the all too tempting scenes playing out before me. I welcome it, exploring her body with my eyes as she sleeps unaware of what's happening and the effect her body is having on me. "Moya iskusitelnica," *My temptress,* I sigh, stifling my orgasm as the pressure inside of me finally snaps, wracking my body with an intense shudder as I violate her sickeningly perfect skin, coating her and claiming her as my own.

    I breathe out heavily as I shove my still rock solid cock back into my pants. Unable to take my eyes off of Adanna's perfect form, completely tainted by my sin. It's alarming how much it turns me on to have my cum coat her unconscious body, and if she were to wake up right now, I'd fuck her raw to coat her insides too. What the fuck is wrong with me? This woman has signed her death warrant, and I'm her executioner. Yet here I am, daydreaming about filling her up with my cum. I need some sleep. I need to clear my fucking head away from her.

    I leave the room, refusing to take another look back at Adanna's body, because if I do, I won't be fucking leaving. I pull the door into the latch, quietly locking it behind me and depositing the key in my jacket pocket before I hastily make my way downstairs. I eventually drink enough that I pass out in the library, underneath the scrutiny of the moonlight that washes over me through the window.

CHAPTER THIRTEEN
Adanna

My head throbbed as I woke from the deepest sleep I've had in days. I swallow, my throat sore and tender, in desperate need of a drink. I shift my weight, feeling the luxury of soft silken sheets beneath me and instantly, I remember where I am. I open my eyes, the door to the room is still closed, likely locked. I glance around, but there isn't anything in the room that stands out, nothing personal, it just looks plain, even the furniture is relatively boring. This isn't someone's bedroom, thankfully.

I stretch out the kinks in my joints and sit up. Most people in my situation would panic, or at least worry, not me though. This isn't my first rodeo, I've been held in places much worse than this, and at least it's a step up from the cage I was in yesterday. Guilt creeps up on me as I remember Lev's head exploding last night. That's an image I won't be forgetting anytime soon. I'll make him pay for it though. He not only stole a friend, he stole my last opportunity to talk about my parents with someone who knew them. For that, I'll never forgive him.

I notice a glass of water and something that looks very much like a sweet breakfast pastry on the small table beside the bed. My aching need for a drink has me reaching out to smell and inspect the water before downing it in seconds. My stomach rumbles at the sight of the pastry, it's been a while since I last ate, but I decide against it. He vowed to kill me. I'm not going to help him do it by snacking on a poisoned pastry.

There's a door on the other side of the room and I'm praying it's an ensuite, I don't think my bladder can wait for someone to let me out before I shame myself and pee on the floor. Swinging my legs over the edge of the bed, I wince at the sight of my feet. These goddamn heels! Give me a pair of boots any day. I groan in relief as I hastily undo the ribbons and the shoes finally fall off. My toes are bruised and sore from being caged in those torture devices all night. An idea comes to mind as I look at the shoes. Grabbing the stiletto heel, I give it a yank and it breaks off with a snap. I quickly hide it under my pillow and kick the other under the bed. Someone has been in here while I slept, I'll be ready for them next time. I hobble over to the door and sure enough it's an ensuite. I pee and turn the water on in the shower. If he's going to keep me here, I'm going to use the facilities. While the water heats up, I look out the bedroom window. It was too dark to see anything last night. This morning though, it's completely different. Like a scene from a book, lush green trees as far as the eye can see. I give the window a yank, just in case, but like I suspected, it's locked. Steam is billowing out of the ensuite now and I can't wait to feel clean again, my body feels disgusting, dirty, sweaty and there's a stain at the bottom of my dress that I daren't think how it got there. I shake it off, shrugging from the dress before I jump in the shower, hissing as the hot water hits my skin. I make quick work of my makeup and thoroughly scrub every inch of my skin until my spine prickles in warning and the hair rises at the back of my neck. From the corner of my eye I see a shadow, someone is watching me. I don't feel fear though, stupid I know, but the gratification of someone choosing to watch you is intoxicating and I already know who it is. My mind says fight but my body says fuck. Nobody has ever made me feel this way, sure I like to fuck, but this is pure desire. Dangerous, deadly desire. Why does he make me feel this way? "I know you're watching me." I say but it comes out breathier than I intended. I turn slightly, giving him a view of the water cascading down my body. I know I shouldn't tease him but I can't help it.

"Just admiring the view." He says, emerging through the steam. His piercing blue eyes shock me, the colour, the intensity, it does something to me, deep within my soul. He isn't shy about staring as he takes in every inch of my naked body and I don't try to hide. My heart is pounding and I'd be lying if I said I didn't love the feral look in his eyes as his tongue slowly swipes across his bottom lip.

"Your presence is of no consequence to me," I say but my voice is a little more shaky than I'd like and I turn the shower off.

A wolf-like grin shadows his face as he moves, ripping the shower door open and pushing me back against the tiles. He captures my wrists and pins them above my head, securing me tightly. "It should be," he whispers, leaning in close to my body.

I'm breathing heavily now, my breasts pressed tightly against his chest as holds me tight. I can feel the slickness grow between my legs but I won't give him the satisfaction. "Fuck you! I don't care who you are or whatever I did to get your knickers in a twist. Nothing you do to me will ever change that. Now, let me go, svoloch!" *bastard!*

He chuckles at me before biting my ear, sending a delicious wave of pleasure straight to my core. "Get dressed and meet me back in the room, I've left some clothes for you, they'll cover your tits better than that dress did. And the names Nikolai, but great pronunciation." he smirks. Just before he releases me, he takes one hand and traces the scar on my arm. "You can tell me about this after." Then he turns to leave the room and slams the bathroom door.

I stand frozen to the spot. What the fuck was that? Why do I have such a visceral reaction to him? Shivering from the cold and the backlash of emotions, I grab a towel and wrap it around myself. I hate the effect he has on me, it's nothing more than instinctual urges, anyone would have them around a man like him, or that's what I keep telling myself.

Smearing the steam coated mirror so I can see my reflection, I check my face, it's a little red and flushed but at least my face is clean of all that make up. I start to smooth my hair with my fingers, realising it's not going to make much difference, there is no brush or anything to tame it so it will have to do. Glancing around, I notice a pile of clothes, a white oversized t-shirt and some grey jogging bottoms that look far too long for me. And how convenient, no underwear. I pull the t-shirt over my head and I debate whether to forgo the jogging bottoms, just to tease him. But it's a risky game to tempt a man who has all the power, at the moment, so as much as I want his eyes glued to my arse, I pull the trousers on, tying them as tight as I can with the drawstring. Giving myself a once over in the mirror, I make my way out to the bedroom.

  I enter the room, my eyes immediately find him sitting in the armchair next to the bed reading a book, like this is just some casual ordinary thing, to have me locked in this room. The stupid arrogant man doesn't even look up at me and it irks me. I squint my eyes in annoyance and take note of the book he is reading. For fuck sake, why is he reading that? Now he's either trying to unnerve me or piss me off. He's reading one of my favourite books, Dracula by Bram Stoker. I tut loudly, "Comfy there?" His eyes don't move from the page he's reading, angering me more as he ignores me. Walking over to him, I pull the book from his hand and throw it on the bed. The look in his eyes is wild. Shit.

  His nostrils flare as I take a step back, but he catches my forearm before I'm able to make it any further away. Nikolai's fingers pinch into my skin causing me to wince and his top lip curls as he snarls at me, "That wasn't very nice, I was just getting into it."

I quickly reach for the lamp that sits on the side table and throw it at him causing him to duck, letting my arm go in the process. His fingernails have marked my arm. Bright red crescents puncture my skin. "Arsehole!" I snap. How dare he mark me again, as if the bruises on my throat weren't enough.

Catching me off guard, he lunges at me, knocking me onto the bed and pinning me down. "Now Adanna, you owe me a lamp and a story. Tell me how you got that scar." He nods to my arm. I stare at him for what feels like forever, his need to know what caused a silly little scar seems so confusing, but I close my eyes as I remember how foolish I was the day I gained it. How I almost got myself and my father killed.

"It's just a casualty of war, you must have some of those. There's no story to tell." I say, finally meeting his gaze again.

His smile is unnerving, "Don't lie to me again, Adanna. I know exactly how you got that scar. Do you want to tell me or shall I remind you?" he says vehemently.

"How would you know anything about me?" I spit, ignoring his question.

"The same way a predator knows how to hunt its prey. I've watched you, I've learnt how you move, how you act, how you kill and how you fuck. I've watched everything you have done since the day you pulled that trigger and inadvertently made yourself mine." He grins. "Now don't make me ask again, tell me how you got that scar." His body pushes down on mine, pinning me with his hips and god I wish I had no clothes on again. I break eye contact, turning my head away but his hand snaps out and grabs my chin, forcing me to look at him. "I am waiting, Adanna, and you should know I'm running out of patience with you."

"You want to know what happened, Niko? I fucked up, okay! I made a poor decision." I scream in his face.

"I know, moya iskusitelnica, admit your sins to me." *My temptress.* Niko whispers to me.

"Why? Are you going to admit yours?" I snarl back at him. How dare he call me his temptress. I don't understand what's happening. He shot Lev, but now he's asking me to admit my sins…None of this makes any sense. Raising my head from the bed, I headbutt him, cracking my forehead against his nose in an effort to get him ro release me.

"The suka." *You bitch.* He groans, but still doesn't release me from his hold. Blood runs down his nose, seeping through his teeth as he grins at me. "You really don't like me, do you?"

I roll my eyes. "Whatever gave you that impression?" I grin at him.

"You're not a fan of the food that was brought to you?"

"I wasn't hungry." I say as my stomach grumbles betraying my words.

Niko chuffs a laugh. "I'll send something more appetising up to you." He smirks just before using his thumb to smear blood over my cheek, his pupils dilating at the sight as he stares at my face. "Next time aim for the balls, I'm more likely to move." He leans away from me seeing the disgust in my eyes and without another word he leaves the room.

Yet again, I'm frozen, stunned into silence by him. I recover myself and sit up, smoothing out my shirt. How is it that he seems to know everything about me and I have no idea who he is other than a nagging voice in the back of my mind. His eyes are so familiar, but I can't piece together where from. I need to find out more about him, I need to arm myself with something, anything I can use against him. I look around the room for any clues I could use, but it's a quick search due to the lack of furniture in here.

Anger gets the better of me as I flip the bedside table over, sending it crashing against the wall. I glance at the broken pieces, the underside of the table now facing up with a piece of paper stuck to it. I reach down, pulling the paper free. It's a photograph, creased and looks like it's seen better days, but I can see clearly that the photo is of Vladimir and Dimitri. My first kill and my last to date. I smile at the picture, pocketing it for later use. I'm not dying here and I refuse to be held captive for much longer. Nikolai thinks he's the one in control here, but he has no idea what I will do to get home.

CHAPTER FOURTEEN
Nikolai

I shift my solid cock in my pants as soon as I lock the door to Adanna's room. I don't know what hurt me more - feeling her naked body against mine or seeing my own blood smeared across her face. I almost snapped as the tempting little devil dared me to touch her with her eyes. Her unspoken plea screamed loudly between us. I know she wants me, no matter how much she tries to hide it. I can see how her body reacts when I'm close, the way her breath hitches in her throat as her thighs clench together and her nipples become stiff. Such a damn tease.

I slam my fist into the nearest wall, roaring like a man possessed at my infatuation. She's getting to me, and I don't fucking like it. My outburst is quickly diluted by a text chime that doesn't belong to my phone. I scramble to retrieve the phone from my pocket.

This was not part of the plan. I trusted you to keep her safe. Clearly you can't. I'll have to make alternative arrangements if you can't verify the exact whereabouts and safety of my daughter, Lev. I know you understand the consequences if anything happens to her under your watch. I will be expecting your reply. - A.S

I read and reread the message over ten times before quickly replying that Adanna is safe, that I would give my life to protect her, something I'm starting to think may just be true, as I walk myself back home.

I finally put the phone down to take a freezing cold shower. Letting the ice water shock my mind and body back into working order, I know what I have to do, but a usually subdued part of me, a part that is so deep down in the darkest depths of my own personal hell, doesn't seem to be able to come to terms with the decision just yet. I need more time with her.

By the time I've dressed in a fresh pair of cargo pants and long sleeve black t-shirt, with each of my blades settled into its sheath, I feel more determined, but there's work to be done first.

I pull on a thick, fur-lined leather jacket as I leave my house, heading towards the large yard at the back of the compound. The air is still bitterly cold this time of year and the ground crunches loudly underneath my heavy boots as I make my way across the gravel. The new buds are shooting through the edges of the grass verges and have a crisp layer of frost threatening their survival.

"Ubiytsa." A jovial voice calls out to me. My head snaps in the direction of the voice, I smile when I see who it is and head over to the garage.

"Chto the zdes delaes, Kirill?" *What are you doing here, Kirill?* I ask, patting the young boy on the back of his shoulder. Kirill is one of the youngest members living on the compound. Through blood he deserves his place among the rest of us here but he's still young at only eleven years old, and is yet to join the men with any real work, much to his annoyance. He spends most of his time working alongside his mother and sister in the kitchen of The Manor and trying to keep himself out of trouble.

"Maksim said I could help him work on the van today," Kirill chirps, the excitement radiating off him is contagious, instantly making me relax.

"You wound me, boy. Don't tell him that. He'll have you peeling potatoes before you can say your name." I hear Maksim chuckle as he crouches underneath the garage door holding a crate of cloths, sponges and a variety of small tools.

Kirill's face immediately drops, the disappointment clear on his face as Maksim drops the crate at his feet and ruffles his hand playfully through his hair.

I smile and shake my head. "If you do a good enough job, I'll let you work on my car next," I say with a playful wink. Kirill shrieks with delight as he grabs a sponge from the crate and runs over to the van to begin wiping over the doors.

"You're good with him," I voice, watching the young boy's eyes sparkle as he drenches the van with his now wet sponge.

"I was his age when my father started to let me work on his car." Maksim begins before letting out a low sigh and turning to face me. "He's only got his mother and sister. Who else is going to teach him?" he asks, not really looking for an answer.

I nod my head then lower my voice ensuring Kirill is out of earshot. "Are you ready for the drop this week from The Facility?"

Maksim nods moving over to the large wooden bench that lines the back wall of the garage. Lifting the lid to showcase the empty space where the delivery will be stored until it's sent out to the buyers. "Plenty of space in here for it, boss," he grins.

"Well then, you'd better get back to your van because there won't be any paintwork left on it much longer." I laugh, pointing over to Kirill who vehemently scrubs the drivers door with a bristle brush.

I crouch my way back under the garage door as I hear a slur of Russian swear words as Maksim runs over to Kirill to take the brush from his hand. I chuckle to myself. That van is Maksim's pride and joy, but I know he'd never berate the boy for defacing it. He's a scary fucker when he needs to be, but he's such a teddy bear at heart.

With myself now taking the lead in the business, I know I'll have to bite the bullet sooner or later and show my face over at The Facility. Since the day I was chosen as Vladimir's new heir, removed from the damp and disgusting conditions of the small room they kept us in, I have hated every single day that I have since returned. Only ever staying there to do what was asked of me and not a moment longer.

My own plan to end Vladimir's life consequently came with the end of The Facility and our involvement with child trafficking and slavery. I've never been shy expressing my feelings about the dealings we've had. However, I'm not stupid enough to ignore the ramifications of my actions in shutting it down. Vladimir made his bed the day he signed a deal with Samuel Anderson. A higher power on British soil with a disgusting taste for dealing in children.

I've only dealt with Samuel a handful of times over the last seven years, Vladimir kept the business as under the rug as he could to keep the police general at bay. When Samuel would show his face on this side of the world, it wouldn't be for long, and more often than not, somebody always ended up dead. If word got out about the true horror of Vladimir's gun factory, there would be no escaping the entirety of the Russian police force with an unmistakable penalty of death.

I shake my head, running my hand over my face in frustration. I have no idea what I'm going to do or how I'm going to do it, but with my last dying breath, I will put an end to it all and I will make sure that no child is ever brought to this godforsaken hell again.

After pulling through the gates with a swift nod from the heavily armed guards, I exit my car and make my way towards the imposing metal doors of The Facility. They open with a loud clunk before me and the shadow of a large figure looms in the darkness inside of the main foyer.

"Ubiytsa." *Killer.* The shadowy figure grunts, lowering his head as I narrow my eyes at him. He slowly raises his head as I draw closer and the dim lighting crested along the walls allows me to take in his face.

"Bogdan." I nod. Taking the corridor to the right, heading straight for the ammunition hall. Bogdan follows my stride. "Anything I should know?" I ask, keeping up my pace as we near the hall.

Bodgan sighs loudly. "We lost one on the first night, another on the second."

"Sick?"

"Agata said the first one caught pneumonia on the journey here, there was nothing she could do to help. And the second tried to escape. I caught her trying to climb through the kitchen window."

I freeze. "How old was she?" I snap, turning to face him. His nonchalant expression makes me feel sick with anger as he shrugs his shoulders.

"Looked around seven, I guess." He states.

Seven. Seven years old and shot dead for trying to escape a life she would be better off dead from anyway. The thought makes me want to stab my blade through Bogdan's eye but I bite back my temper and continue into the large ammunition hall, shoving the double doors open as I enter. The room draws to a sudden stop at my intrusion.

The tables are lined with children who all stand stock still staring wide eyed at me.

"Let me make this as clear as fucking possible for you all." I bellow, forcing myself to meet the eyes of each and every child in the room. "You are no longer yourselves under this roof. Forget what you know, forget your previous lives. Forget your families. You belong to me now and I will ensure that your lives are a living fucking hell if you decide to disobey my rules." Most children have already begun to cry as I pace the worn wooden floor, keeping my emotions at bay, simply playing the part I need to, to ensure these children stay alive. "You are here for one reason only, and that is to build my ammunition. Do not be fooled into ever thinking you are safe and if any of you ever feel brave enough to attempt to escape, you will be killed immediately. There are no second chances here." I stop walking. "Do I make myself clear?" I call out and am immediately met with silence. I notice Bogdan smirking to himself from the corner of my eye. He must have already given them all direct orders not to speak. I simply nod, "Good." I make my way up to Vladimir's office that overlooks the entire hall from the mezzanine floor above, I guess it's my office now. I entire the room and slam the door behind me, causing the glass windows to shake between their frames as I throw myself onto the leather sofa and wrap my arms over my head. I have to shut this place down.

After what feels like hours upon hours of paperwork, checking inventory and ensuring to show my face among the children again before I leave, I finally make my way back to my car, advising Bogdan to inform me immediately if anybody else tries to escape before flooring it through the gates and back down the mile long driveway.

It's late by the time I arrive back, the moon is rising slowly to its place in the sky. I park my car, my feet automatically walking straight to The Manor, to the woman who's been haunting my mind all fucking day. I purposefully forgot to order any of the staff to take her food or water while I was away, hoping it would make her more appreciative when I delivered her next meal. I make my way to the kitchen, fixing a bowl of hot beef stew with a fresh buttered roll and a glass of milk. I'm not sure what possessed me but the thought of Adanna's only meals being passed through my hands makes me feel an addictive sort of power.

I take the tray and make my way back up to her room, carefully unlocking the door, pushing it open slowly to reveal Adanna sitting on the bed with a smug grin plastered across her face. I walk into the room, taking in the scene around me. The entire room has been thrown upside down. Completed trashed. The furniture is fractured into pieces and the bed sheets are strewn across the room. But she sits there, as still as a statue, watching my every move like a hawk. The fucking bitch. I drop the tray to the floor, the bowl and glass shatters across my boots. Adanna doesn't flinch and it's only when I lunge my body at her that I see her eyes flare at all. She tries to dodge my advance but I'm too fast, throwing her over my shoulder with little effort.

"The prosto nay mozhesh vesti sebya dostojno, nay thuck lee, printsessa?" *You just can't behave yourself, can you, princess?* I snap, slapping the palm of my hand across her backside causing her to gasp.

"Get your hands off of me, you prick," she wails, flailing her arms into my lower back as I haul her through the halls. I'm unaware of the exact moment I made the decision but I haul her ass, hitting and kicking, across the compound back to my house. Carrying her up the stairs and straight into the second bedroom.

I throw her onto the bed, circling back to the door as she goads me. "You know, this photo sure is sweet." I spin on my heels, my eyes immediately narrowing in on the photograph of Vladimir and Dimitri that she waves carelessly for me to see. "If I close my eyes tight enough, I can still feel the rush of excitement I felt as the bullet pierced through his skull," Adanna sighs, pointing to Dimitri in the photograph. "And I can still feel Vladimir Sidorova's warm blood trickle over my hands as I punctured his carotid," her finger moves over to Vladimir.

I'm across the room in less than a second, slamming her into the bed with my hand squeezing tightly around her throat. I snatch the photo from her hand, holding it inches from her face, forcing her to take a good look at what she's done. "Do you think, even for a second, about the consequences of your actions, Printsessa? Hmm…Or do you just kill for the fucking thrill of it?" I snarl, leaning the full weight of my body against hers.

I'm met with a smile, her throat tightening beneath my fingers as she chokes out her reply. "I know you want me. I can feel your cock rubbing against me." As the words leave her mouth, she wraps her thighs around my waist, clenching them tightly, making my treacherous cock twitch against her. Fuck. "You can try to keep this act up all you want. But you and I both know that you're dying to fuck me, Nikolai." she whispers, her hooded, lustful eyes daring me to do exactly what she says.

What little restraint I thought I had snaps as she grinds her crotch against my dick. I slam my mouth to hers, capturing her lips between my teeth. It's a toxic mix of tongues and teeth as our mouths collide and she kisses me back with equal ferocity. I force my tongue between her lips, exploring her mouth, tasting her and immediately needing more. I swallow her guttural moan and fuck if it doesn't turn me on. I thrust my hips forward, squeezing her neck until I feel her begin to panic. I bite down on her bottom lip until a coppery tang floods my mouth as I pierce the skin. Pulling back, I swipe my tongue across the broken skin, sucking her blood into my mouth until Adanna's moans make me freeze. Fuck fuck fuck. I rip myself away and leave the room, slamming the door behind me and locking her in. Jesus fucking Christ, that was not supposed to happen. I slam my fists into the wall leaving two fist shaped holes in the plaster. This is fucked up and I have just crossed a line.

I leave the house with rage and pure fucking sexual tension radiating through my body and I have no idea what to do with it. I shouldn't have kissed her. Now that I've had a taste, I need more. I want to fucking devour her, to bend and break her body until she submits to me, and may the devil help her, because once she does, she'll never be able to escape from me.

I shake my head, scrubbing my hands over my face in frustration. I need to focus. I grab my phone from my jacket, sending a text to Dodge and Tolya to get over to my house with strict instructions to keep guard at the front door. Since Vladimir's death they have sensibly kept their distance from me but now it seems their guard duties will come in quite handy. I also text Jane, instructing her to take some fresh food and clothes over to Adanna, ordering her not to let her out of the room or entertain her by any means. Jane tends to have a 'take no shit' personality so in the back of my mind I'm hoping she'll put Adanna in her place.

I glance at my phone for a moment, realising I haven't heard anything back from Alexander since I replied to his message this morning and alarm bells begin to ring. I remove Adanna's phone from my pocket and double check it's still switched on. It is. Fuck. Does he know it isn't Lev who's been messaging him? It wouldn't surprise me if he did, Vladimir always said they were not to be underestimated. I swallow thickly, I need to know their movements. I ring T, he answers on the second ring.

"Mr Sidorova," he says, his monotonous voice calming me instantly.

"Has there been any movement from the Sinclairs this week? Any flights booked or large outgoings of money?" I ask, making my way to The Manor.

"Nothing out of the ordinary, Mr Sidorova. Is there something I should know?" he asks. I contemplate telling him that Adanna won't be making it home but I decide against it. It's not necessary information at the moment.

"No. Keep watching, I want to know the minute you suspect anything."

"Yes, Boss." he confirms before ending the call, leaving me feeling slightly better. Maybe they're buying this shit after all. This will all work out. I make my way to the drawing room where I meet Ivan, already waiting with a large glass of vodka for me at the bar.

"Fuck. I needed that." I gasp after taking the drink in one.

"Rough day?" He asks, cocking his brow at me while pouring another drink.

I keep the information about kissing Adanna to myself. The thought of any other man thinking about her in that way sends a fierce wave of jealousy through my body. I should be the only man allowed to see her and think of her that way. "I went to The Facility," I sigh, taking note of the way Ivan casts his eyes down at the mention of our former home. "Bogdan shot a young girl he found trying to escape." I recite. "This needs to come to an end."

"At what cost? You know what will happen if we pull out of Vladimir's deal. Anderson will bury us." Ivan chokes, taking a large drink of his own.

"Then I guess we need to bury him first." I state, with pure conviction in my voice.

CHAPTER FIFTEEN

Adanna

What the fuck just happened? I lie back on the bed, but the cool silk sheets beneath me do nothing to cool my body. I'm shaking with anger, but worse than that, I'm shaking with need. I can't decide whether I want to fuck Nikolai or kill him. And then I realise that I want to do both. Remembering the split second before his touch, every nerve in my body and brain electrified. The anticipation of being together had my mind spinning, and when his body pressed against me, for the first time I wanted to let him take control, to do with me as he desired. I wanted him to take me and use me in every way imaginable. And I knew he wanted it too from the feel of his rock hard cock between my legs. The thought sends warmth through my body, from the very top of my head to the tips of my toes. I groan at the feeling, grinding my hips up into nothing, desperately needing to come. I can't fight it anymore.

I move my hand down my body, taking my time to caress my breasts, my stomach and hips, imagining his hands in place of mine, until I slip my fingers beneath the waistband of my bottoms. I'm already soaked. Slowly I drag my middle and forefinger between my lips, inserting them deep into my cunt before dragging the slickness up to my clit. I circle my fingers slowly, gently teasing myself, fantasising about Niko's body holding me against my will, whispering how much he wants me and how much of a good girl I am for him as I reinsert my fingers deep into my pussy. I gasp, pumping my fingers in and out as I use my other hand to rub my clit, applying more pressure as I increase the pace of my fingers. I feel my orgasm building, winding itself around every nerve in my body as I grind my hips against my hands and I can't help wondering how it would feel for Nikolai to fill me with his cock instead. I could feel how big he was even through our clothes and it makes my pussy throb. I insert a third finger, stretching myself against my hand as I close my eyes, his bright blue's piercing my mind as my body clenches, building, building until snap. I cry out as my climax peaks, "Fuck Niko!"

My fingers are coated with my release and my body still shudders with aftershocks as I slip my hands from my trousers. I have barely caught my breath when a knock at the door startles me from the bed. "Who's there?" I shout horsley, my throat still sore and aching. No one replies but the lock turns and the door slowly opens, and to my surprise, I see a woman, she must be a similar age to me although she's shorter and fair haired. She regards me closely, her eyes judging me as she enters, still not speaking. Rude! "Not going to answer me then?" I snap. Her eyes immediately flick to mine, a dull blue in comparison to Nikolai's bright blue orbs.

"Tebe nay nuzno znat, kto ya takoy, ubiysta!" *You do not need to know who I am, killer!* she spits venomously at me.

I notice she has what looks like a sandwich and a jug of water. "Thank you for the food and water," I say, ignoring her harsh words. I am a murder, I suppose. I can't deny it and neither do I plan to. I assess her carefully, noticing she isn't armed with any weapons. She left the door unlocked as she entered, too. How silly. I move slowly, preparing myself for the chance I'm about to take. I would be stupid not to. I smile sweetly at her before saying, "Vy prava, ya ubiytsa. Noh yi vas bosse toze. Raznitsa vie tomme, chto ya sdelayu eto bystro dla vas vie blagodarnosti saa to, chto vy ostavilly etu dver nezapertoy." *You are right, I am a murderer. But so is your boss. The difference is I will make it quick for you as a thank you for leaving that door unlocked.* Her eyes widen with horror, realising her mistake. She looks at the door before making a run for it but I was already prepared. I stop her before she even gets close, grabbing her by her ponytail and smashing her head into the wall. She falls to the floor, blood trickling from her nose and forehead as she cries out in pain. I could kill her but I don't have the time, I need to get out of here while I still have the chance. Looking at the tray she brought in, I noticed some cutlery, a butter knife. It's blunt but with enough force it will do damage. I take the fork as well before making my way to the front door. I open it slightly to check my path is clear, but standing on the other side are the two big, muscly lap dogs that Vladimir had with him at the club.

Fuck it. I need to move now. Yanking open the door and taking them both by surprise as they turn their heads to me I give them both a feral smile. "Kazhetsya, u nas byli nebolschie raznoglasiya." *It seems we had a little bit of a disagreement.* They lunge for me but I'm much quicker and smaller than them, dodging their advancements before bringing the knife down on the one on my right's thigh, piercing his skin and making him fall to the floor. Blood spurts out of his leg as he cries out in pain and I kick him hard in the head, using the heel of my foot for impact, knocking him unconscious.

Knowing I need to run, I don't bother attempting to take on the other guard as he tries to grab me. I dodge him easily, making a break for the wooded area opposite the house. I run, as fast as my bare feet will allow me, into the forest, the rough, uneven ground already ripping apart the soles of my feet. They're going to be in a horrendous state after this, but if I can get away from here, I'll happily settle for it. I run deep into the maze of trees before I stop to catch my breath. I look around, desperate to work out which direction I should take but it all looks the fucking same. I take off again before I spot an opening about 20 metres north of me, and that's when I hear him shout.

"You can run, Printsessa. But you can't hide in my woods. I will catch you." Nikolai's taunt freezes me on the spot as it echoes through the trees. If he catches me now I will never escape. I spin around trying to narrow in on where he is, but I can't see anything but trees and darkness. I refuse to move, knowing if I do he'll hear me, but everything around me screams loud with a deafening silence impairing my senses. I swallow nervously, my heart hammering in my chest as I dare to take a step forward toward the opening. Nothing. I take another step, and another, and another before a dark figure emerges from the trees. He found me. I dart behind the closest tree, pressing myself into the bark and taking a slow, calming breath. "Come out, come out wherever you are," he goads as I hear the crack of sticks as he stalks closer to me. I stifle my breathing and close my eyes, willing him to keep moving. "Gotcha!" he shouts as he jumps around the tree.

I don't wait as I break out into a sprint, but he merely stands back and laughs, the deep, guttural sound taunting me through the trees. It doesn't take long before he's right behind me. "There's no way out of here, Printsessa," he calls and a sharp pain pierces my arm as the sleeve of my shirt catches on a branch. Fuck. I keep going, my feet cause me to wince everytime I move and my lungs burn for reprieve but I am not giving up without at least trying. "Are you getting tired yet, Adanna? Are your lungs burning for air? Or is it your legs that are growing weaker? I can keep going Printsessa. I just want to see how far you get before I drag you straight back to hell."

He's taunting me and he's fucking enjoying every minute of it. I refuse to glance back, he's too close, I can hear the heavy thud of his boots as he chases me and I can't figure out whether it frightens me or, in some fucked up way, excites me.

"Fuck you!" I spit, making him laugh again. I try my luck, quickly shifting my weight and switching directions, hoping it'll give me some time but I don't see the tree stump hidden beneath the leaves. I panic as my foot catches against the stump and I land hard in the dirt, pain radiating through my knees and palms that took the brunt of the fall. No, no, no. I try desperately to get up but Nikolai is on me before I have a chance, his heavy, muscular body pinning me to the ground, roughly locking me into the dirt with his hips and hands as he restrains me, making it impossible to escape. "You made a mess of things back at my house, Printsessa," he whispers into my ear. "How will you repay me?" he asks, running his tongue up my neck. "Mmmm, your fear tastes so sweet." Nikolai sighs as he presses his cock into my groin. There's nothing of the man that pinned me onto his bed, as I lock onto his eyes, they're no longer human, just deep and dark, filled with a hunger that I'm sure is mirrored in my own. "You're mine now, Adanna Sinclair. But you already know that, don't you?"

I try to push his body but he's unmoving as I struggle. "Let me go, I am not fucking yours, you psycho!" I scream at him.

"Yes, you are," he growls, the sound so deep and threatening that I freeze. He's like an animal possessed and I need to handle this carefully if I'm to survive. He likes me fighting him. I can feel his length hardening the more I struggle, and I would be lying if I said I didn't like it. If I said that I didn't want him just as much as he wants me. I'm not only fighting for survival, I'm fighting my own unfiltered lust for him.

"Who are you, Nikolai?" I ask, my breath ragged and desperate, trying to not moan as I feel him against me.

"You know exactly who I am. I'm your worst nightmare, Adanna, I'm disappointed that you don't remember me." he snaps.

"What's your surname?" I ask, not sure I really want to know the answer.

Niko regards me before curling his lips into a viscous smile. "Sidorova."

One single word and my mind reels at the revelation of it, my world suddenly tipping on its axis. Why did my father not mention a son? Why wasn't this in the file Lev gave me? Before I have a chance to respond, his lips crash down on mine, and although I know deep down that I should fight him, I can't help but give in, allowing myself to let go and in that moment, everything else melts away as I lose myself in him.

Niko's tongue dances with mine as his hands move down my body to my joggers where he makes quick work of pulling them down my thighs, and I let him. His hands expertly caress my body before his fingers glide across the wetness of my pussy. My earlier imagination induced orgasm had nothing on this man's skills. I want to stop him but my body is craving everything that he wants to take from me and I open my legs further for him as he inserts two thick fingers inside me. I can feel myself getting wetter the more he touches me, my moans grow louder, more needy, more desperate and I can't help myself as my hands reach for purchase on his shoulders, digging my fingers into his skin. I moan loudly as Niko curls his fingers, fucking me with deep thrusts of his hand against the forest floor. I need more, I need him inside of me. "Niko." His name leaves my lips like a whimper, but he cuts me off, moving so fast I choke as he grabs my throat.

"No. When you behave like a good girl, then you will get what you want, but until then you will take only what I give you. And you will scream only for me when I allow it, whether it be from pain or pleasure," he snarls, reaching a hand to his hip. I focus my eyes on the blade he flicks between his fingers, and only then do I realise exactly what he means. Fuck, no. I panic as I try to move away from him but he smiles, digging his fingers into my windpipe. "You aren't going anywhere." He slowly and precisely drags the sharp point of his blade against my inner thigh, the tip of it making me freeze to ensure I don't get cut. "That's my good girl. We wouldn't want to scar up your pretty skin now would we? Stay still and I promise this will feel good." Niko whispers against my cunt before slowly and painfully dragging his tongue between my wetness, groaning as he swallows me down. I close my eyes, the pleasure his tongue grants with just one swipe is otherworldly and it's hard not to beg for more. But quickly his tongue is replaced with the cold hard handle of his knife as he carefully inserts it into my pussy making my walls to clench around the unfamiliar object. Oh fuck. I immediately feel full as he pushes it all the way to the hilt and I gasp at the intrusion though unconsciously, I open my legs more as he allows me time to adjust, whispering sweet praises that fall onto deaf ears as he slowly begins to fuck me. Pumping the handle in just the right way that it hits the sweet spot deep inside of my cunt, sending dangerously intoxicating shockwaves straight to my core. I moan and writhe beneath him, his hand still choking the breath I desperately need, only allowing me to breathe when he says. Niko slowly increases the speed of his hand, thrusting the knife into me. I throw my head back into the dirt, closing my eyes, my orgasm barreling towards me at an unprecedented rate. It's then that I realise that I'd let this man do absolutely anything he wanted with me. "Look at me when you cum, Adanna." he demands, and immediately I comply. I snap my eyes to his, the precipice burning through my body. I can't hold on any longer, I can feel the last of my restraint snapping as I freefall into ecstasy, halted suddenly by a voice calling out in the darkness.

    "Ubiytsa, have you found her?" Reality hits me like a fucking boulder, along with the realisation that the man who has threatened to kill not only me but my entire family, is between my legs and I was seconds away from completely coming apart on his knife.

    Nikolai freezes, his jaw tenses as he snaps his head in the direction of the voice. It's only then that I see a thin chain dangle from his neck. His shoulders shift and the necklace falls free from his shirt and my head swims with realisation. The ring at the bottom of that chain is my mothers, the one that Vladimir stole. But why does Nikolai have it?

Nikolai carefully pulls the knife from my pussy, bringing the handle to his mouth as he licks the length of it, keeping his heated gaze locked on mine as he does, clearly enjoying himself. "If you want to live, stay quiet." he finally orders, before sheathing the knife and standing.

I'm not listening anymore. I should never have let him get this close to me. I reach up and yank the necklace from his throat, the chain snapping easily. Nikolai's eyes flare as his hand instinctively goes to his neck and I shove my hands through the dirt, feeling for anything I can use as a weapon. I quickly scramble from between his legs, pulling my trousers up in a fluster, and then I remember the fork. Praying this works and at least allows me a minute or two to get ahead, I grasp the fork and stab it down with brutal force into Nikolai's thigh. His cry of pain floods me with adrenaline and I kick up to my feet, using every single ounce of it. As Niko clutches at the fork still wedged through his leg I swing my knee, landing it straight between his legs. "You did say to aim for the balls. Better luck next time." I mock before running, leaving raised voices and Nikolai's anger in the distance.

I run with blistering feet and scorching lungs until I enter a small town a few miles away, and even then I don't stop long enough to get caught. I move from building to building, hiding in and behind what I can, trying to keep my face hidden from the locals. I can't believe I've gotten myself into this fucking mess, all for my own selfish satisfaction. My father will never forgive me for what I've done, the thought of his disappointment almost makes me not want to return home. I can never admit to him what really happened, the severity of it anyway, to any of my siblings either. They would never understand how I let Vladimir Sidorova's son get to me the way that he has, and worse, willingly let him between my legs. I can try all I want to convince myself that I didn't want it, that the fact that he took away my ability to breathe while forcing that knife inside me was everything I didn't want, but at the time, I needed more.

    I crouch behind a small wooden hut, ignoring the searing pain through my feet. Thankfully the sun hasn't risen yet but there's plenty of people milling through the street, setting up for what looks like a market. I take my time, not wanting to ruin the only chance I've got at freedom, watching closely before finally encouraging a young girl to let me use her phone, and with shaking hands and a deep meaningful breath, I call my father.

CHAPTER SIXTEEN
FOUR WEEKS LATER

Adanna

The strobe lights flicker around the dance floor, reflecting off the bodies as they sway to the heavy, intoxicating beat of the music. My sister's Niamh, Lyssa, Ottie and Narcissa are dancing away, attracting every warm-blooded male in the club. As much as I enjoy having all eyes on me, my mind has been occupied tonight and every night since I arrived home. I haven't been able to unwind for so long and had hoped that with this rare night off, I'd be able to forget the eyes that stalk me through my dreams. To find someone to fuck, so I can feel like me again, so I can forget about the way he made me feel. I want to erase his touch from my body, but no amount of showers seems to be able to do that. So this is my next option, find a warm body to do it for me.

I need alcohol, that will help. I stalk off, leaving my sisters in the middle of the dance floor, weaving my way through the mass of entwined limbs as I make my way to the bar. I haven't been waiting long when a rough hand lands on my hip, startling me, immediately raising my guard. I jump from the touch, turning to face a guy a little taller than me with dark hair and dark brown eyes. Brown, not blue. His eyes are as dull as the dirt in the forest I escaped from. Shit, here we go again. Stop thinking about it, stop thinking about him. This is what I need, what my body is craving. I smile up at him, fluttering my lashes as he pulls me into his body.

"Hey gorgeous," he smiles down at me. "What are you having? I'll get it for you." What a gentleman, but right now, I don't need to be wined and dined, I need to be fucked, and like a whore, my body is all but screaming for it. I glance down at his hands on my hips. No tattoos. Fuck it, maybe I do need a drink to go through with this. My body feels on edge and my mind is playing tricks on me. I want to run. I want to be anywhere else but here right now.

"Well, I was ordering tequila shots, do you think you can handle a few with me?" I look up through the thickness of my lashes and lay on my sweetest smile. His eyes light up at my flirtatious tone as he waves over the bartender and orders two tequila shots with lemon and salt. Our shots are placed in front of us and only when I know that he's watching do I slowly suck on the top of my hand before covering it with salt. He mirrors my action, though not making it quite so sultry and when our eyes meet I smile, swiping the salt from my hand with a slow lick of my tongue before throwing back the tequila. I swallow it down too easily before I suck on the lemon wedge, letting the buzz of the alcohol clear my mind as I close my eyes and enjoy it. But behind my eyelids I'm haunted with eyes that ignite my soul and set my whole damn world on fire. I gasp, and as I open my eyes again, disappointment floods through my body as the only eyes staring back at me are those of this dark eyed stranger. I open my mouth to thank him for the shot, but before I have a chance to say anything, his lips come crashing down on mine and his tongue forces its way into my mouth. My first instinct is to push him away but the more he kisses me, the more I see him, Nikolai, and the more it makes me angry at how he's poisoned my mind. I feel the stranger's body shift, his hands fall to my ass and he squeezes my body against him, but I lock up, my body freezes. I just can't do it. It feels wrong, this guy is not who I'm looking for. He isn't him, he doesn't even come close. Fuck him for ruining this for me, it's been four weeks and I want nothing more than to be beneath his body as he fucks me into the dirt with his knife again. I pull away, placing my hands against the stranger's chest. "Thanks, but I am not interested."

    His demeanour changes immediately as his lips pull up into a scowl. "Bitch, I brought you a drink!"

    What a fucking cunt, how dare he expect me to give out for what, a tequila shot? I shake my head and scoff, "How charming of you." I bring my arm back, clench my fist and punch him straight between the eyes, feeling a deep sense of satisfaction as he stumbles back into the people behind him as his nose spurts with blood. I don't bother to wait for a comeback or to hear his threats to get me arrested for assault, I turn and walk back to the dance floor to find my sisters, all of whom are looking at me like I've just hurt a baby. "What? He pounced on me," I shrug, not trying to hide my smile.

They all look at one another before Niamh raises her eyebrows at me, "Well you looked okay when he was putting his tongue down your throat. What happened in those two seconds to make you want to knock him the fuck out, Adanna?" she chides.

I want to say Nikolai, but I can't. No one can know what happened between us. After calling my father from a stranger's phone while I was hiding from Nikolai, I was on a plane home within the hour and back home to an extensive assault of questioning not long after that. I was a mess, covered in blood, my feet were ripped apart from running barefoot through the woods and my arm had a large gash. My father probed me daily on what happened while I was there but I refused to say. I couldn't. He would never forgive me for what I did. He got the need to know details, and although he wasn't happy with it, he eventually stopped asking.

"He caught me off guard. I didn't want it." I sigh, knowing I can't tell them why this perfectly nice guy couldn't fuck me in the alleyway tonight.
"I think I'm going to call it a night, I'll call a taxi to come and get me." I say without waiting for their replies. I hear them shouting for me to wait but I can't stay here any longer. It's too loud and I need my bed. I need a moments reprieve from my own intrusive thoughts, of a man I should want to kill, not fuck.

Stumbling out of the taxi, I make my way to the front of our home, The Mansion. I look up and think how it's given me everything I have ever wanted, safety, family, a purpose. Movement catches my eye from the gardens and I freeze, narrowing my eyes on the place I thought I saw the shadows move but I can hardly see anything through the darkness. Scolding myself for letting my imagination run wild, I put my key in the door and push it open, it's just my mind playing drunken tricks on me. I tiptoe through the house as quietly as I can, I don't want to see my father tonight, I've had far too much alcohol and I just want my bed.

    I make it to my room without interruption and kick off my heels before closing the door behind me. I unzip my dress, leaving it where it falls and climb into bed, not caring to wash off my makeup. I hate that I didn't achieve what I wanted tonight. I wanted to replace his touch with another and prove to myself that he means absolutely nothing to me. I close my eyes and let the memories of Nikolai's hands wandering over my body consume me, unable to stop myself anymore. I let my hands explore my body, pinching my nipples, gasping at the pain before it melts into pleasure. I follow the curves of my body, moving my other hand down to my pussy. I rub my clit softly at first, teasing myself and spreading my slickness over the sensitive area as I circle my fingers faster. With my other hand I insert two fingers, my cunt warm and wet and needy. I moan as I curl my fingers, wanting him to be here with me, wanting it so desperately to be his cock stretching me out. My fingers glide in and out with ease, the closer I push myself to orgasm. I fuck my hand, fast and presice as I picture his cock filling me up, pounding into me so hard I cry out from the pain of it. Fuck. My body tenses and my walls clench around my fingers as I turn my head and cry out his name into my pillow. My orgasm drowns me, ripping straight through my body like a viscous tornado with no thought for the destruction it leaves behind. Waves of pleasure roll through me until my body sags as I come down from the high, leaving not only my heart racing, but my mind too. I'm completely and utterly fucked. I lay spent, regaining my breath but finally sated, and close my eyes, letting the bright piercing orbs that usually haunt me, soothe me into a restful sleep.

 Loud continuous banging wakes me from a deep sleep. I rub my eyes as I squint around the room seeing my father standing next to my bed with a disapproving look on his face. I pull the sheets up covering my body. "Good morning Adanna. I must say, it makes a change for me to be waking you up from a night of alcohol, rather than your brother." He voices. I close my eyes, wanting the world to swallow me whole. "Get up and get in the shower. We have a guest downstairs who has an important job for us," he barks as his eyes flicker over my dress and shoes strewn haphazardly across the floor before landing on my neck. He frowns, a deep worry line etched between his brows before leaving the room, leaving me to wallow in self pity. Instinctively I reach to my neck, my fingers finding the ring that I snatched from Nikolai's neck, my mothers ring. I smooth my finger over the band, letting it calm the storm brewing as it brings back all the anger from a few weeks ago.

Forcing myself out of bed, I head to my ensuite and turn the shower on, letting the water warm up before I remove my underwear and get in. I lather my body, my mind wandering over what job father has in store for me now and why it seems so urgent. I scrub at my skin, washing away all of the evidence of last night, letting my shame wash away with the bubbles as they disappear down the drain. I step out of the shower, feeling more human than I did ten minutes ago, quickly drying and dressing in the first things I grab, a plain black tank top and dark navy jeans, boring but comfortable. I apply a small amount of mascara and brush my hair until I'm satisfied with my appearance. Work is the last thing I want to be doing right now but when Father says jump, we don't ask how high.

Bringing my hand to the door, I knock at my father's office, knowing better than to just walk straight in. "Come in." My father shouts. I push the door open, smiling as I enter the room, seeing my father sitting behind his desk. A split second later and the entire energy of the room changes. One second, that's all it takes for my whole world to flip. My stride falters as I take in the man sitting opposite him. His short buzz-cut hair, large imposing frame and strong tattooed hands. Before he turns to look at me, I already know who it is, but that doesn't make it any easier to accept as his eyes threaten to set me on fire. I blink rapidly, praying that this is just a cruel dream brought on by the amount of alcohol I drank last night. I do my best to remain calm and keep my composure but everything inside of me wants to run. I barely register my fathers words over the rush of blood whooshing in my ears. "Ah, here she is. Adanna, this is Nikolai Sidorova. Come, take a seat so I can brief you on the job Mr Sidorova has requested your assistance with. Mr Sidorova, this is my daughter, Adanna."

My body moves like a robot, doing what is asked of me, what is expected. I sit next to Nikolai, doing everything I can not to look at him as I focus on regulating my breathing, staring directly at my father. I feel flushed as a white hot sweat breaks out across my body and my heart is hammering so hard against my chest I'm sure the entire house can hear it. And to make things worse, all I can feel are Nikolai's eyes burning into me, watching my every move.

"Mr Sidorova has asked for the best of the best to help take out a very large target. That would be you, Adanna. You are to accompany Mr. Sidorova on his mission and assist him with whatever is necessary to get the job done" My fathers words pull me back into the room. Wait, what? Work with Nikolai? No way in hell am I doing that. My father may not know the truth of what happened in Russia but he's Vladimir's replacement, he's Vladimir's son for fuck sake, they share the same surname! I can't do it. I finally allow my eyes to flicker to Nikolai and back to my father before I'm able to speak.

Nikolai clears his throat before pulling a knife from his sheath. "This is a gift for you, Adanna, a gift of our union, our pledge to work together. What do you say?" he smirks, holding out the knife in the palm of his hand. My gaze casts down, fixing on what he's presenting me and I gasp. This mother fucker, he's handing over the knife he fucked me with, the one he put inside of me instead of his cock.

I stand abruptly, "No." Is all I say before I leave the room, moving my legs as fast as I can to get me as far away as possible.

"Adanna Sinclair!" My father bellows as he chases me from the room. I freeze in the hallway and turn to the man who has protected me since the first moment he laid eyes on me, but right now he has no idea of the danger he's putting me in, and I can't even fucking tell him. "I know his last name must have caught you off guard but he's paying well and we need this assignment to go smoothly to keep all whispers of us taking Vladimir out, off our backs, okay?" He tells me in hushed words as he pulls me into a tight hug. I close my eyes letting myself sink into the safety of his arms, like I used to when I was a scared and timid little ten year old girl, and finally, I nod, agreeing to his demands. "Good, now go get yourself together." he orders, releasing me from his hold, but not before passing me the blade that Nikolai gifted me. I have no option but to accept it. I take it into my hand and smile at my father, feeling an imposing sense of dread that makes me want to scream. Father nods with a half smile before he returns to his office, to no doubt make excuses for my behaviour. But Nikolai knows better. He knows exactly why I panicked and ran.

CHAPTER SEVENTEEN
Nikolai

The look on Adanna's face was priceless as her eyes locked with mine when she entered her father's office. She was shocked, horrified even, and I was trying my hardest not to rake my eyes down the length of her body, enjoying the way her breath hitched and her cheeks flushed. It's only been four weeks since she escaped me, but she has plagued my mind every single day since.

Adanna failed to explain the truth behind what really happened back in Russia to her father and the rest of her family. She simply played it off, making excuses that led to the extension of the length of her job. I've become something of a mad man over the last month, becoming utterly obsessed with her every movement, watching her every waking moment throughout the day. T hates me after hounding him repeatedly for new information on her daily activities, her whereabouts and as a new sick addition to my fixation with her, I suddenly needed to know of every man she came into contact with while we were apart, because I vowed to kill them all for touching what is mine.

I knew I needed to see her again, to have her body writhing beneath mine. I just needed a way to make it happen. With shit escalating back at The Facility, I became more determined than ever to end our side of the deal once and for all. I wanted nothing more to do with the sick child slavery deal Vladimir signed us up to. I don't care who Samuel Anderson is or what connections he has. I will slit his throat and bathe in his blood before I let another innocent child be slaughtered for their own sick gain.

Ivan and I planned every moment possible over the last two weeks before I finally set the ball rolling, using my connections in the UK to reach out to Alexander Sinclair, asking him for his help and expertise in eliminating a man of such a high social calibre without any backlash. Mr Sinclair agreed to meet with me, agreeing that Anderson's business needed to be eradicated and the sooner the better. He was also more than happy to offer out his pride and joy to help finish the job.

Which leads us to today, here and now. I had the desired effect taking her by surprise like I did. But her refusal shocked me. After years of surveillance, I've come to learn that Adanna is the apple of her father's eye and to him, she can absolutely do no wrong, but in this instance, I was wrong. My arrival stirred up something deep inside her, and she can deny it all she wants, I know she wants me just as much as I do her. Her denial will only make it that much sweeter when she's calling out my name.

 As Alexander ran after her, scolding her for her insubordination, I had to stand and rearrange my crotch, making my raging hard on a little more bearable. Naughty little *printsessa,* opposing her father like that. She needs to be taught a lesson in obedience, and I'll gladly deliver it.

 The look on Alexander's face as he walks back into the room tells me of how pissed off he is, and if I look closer, the disappointment is unmistakable.

 "I apologise for my daughter's manners, Mr Sidorova, she hasn't been herself for a while," he sighs, leaning back into his office chair.

 "There's no need to apologise. But please, call me Nikolai. I no longer wish to be associated with my fath…with Vladimir Sidorova's name."

 Alexander raises an eyebrow at me, contemplating his next word carefully. "Why exactly are you here, Nikolai? I understand your need to execute Samuel, however you must forgive me for asking why you aren't able to fulfil this job by yourself?" Alexander leans forward in his chair, linking his fingers together and resting his hands across the desk. "Why are you *really* here?"

 "I didn't choose this life, Mr Sinclair. Neither did the rest of the children that were snatched from their beds in the middle of the night and brought to a country where they didn't speak it's mother tongue. The actions of men like Samuel Anderson are the reason I'm here." I show no sign of intimidation as he bores into me with eyes the colour of burning ash. "Due to recent events, I can't be linked to this job in any way. The retaliation will be its own death sentence."

"And you think I want that retaliation brought to my own door?" he asks, straightening his shoulders.

"The operation you run here is the best, is it not? Your family is renowned for what you do. I've come here asking for an alliance, a deal to end Vladimir's child slavery facility and to take down one of the biggest child traffickers known among our kind…"

"Our kind?" Alexander stands, scraping his chair across the floor. "You don't have the right to marry us into the same category as you. I know who you are, Mr Sidorova." He slowly stalks towards me until his body is only a few inches from my own and I can feel his hot breath against my face. "Don't you think I've done my own research on you, boy? Before allowing you into my home, and close to my daughter. I know exactly what you did to get to where you are now, Ubiytsa." *Killer.* My nickname is like poison on his tongue as he hisses the word. How the fuck does he know? I grind my teeth, desperate to put my fucking blade through his throat, to spill the blood pumping through his veins.

I step back, letting out a long breath before squaring my shoulders. Immediately, my mind flicks to Adanna. Does she know? My nostrils flare as I shove into his chest. "You can't tell her." I snarl, feeling an overwhelming mix of anger, trepidation and something I can't put my finger on. Before I have a chance to think of anything else, Alexander rushes me, pinning me against the wall by the collar of my shirt with his face too close for comfort.

"May I remind you, Nikolai, that you are under *my* roof. You play by *my* rules now." Alexander hisses, shoving me roughly before releasing me. "You have no say over what happens here. You'll do well to remember that." I stare at him, regulating my breathing as he walks to the door to his office. "Are we going to have a problem?" He asks, facing me with one raised brow.

I shake my head, biting back the urge to tell him to go fuck himself. If I thought there was any other way through this without total annihilation, I would kill the fucking lot of them and take Adanna for my own selfish needs. "So long as you keep your information to yourself, Alexander. I won't cause any problems for you or your family."

I take in the slightest flare of his pupils and he smiles. "For the sake of my daughter, I expect your complete professionalism until this job is done. If she utters a single word about you treating her with anything less than the courtesy she deserves, I will personally remove your liver and make you choke on it. This is strictly business, understood?" Alexander narrows his eyes at me before beckoning me to follow him from the room.

"We both want the same outcome." I nod, smirking to myself. I've had my taste of her now, there's nothing I won't do for seconds. I follow his lead down the too-wide hallway to the furthest door at the end of the wall.

"This will be your room until the job is complete. We can offer you safety while you're here and it will be easier for you to keep me updated with your progress. I took the liberty of having your bags sent over from the hotel. Your friend Ivan will be expected to stay there. I'm sure you can understand that having one stranger in my house is already one too many."

I stay silent, my eyes growing wide. What the fuck?

Alexander chuckles at my expression. "I told you, Mr Sidorova. I did my research." He smirks before striding back to his office, leaving me alone. I wasn't expecting to be offered a room here, but I'm definitely not refusing it. I glance back down the hallway, wondering which door leads to Adanna's room. This is going to be a lot more fun than I thought.

CHAPTER EIGHTEEN
Adanna

Pacing back and forth in my room, clutching his damn knife. That bastard. How dare he offer me this knife as a partnership, an alliance. Uhh I am fucking livid. Anger burns through my veins, encompassing every cell in my body and burning them with white hot rage. I grasp the knife, envisioning his smug fucking face as I hurl it through the air just as my bedroom door opens. Niamh ducks at the knife propelling towards her, letting out a high pitched shriek. "Bitch, mind where you're throwing your weapons." The blade lands in the wooden frame of the door above her head. Perfectly piercing it, but I wish it was piercing his godforsaken face instead. "So, are you still cranky from last night or is the hangover that bad?" Niamh asks.

I don't want to tell her about Nikolai. I just want him gone. "No, I'm fine. Just tired, that's all. How was the rest of your night?" I smile at her, trying not to let my true emotions show as I slump down onto my bed.

She frowns at me, I don't think she's buying it. "Yeah, it was good, we had fun. It was a shame you left early." Then she smirks at me, the fact I almost pierced her head with a knife, seemingly forgotten. "Have you seen that tall piece of Russian God that Dad has in his office? I tell you what Adanna, I want to climb him," she giggles, wiggling her brows at me. Immediately I fight the urge to slap her and tell her she has no fucking chance, because he's mine. The sheer audacity of that thought floors me just as much as the foreign jealousy that's embedded itself into the squishy fabric of my brain. She can keep her hands to herself, and just as I'm about to tell her exactly that, father appears in the doorway, looking pissed off to say the least. Great, he's here to give me a dressing down.

"Niamh, I need to speak with Adanna. Privately." He states, staring at me as furious as I feel. Niamh looks between us both, clearly unsure of the situation before quickly leaving the room. She knows not to question him but it doesn't stop her worrying about us arguing. I might be his so-called pride and joy but I challenge him more than he cares to admit, but he challenges me more. Once Niamh is out of sight, Father closes the door, sitting on the bed next to me. He takes me by the hand, his hard composure suddenly gone. "Adanna, you know what's expected of you. You *will* work with Mr. Sidorova." he begins and I breathe in at the very mention of his name. "He assures me that he's not like his father and wants to undo his wrongs," he explains. I don't believe him, if my father knew what I knew, he wouldn't let that man anywhere near me or his family, he'd have killed him four weeks ago and not thought about it for a second after. Nikolai is a liar and has my father caught in his intricate web of deception. But no matter how much I want to tell him, I simply can't bring myself to do it. So I stay quiet. "He wants you to assist him in assassinating a man named Samuel Anderson. He's a target that we've known about for many years but nobody has ever been stupid enough to challenge him. He's a dangerous man with ties to high society, but he's responsible for the forced abductions of children who have been sold out to various slave houses throughout the world and Mr Sidorova wants to finally put a stop to him." My father looks me in the eyes, takes my face into his hands and smiles. "We can help put a stop to what you and so many others have endured." I close my eyes, I want to believe him. I want nothing more than to take this Samuel guy out, if what father says is true it will save hundreds of children if not thousands and that thought alone lets me know it's the right thing to do. Even if it were to save only the life of one child, I would put aside everything else to help. Nikolai is an inconvenience and I'll treat him as such to get the job done quickly. I suck in a deep breath, open my eyes and nod. "That's my girl, now go blow off steam at the shooting range or whatever else it is you do." he says with a smile before releasing me and walking back to the door. He pauses on the threshold as he notices the knife penetrating the door frame and yanks it from the wood before handing it to me. "Maybe you need target practice with a blade. I hear Mr Sidorova has an excellent throw. At the very least this will be a good opportunity to learn from someone new, Adanna." He turns to leave. "Just remember that this is strictly business. If he does anything that is less than that, you let me know." And with those last words, he's gone.

  I tighten my hold on the handle of the knife before letting it fly through the air again. The sharp point of the blade sinking way off its original mark. Fuck. I lay back down on my bed wondering how on earth I'm going to keep myself out of harm's way with that snake slithering in such close proximity. I need an extra pair of eyes to keep a close watch on Nikolai when I'm not around. I sit up, going back and forth about the idea knowing I'll need to explain myself and finally speak about what happened back in Russia. But fuck it, I need this, I need to know. I bite the bullet, making my way to Narcissa's room. If anybody can help, it's going to be her.

  Knocking on the door, I swear I hear her talking to somebody, and then silence before she shouts, "Ada, what do you want?" I smile, of course she knew it was me, but I ignore the question and open her door. She's still in her pyjamas, sitting at her desk with multiple computer screens displaying various web pages. The sight hurts my eyes through the darkness of the rest of the room. She doesn't bother to look up as she frantically taps away at her keyboard. "Can't you see I am in the middle of a job?" she mumbles as she continues to do what looks like coding on the computer. I frown, this girl is amazing at what she does, well that's when she actually puts her mind to it.

"I can see, I need a favour." I start, moving into the room and closing the door behind me.

"You want me to watch Father's new friend, Nikolai Sidorova?" She says without breaking her stream.

I smirk. "And how did you know?"

"Because I didn't buy your story about the lost communication in Russia, and I've been informed that Lev's death happened *before* you said it did. Things don't add up Adanna but I'd never call you out because you're my sister and that means something to me, even if you can't tell us the truth." She stops typing and turns to give me her full attention, wiping the smile from my face. Shit. How does she do that? Make me feel insanely awful and guilty at the same time. Here goes nothing.

"You're right," I explain, breathing out and running my hands through my hair before continuing as I perch on the edge of her bed. "I ran into Nikolai in Russia, he knows I killed Vladimir. I don't trust he's here just to kill some slaver. It's too much of a coincidence" Raising my eyes to look at Narcissa so she can see the truth, I decide to keep the other details to myself for now.

I can see she expects me to tell her more but she nods, refusing to pry. "What do you want me to do?"

"I need you to keep surveillance on him and whoever he's here with. I don't want him to stab me or any of us in the back, literally or figuratively," I tell her.

"I can do that, is this something that Father knows about?" she asks, like she doesn't already know the answer.

"He knows nothing of this, just me and you, Cissa."

"Okay, consider it done, but if you start fucking him, I'm not watching that. I'll turn it off and you'll need to watch your own back then, okay?" She smirks before turning back to her computer and continuing her coding, silently dismissing me.

It dawns on me that she might know what really happened between us. My sister is good at what she does so it wouldn't surprise me, but I'm grateful for the fact that she isn't pushing it further. "Not happening, thanks sis." I say, not sure who I'm trying to convince more, before leaving her room and heading to the kitchen. I need coffee and some food. This morning has been far too long already without caffeine.

CHAPTER NINETEEN
Nikolai

I stride into my assigned room, taking in the decor. It's a polar opposite to The Manor back home. Where the furniture there is dark and harsh, this room is light and airy, even the curtains have an intricate pattern of cream and gold weaved within them. There's a large wooden wardrobe opposite a matching dresser, the wood stained lightly to enhance the bronze handles that fashion the drawers. The room itself is bigger than I expected. Though I'm not really sure what I expected. It surely wasn't to have been left alone in this house, that's for sure. To be trusted amongst Alexander's most precious possessions, his children. I sink into the bed, the plump pillows encompassing me as I sigh, staring up at the oddly patterned ceiling. I need to call Ivan. I grab my phone and hit call. He answers immediately.

"Ubiytsa," *Killer,* he answers, sounding a little irritated.

"Is everything alright, Ivan?" I ask, my hackles immediately rising. It hasn't been an easy choice to fly over here. I would've been happier to come alone but Ivan insisted that I needed another set of eyes and ears on the ground. I'm not sure how happy he's going to be now that I'll be spending the rest of my time here under Alexander Sinclair's roof.

"Everything is fine. Are you in? Have you spoken to Alexander?" He asks, a little too eager for my liking.

"Yes. He has agreed to help. It will take a few days to come up with a plan but he's offered me a room here in the meantime."

"Brilliant, I'll collect our..."

"You're to stay at the hotel, Ivan. I need you outside of the house. I need you to keep a close watch on Anderson while I'm here." I interrupt before he gets too carried away. There's no point in telling him Alexander didn't want him here. It would make very little difference, he's of much more value to me out of the house anyway.

"What about you?"

"I'm going to play my part, they need to trust me. I'll contact you via message unless it's an emergency. You shall do the same."

His tone sounds off. Disappointed or annoyed. It's difficult to tell through a phone call but something definitely isn't right. "Of course," he agrees, before hanging up.

I throw my phone down onto the bed and close my eyes. Racking my brain through that quick conversation. He should know the job by now. It's what we came here for. I relax for a short while, thinking hard about Alexander wanting to keep me close. It makes sense when I think about it but…oh shit. Could this be a test? This has to be a test. I spring from the bed on high alert, scanning the room from top to bottom, trying to decipher the best locations for hidden cameras. I glide my fingers over every surface and ensure to check each small crevice that one could be hiding. It's been fifteen minutes and I've come up empty handed. I rise to my feet after scouring underneath the bed to be met with a small giggle coming from the doorway.

"You lost something?" The blonde bombshell giggles as I glance over the bed, taking in her small stature, even with the deathtraps she wears on her feet. Damn, she's hot. I stand to my full height, eyeing her warily. "I'm Niamh," she offers, though I already know who she is.

"Nikolai," I smile. Leaning against the wooden doorframe. I watch as her eyes slide down the length of my body before she returns her gaze to my eyes. She likes what she sees. Maybe I can work this to my advantage.

"Would you care for the grand tour, Nikolai?" she smiles, fluttering her long thick eyelashes at me. The action makes me cringe but I style it out with a fake cough.

"I'd love that, beautiful." I wink, keeping her sweet and blissfully unaware that she's setting herself up for failure. Her cheeks flush as she pulls her bottom lip between her teeth before spinning on her stiletto heels and signalling for me to follow her.

I walk beside her as she points out the different rooms for me, and pretend to listen as she garbles on about meaningless tripe that I really couldn't care for.

"That's great, now…tell me about Adanna." I interrupt, flashing her my sweetest smile.

Niamh's brows draw together and her step falters ever so slightly. "Adanna? What do you want to know about Adanna for?" she asks, obviously feeling a little putout that she's not the one I'm asking about.

"Well, since we're going to be working together, I figured it would be best if I get to know more about her." I say with a shrug.

Niamh lets my words sink in before allowing it to make sense. "I guess that would make sense. What do you want to know?"

"Everything." I smile, my eyes hounding her for information.

"Alright well, her favourite colour is purple, she's an Aries you know. Very hot headed, has a very mean temper when somebody pisses her off, and as I'm sure you're aware, she's a killer shot." Niamh skips ahead of me, twirling her too short skirt, trying desperately to get my attention. It doesn't work, my eyes are glued directly at her bleach blonde head.

"What's it like having Adanna as your sister?" I ask, wanting to know more about her personality. What she's like to those that she loves. She's a fierce protector, I already know that but families have their own unique way of surviving with one another.

"She's like the mother we never had." Niamh's words halt me, twisting my insides and forcing a feeling within me that is almost unnatural. "She is always the first to sacrifice herself whenever anything goes wrong and Father is looking for someone to punish. Ada would never let the rest of us take the blame, even if it was entirely our fault. She looks after us all, she always has. She has always been Father's favourite for it. For her ability to push aside her own pride for the sake of the rest of us." A sad smile crosses over Niamh's face before she shakes her head. I'm not sure she meant to tell me that piece of information, but I'll hold it close to me for safekeeping. "Anyway, shall I show you where the kitchen is? I'm sure you're hungry. I could make you something to eat if you'd like?" Niamh closes in on me, dragging her finger down my chest, batting her lashes at me once again. I'm sure this must work with every other male within her reach but there's only one woman I want, and it sure to hell isn't her.

    I push her hand from my shirt and side step her, ignoring the disappointed look on her face. "An offer I can't refuse," I call over my shoulder as I make my way to the other side of the house. She's beside me in a second, frolicking around, swaying her hips as seductively as she can as I follow her, rolling my eyes at her lack of decorum.

    "Here we are, the heart of the house." Niamh smiles, spinning around with her arms out wide. "Now, what can I make you? I've been told I make a delicious cheese toastie. Would you like to try one, honey?"

    I cringe at her use of a pet name for me but playing the good house guest that I am, I smile sweetly at her, denying myself the pleasure of snapping her neck. "Sure thing."

A few moments pass while the blonde busies herself around the kitchen and my concentration is drawn elsewhere to the family photographs that line the walls. I move closer, studying each one carefully, internally timestamping the ones taken within the last seven years. Most I was already aware of, which day they were taken and for what occasion.

Suddenly, bringing me back into the room, a solid weight hits my body causing me to swing round, just in time to catch Adanna by the waist as she stumbles backwards. Her eyes flare wide as she takes me in, clearly shocked and annoyed at what just happened.

"What are you doing, Niko?" she gasps, pushing my hands from her body and taking a step back, clearly flustered at our close proximity.

Right on cue, Niamh's voice breaks through the tension building between us. "I was just giving our guest the grand tour and treating him to my famous cheese toasties."

Adanna spins to face her sister. I can tell from the bunch in her shoulders how frustrated she is and I can't help but smile, knowing I'm the cause.

"I wouldn't bother showing him the entire house, Niamh. He won't be staying long" Adanna snaps back at her sister.

I scoff, taking slow and deliberate steps towards Niamh. "Well at least one of the Sinclair sisters was kind enough to offer. I guess it's just my luck that it happened to be the most beautiful one, too." I smirk, raising my brows as Adanna's cheeks flush a delicious red hue before she leaves the room with a resounding huff.

I stare after her long after she's gone, forgetting where I am until Niamh sighs heavily against me, swooning at my compliment. I shift my body, stepping away from her and clearing my throat. "Shall we continue with the tour?" I ask, not waiting for her to agree as I leave the room in the direction that Adanna went.

"Wait, Niko, what about your toastie?" Niamh calls, causing me to freeze, spinning so quickly I catch her off guard, making her gasp.

"Nobody calls me, Niko." I snarl getting into her face.

"But…Ada…" her bottom lip trembles slightly.

"Nobody." I snap before moving away, holding my arm out for her to move forward, she hesitates slightly but moves on, showing me each room on this side of the house with decidedly less enthusiasm until we reach my intended destination.

"Wait, you can't go in there, that's Adanna's room." She tries to stop me but I push past her.

"I can do whatever the fuck I want," I say. Niamh scowls at me, throws her hands up in the air and then leaves, stomping back through the house.

"Fine, whatever. Do whatever the fuck you want. You're not that hot anyway." I hear her mutter, and I chuckle to myself.

I close Adanna's bedroom door before slowly stalking around the bed. Her room is sparse, lacking any identity, clean and tidy but lacking something. I slide my hands across her plain black dresser, picking up a small bottle of perfume and bringing it to my nose. Beautiful. Her scent in a bottle, sweet but with a hint of spice, just like she is. I return the bottle, opening the top drawer of the equally black cabinet to find an array of lace underwear. Fuck. I hold out a black lace thong that leaves very little to the imagination. My cock instantly comes alive at the thought of her in nothing but these, throbbing painfully against my trousers. I don't realise what I'm doing before I bring the flimsy material to my face and inhale. Oh fuck. My cock twitches in desperation as her scent surrounds me. If she has ever worn these for any other man, I will ensure to hang him from the front gates of this property by his scrotum to ward away any other fuck who likes to think they have a chance with her. She belongs to me now and I want every fucker to know it. I slide the underwear into my back pocket, unable to comprehend the thought of her wearing them without my knowledge, and just as I do I hear the door click behind me.

"Niko?" There it is again, that name. Nobody calls me that name. But on her lips, it's sure to be my undoing. I rush her, completely capturing her body between my own and the door behind her back. I have her arms pinned above her head, her small wrists easily imprisoned by a firm grip.

Adanna's breathing is heavy, pushing her tits against my chest as she tries to compose herself, but I know her better than she knows herself. Her eyes deceive her as she tries to free her wrists from my hold, they're burning right through me with a wanton desire for more. "Let go of me," she snarls.

I snap my head to the right, catching the glint of something from the corner of my eye and I tut loudly, shaking my head.

"Didn't you like my gift, Printsessa?" I smirk, ripping the knife from the door frame and bringing the sharp tip to her throat. "Don't tell me I haven't plagued your every waking thought over the last four weeks. And even when you've lain in bed at night, you've thought of me, haven't you? You've fucked your fingers wishing they were mine." I trace my lips up her neck before angling my head to watch her reaction. "Just like you did last night." Adanna's eyes flare as the realisation kicks in. It was me she could sense watching her through the darkness of the garden last night, and long after she had entered the house. I waited, needing to know which room was hers when she finally flicked on the light. I could hear her, perched underneath the window to her bedroom. As the rest of the house was deathly silent, her moans echoed through the night as my name became a whisper on her lips as she fucked herself to sleep.

I drag the blade slowly down her body until I reach her knee, then slowly I start stroking it back up, tracing the inside of her thigh. "I seem to remember last time we were together that your pussy liked my knife alot." Adanna moans, closing her eyes and thrusting her hips against me as something inside of me snaps. Just like it did back home. I slam my lips to hers, capturing her whimpers as she bucks against me. I've twisted the blade, angling the tip away from her body as I become lost with my own desire to take her right here and fuck her for her entire family to hear.

Adanna's tongue fights for dominance against my own but her hips continue their delicious dance against my body. She's as caught up in this as I am and no matter how much she tries to deny it, her body begs for me. She groans again and my cock responds, jutting out against her. I thrust my hips forward, letting her feel the effect she's having on me.

Kissing her harder, I flinch as Adanna sinks her teeth into my bottom lip, making me pull back. Her eyes are wild as she stares at me with a smear of blood across her mouth that slowly drips down her chin onto her exposed cleavage. I growl at the sight, flexing my hips and pinning her. "I shouldn't enjoy the sight of you covered in my blood, Printsessa, but fuck I would be lying if I said I didn't want to fuck you in it." Adanna pulls her head back and spits directly into my face, covering me with a mixture of saliva and my own blood. "You're disobedient, Printsessa. Do you know what happens to those who disobey me?" I growl, bringing my hand to her throat, restricting her breathing. "I think it's about time your new daddy taught you a lesson." I have no idea where the words came from but the way her thighs clenched together and her pupils dilated as I said them told me everything I needed to know. My little printsessa has a fucked up daddy kink. "Get on your knees, sweetheart." I demand, shoving her down between my thighs.

"Fuck you, Niko. I will bite your fucking cock off if you dare." Adanna hisses at me, her usual composure has completely vanished, but the way her tongue swipes her bottom lip urges me on. I fist her hair, yanking her head back to face me.

"You won't get the fucking chance. Now open up those pretty lips of yours. I'm going to fuck your throat so raw you'll feel me inside of you every time you have to swallow." I reach for my cock, frozen as my phone starts ringing. You have got to be fucking kidding me. I lock eyes with Adanna who smirks at me.

"Aren't you going to get that?" I tighten my hold in her hair, making her wince as I have a full on internal war with myself. The ringing cuts off, only to start back up again. Groaning loudly with a raging hard on that threatens to cripple me, I remove my phone from my jacket and answer the call giving Adanna a warning look to keep her mouth shut.

"Chto, Ivan?" *What, Ivan?* I shout, my patience non-existent.

"It's Anderson. You may want to get over here, looks like he's planning another oversea's shipment from the ferry port in Portsmouth."

I suck in a breath. "Ebat." *Fuck.* I flick my eyes down at Adanna, she hasn't taken her eyes off me since I answered the call. I want nothing more than to give her a new meaning to the word daddy but this is something that cannot be ignored. No matter how much I want to fuck her, the need to do what I came here for trumps all else. Despite what Adanna may think of me, I am here to put an end to Samuel Anderson.

"Ya idu." *I'm on my way.* I end the call, sliding my phone back into my pocket before leaning forward, so close to Adanna's face that I can taste her sweet breath on my tongue.

"You just got lucky, Printsessa." I whisper before shoving her away from me and standing tall. It's the only way I'll leave. If she continues to look at me with those fuck me eyes I'll die a happy man in this room because I will never leave it once I'm finally inside of her.

"Keep dreaming, asshole," I hear her shout as I make my way out of her room to the front of the house. I smile, knowing soon enough that my dreams will become reality and Adanna Sinclair will answer to a new master.

CHAPTER TWENTY
Adanna

The sunshine streams into the room, casting a warm glow over everything it touches. I sit up slowly, stretching my arms over my head and I close my eyes. I spent the rest of my day at the shooting range yesterday after my altercation with Nikolai, but no matter how many targets I destroyed or how many magazines I emptied, I couldn't erase the feel of his body against mine or the dirty words he'd said. The way he held me against the door as his lips devoured mine. Tasting him on my tongue felt like a burning inferno that I never knew I needed. I wanted more of him and when he wanted to punish me, I was done for, eagerly sinking to my knees, practically salivating at the thought of his cock down my throat. I wanted to beg for everything he was offering but I can't give him that much power. I don't trust him and as much as my instincts scream for it to be just sex, I don't think it will ever be that for me and Niko.

This is torture. Pushing the thoughts from my mind, I move to the bathroom and get myself washed and dressed, making the decision that I need to get rid of this fucking itch. It's not Nikolai I need, it's anybody. I just need the release. I grab my phone as I make my way to the kitchen. I need to hook up with Tony, I know he's a good and easy lay and he always says yes. I type a quick message out and hit send. I don't have feelings for Tony and maybe, just maybe it will make being around Nikolai just a bit more bearable until the job is done.

Entering the kitchen, I see Nikolai sitting at the breakfast bar drinking a coffee, like he's already made himself at home. Everything about him angers me and turns me on at the same time. I've never felt this way about a man before, especially one that I know wants to kill me. I definitely need to fuck Tony and get this sick fucking infatuation out of my head. His eyes lift to meet mine automatically, like they are as drawn to me as I am to him. "Good morning, Printsessa, did you sleep well?" He asks like it's a simple everyday conversation and he didn't almost force me to suck his cock yesterday. I roll my eyes and make my way to the coffee machine, refusing to acknowledge him with an answer. "Not a morning person before coffee then?" he asks. I don't have to turn around to know he's watching my every move. I can feel the searing heat of his eyes all the way to my bones, making my whole body tingle.

"I am not a you person before coffee," I snap.

"Right, you don't want to be civil with me. We have a job to do, Adanna, you need to show some respect at least for that and learn to hold that sharp tongue of yours before it gets you into trouble" he barks, clearly annoyed at me now. I slowly turn to face him but I don't answer as I sip my coffee, watching him with an unamused look on my face. "Anderson has a shipment due today. We need to do reconnaissance. I want to know his every move before he even makes it. It's the only way this job goes smoothly," he continues.

"I am a little busy today," I sigh.

"Busy? What with? You're being hired to do a job, Adanna, do I need to remind you of our arrangement?" He moves from the bar, glaring at me as he encroaches on my personal space, making it difficult to concentrate. I know I have a job to do, neither Father nor Niko will let me forget it, but I need to shake him from my body first. In order to do my job efficiently, I need to be able to stand within an arms length and not want to fucking jump on him.

"Not that it's any of your business but I planned to see my uncle and my sister Ottie today, then I have a date with my boyfriend. Surely you don't need me to watch Anderson's movements with you. Once you suss him out, I'll be there to assist with the hit." I smile sweetly, knowing I shouldn't have said Tony was my boyfriend when he's damn well not but I couldn't help myself. I want him to get the message, I am not his, no matter how right it feels everytime he touches my skin and lights up my body like an exploding firework.

Nikolai's fingers grasp my chin with a bruising force, tipping my head back as he stares directly into my eyes. Churning my stomach with his beautiful blue pools of sapphires. "Have it your way, Adanna Sinclair." He growls, digging his fingers into my skin before storming out of the room, almost knocking Narcissa over on the way.

"Jesus, careful! What crawled up his arse?" She snaps, throwing her hands up in annoyance.

I shrug, looking away from her and downing the rest of my coffee. "I'm off to see Uncle George and Ottie for breakfast. Do you want to come?" I ask, knowing full well she has every intention of going back to bed after she's eaten. Unsurprisingly, she shakes her head so I grab my jacket and make my way to my bike. I need to clear my head and maybe catching up with Ottie and Uncle George will help me get my priorities back on track.

The adrenaline rushes through my veins as I race through the winding streets. The ride to the city doesn't take long this early in the morning, the traffic being on my side this morning is much quieter than usual. I arranged to meet Uncle George for coffee and Ottie asked to join us. They work together at our family's law firm with Uncle George teaching Ottie everything she knows with the plan to one day take over the business. Ottie has always been so focused, I guess her and Uncle are similar in that way. Sometimes I think working together as closely as they do causes tension but I don't miss the way Ottie looks at him, she admires him and I'm not sure how healthy that is for her. I keep my thoughts to myself on the matter but I know our other siblings see it too, they see what they're trying to hide, the only one who seems oblivious is Father.

Parking my bike up opposite the cafe and securing my helmet, I make my way over. Uncle George is already sitting at one of the outside tables, underneath a large white and blue striped awning. I wave as I walk over and he immediately gets up and pulls me in for a tight hug. "Adanna, it's been too long," he smiles down at me with a familiar warmth in his face that he shares with my father. It must be a Sinclair family trait.

"I know, it's been ages. How are you? Where's Ottie?" I ask, looking around and noticing only two cups of coffee on the table, one black and the other, his usual latte. No third cup. Where is she?

"Ottie has a big case this afternoon and decided she needed to prepare. I told her I'd help her after but she won't let me. Insisting she had it all under control. She told me to pass on her apologies" he says, his eyes briefly moving from mine. A tell that he's not giving me the whole truth, but I know I would be stupid to pry.

"Oh, that's a shame, I was really looking forward to catching up. Anyway, how are you?" Ottie takes her job very seriously and so does our uncle. I'm sure they butt heads as we all do, but I know that isn't the reason for this, there's something off and it begins to taste bitter the longer I dwell on it.

"I'm good, I can't stop long, I need to be in court shortly. Alexander tells me you've taken a new job with Mr. Sidorova?"

Wow, straight to it. My hopes that this would distract me from Nikolai diminished as Uncle George probes me for answers. Father has set him up to this, I just know it. "Yeah, I have. It should be an easy one though. What time do you need to be in court?" I ask, it's obvious neither of us are comfortable with the conversation this morning, both of us giving very little in terms of answers.

George glances at his watch and frowns. "I'll have to make tracks in the next ten minutes if I want to get there in decent time to prepare" he sighs

"Tell me about the case before you go? Are they pleading guilty?" I ask. Knowing he won't give me too many details but needing to change the topic of conversation. He and Ottie are all for the confidentiality of their jobs and I understand it completely, but sometimes I can't bring myself to understand how they can represent guilty parties in the heinous crimes they committed.

He shakes his head and smiles, "You know I can't say too much, but I will say that I'm confident in them walking free today. After all, they have me defending them."

"They have the best lawyer for the job then," I smile, taking a quick slurp of my coffee. "I have to shoot, George. It was really good to see you, maybe we can arrange a get together with everyone soon? You haven't been home in ages." I say.

"I would love that," he finishes his coffee and then we say our goodbyes. That was a little more uncomfortable than usual, something is up but I don't have the brain power to fathom it out now.

Making my way back to my bike my phone pings. Glancing down, I open the message.

Hey babe, fancy coming over now? - Tony

I smile, this is exactly what I need. I need to lose myself and stop being consumed with Nikolai and this job and just feel like me for a moment. I type my reply quickly before jumping on my bike.

On my way. - A

Revving the engine loudly, her beautiful roar sends a thrill of excitement through me before I speed off in the direction of Tony's apartment. I've been here a few times when I've needed a quick and easy hookup so my brian autopilots as I weave through the city. The apprehension of what I am about to do wages war in my mind. I need to get rid of this feeling, but a part of me feels like I'm betraying, not only myself, but Nikolai too. It's ridiculous this hold he has infected me with. Like a disease, he's a cancer that's spreading through my bloodstream and I feel like I'm drowning with it, hopeless and desperate to find the cure before it's too late and I've completely succumbed to the monster. Before I know it, I'm parked outside of Tony's apartment building, staring up at the high rise flats, contemplating backing out and heading home. I shake my head. Fuck that! I enter the building and make my way to Tony's door on the fifth floor. I knock waiting for an answer when my phone beeps again.

Doors open, come in. - Tony

I smile, it's odd though, he never leaves the door unlocked but I don't think much of it as I turn the handle and enter his apartment. It's dark, the thick curtains are pulled together letting no light in and it's unnaturally quiet. I frown as I shout out to him, "Tony, are you here?" A muffled grunt from his bedroom immediately sends my brain into overdrive. I dash in, unsure what to expect but am horrified by the sight. Tony is half naked, wearing only a thin pair of lounge shorts, tied to a dining chair with a dirty rag shoved into his mouth. His eyes are wide, terrified, desperately pleading for me to help him. There's blood dripping from his nose that looks like it's been smashed repeatedly and his body is covered with red and purple bruising. He looks fucking awful. Who the fuck would do this?

I dash toward him but the loud bang of the door behind me stops me in the tracks before I can help, and what comes next turns my blood to ice. "Hello, Adanna." That voice. Nikolai. I spin quickly, but it isn't Niko that stares back at me. No, this man is a fucking monster. A devil in human form. He's not just angry anymore, he's gone fucking insane.

"What the fuck is this, Niko?" I bark at him.

"What the fuck is this? This is me showing you what happens when you defy me. What happens when you even consider letting someone else touch what is mine!" he growls. Before I can counter, he moves into my space, his face so close to mine that I can feel his breath hot and tempting against my skin when he taunts me. "This is your boyfriend, Adanna?" Tony grunts in protest behind me and I want to tell him to shut the fuck up but I can't seem to break eye contact with Niko, caught like a deer in the headlights, completely captivated by him.

"He's who I want to fuck, yes." I say, hoping the shake in my voice isn't as loud as I heard it.

"Really? This guy that's about to piss his pants? You really want to fuck him?"

"Well I wouldn't be here if I didn't, would I?" I snap.

"If you need to fuck someone, you fuck me, Adanna. You're mine. Nobody else gets to fuck what belongs to me." He snarls, grabbing my hair and forcing my lips to his. His tongue battles mine as he invades my mouth and I can't fight the feral moan that escapes as he continues his assault on me until Tony's muffled cries force me to pull away as he fights his restraints. Niko growls furiously, as he strides across the room stopping at Tony's side. For a brief second he looks me in the eye, no other emotion than pure unfiltered hate before he pulls a knife from his waistband and brings it to Tony's throat.

"Niko! Stop!" I scream at him. Fuck, I don't want Tony to die because of my own selfish need for a fuck. My heart thunders against my chest, I'm completely unarmed here and I know exactly what Niko is capable of.

I take a step forward but Niko snarls, pushing the edge of the blade into Tony's neck, "Take a step towards him and I will cut his fucking head off. Now I want you to think carefully about your little boyfriend here before you answer me…What will you give me to save him? What does his pathetic excuse of a life mean to you?"

My mind races as I look at Tony and back to Niko. The truth is, Tony could die right now and I would feel awful but I wouldn't grieve him, I wouldn't shed a tear. His life isn't of any importance to me. "What do you want, Niko?"

He smirks, his face shadowing a cruel and dark look. "I want you to do so many things. In time you will learn what it means to be mine and you will beg me for it. But until then, I'll keep this simple. All you have to do to save Tony's life is go on a date with me. Take me to your beloved shooting range, let me into your world, Adanna, open yourself up to me. Or we get to see if Tony's blood paints a nice pattern on his cream carpet. What will it be, Printsessa?"

I want to refuse him. To tell him to get fucked, that place is sacred to me and he seriously wants to threaten somebody to go on a date? This man is more unhinged than I thought possible. I look at Tony, his eyes are red and raw with tears as he silently begs me to save him. I can't allow him to die. I nod, "Fine, we go tomorrow."

"Good choice." Niko's face morphs with a sinister grin but I notice he is yet to move the knife from Tony's throat.

"Put the knife down now, Niko." I demand. He laughs and moves away from Tony before he whispers something in his ear that I can't quite catch.

"Are you going to untie him?" I ask.

"I will but it's time you go home now Adanna. Me and Tony need to have a serious conversation before he's set free." Tony looks like he's going to be sick as his eyes widen in horror and he pulls against the chair.

"Nikolai, I agreed your terms, you said you wouldn't hurt him." I snap.

"No Printsessa, I said I wouldn't kill him. He needs to learn not to touch other people's belongings. Now go or my offer will be rescinded." He growls.

"Niko…" I plead slowly inching forward. I don't trust him not to kill Tony the moment I leave the room.

"Now Adanna!" Niko growls, his body tensing with violent anger that causes me to falter. "We're just going to have a little chat, I promise."

I hesitate, fighting every instinct within my body, before forcing my gaze back to Tony. His body trembles as he sags, almost as if he's given up and I hate what I've dragged him into. He closes his eyes as I turn for the door and I catch the smirk on Nikolai's face just before I leave the room. I don't trust him but what choice do I have? I pray I've done the right thing, that I'm not going to regret agreeing to his irrational terms to spare Tony's life, but something inside of me says I'll regret it more than I could imagine.

CHAPTER TWENTY-ONE
Nikolai

After Ivan helped me dispose of Tony's mutilated body and we conducted a thorough clean of his apartment I tossed and turned all night, furious at my little sinner for taunting me with that sorry excuse of a man. After she named him as her boyfriend there was no way I was willing to let him live. Besides, she doesn't want him, she's using him to try and satisfy her need for me. She still doesn't understand how willing I am to end the life of any man that dares to even look at her. Maybe now it'll be clearer for her. Maybe when she finally realises that Tony is the first of many men who I'll end in the blink of an eye, she'll know i'm not fucking around.

I barely sleep at all with the thought of her and him together ravaging my mind as soon as I close my eyes. That and the gnawing feeling in the pit of my stomach about Anderson's plans for a new delivery of children is enough to keep anyone awake. No matter how hard I try, it's futile, and the only thing I can think to do is run. I need to clear my head before I kill somebody. I quietly slip through the front door of the Sinclair Mansion, it's still early and the sun is barely breaching the horizon as I begin to pace myself across the gardens around the house. Other than my first night here, when I watched Adanna through the darkness, I haven't spent much time taking in the tranquillity of the surroundings here. It's not the usual heavily-trafficked area that blankets the majority of London, but rather quite peaceful as I allow the earth to forge my path forward.

     I lose myself in my rhythm, letting my feet land where they may, not daring to think of anything other than the open space before me, and it works. After the sun has risen and the birds are singing their morning songs, I've circled the entire property three times over.

     I make my way back inside feeling weightless, with noticeably less tension constricting my body. That is until I hear Niamh's highly pitched voice coming from the kitchen. I strip my vest over my head and use it to wipe the sweat from my face as I enter the kitchen to grab a glass of water.

     I hear a sputtering noise as Niamh chokes on her drink as I saunter straight to the fridge.

     "You're up early," she chokes, slamming her glass to the table.

     I glance her way to notice her eyes roaming over my topless body, tracing the lines of my tattoos as I fill my glass with water. "That's because I don't like to talk to anybody before I've had my breakfast." I offer, pulling my lips into a tight smile which causes Niamh's face to straighten.

"Well fuck you, you miserable Russian god. Just because you're hot doesn't mean you get to be a cock," she sneers before storming from the kitchen. Oh how easy it is to piss her off. I finish my drink and make for my room. I'm in desperate need of a shower before I join Adanna at the shooting range today. It was her part of the deal. I let the slimy fucker live, and she takes me to her shooting range, little does she know, I didn't keep up my end of the deal. I already know how to shoot, but if this is how I get closer to her, I'll happily play dumb. She also needs to be reminded why I'm here. Her refusal to join me with her father yesterday was immature and selfish.

I fill the entire door frame to Adanna's room as I wait silently for her to lace her boots, her thick thighs tempting me as they stretch the fabric of her leggings. I stifle a groan, scrubbing my hand over my face to distract me.

"How long have you been standing there?" I hear her ask before opening my eyes to reveal her standing closer to me than I expected.

"Long enough. Come on, you owe me a date." I smirk, noticing my knife nestled at her hip.

Her eyes travel the path of my own and she tuts loudly. "It's not a fucking date. I'm just not willing to have Tony's blood on my hands."

I take the one step that's between us and wrap my fingers around her neck, feeling the bob of throat as she swallows. She immediately flattens her palms against my chest attempting to push me back. "Don't fucking speak his name. The only man's name you're allowed to speak is mine." I growl low into her ear.

Her eyes heat for a moment before a scowl adorns her face. "Don't be so fucking…"

"I mean it, Printsessa. The only man's name I want on your lips is my own. Do you understand?" I ask, pulling her tight against my chest and flexing my fingers around her throat

Her body fits against mine perfectly. So perfectly it's hard to think of anything other than ripping the clothes from her body and plastering myself on top of her.

"Yes. Yes, I understand," she chokes, gasping for air as I release her.

"Good. Now let's go." I order, holding my arm out towards the door for her to take the lead.

It takes longer than I expect to drive out to the large brick building. I step out of the car, glancing around the large empty car park. It looks more like a warehouse than anything else and I almost want to ask her if this is some sort of joke.

But she gets out of the car and heads towards the large wooden door on the front of the building. "What are you waiting for?" She calls and I quickly stalk after her.

The interior is a vast difference from the way the building looks from the outside. I walk in step behind

Adanna, subtly watching her ass as her hips sway back and forth, taunting me to grab them.

"Good morning, Miss Sinclair. I made sure to block out the entire morning for you so you're undisturbed." A petite brunette with large wire frame glasses and a horribly pink jacket smiles as we enter the building. I side-step Adanna coming into full view of the woman behind the desk and smirk as her eyes grow wide at the sight of me and her pen drops from her hand, clattering to the floor.

"Thank you, Emily. We'll be needing two sets of defenders and goggles today." Adanna says, raising her chin and ignoring the now blushing receptionist as she scrambles to retrieve her pen.

"Of...of course, Miss Sinclair." Emily stutters, shakily placing two sets of ear defenders and safety goggles on top of the reception desk as well as a key with a white tag with the numbers 1-4 written on it.

Adanna walks off down the only corridor off the main reception but I can't help myself as I face Emily and wink, flashing her a devious smile. "Thank you, Emily." I nod before walking in the same direction as Adanna.

"Do you have that effect on all of the women you come across?" Is the first thing she says when I find her grazing her fingers over the ammunition selection in our numbered booth.

"Are you jealous, Printsessa?" I smirk, causing her attention to snap back to me.

"Oh please. You're nothing special." She scoffs, quickly breaking eye contact as I move towards her, stalking her backwards until her ass hits the ammunition cupboard and I've caged her between my arms.

"Adanna's breathing becomes rapid as I lean closer. "What are you doing?" she whispers. The effect I have on her without even touching her body drives me crazy.

"I'm simply picking my poison." I grin, reaching over to grab the Glock 19 and two extra magazines before pushing away from her, leaving her staring after me trying to gather herself.

"We both know you're not inexperienced with a gun, Mr Sidorova. What exactly do you aim to get out of this?" she asks, coming to stand beside me with her own choice of a Glock 17. The pistol looks bulky against her dainty hands but as she flicks the magazine catch, checks the magazine, loads it back into the well and pulls back the slide to load, my dick stiffens against my too-tight cargo pants. I've come across many women in my life who know how to wield a gun, but nobody has made it look that sexy without even trying. I have to shake my head, staring down to the target to try and distract myself from my already throbbing hard-on.

"If we're going to work together to take down Anderson, I need to know that I can trust you."

"Trust me?" She scoffs loudly before pulling me around to face her. "The last time I saw you with a gun, you killed the only man who knew my parents before he had the chance to tell me about them!" She shouts, her face reddening with a deep blush of anger. The sudden plummet of my stomach hits me hard as I realise she's talking about Lev. Fuck. The hurt in her eyes is too real for me to ignore. I find myself wanting to comfort her, to apologise. But what good would it do? He's dead. It won't bring him back, and it won't bring back her parents.

"What happened to them?" I ask.

Adanna's face scrunches with confusion. "What?" she baulks.

"The night you were taken. Do you remember what happened to your parents?"

Her eyes tighten as she holds back her emotions. "No, I don't. I was told I was sold to Vladimir in place of my parents' debt to him. But I later found out that he murdered them. For what reason, or how, I do not know. Neither do I wish to. It's the past, it can't be undone. I was granted my revenge and I took it with great pleasure." Her breathing hitches and our eyes meet. "Until I met you," she whispers barely loud enough for me to hear.

There's a deafening silence between us as we weigh each other up. I'm not sure what Adanna is expecting me to do, but by the way her finger flexes around the trigger of her gun, I'd assume she thinks I'm going to hurt her. But in this very moment, I feel sorry for her loss, because I know the exhausting pain of losing the ones you love.

I sigh loudly at what I'm about to say out loud for the first time in seventeen years. "Vladimir killed my entire family." An audible gasp leaves her lips as I share with her the worst moment of my life. "The day of my fifteenth birthday. I remember we were all at home celebrating, me, Mum, Dad and my younger brother.

There was a knock at the door and Dad went to answer it. He was gone for a few minutes before he walked back into the room with a gun held to his head. I don't remember what words were said between them, only the haunting sound of my mother's screams as Vladimir shot my father and brother through the head. Her screams died with her as he slit her throat shortly after and she died in a puddle of her own blood right in front of me. He took me to The Facility that day, and I've never spoken about it since."

"Niko," Adanna whispers, her small hand cups my cheek, startling me. I hadn't even noticed that she'd moved. "Your last name. I don't understand," she urges, wanting to know why I bear the same name as the monster who slaughtered my family.

I lower my head, hovering inches above her. "I did what I needed to do to gain his trust. He wanted an heir, I had no other choice but to let him mould me. The day that you left, was the first day of both our new lives. Only yours had a much happier ending, Printsessa." I reach her hand with my own, squeezing it gently as her eyes mist over. "I have seen things you could never imagine, things that Vladimir subjected those children too. I need this to work Adanna, we need to put an end to the slavery unit back in Russia and we need to take out Anderson before he transports another bunch of kids across the world." I sigh. "I need you to put your pride aside for once and work with me. This is bigger than you and me."

Adanna steps back from me, whatever I said has clearly pissed her off but I hope she can see that this isn't about revenge anymore. It's about justice and survival. Those children need help, and with or without her, I'm going to give it to them.

"I'm not so conceited that I would bury my head when it comes to helping innocent children. I was in that place the same as you were. My parents were killed too," she snaps, clearly offended at my choice of words.

"Adanna, you were there for mere months. I lived the better part of my life there. I have…" I shut my mouth quickly. There's no fucking way I'm admitting my greatest sin to her. It's a burden I will take with me to my grave, I don't need her to think any less of me for it. "Just stop fighting me on this." I exhale, lowering my shoulders as she regards me.

In a split second she holds up her Glock, aiming with both arms outstretched, her face is void of emotion as she fires, demolishing the target straight through the head, until she empties her magazine. My ears ring as the wooden cut out of a man automatically replaces itself with a new one at the end of the gallery. My lips twitch into a smile and I subconsciously drag my thumb over one of my blades concealed across my chest.

"Blades are much quieter, you know." I say before launching the knife between the eyes on the next target. "Much cleaner, too."

Adanna's jaw clicks with irritation as her eyes narrow in on my perfect kill shot. "I prefer to work from further afield. A blade simply wouldn't travel the distance," she scoffs as if it's a well known fact. I press the button for a new target and shake my head, tutting loudly.

I slide behind her body, gliding my hand down her arm that still holds her gun. Her entire body is tense, solid almost as I push my chest into her back and claw my fingers into her hip holding her against me. "Drop the gun, Adanna." I whisper, gently dragging my nose along the length of her neck.

I feel her sudden inhale before the Glock clatters against the cemented floor. "Good girl." I praise, noticing the way she pulls her bottom lip between her teeth, trying to stifle the whisper of a moan as it escapes her. I smile against her neck, kissing the tender spot below her ear before I place one of my blades into her empty hand. "I want you to land it between his eyes." I ghost across her skin, switching sides and mimicking my previous actions.

"I've never…"

"I'll teach you." I cut her off, closing my palm around her as she clutches the blade. "Feel the weight of it, balance it between your fingers. Feel the sharp tip against your skin, the smoothness of the blade." I bring her hands in front of her, balancing the knife against her palm.

"It's heavier than I expected," she notes quietly.

"To travel a further distance the blade needs a little more weight behind it. Too light and it'll be harder to control through flight."

Adanna nods her head taking in my advice. I take her pointer finger and hold it against the tip of the blade causing her to wince as a small drop of blood beads where it punctured the skin. "The sharper the point, the easier it will pierce its mark." I bring her finger between my lips, sucking the blood from her wound as she gasps, tilting her head to watch me as I suck on the tip, pulling it out with a resounding pop. Adanna's tongue darts out over her bottom lip and her eyes quickly flick over my mouth. Fuck I want to kiss her so bad right now, to fuck her so hard that Emily can hear her as she begs me for more, but I'm trying to restrain myself, for once.

I clear my throat, breaking the tension and Adanna snaps her head back to focus on the target. "These are blade-heavy, meaning there's slightly more weight in the blade than there is in the handle. You should always throw with the weighted end first, this means you need to hold the blade and release the blade without slicing your fingers open in the process." Adanna nods, pinching the tip of the blade between her pointer finger and thumb. I guide her arm up over her shoulder with her elbow forwards, twisting her hips slightly to the right. "Steady." I whisper.

Adanna sucks in a long breath before releasing her arm, and flicking the blade. It spins beautifully but misses the target completely.

"Fuck," she mutters, her pride clearly diminished by her lack of ability.

"Again," I order, handing her another blade. "Follow through with your arm. Don't flick your wrist."

Adanna narrows her eyes at me with a tight lip but doesn't say anything as she positions herself as I showed her. I slide my hands up her stomach as she inhales and the blade flies from her hand hitting the clear section between the galleries.

"You're distracting me!" she snaps stepping away from me.

"You think you won't face distractions when the time comes, Printsessa?" I growl, pulling her back into me with a bruising force to her hips.

"Not as infuriating as you," she snarls, grinding her ass into my dick whether she means to or not.

"Again, Adanna. We're not leaving until you hit your mark."

Six more failed attempts as I roam my hands across her body leaving us both tense and frustrated as I hand her my last blade.

"Last one, Printsessa, make it count." I whisper, sliding her hair to one side behind her neck as she brings her arm up and behind her head. She aims with a deathly serious expression on her face. She's trying to block me out, but I'm enjoying the way her body squirms against mine each time I trail my fingers just above the waistband of her pants. "Do you know how sexy you look handling my knives? It's been a real test of my restraint not to fuck you. Do you know that?" I purr.

Adanna's arm extends fully as she releases the blade. I watch with a smug grin as it spirals through the air and the tip sinks directly into the mark just above the brow. "Such a good girl."

I spin her body around to face me, pulling her flush against my chest. Her breathing has accelerated and her eyes are wide with adrenaline and need. Our lips smash together, a fury of thrashing tongues and knocking teeth. I'm unapologetically brutal as I lift her from the floor, wrapping her thighs around my waist as I slam her up against the section wall. Adanna cries out in pain but I swallow it down, enjoying the sweet taste of her mouth on mine. "Such a temptress, teasing me with that weasel of a man last night." Adanna grinds herself against me, gasping as I thrust my solid and throbbing cock into her ass, kissing my way up her throat. "You are mine, Printsessa. Anybody who stands between us will find themselves in a shallow and unmarked grave."

Adanna shakes her head, and with a feeble attempt, tries to shove at my chest with all her strength. "You don't own me, Niko. I can fuck whoever I want," she spits, slapping me hard across the face. The sting travels all the way to the tip of my cock, and like the sick fuck I am, it only makes me harder. This woman will be the death of me if I don't empty myself inside of her soon.

I snake my hand around her neck, squeezing tightly as a feral growl rips its way through my throat. "Then you will be the cause of death for many men, Adanna. I'll rip through the chest of any man who dares touch what is mine and leave his bleeding heart at your feet as a reminder that you belong to *me*."

"You wouldn't."

"I wouldn't even blink."

"This is business, nothing more. Once Samuel is dead, we go back to our own lives." Adanna says with a look in her eyes that tells me she doesn't believe it is possible even as she says it. I shake my head and drop her body.

"If you believe we can live a normal life after this, Printsessa, then I seem to have mistaken you for a fucking idiot." I argue. My words clearly hit a nerve as she flinches away from me. "There is no going back from this. From whatever this is." I shout, waving my arms between us.

Adanna laughs before schooling her features. "Then I guess I am an idiot."

I watch after her as she walks away and leaves me alone with my thought running riot. What the fuck just happened? What am I doing? I've never been so hot and cold over one woman before, but I know she's feeling it too. I can see the trepidation in her eyes, mirroring my own. We're spiralling through dangerous territory, but I refuse to let it end.

CHAPTER TWENTY-TWO
Adanna

"Daddy please, I just need something small, easy, anything to get me out of this house." I plead. It's been days since Nikolai and I have spoken, every time I see him at the house he's on his way out or hauled in my fathers office and barely looks in my direction. Part of me is glad, I don't trust myself around him, and I definitely don't trust him around me. I remember the feel of every kiss, the way my body reacted to every touch and every look he gave me. How his words had me melting for him, distance is a good thing. It gives me clarity to complete the job I have been hired to do. Afterall, Nikolai is a client and nothing more. But I need a distraction. Father hasn't sent me on any jobs since Niko's arrival and the tension chipping away at my resolve fractures by the hour. I need to get a hit.

"I'm sorry Adanna, but this job takes priority. No more hits until it's taken care of."

"Come on brother. What's the problem? You know she's capable of handling more than one job at a time." Uncle George objects, flashing me a devious smile. He's here for a last minute meeting about a potential client of his that flags up a huge warning sign with multiple murders under his belt. I knew he'd have my back so I interrupted their meeting, pretending I hadn't known.

My father narrows his eyes at his brother. "I have no doubt that she can handle it but this requires more attention than everything else we have waiting right now" he states.

George rolls his eyes. "You're too uptight big brother. You need to relax. Let her get in an extra job before she nails this fucker." his gaze lands on me as I wait by the door. "She looks like she needs it."

I don't think about what that means. Do I really come across as desperate for it? It's been just over a week since I last fulfilled a contract and already my palms are twitching for blood. I look away, catching my fathers quizzical stare before he sighs, resigning himself to the fact that he created the monster in me, and he can not be the one to lock her away.

"There's a known drug dealer about two hours from here who has been caught selling cocaine to minors. His latest batch was tainted with what was presumed to have been rat poison. He sent four kids to the hospital and another six to the morgue. One of these kids was a chancellor's son. Him and his wife have reached out twice for immediate action to be taken, and the money they're willing to pay has tripled"

"Money means nothing. Give me the file" I demand, holding out my hand.

"Make it quick Adanna" My father orders as he hands over a manilla envelope. I take my leave, but I know he doesn't mean his death itself. Because for that, I vow on making him suffer.

I don't wait to make a plan after quickly reading through the file my father gave me, I drop the target, Billy Treskin's, last known address into my phone and get ready. I grab my handgun and secure Niko's knife to my hip before shoving several cable ties, my black leather gloves and a pair of pliers into a bag and then make my way to my bike.

I shove my helmet over my head, snapping my head as the front door opens and Niko comes barreling towards me. Oh fuck. "Where are you going?" He demands, blocking my path.

"Get out of the way" I snap, my voice slightly muffled by my helmet.

"Tell me where you're going Adanna." His eyes are wide and wild and I'm suddenly worried that his outburst may draw unwanted attention from the house.

I bring my bike to life, feeling the deep vibrations rattle through my body, letting them calm me. "I've taken an extra job. I'll be back in a few hours" I sigh, seeing the tension in his shoulders relax before his face hardens into stone.

"Where? What job?" He asks as he side-steps the bike wheel and stands beside me.

Even through the tint of my visor I can feel the intensity of his burning blue eyes as they search for answers.

"That's need to know" I start before he snaps back at me.

"And I need to know that you're coming back." The truth and vulnerability behind his words leaves me breathless, completely and hopelessly torn as I fall deeper for this man who is strictly off limits.

I swallow a thick lump of sickly sweet emotion as I reach out and place my hand against his chest. "I promise," I sigh, pushing him out of the way and tearing my bike down the driveway and out through the gates. He'll be pissed, but he has no right to be. He's the reason I'm taking this job. He's the reason I need to get away.

Leaving my bike down the alley at the side of Billy's apartment block, concealed behind a large waste container, I pull on my gloves before using the fire escape ladder to make my way up to the seventh floor. The window to Billy's living area is open when I arrive so I climb inside, quietly placing my bag onto the small dining table and removing the cable ties. I grab a cloth from the kitchen sink, ignoring the dried food stains that cover it and throw it on the table too, then slowly, with my knife drawn and ready, I creep through the apartment. With only the light shining through from the street outside I step over several piles of dirty clothes, rubbish and empty food containers. What a disgusting way to live. I push open the first door to reveal a bathroom, then the second, a dingy little room with nothing more than a mattress in the corner and more rubbish strewn across the floor. If this fucker isn't here I'm going to be so pissed.

    I make my way to the last door, pushing it open while holding my breath. Jackpot. He looks completely comatose as I step inside. His body is still dressed in what looks to be at least four day old clothes, covered in stains and is that blood? I grimace at the sight of him. This man has killed six children that we know of, probably more and the sight of him makes me want to set the building on fire. I glance down, my eyes catching on the needle that lies beneath his hand.

    I grip my knife, pressing the blade against his neck as I order him to get up. "Wake the fuck up Billy. You've got a date with destiny"

    Billy immediately opens his eyes, taking me in and flinching as he realises what's in my hand. "What the fuck is this? Who the fuck are you? How did you get in here?" He stutters, sitting up and raising his hands.

    "No. No questions. Get up and get in the front." I order, shoving the blade to his back and pushing him down the hallway.

    We enter the kitchen and I guide him onto a chair, quickly securing his arms and legs with cable ties. "What do you have to say for yourself Billy?" I ask, taking my phone out and setting it up against the shelf opposite his chair. I switch on the video, knowing that's what the chancellor and his wife requested. To see the man who murdered their son suffer before he dies.

    "I don't know what the fuck is going on you crazy bitch. Let me go" Billy spits, his pupils blown. Either from his high or fear, I can't tell which.

"This is about you selling drugs to underage children. Drugs that were laced with poison." I sneer, walking towards him with my knife, carefully keeping my back to the camera.

"That wasn't me. I didn't fucking do it. I swear"

"Wrong answer Billy." I grab the kitchen cloth, shoving it between his teeth to muffle his cries as I press my knife into the knuckle of his forefinger and force it through the skin. Billy screams as I repeat it on his middle finger and again on the next, hearing the snap and crunch of tendon and tissue as the appendages drop to the floor one by one. "Shall we try again? Did you or did you not sell those drugs to minors?" I bark, as the colour drains from his face and he looks as if he might throw up. I remove the cloth, pushing the blade to his throat. "We both know it was you Billy boy so you may as well admit it and save yourself while you can" I tease.

"I…I…Yes it was me…I sold the drugs…I didn't know they were underage, I swear! I'm sorry…I'm sorry!" he stutters. "Now please…let me go"

I shake my head, tutting loudly. "Oh Billy, Billy, Billy. What a silly, sorry little man you are." I swap my knife for the pliers and grab his head, forcing it back while squeezing him tight. "Now smile for the camera, won't you?" Billy's eyes flash with panic as he pulls to get away, but I'm stronger than him, the drugs running through his system make him weak and easy to overpower as I force the tool between his teeth and clamp it onto the thick pink muscle of his tongue. It's tough, but I use every ounce of anger that's built up inside of me and while Billy screams, flailing his head to deter me, I tear his tongue from his throat, dripping blood across the linoleum floor before dropping the useless fatty organ to the floor .

"No more lies from you" I smile as he chokes on the thick, dark red blood that pours from his mouth, coating his body. He makes a pretty scene for such a disgusting human being. Billy sobs, retching heavy and panicked breaths as he tries to breath but the longer it continues, the angrier I become.

I swap back to my knife, plunging it deep into Billy's stomach causing him to lurch forward, crying out the best of his ability. There's a thick gush of blood, pooling from his open mouth as I sink the blade into his body for a second, third and fourth time until I notice the final sag of his head. He's dead. I remove my knife from his gut, wiping the blood with the dirty kitchen cloth before putting that and the pliers back into my bag along with my blood-covered gloves.

I stand and stare at Billy's body, my hands shaking from the rush of adrenaline still coursing through me and I realise that I'm no different than Nikolai. A cold blooded killer. I shake the intrusive thought away the moment it materialises, grabbing my phone and ringing Narcissa.

To my surprise she answers on the first ring. "Ada, what's wrong, are you okay?"

I smile at her concern. "I'm fine. I need a clean up ASAP, I'll send you the address. Just tell them there's quite a lot of blood."

"I thought Father banned you from jobs until Samuel had been dealt with?" Narcissa asks.

"He allowed this one. There's a video I'm sending you, make sure I'm cut from the beginning and end and send it to Father, he'll know what to do with it." I instruct, taking a final look around the room ensuring I have everything I came with before making my way back out of the window and down the fire escape to my bike. I can't be bothered to wait for Cissa's clean up crew to arrive today. I trust they'll do a good enough job. I need to get out of these clothes, so I send her the address and floor it.

I walk back into The Mansion a little after midnight to find Nikolai standing at the bottom of the main stairwell, and even though he doesn't voice it, I can see the way his eyes take in my bloodied appearance and the way his jaw tenses at the sight. I move past him, walking straight to my bedroom and into my en-suite, locking the door behind me as I strip and shower, watching Billy's blood circle the drain until the water finally turns clear and I get into bed and close my eyes.

CHAPTER TWENTY-THREE
Adanna

Over the next two days Nikolai stays clear of me and deals with his business remotely, while I work with Narcissa to gather intelligence on the routes that Samuel Anderson uses when he picks up his 'goods'. It's been hard to watch and not intervene. He's transporting tens of children at a time. I have already watched five pick-ups so far but each time he uses a slightly different route and location depending on the area. I know Nikolai and I have to go on a physical stake out soon. The clock is ticking and more and more children are being put in danger. Deciding I need to take action and get this over with, I send a message to Nikolai asking him to meet me.

Meet me in the brunch room at 9 o'clock. We need to talk. - A

Within seconds a reply comes through.
I'll be there. - Nikolai

Checking my watch, it's 08.15am. I have time to get washed up and dress before heading down to meet him. I decide on wearing my tight leather trousers with a simple black t-shirt and as I take my brush through my hair I can't help but wonder if Nikolai really intends to do this job for the children or if it is just to get to me. I guess there's only one way to find out, we need to stop avoiding each other and get the damn job done so he can leave.

Making my way downstairs, I head for the kitchen. I have a few minutes before I meet with Nikolai and I intend to use it for a much needed coffee. As I pour the rich black liquid into my mug, I hear the door open behind me, and without turning to see who it is, I already know that it's him. My body always seems to know before my brain catches up. I take a deep breath and turn to face him. His eyes meet mine for what feels like the first time in so long and I'm lost all over again, held captive for a long, agonising moment, unable to move from my spot.

Niko's eyebrows pinch together like it physically pains him to talk to me and it causes my stomach to roll. "What did you need to see me for Adanna?" His tone catches me off guard, cold and stern and utterly confusing. A few days ago he had me pinned to a wall with his cock pressed up against my ass telling me how much he wanted to fuck me, and now he's talking to me like somebody's forcing a gun to his head. I don't get it. I don't get him and his fucking testosterone infected mood swings.

"Well, I was thinking we need to make moves on Samuel. I've been tracking his routes, his pick-ups and his clients for the past few days. I'm confident we can take him out on his next run." I explain as I take a sip of my coffee, breaking eye contact with him.

"I'm well aware we need to speed this job up, Adanna. I have information on his next exchange. But it won't be a pick-up, this will be a delivery. He's shipping them out on Friday morning, at the Portsmouth docks," he says, leaning back on the counter, looking so god damn handsome it's hard not to stare.

I turn and busy myself with my coffee to stop from ogling him. "Okay, shit. That's tomorrow. If we travel this afternoon, we can be there by nightfall. It would mean a stop over so we can get a feel for the place though." I suggest, realising how little time is before the exchange. There's no time to do a full recci like I planned.

"I have a few things to tie up but let's leave at 14:00." Nikolai barks at me as if I'm one of his soldiers.

I roll my eyes and look at him as if he's lost the fucking plot. "Yes, sir!" I obey sarcastically.

His lips curve up and his brow rises as he smirks at me, "So you can follow orders, good to know." As annoying as he is, another part of me is glad to have playful Nikolai back, but I will be damned if I admit it. I have not missed him at all.

"Right, whatever. I'll go and sort some equipment out and get a car ready." I say as I go to leave.

Before I can make it past him, he grabs my wrist making me stop dead in my tracks. My skin burns from his touch, and his thumb rubs over my flesh in a soothing motion, driving me insane. "We need to be professional, Adanna. What happened before can't happen while we are on the job. We can't afford a wrong move." My head wholeheartedly agrees, but my heart feels crushed. I know it's for the best, nothing can happen but the pull between us is magnetic, like two broken pieces of a single soul, destined to be together. I frown at him though my brain tells me it is pointless fighting the urges, this chemistry between us. For now, until this job is complete, we need to be professional and then I never have to see him again, and hopefully, maybe one day, I won't wish it could have been different.

I nod and pull my wrist free, not wanting to speak, because honestly, I don't trust what I'll say. I all but run from the room and focus on getting shit sorted before we leave but the entire time the ghost of his skin against mine awakens a deep and scary revelation that makes me wish I had never accepted this job. I'll miss him when he's gone.

It hits 14:00 and I have the car loaded with equipment, weapons and an overnight bag packed with spare clothes for tomorrow. I take a deep breath and lean back against the car, basking in the sunshine, enjoying the warmth on my face and my last few moments of solitude before his footsteps creep up behind me. "Enjoying the sunshine, Printsessa?" he mocks.

"Actually, I am. The sun doesn't always favour me and my skin tone though." I sigh, moving towards the driver's side of the car. Niko's large hands pull me back and his body immediately pins me against the door.

"I have seen you ride that death trap of a motorcycle, I would like to out-live Samuel." He says, pushing me aside and jumping into the driver's seat. I stand staring after him, shocked and a little pissed off that he criticised my bike and my driving skills. What an ass. I stomp around the car and reluctantly get into the passenger's side, not bothering to grace him with a reply. "Look, you're a better shot than me. It makes more sense for you to keep your hands free, incase of any trouble." He says, trying to explain away his need for control as he starts the engine and pulls away from home. I roll my eyes, staring out of my window with a deep rooted sense of gratification swelling in the pit of my belly and I can't fight the smile that it brings.

The journey is mostly silent as we make our way down the A3 to our destination. We exchange a few glances along the way but I can feel his eyes on me every few miles, gazing over my body. The tension between us is thick and heavy and the only way I can stifle it is to keep my window open, letting the fresh air keep me grounded. We hit heavy traffic along the way so I keep myself occupied by reading my book and messaging my sisters. Narcissa is tracking the car and panics anytime we're stationary for too long and so I send her photo reassurances that we haven't killed each other on the journey.

We eventually arrive in Portsmouth, although it's later than anticipated and Niko's mood has soured to somewhat of an unbearable degree.

"Let's stop for food" he grunts as we pass through the town. My stomach growls at the mention of food and Nikolai smirks without saying a word.

"Sure, food sounds good. Where are you thinking?" I ask.

"What about this place?" He nods towards the Beefeater pub that also has a Premier Inn hotel attached to it. "We can grab some food and drink before getting a room for the night. Samuel's next delivery isn't until 05:00 at the docks so we will need somewhere to rest." he explains.

"Okay, Beefeater and two separate beds, sounds good." Making a point of requesting that before he has any ideas of anything else.

"You don't want to share a bed with me, Printsessa? Scared you might like it?" he mocks.

"This is business not pleasure, as you reminded me this morning Niko." I snap. He chews at the inside of his cheek with a slight smirk but decides to say no more on the matter.

He pulls the car into a space close to the adjoining hotel. "I'll go and get us a room. Why don't you go and get us a table?" He suggests before stalking off toward the hotel reception.

"Sure Niko, not like you gave me much choice." I mumble even though he can't hear me. As I get out of the car, I hear the click of the electronic fob locking it. Guess I'm not taking anything other than myself and my phone then either. I turn to curse him out but he's already inside so I compose myself and head for the pub.

I make my way inside, taking note of the recent makeover the place has been given with cool blue tones, dark wood and fancy new furnishings. I don't wait to be seated like the sign instructs, instead I head straight to the bar. I need a drink if I'm going to get through a meal *and* share a room with him because I have no doubt that that is exactly why he chose to sort the hotel rooms and ordered me to come in here alone. So that he could make sure we have a single room. How is it only just dawning on me how much of a control freak he really is? I lean against the bar and smile at the bartender, he's cute with messy blonde hair and brown eyes that scream gentle. I'm not sure how, but I know he's vanilla and it makes me feel a little sorry for him. Definitely not my type but I can't help but notice the way his eyes track over my body, appreciating every dip and curve of it.

"So what can I get you, love?" He asks, maintaining eye contact. The guy is confident, I'll give him that. He's very attractive, and has a smile that I'm sure would melt any woman's heart, but he's just not the guy I'm craving.

I reciprocate his smile, not wanting to be rude. "What whiskey do you have?"

"A whiskey girl. I like that," he grins. "We have Jamesons, Jack Daniels, Johnnie Walker Red Label, Johnnie Walker Black Label, Glenfiddich and Woodford Reserve. Any of those up your street?" he asks.

I smirk, appreciating him with my eyes, yeah he's definitely easy to look at. "What would you recommend?"

"Well you can't go wrong with JD or Jameson but my favourite would be the Johnnie Walker Red Label." He explains leaning himself over the bar as he rolls his sleeves up to expose his tattooed forearms. That's a shocker. They're pretty impressive but not as impressive as a certain Russian guy whose arms could crush a boulder they're so strong.

"Well as it's your favourite I'll give it a try," I say, fluttering my lashes. I shouldn't flirt but I like the way he looks at me, I like the way it makes me feel, getting a kick out of the reaction I can get from other men.

"Neat, or with coke?" he asks. Flashing a flirty wink. I can't help but giggle. Fuck I'm turning into a soppy idiot! What's wrong with me?

"On the rocks-" I look at his name badge, "Ethan."

He places the glass in front of me and I take a slow meaningful sip. "So, what brings such a beautiful girl like you here?" I laugh at his attempt at flirting but my good mood is soon dwindled by a loud cough a few feet behind me.

"Yes Adanna, what brings a beauty such as yourself to a place like this?" Nikolai asks darkly. The bartender frowns at me and then looks at Nikolai. I breathe in and roll my eyes at him, shaking my head.

"Niko, Ethan here was just getting me a drink, what would you like?"

"First name basis already Adanna? You are far more chatty here than on the journey. Ethan must be something special."

Ethan looks uncomfortable but smiles at me before recovering his professionalism and turns to Niko. "Anything for you, sir?"

"I'll have the same," he grunts. Ethan nods and prepares Niko's drink.

"Will that be all?" Ethan asks, looking like he'd rather be anywhere but here, the flirtatious vibes long gone between us.

"We'll be eating too, put these on our tab." Niko says before I have a chance to speak. Great, the master controller is at it again.

I smile at Ethan and grab my drink before heading over to a table. "His name is Ethan and we were not flirting."

"Sure, why don't you tell him that." Nikolai grumbles, pointing his chin in the direction of the bar. He's such an insufferable ass.

Taking the menu I look it over and decide on a cheeseburger and chips. It's easy and usually hard to get wrong. I look up to see Nikolai glaring behind me. "So what are you going to have?" I ask, trying desperately not to turn and see who Nikolai is murdering with his eyes.

"Steak. Rare." he says, refusing to break his line of vision.

"Well I hope they cook it right. You look like a steak kind of guy." I comment and his eyes snap back to me as his eyebrows pinch together.

"What does a 'steak kind of guy' look like?" he quizzes.

"I don't really know. I suppose someone who knows what they want. A man who likes what he likes and how he likes it." I shrug.

"I know exactly what I want, Adanna. Do you?" he asks, taking a sip of his whiskey, his eyes burning into me, sending a delicious wave straight to my core. I get the feeling he's not talking about the food anymore. My heart pounds against my chest as I take an encouraging sip of my drink, letting the burn settle before I respond.

"Yes, I do." I say with less confidence then I'd intended. I look down at the menu once more before placing it back in the holder, feeling my whole body flush underneath his unyielding stare until a perky blonde waitress comes bounding over like a little puppy eager to impress.

"Hello, my name is Gemma, I'll be your waitress today." She can't be more than twenty but her eyes roam all over Nikolai making my blood boil and he gives her that smile. My smile. I want to tell her to fuck off but I keep my calm, she's young and doing her job. She's probably scrounging for tips. "So what can I get you?" She continues to eye fuck Nikolai before her eyes jump over to me with disdain. I gave her a chance but now she's just being rude.

"I'll have the Beefeater double stack," I say, sharply. She is quick to scribble it down and turn her attention away from me. "And for you, sir." She leans closer to him, her breasts practically in his face as she purposefully pushes them together.

 Nikolai's eyes don't move from the menu as he orders, "Sirloin steak, rare, with triple cooked chips." She takes a step back at his tone but doesn't fully move away from him, which makes me want to stab her in the eyes for even looking at him like she wants to fuck what is mine. Woah, mine? Where did that come from? What am I thinking? He definitely isn't mine, she's welcome to him for all I care.

 "Will that be everything?" She asks, smiling at Niko.

 "I think we have everything we need." I snap, making her jump before hurrying off to the kitchen to place our orders. I watch her leave until she retreats out of sight and as I look back to Niko his smirk pisses me off.

 "What are you looking at me like that for?" I hiss. Still not impressed by her flirting.

 "Didn't you like Gemma?" He asks. No, I wanted to rip her eyes from their sockets I think to myself but I don't want to give him the satisfaction. Shit. That's it, I'm jealous. The realisation hits me and my face burns with the heat of embarrassment.

 "I need to use the restroom," I say, excusing myself from the table and walking away to find the ladies room. I turn the corner, passing the entrance to the kitchen and freeze when I hear Gemma's voice.

 "He's so fucking hot. The woman he is with though, she looked at me like she was going to kill me. I doubt he's even interested in her, he didn't even look at her the whole time I was there, he just stared at the menu. I'm going to try to get his attention, it shouldn't be hard. What man wouldn't want this?" I peer around the corner and see her gesture to her body, pushing her boobs together and pulling down the front of her t-shirt. She's a good looking girl, I'll give her that, but she's not me. There's no way Niko would lower himself to her level. Would he? I step away and go to the bathroom, stopping at the sink, to splash my face in a failing attempt to cool down. Why am I letting her get to me? She's nothing, there's nothing between me and Niko, professionals that's it. This feeling of jealousy is uncharted territory and its freaking me the fuck out.

    I return to the table after giving myself a talking to and as I round the corner, I'm stopped in my tracks. I watch the blonde standing with her hand on Nikolais' shoulder, laughing as she digs her freshly manicured nails into his shirt. She's actually touching him. So much for talking myself down. My mind goes black and my vision turns red as I march over and slap her hand away, making her flinch and all Niko does is laugh. He fucking laughs.

    "Keep your hands off him, this is your only warning. Next time I'll start removing your fingers. Understood?" I spit at her as her bottom lip trembles.

    Her eyes dart to Nikolai, like he's going to help her, and to my surprise, he reaches out and grabs my waist, pulling me to his lap.

    "Would you like my knife, Printsessa?" He coos, dragging his tongue up my neck before he smirks a shit eating grin at the girl. Fuck, its hard to remain cool when he does things that set my insides on fire. I wriggle uncomfortably, ignoring the way my pussy pulses. Gemma looks ready to burst into tears as she runs off and Instinctively I try to move from Nikolai's hold, shifting my ass against his thighs. "Keep struggling, Printsessa and I will spank you until your ass is red raw before pinning you onto this table and fucking you for the world to see." I stop moving as he lowers his voice and his fingers dig deep into my hips making me wince. "You didn't like her touching me." He says. it wasn't a question, he already knows the answer.

"Let me go, Niko. I want to sit in my seat." I snap, ignoring his question.

"Answer me and you can. Stop denying us this, Adanna." he whispers softly as he takes my ear lobe into his mouth, sucking and biting his way up my neck as his hands begin to caress my thighs, making me whimper. I'm a mess, my pussy weeps at his every touch and this is fucking torture.

"No, okay? I didn't like her hands on you, I didn't like the way she fucked you with her eyes and I sure as hell didn't like the way she was gossiping about you back there. Saying you weren't interested in me and that she could easily have you instead" I admit, leaning my head back onto his shoulder. The feel of his hands are driving me wild. I know I'm already playing a dangerous game but it feels too good to stop.

"That's very territorial of you, Printsessa" he says, letting his hands fall from my body, freeing me up to move, but I don't, not yet. I turn to look at him, shifting my body so we're face to face. His bright, wild eyes stare back at me as I take in all of him, his rough layer of stubble that coats his chin, his tattoos that decorate every inch of his body that I've been able to see, his thick, broad shoulders and those eyes. The eyes that hold me hostage everytime I'm caught in them. I could die happy having known what the entire universe looks like simply by looking into his eyes.

    I swallow nervously, going back and forth between his eyes and his lips, eyeing him up like he's my next meal and what makes it worse is that Niko is staring back with the exact same look in his eyes. I am his, and he is mine. I may not want to admit it but I know it's true, I'd be stupid not to admit it. There's nobody else that plagues my mind the way he does and nobody else I want. A feeling of calm comes over me, like finally admitting it to myself has somehow soothed my soul.

    Reluctantly I move from his lap, returning to my seat opposite, and taking a much needed drink of my whiskey, relishing in the burn it leaves behind. "I am when I need to be." I say in reference to his earlier statement.

    "I must say, I liked the violence. I want nothing more than to see you use my blades on her, and then when you were done, I want to fuck you in her blood, Adanna, so feel free to be blood thirsty and show her what happens when she touches what is yours. If a man dared to touch you like that, I wouldn't let him live another minute. Luckily for him, the bartender didn't touch you, otherwise we would fuck in both of their blood." Nikolai says, like it's the most normal topic of conversation to have over the dinner table.

I can't help the coiling heat building between my legs, hearing him talk so freely makes me want it too, exactly the way he said. To fuck in the blood of all that try to come between us. "I wouldn't take her life, fingers or eyes maybe, she has her warning." I shrug, and just like that, Gemma appears with our food. She doesn't speak or make eye contact this time. Maybe she heeded my warning afterall. She carefully places our order on the table and leaves as quickly and quietly as he came. "Well this looks good, I'm starving, are you?" I pick up my burger and bite into it as I wait for his response.

"I am starving Printsessa, but not just for food." He sighs before he tucks in to his meal.

Choosing to ignore his comment, for now, I stick to safer topics of conversation. "So tell me Nikolai, what was it like to grow up in Russia?"

"Harsh, cold and bitter. How was growing up in a mansion?" he snarls. Maybe this wasn't a good choice of topic afterall. But does he honestly think I always had it easy? He doesn't know my life before this or the life that I had in that place.

"Well, for someone who claims to know so much about me, why don't you enlighten me. What do you think it was like for me?" I snap, taking another bite of my burger though I can't say I'm really that hungry anymore.

"You are the printessa of the Sinclair family, your father's pride and joy, or so they say. You were rescued from the hell hole that Vladimir ran, but you left behind your friends and didn't once try to save them, did you?" He taunts.

I baulk at his accusation. "I went through hell and was given the opportunity to grow stronger, learn skills that would help me one day get the revenge I so desperately needed. Maybe I didn't go back and save the others and I regret not being able to, but I'll make sure no other child has to go through that by stopping Samuel with you. I have many failures, Nikolai, but I have more successes and if you really knew me and my past, you would know each of my victims deserved what they got. Even your precious Dimitri. Did you know he burnt alive a mother and her new born baby because he wanted to take out the family line of one of Vladimir's rivals? That isn't even the worst one but it was one of the reasons why I chose to take the job to assassinate him. I kill the monsters for other monsters, and if I have to become someone else's monster to do it, then so be it, Nikolai. I never once proclaimed to be innocent." I finally break eye contact with him, no longer wanting the rest of my meal.

"I know of Dimitri's loyalty to Vladimir. I know what choices he made and the ones he made to protect others. You, Adanna Sinclair, always so full of pride. I wonder if you knew the reasons behind the actions of others, and if you would still be so quick to pull the trigger." He says calmly as he takes a sip of his drink.

"I knew more than enough to pull the trigger, maybe to you he was a good man Niko, but to many he was the face of evil." Nikolai doesn't say anything else as we sit in silence and he finishes his meal, my appetite completely dissolved.

"I'll go pay," Nikolai says, moving from the table as soon as he places his cutlery onto his plate. I take one last gulp of my drink before I follow him. I make my way to the servers station, but Niko is nowhere in sight so I head outside, hoping some fresh air will make me feel better about whatever the fuck just happened at the table. However, what I see only makes me feel ten times fucking worse.

"Nikolai, that is such an exotic name. Where are you from?" I hear Gemma giggle. This woman is either deaf or incredibly fucking stupid. I watch her leaning into Nikolai, looking up at him like he's her world and my resolve snaps. Before I know what I am doing her hair is in my hand and she's screaming at me as I rip her away from him.

"I warned you not to touch what is mine." I whisper as I yank her body toward me. She whimpers in pain but doesn't reply, looking at Nikolai again for help. But he crosses his arms and watches on with a satisfied grin, waiting to see where I take it. I've already started moving as I shout back at him. "Room, now." and he quickly follows, laughing as he does.

"Konieczno, moya zhestokaya printsessa, room 19." *Sure, my violent princess, room nineteen* Niko informs me, holding open the door to the reception for me to pass.

I pull Gemma close to my face, tightening my hold on her hair. "You will do well to remain quiet, and not make a scene, otherwise it might be a very long night for you."

"Please, I'm sorry!" She whimpers, her bottom lip trembling as she begins to cry.

I'm not sure where this insane amount of possession and anger has come from but I can't hold it back any longer. "No. I told you once and you didn't listen. Now, keep quiet." Gemma sniffs and wipes away her tears with the back of her hand but nods at me before I pull her through the lobby of the hotel and shove her into the waiting lift. She stumbles, catching the heel of her shoe and falling to her knees where she crawls away from me, trying to get closer to Niko. Yeah, like he's going to protect her. What a moron. When the lift gets to our floor, I wait until Nikolai opens the door and drag Gemma into the room by her shitty hair extensions.

Gemma struggles against me as the door slams shut behind us and Nikolai engages the lock. "Please, I'm sorry ok. You don't have to do this. I get it, he's yours, I should've listened, but this is going too far. You're insane." The beautiful flirty girl is gone and in her place is a snot-covered wimp, cowering on the floor. Pathetic.

"You were told, multiple times. I told you there was only one woman for me and it was not you." Niko interrupts, before turning to me, cupping the sides of my face and staring straight into my soul. "You are mine, as I am yours. Show me what that means to you." He demands as he captures my lips with his. The feel of his body is solid against mine as his tongue invades my mouth and I can't stop the moan that tears through me as his hands lower to my throat and tighten around my neck. Every damn time he chokes me I almost come, the fucking pressure of his fingers being the only thing that allows me air sends a wild frenzy straight between my legs and everytime, I instantly become wet, soaking my panties. Nikolai pulls away leaving me breathless and needy for more of him, but maintains eye contact. "What is her punishment, Printsessa?" I had almost forgotten about our little visitor under the power of his touch.

"Gemma, that's your name right? I told you if you touched him, I would slice your fingers from your hand. Correct?" I ask, turning and kneeling in front of her. She looks petrified, shaking from head to toes as she scrambles away from me. I don't condone this, and it isn't like me to punish a person who hasn't committed a crime, but the way Niko stares at me, with lust and fire burning through his eyes, dissolves the usually humane and logical part of my brain. He wants me to make her suffer. I smirk as I grab onto Gemma's ankle and pull her back across the carpet. Climbing over her hips, I pin her body beneath me and whisper low in her ear, "I am not a cruel person, so I will let you live, but I will take one finger for every time that you touched what is mine." Gemma's eyes widen in horror and she begins to panic.

"No please don't! I will do anything," she begs with fresh tears streaming down her cheeks. Niko flicks the TV on behind us and turns the volume up. Using the sound to drown out her wretched screams.

I can't help the smile on my face as I reach my hand out. "The knife please, I have a promise to keep to little Gemma here." Niko places his blade in my hand.

It's the same blade he fucked me with. How fitting. He must have taken it from my bag before we got back to the hotel. "This is going to hurt, alot." I promise as I grab a cushion from the bed, tear the cover off and shove it in her mouth. "Bite down, we don't want you to bite off your own tongue now, do we?" I smirk. I'm running on pure adrenaline now, my inner demon is rearing her vicious head and coming out to play, with her new master watching on with an intoxicating look of pure fucking lust blazing through his eyes.

  I shift my weight and kneel onto Gemma's arm, pinning it to the floor before counting to three in my head and lining up the sharp edge of the knife against her knuckle. Just like I did to Billy I force my knife through the bone, sawing away at the flesh and tendons. The rush of blood mixed with the sweet sounds of Gemma's agonising screams and the way Niko looks on with nothing but radiating pride sends a ripple of pleasure to the deepest parts of my body and fuck does it turn me on. I have never wanted to do this for anybody else but me, but the way Nikolai watches me like I'm the only woman in the world makes me want to do it all for him. He is quickly becoming my reason for more, and I'm not sure how to cope with that.

  Gemma bucks underneath me. Her screams are mainly muffled by the cushion cover shoved between her teeth but her tears have stopped now, the shock is starting to set in. I notice Niko has crouched near her head, holding her head still and ensuring the gag stays in place. Her eyes are wide, and the blood from her finger is staining the carpet. I smile at her pale and panicked face. "Because you did so well, I think I'll stop at just one." I say as I bring the bloodied knife to her throat. She whimpers pathetically but doesn't scream so I remove her gag.

"Please let me go," she whispers. "I won't say anything. I promise. I know I was wrong now, please! Please don't hurt me."

"Soon." Is all I say as I raise the handle of the knife and whack it against her temple, knocking her unconscious. She'll wake up comfortable, with nothing missing except her pinky finger. She should be grateful I left it at that.

The sudden silence that engulfs me is deafening. I realise Niko has turned the TV off but before I have a chance to come to terms with what I just did, Nikolai picks me up and throws me down on the bed. "Stay there while I move our guest to the bathroom. She can sleep in there while I fuck you in her blood." Without another word he effortlessly hauls Gemma's body over his shoulder and drops her in the bathtub. Within seconds he's on me, the blood from Gemma's wound covers my hands and stains my skin as he pins me to the bed. I still have his knife clutched tight in my hand as he grabs my wrist and forces me to drop it.

"You did so well, Printsessa. Showing me that I belong to you. Such a good girl…My good girl." His hot breath warms my neck as he kisses me, and I'm gone. All I can think of is his body on mine and how his lips set my skin alight as he covers every inch of exposed flesh with his tongue. I gasp as he nips my shoulder, my eyes meeting his and he smirks. He crawls down my body making quick work of removing my trousers and underwear, leaving me in just my t-shirt and bra. I feel exposed as he stands back from the bed, admiring the view as his tongue swipes across his bottom lip and his pupils dilate as I spread my legs for him. "Take the rest off now, Adanna, I want to see all of you." I don't question him as I quickly strip down to nothing. He removes his clothes, not tearing his eyes from my naked body for a second until he stands before me, as naked as I am. Holy shit, what a man. I always knew he would be big, in every aspect of the word, but the way this man is built is something unnatural. I trace his body with a hunger building deep inside of my cunt and I can already feel how fucking wet I am for him. The mass of artwork covering his skin only enhances the grooves of his muscles, leading down to that deep V shape of his adonis belt. Fuck. I lick my lips, my mouth all of a sudden dry as I take in the length of his cock. A solid 8 inches with a deliciously thick girth. That's going to hurt. My eyes snap to his and he laughs at my horror.

"Don't worry Printsessa, I'll be gentle with you" Nikolai coos as he climbs between my legs and settles his hips against mine, his rock hard cock sticking into my ass cheek. His lips crush mine, snatching my breath as his hands caress every inch of my body. And I love the way they feel against my skin, callused and rough, leaving gooseflesh in their wake. He breaks away from my mouth leaving me panting as he shifts his lips to my nipple, licking, suckling and nibbling with the perfect pressure as he pinches the other, sending a jolt of pain straight through my body. I suck my bottom lip between my teeth, trying desperately to stifle my moans, but it's no use against his expert handling. "Let go Adanna, I want to hear you!" Niko growls as he glides his hands lower and without warning, begins to tease my clit, rubbing in slow and torturous circular motions, making my hips jump at the contact. "Don't fight it, don't fight me" he whispers as he slowly inserts his fingers into my pussy and bites down on my nipple. I gasp loudly because the pleasure of his fingers mixed with the pain of his teeth causes my pussy to clench around him. "Breathe, Printsessa, I need to stretch you out before I fuck you, are you ready for another?" I bolt up, unable to believe he has any more fingers to give me at how full I feel, but I watch as he pushes another inside me.

"Fuck that feels good," I groan as I fall back on the pillows and let him stretch me out, scissoring his fingers against the tight walls of my pussy.

"I never took the time to fully appreciate how good you felt on that forest floor" Niko whispers as he thrust his fingers faster, curling them in just the right way to hit that spot until I can barely focus and the desire builds hot and heavy, racing me towards my orgasm. "I won't make that mistake again." Niko moves faster, fucking me hard with his fingers until his tongue swipes against my clit. Oh fuck, yes. I can feel my body burning, the fire sparking as I approach the precipice, rolling my hips to meet his mouth. His tongue works against my sensitive clit, lapping and sucking, applying just the right amount of pressure to drive my body wild, and just when I'm about to explode, Niko pulls away.

"What the fuck, Niko, I was so close!" I snap.

He smirks at me with a glistening sheen around his lips as he pops his fingers into his mouth and sucks them clean. "You taste divine," he smirks. Niko crawls back up my body and kisses me with renewed fever. I can taste myself on his tongue, sweet and tempting and it makes my body shudder. I drag my nails down his back as we battle for control, our tongues thrashing against each other. I'm sure he'll be left with my marks on his body after we are finished, and I'm ok with that because equally, I know he'll leave some of his own on me. "You take my fingers so well. But I want to feel that tight little cunt strangle my cock as you cum, Printsessa. So now I'm going to fuck you, hard and fast," he breathes out as he breaks our kiss.

Niko doesn't give me a second to brace myself before he pulls his hips back and lines the swollen head of his dick with my entrance and thrusts inside of me so deep that I cry out at the intrusion. His nostrils flare as he feels how tight I am, and through gritted teeth he groans as he's met with resistance. "So. Fucking. Tight!" he grunts as he thrusts forward and tries to bottom out. I cry out again at the pressure, the way his dick stretches me out dances the fine line between pain and pleasure and my body shakes as he tries to shift his hips. "Breathe, Adanna, you need to let me in baby. Just relax." Niko's eyes search mine and for a moment I wonder if he's scared of hurting me with the way his face contorts. I let out a deep, shaky breath and relax my hips, feeling the stretch of Niko's dick as he pushes further inside me.

"Okay." That's all I can say as I dig my nails into his shoulders, covering them with Gemma's blood and brace myself for what happens next. Niko grabs my thighs, wrapping them around his waist before gliding his hands under my ass and lifting up my lower body. I hook my ankles together around his back and push my hands against the headboard for purchase. With a deep and powerful thrust Nikoai buries himself inside of me, allowing me a breath before he fucks me with dangerous and delicious brutality. Oh Jesus Christ. I'm not sure how it's possible but he's hitting a spot I didn't even know existed. And with each thrust, he pulls out a feral cry from my throat. His grip tightens and his nails dig into my ass, spreading me open as he speeds up, fucking me like his life depends on it. Like nothing else matters. I close my eyes, arching my back and meeting him thrust for thrust. The pain long forgotten as pure ecstasy winds its way up my spine. I lose myself in the scent of leather and pine, and sex and the feel of his skin against mine, the power of him, the sound of our bodies as they collide over and over again.

"Look at me Adanna. I want to see the submission in your eyes the very moment you give yourself over to me." Niko barks, and I easily comply. "Good girl. Now come on my cock Printsessa. Come for your new daddy, because I fucking own you now."

Oh fuck. Those words. They shouldn't sound so good coming from him but they do and the effect is cataclysmic. Niko snaps his hips, growling with a deep, guttural ferocity and my body fucking sings. The tight winding snake wraps around the last of my restraint and strikes, stabbing its venomous fangs into my skin and everything explodes.

"Fuck!" I scream as my head pushes back into the pillow. My pussy clenches savagely around Niko's cock as fireworks explode through my body and the intensity of my orgasms crashes through me. I tighten my thighs around Niko's hips and use my heels to pull him into me, grinding our bodies together, dragging out every second of my own pleasure. Niko's eyes are wild as he stares down at my body. But there's no reprieve as he brings a hand to the front of my body, pinching my nipples and pulling at them one after the other until he shoves his fingers between my lips.

"Suck" he orders, and I do before his fingers find my clit and he adds a delicious friction to the swollen bundle of nerves.

"Niko…Fuck" I cry out. My voice doesn't even sound like it belongs to me as I feel another orgasm sparking in the wake of the first and my body feels as if it's on fire. I scream loudly as I cum quicker than I ever have, my pussy gushing around him as he pounds me harder and harder, racing towards his own release.

With all rhythm gone, he thrusts his solid cock balls deep inside of me, causing me to gasp as he reaches his climax with an inhuman growl. Niko pushes himself against my body, pinning me to the bed, forcibly capturing my mouth with his, biting my lips and tongue with his dick twitching deep against the tight walls of my pussy as he fills me with cum.

"You belong to me, Adanna Sinclair" he growls. And I do, I can't deny it any longer. I dig my nails into the flesh of his strong muscular back and pull his body into me. Nothing has ever felt so right but so fucking wrong at the same time before. But at this very moment, I don't want it to end.

CHAPTER TWENTY-FOUR
Adanna

We lie together for what feels like a lifetime, entwined and at peace, covered with blood, sweat and the mix of mine and Niko's cum steadily seeping out between my legs.

With my head against his chest I let the steady rhythm of Niko's heart lull me until my eyes grow heavy and I have to fight hard not to fall asleep. That is until Nikolai reminds me that Gemma is still in the bathtub. Fuck. I groan, not wanting to burst the perfect little bubble that surrounds us, but I know he's right, we need to deal with her before she wakes up, and we're already pushing it. "Get dressed, the key for the room next door is in my jacket. Take it and go get yourself cleaned up." Nikolai instructs me as he slips out of bed, leaving my body cold in his absence. I sit up and frown as he pulls on his clothes. Has he gone mad? What about the girl? I open my mouth to ask but he cuts me off. "I'll arrange for somebody to clean up this mess but you need to leave. I don't want them to see you freshly fucked with my cum dripping down your thighs. That sight is for my eyes only." Gooseflesh prickles over my skin at his words and the way his eyes darken as he drags his gaze down my exposed body. Fuck. If he keeps looking at me like that I'll never get out of bed. Thankfully he quickly turns and fishes the room key from his jacket on the desk before throwing it at me. I have questions but now isn't the right time so I nod and get dressed. Niko makes a call as I pull on my trousers and has a quick one sided conversation before walking into the bathroom.

  I leave without saying goodbye, quickly slipping into the room next door. It's not until I close the door behind me that I realise how exhausted I am and I aim straight for the bed, collapsing into the pillow. I can't keep my eyes open any longer and I let myself drift into a deep slumber.

  "Adanna, wake up." A low voice whispers against my ear. I feel his hand gently caress my cheek and I smile. My eyes flicker open and Nikolai smiles down at me. "We need to go, the drop is in just over an hour." Oh crap. I sit up and rub my eyes and try to pull myself together.

  "Uh okay, do I have time to shower?" I ask, glancing at the clock beside the bed.

  "I'd rather you didn't, I like the smell of my cum drying on your skin" he says as he pulls me up against him. "Unfortunately I don't think we have time, it took longer than expected to clean the blood from the carpet next door and keep our friend quiet, otherwise I would've been waking you up with my tongue deep inside of your pussy." I shiver at the thought of it. "But there is always later," he says with a promise, nipping at my neck and groaning into my ear. "Fuck, you make me so hard it hurts my cock" he growls, biting my ear lobe and pushing my hand against his crotch.

"We'll never get there if you carry on" I breathe out, wanting nothing more than to climb onto the steel rod beneath my fingers.

"Then you had better stop teasing me" he snarls, and I smirk, ripping my hand away and jumping from the bed, squealing as Niko spanks my ass on the way to the bathroom.

"I'll just freshen up quickly," I state as I grab my bag that Niko had brought in and close the door behind me. I'm wide awake and infuriatingly horny but I get ready quickly, making sure I wash away the remaining blood that still stains my hands.

"Adanna, come on we need to go." Niko bangs at the door as I pull on a clean t-shirt.

I open the door to an angsty but gorgeous looking Nikolai as he scowls at me from the bed and I smile. "Let's go take out the bad guys." I wink.

Nikolai shakes his head and huffs out a laugh as we make our way down to the car. "Do you think you're a good guy?"

"I'm a monster to some, a hero to others. I don't give much thought to what I am, I only care about getting the job done." I answer truthfully. Because if I'm honest, I don't care who I kill, or who my next hit is, as long as I do it to the best of my ability. My conscience has always been dependent on my pride.

We're ahead of Samuels schedule as we pull up at the port, and ensure the car is parked in an inconspicuous spot that still gives us a good vantage point. Luckily the windows are blacked out as we settle into the seats, get comfortable and wait for Samuel to arrive with his men.

"Now we wait" Nikolai states as he stares ahead. I nod, and we sit in comfortable silence until 05.11am, when a black van pulls up followed by two grey cars. We watch through binoculars as two armed men exit the van and walk over to the first grey car, exchanging something through the window. I notice Samuel take the package in his hands, it's a set of keys and a thick lump forms in my throat at the thought of what is in that van. I try not to let my feelings get the better of me but it's becoming difficult. I glance over to Nikolai's who hasn't moved an inch since Samuel arrived.

I move back to my binoculars as Samuel moves out of the car, followed by the rest of the men from the second car. They are all visibly armed. I feel my hands itching to reach for my gun and have to flex out my fingers to try and expel it. Removing the piece of shit from this world will be a blessing and an honour. I watch on, wishing I could hear the exchange as the men exchange a handshake. The smug look on Samuel's face is sickening. This vile excuse for a human being needs to be put in the ground.

Our plan was simple; wait until the exchange had taken place and the kids had been transported into a shipping container. Once we had eyes on and were able to ensure the children were out of range, I would take out Samuel with my sniper rifle from the car, along with anyone else who got in my crosshairs. Once it was clear, we would make a call and get the children rescued by the local police. The plan was dependent on Nikolai not being involved and being able to take the men out without being seen but this waiting around is becoming too much for me. I don't understand why I can't just take him out now.

"Ok, that's enough show and tell for me, I'm heading up," I snap as I reach for the door handle. Niko's hand grabs my thigh and his fingers dig into the muscle, freezing me in place.

"Be careful, Printsessa." Is all he says before releasing me and lifting the binoculars back up to his eyes. I guess that was his way of saying he cares about me.

"Always am," I whisper as I climb out of the car and up onto the roof where I quickly set up my rifle. I lay down on the rubber matting and lift the butt of the rifle to the crook of my shoulder and focus the sight. I'd prefer to use a laser sight but the red dot is a little bit of a give away. Thankfully there is no breeze to contend with and my calculations seem on point, I adjust slightly for the distance but the 7.62mm bullets I have will definitely do the trick.

As I watch the exchange unfold down the scope of my rifle, I see one of the men drag a young girl from the back of the van. She can't be more than six years old. Her hair is lank and dirty, her skin covered in purple welts and I may be far away but I can see she's been crying. I feel like an imposter watching from the safety of my gun sight as Samuel grabs her by her hair and spits in her face but my anger quickly quietens as my inner demon takes over. A film reel of horror plays out in my mind as it replays the things men like Samuel did to me and so many others. Never again. Taking a deep breath and blowing it all the way out I settle and focus, watching the sick piece of scum man-handle the girl as the rest of the men watch on, laughing. I can't get a clear shot on Samuel without risking the girl but I can't watch any more and the need to shoot is like a drug addiction and even I am no match for the rush it gives me. I make a split decision to take out one of the henchmen first, clearing the field before taking out Samuel.

"What are you waiting for, Adanna? Take the shot!" Niko hisses from below me.

Another deep breath in, out and hold. My finger sits on the trigger, ready to squeeze as a sudden gust of wind hits as I slip. I fucking slip. "Fuck!" The bullet misses its target and hits the van door, the force of the impact echoing through the distance.

"What the fuck, Adanna!" Niko shouts and I can't tell if he's worried or angry.

"Fucking wind! We need to abort, they know we're here now. Start the engine Niko, we have to go, you can't risk being seen." I shout as I grab my gear and slide off the roof, yank the back door open and throw it all in.

Gunshots ring out as our position is blown. "Shit! Get in the fucking car Adanna!" Niko shouts.

"I can still shoot, you focus on getting us out of here and let me do my job. This is why I always have a Plan B." I say with a smile that doesn't quite reach my eyes.

The scene at the docks is sheer pandemonium. The cries of children, the firing of guns, the screech of tyres and the shouts of men. As my bullet hit the van, everyone dropped to the ground, thinking that would save them. The only reason I stopped shooting was the risk to the children in the van, that first bullet was too close for comfort. Although they couldn't see me, they knew the direction my bullet came from as the henchmen opened fire and Samuel, like the weasel he is, lifted the girl to cover him as a shield and ran for his car, speeding away in the opposite direction.

Niko floors it, turning left, right and then left again, racing from the dockyard and into busy traffic to get us away from the disaster we've just caused. I've caused. Fuck, I should have waited. I turn in my seat, chancing a look behind us to see one of the grey cars following and quickly closing distance. I turn back, covering my head as bullets hit the back of the car, smashing through the back window, spraying glass everywhere.

"Shit! What's this Plan B then Adanna, care to share?" Niko asks through gritted teeth as he weaves between vehicles.

"Ok, not a Plan B, more like an off the cuff plan, a last minute sort of thing." I admit, grabbing my gun from the back seat and subconsciously opening my window. "When I say, I need you to turn hard left, alright? I need you to trust me." I say as I ready my gun. Niko is silent as he races between traffic, narrowly missing a bus at a crossroads. "Niko. I need to know you're going to turn when I say!" I snap and his jaw clenches.

""Fuck no, Adanna! I know what you're going to do and I can't fucking let you. You could get hurt!" he shouts, keeping his eyes narrowed and on the road.

"Niko, you have to trust me. There's no other way out of this right now!" I plead. "I can do this. You have to trust me." The car is getting too close and if they don't shoot us dead, they'll end up eventually capturing Niko and torturing him for Samuels attempted assassination. That's something I can't even begin to imagine. Another round of bullets pierces the back of the car, narrowly missing my head as my seat takes the impact. "Nikolai!" I scream.

"Fine, do it, but this conversation isn't over Adanna. You hear me? I'm not fucking happy about this" he bites back furiously.

I roll my eyes. "Yes, yes, I hear you." I take a deep breath and steady myself, as I watch for the perfect moment. Three. Two. One. "Now!" I shout and Niko pulls hard to the left. Leaning through the window into another round of incoming bullets, I flinch as a sharp pain slices through my arm but I hold it back, biting into the flesh of my gum to stop from alerting Niko. I blink away the blur as my head swims and take my aim while everything around me slows down. I rapid fire as I get the perfect line of sight, and take out the left tyres of our pursuers. Their car careens to the side as the driver over steers to compensate and smashes through the front of a building. I smirk as I sit back, slumping into my seat but something is off. As my adrenaline burns away, the pain in my arm doubles. I glance at Niko who studies my face with worried eyes. His mouth is moving but I can't hear the words. I don't know what he's saying but I think he might be shouting. I blink slowly, my eyes growing heavy as I glance down, there's blood seeping through my t-shirt but fuck I'm to tired to think about where it's coming from. I think I may just take a nap.

CHAPTER TWENTY-FIVE *Nikolai*

I was beside myself when I realised Adanna had been injured. How could I have been so fucking reckless to involve her in all of this? I almost crashed the fucking car when I noticed the blood. She assured me she was fine, but her blood just kept oozing. I'm not even sure she realised she was talking to me or that she'd been shot, and then she blacked out. I had never felt so scared in my life that I would lose somebody I cared about and as I raced us to the nearest hospital it dawned on me. A huge fucking reality check just smacking me straight in the face. She meant too much to me now. I couldn't see her get hurt again. And in that moment, I made a promise to her and myself that she would only ever bleed under my own blade.

Alexander was beyond furious when I rang to let him know that Adanna was in the emergency room, and that she needed stitches for a gunshot wound, but he eventually settled down as Adanna took the phone and reassured him that she was fine. I watched her from the foot of her bed as a nurse stitched her up and I hated every fucking second of it. I had never felt so angry. At her for putting herself and risk, and at myself for letting her do it. Adanna was given the all clear to leave as soon as her arm was dressed and the Doctors were happy that there was no lasting nerve damage. She answered their questions perfectly as they asked how she had obtained the injury but neither of us wanted to stay for longer than we needed too. I carried her back to the car and the pain meds they'd given her soon kicked in and she slept the entire way home.

    I couldn't help but creep into her room tonight. I lay staring at the ceiling above my bed for hours, allowing Adanna to fill Alexander and her siblings in on what had happened and to let her get some rest. But my mind refuses to rest while she's under the same roof and so far away. I need to ensure she really is okay. It was just a little flesh wound, the bullet sliced through the skin, nice and clean, thankfully it didn't hit anything dangerous but still, I needed to reassure myself that her injuries wouldn't cause her to slip into an eternal slumber through the night, snatching her away from me before we even had the chance to thrive.

    I barely managed to walk myself to my own room when we returned home. After a night spent between Adanna's legs and her near brush with death, the thought of being so close to her yet so far away made me feel something unfamiliar and I didn't like it one bit. I gave Alexander my word that this was strictly business. But fuck, I've already crossed the line. Gone so far past that line it's now non-existent so why stop now?

I move closer to Adanna's bed, quietly closing the door behind me, wholly entranced by her beauty and my overwhelming need to feel her naked body against my own again. Slowly pulling the sheets back, I stifle my heavy breathing as I expose her choice of sleepwear. A thin strappy vest and a tiny pair of red lace panties. Fuck. I drag my eyes over her body, relaxing as her chest rises and falls. My eyes catch on the bandage wrapped around her left bicep and I hate myself all over again for letting her get injured. I've known for a very long time this woman meant something to me, but in all the years I've watched over her, I mistook my feelings for anger. I was conditioned to hate her, to hate everything she represented. But the more I allowed her to break down my walls, the more my wretched heart beat to the tune of her and her alone.

I quickly strip from my cargos and pull my t-shirt over my head before I gently slide myself beside her with my body facing hers. Adanna's body is a work of fine art next to mine, one I long to get lost in. I travel my eyes over her body, examining every inch of her, her scars, her tattoos, and the bruises that mottle her skin from our night of brutality together.

I reach my hand up and carefully begin tracing my fingers across her waist to her hip, failing to notice that she's woken up until her loud gasp startles me. "Niko. What the fuck are you doing in here?" Her eyes snap down to my hand resting on her stomach and then back up to mine. I watch as she swallows nervously. Trying to ignore my cock that's growing harder against her hip.

I look away from her. I should leave, I know I should but fuck, the darker side of me wants to fuck her into the bed while she screams my name. To ravish her body, covering her in my marks. To wrap her thighs around my face and drink from her sweet cunt and spend the night drawing out every drop of ecstasy from her body until she's wrung out and pleading for me to stop.

"Niko." Adanna's small hand settles on my face, pulling me back to look at her. "What's wrong?" she asks, searching my eyes for answers I just don't have.

"I needed to make sure you were okay." I admit through gritted teeth. Adanna's eyes soften and I can't fucking stand it, I don't want her to look at me with sadness and sympathy in her eyes. I don't fucking deserve it. In one fluid move, I grab her hips and pull her on top of me. Her thick thighs straddle my waist as her hands come down to my chest. "Niko!" she half squeals, half gasps as my cock throbs beneath her pussy. The thin fabric between us doesn't hide the way her pussy craves me, I can already feel the dampness between her legs that beckons me in.

I bite back a groan as I grab the back of her neck, pulling her into my chest and slam her lips down to mine. She reacts immediately, moaning into my mouth and grinding her hips against me, teasing me with a friction I can't fucking stand as she rubs her soaking panties across my covered dick.

"You're going to be the death of me, Printsessa." I growl, pulling her bottom lip between my teeth, causing her to gasp as her coppery blood floods my mouth.

"Niko, we can't," Adanna whispers, her hips still savagely grinding against my solid cock. "My father will kill you right here if he hears us." I snap my gaze to the small table beside the bed, noticing my knife so carelessly left within reach.

I shake my head as a deep guttural chuckle erupts from my throat. I reach up and I squeeze her throat making her squirm even more. "No, Adanna…I'm your fucking daddy now. And daddy wants you to ride his cock like a good little whore."

Adanna's eyes flare as she whimpers, making me smirk. I grab my knife, slicing through her vest and panties before pulling the fabric strips away from her body and throwing them to the floor.

"Fuck, you're so fucking perfect." I groan, sitting forwards, pulling her to my chest and biting her neck, making sure to bite hard enough to leave another mark against her skin. "Ride me, Printsessa. I want you to take my cock out and ride me like you fucking hate me." Adanna shoves my chest hard, pushing me back to the bed as she makes quick work of pulling off my shorts.

I hiss out a groan as she crawls over me, flattening her tongue along the underside of my steel erection. Adanna never takes her eyes off mine as she trails up and down my length before taking me whole to the back of her throat. It's the most beautiful kind of torture. I could watch her swallow me all day if I wasn't so desperate to get inside of her again. I thrust my hips, hitting the back of her throat making her pull back slightly but I hold her in place. She hollows her cheeks, sucking me hard before twirling her tongue around my head and popping my dick from her mouth. A small trail of saliva drips from her lips and coats her chin, I've never seen anything so beautiful.

Adanna crawls forwards, straddling my thighs as she places one hand on the headboard above me and simultaneously reaches back to line my cock up with her deliciously drenched pussy. Her eyes burn wild as she gazes down at me. "I do hate you," she whispers with a moan as she slides herself back until she's fully seated on me, her hot, wet channel enveloping me as her pussy lips surround my cock. "Oh fuck!" She gasps, rising her hips before slamming herself back down to repeat the movement.

"You're so fucking tight." I hiss through my teeth, digging my fingers into her hips with bruising force. "So fucking perfect." Adanna throws her head back, finding her pace as she bounces on my cock. I glide my hands up over her stomach to her tits, caressing them with my rough, calloused hands before rolling her nipples between my forefinger and thumb. She whimpers, her movements becoming erratic as I pull on the sensitive little bud. "Do you like that, Printsessa? Do you like it when I play with your tits?" I croon, pinching her nipples harder.

"Yes, Niko. Yes!" She cries, clenching her thighs as her pussy tightens around my cock and her hips shudder against me. Adanna rides through her orgasm, grinding her hips, pushing me balls deep inside of her.

I'm not small by any means, my cock is well above average with a thick girth. I have no idea how she's taking it but she's taking it so fucking well.

"Good girl. Now let daddy take care of the rest." I praise before grabbing her hips and flipping us over. I stand, pulling Adanna to the edge of the bed on her knees with her legs either side of my thighs.

"Hold tight." I warn before lining my head up with her slick cunt and burying myself inside her from behind.

"Ahh!" Adanna cries, grabbing the bed sheets with a white knuckle grip.

"Take it, Adanna." I growl, holding her hips, digging my nails into her skin hard enough to leave small crescents of blood. I pound into her, watching the ripple of her ass cheeks as our bodies collide with each thrust and the slap of my balls smacking her clit reverberates through the room.

"Niko…I'm going to…" She cries, pushing herself back to meet my onslaught of thrusts against her cunt as it swallows my dick over and over again. What a sight. I lean forwards, sinking my teeth into her shoulder and wrapping my arm around her body. I pound into her fast and hard as I pinch her clit with a brutal force. "Fuck!" Adanna buries her face into the mattress as she coats my cock with her cum, clenching her thighs around my hand while her body threatens to collapse beneath me, but I'm not finished. There's a full length mirror opposite Adanna's bed and I intend to use it.

I guide her body up by her hair so her back is flush to my chest and as I bring the blade of my knife to her throat, I bring my other hand to her mouth, parting her lips with my fingers. "Suck." I order and she does immediately. Her silk soft tongue caresses my fingers, coating them with saliva before I pop them from her lips. "Open your eyes, Printsessa. I want you to see who you belong to while I make you scream my name." I whisper, before clamping my teeth into her earlobe and gently circling her clit with my lubed fingers.

"Oh fuck, Niko," she whines as I thrust my hips with deep and precise movements, burying my cock deep inside her. I gaze up into the mirror to see her eyes burning straight back into mine, wide and completely blown with lust. Her hair is a hot mess, sticking to her face with sweat and her body is quaking against me.

"Do you see who you belong to, Adanna?" I ask, pressing the sharp edge of my knife to the bottom of her neck where it connects with her collarbone. "Me. You belong to me." A single line of blood slowly oozes from the pressure of the blade and Adanna's face scrunches with pleasure. She cries out as I apply more pressure to her clit, stimulating the bundle of nerves as I continue my ministrations. I'm about to fucking blow, I swear she's the most beautiful fucking creature I've ever seen. My cock is solid and painful with the need for release as I pull back all the way before slamming back in. "I want to hear you say it, Printsessa. Tell me who you belong to. Tell me who fucking owns your sweet little pussy." Her whimpers are heavenly as her eyes fly open.

"You. Niko. Only you." She gasps, barely able to control herself as I hold her hostage against my body, fucking her deep and brutal just like she deserves. Her hands come up to her tits where she pulls and tugs on her nipples, fighting the line between pain with her own pleasure she pulls her lip between her teeth to stifle her moans.

"That's right sweetheart. You're my fucking pride and joy now. Now let me hear you scream my name as I fill up your delicious cunt." I release my knife, replacing it with my hand and wrapping my fingers over her wound, pressing firmly, covering my fingers with her blood.

Adanna hisses out in protest before a wave of pleasure washes over her body, and as I watch her come apart for me and only me, my body feels it. The overwhelming pleasure, the burning desire to own this woman in every single way possible. I force her forward, face down into the bed with her ass up high, bending myself over against her back and tightening my hand around her throat. "Cum for me, Printsessa. I want another one." I squeeze hard while simultaneously slapping her swollen and over sensitised clit. I feel her body shifting as the sudden gush of her orgasm coats my cock and gushes between us, covering my thighs as I hammer into her tight hole, hitting her sweet spot deep inside from my new angle.

I release her neck, the sudden rush of air overwhelming her as she screams out beneath me and her body breaks, "Fuck, NIKO!"

Her undoing pulls me right along with her, with one deep thrust I bite down hard onto her shoulder and unload myself inside of her. My thick cock spasms uncomfortably as I fill her up with my cum until I'm completely wrung out, and nothing but our rapid breaths can be heard between us.

    I lay us down, pulling her into my chest as we try to regulate our breathing. "The thuck choroso spravilas, printsessa." *You did so good, princess,* I whisper, placing a single kiss into her hair. "Get some sleep." I feel her body release a long and heavy breath before she finally falls into a peaceful slumber with my body wrapped around her and a mixture of our cum drying between us. There's no where else I'd rather fucking be, but I know this is risky. I don't intend to push Alexander any more than I already have, I know full well that he has the ability to kill me before I even see it coming. I was stupid and reckless to fuck her like that here, but I'm enraptured by her, my little temptress. If her father ever wanted to keep us apart he would have to commit me to death, because while I'm alive, there is nothing that will stand in my way from getting back to her.

    The following morning I'm already up and showered, sitting at the breakfast bar when Adanna finally makes her way into the kitchen. It was the most restful night I've had in weeks. But, as I lay watching her sleep for longer than I should have, I knew I couldn't be found in her bed, and the longer I lay there, the higher chance there was with one of her siblings or her father finding me. So, reluctantly, I slipped my arm from beneath her battered body and quietly made my way back to my own room where I began to put together my own plan to take out Samuel.

Our eyes meet for a brief second before she lowers her head and walks past me to make her coffee, a hint of blush creeping into her cheeks.

"We need to get back on Anderson." I state, taking a sip of my coffee as I watch her make her way around the kitchen noticing her specific choice of clothing covers up the marks I made on her body last night, including the cut on her neck.

She responds with an acknowledging hum, her hand freezing slightly as she reaches for the milk, before facing me again. "Let's go then. The quicker we do this. The quicker you get back home." She says with an unconvincing smile.

I frown, confused at her words, but shake it off. We can talk about it later. We've got shit to do. We need to find Anderson.

"Eat. You need your strength after yesterday, then we leave." I order, taking my coffee and leaving the room. Her mood swings are too confusing this early in the day. I need a clear head for what happens next. I have a feeling she isn't going to like what I have planned, but there doesn't seem to be any other choice. Samuel Anderson must be stopped.

I make my way to Alexander's office on the chance that he'll already be up and working. After a rapt knock, he calls me in.

"Mr Sidorova, what can I do for you? Come to almost get another one of my children killed?" he asks without looking up from his morning paper, the tick in his jaw almost palpable.

He's pissed, I don't blame him. I'm still fucking furious at myself too, but I need to keep him in the loop. For Adanna's sake at least.

"I'm going to use myself as bait. I'll set up a meeting with Samuel to discuss a new shipment of children for The Facility and while we're there Adanna will take him out. A clean shot to the head, neither of us will be tied to the murder, but the business will crumble and his fucked up traffiking ring will come to an end." I pause, waiting for any sort of acknowledgment to pass before I continue. "Your brother will see to that. Won't he, Alexander?" His head snaps up immediately.

"I will not bring my brother into this."

I crease my brow. Surely they would want to take down the largest child trafficking organisation that's led by a fellow Londoner. His brother, the name and face on every damn bus poster you see representing his law firm would do well to be connected with the demolition of such a thing. "No association, Mr Sidorova. Or have you forgotten our deal?"

I bite my tongue, literally to stop myself from telling him to go fuck himself, but instead I simply nod. Adanna would never forgive me if I were to kill the man that saved her from a life much like my own, if not worse. Who's to say Vladimir wouldn't have made me kill her instead of Polina.

"Can you assure me of my daughter's safety?" he asks, rising from his chair.

I scoff at the question before my mind reels back to her getting shot, but I shove it aside, rising to meet his height.

"I would protect her with my life." I admit.

"That is what worries me, boy. She doesn't need somebody like you looking out for her, she has all she needs in her family. Don't forget your place. I welcomed you into my home and agreed to help you with your job for the sake of thousands of innocent children, but do not mistake my kindness for weakness. I have no reservations in spilling *your* blood. Do you understand?" His eyes have darkened, their usual ash grey colour now a devilish shade of black as he broadens his chest and bares his teeth.

"I know nothing of the word weakness, Alexander. I would've thought with all of your research on me, you would have known that. Don't think I had any other intentions of coming in here than to let you know what I have already decided. My courtesy is not to be mistaken for seeking permission." Alexander's jaw flexes as his eyes burn with fire at my comeback but as he opens his mouth to reply, raising his finger towards my face, the door to his office swings open and in saunters Gulliver.

He takes in our offensive stances and both of his brows shoot to his hairline before a cocky one-sided grin pulls up the side of his mouth. "Am I interrupting?"

Alexander clears his throat before sliding back behind his desk where he takes his seat. "No, son. Mr Sidorova here was just leaving," he states, returning back to his paper like our conversation never happened.

I stare at him, and then at Gulliver who holds his hand out in front of the door, pointing me out.

Over all the years I've watched Adanna, this fucker has always made me wonder what the fuck goes on inside his head. He almost seems delusional and I can't help but wonder how the hell Alexander puts up with him. Although he matches me in height, we are the complete opposite with everything else. My hair is short to my scalp and dark, whereas his is blonde and long enough to style. His eyes are pale green unlike my piercing blue ones I inherited from my mother. He's toned, that's for sure, but his body doesn't seem to hold the scars like my own and as far as I can tell, conceals no weapons either.

"This way," he grins, and I want nothing more than to put his cocky fucking grin through the floor and to stomp my boot into his neck until I feel the bones crack beneath me.

"Nikolai. If my daughter comes back with one more scar on her body, I will personally see to it that you fail to make it back to Russia." Alexander voices as I walk through the door, pausing my steps to hear his threat before I make my way back to the kitchen.

"Are you ready to go?" I snap, interrupting the conversation between Adanna and Narcissa who both snap their heads in my direction.

"Where are we going?" Adanna asks, glancing sideways to her sister who narrows her eyes at me.

"We're going to meet a friend. Get ready. I'll wait by the car." I add before walking out of the room, leaving them both staring after me.

I'm too riled up to be conversing. What the fuck is wrong with me? I have a reputation back home, and this isn't it. I'm known for not caring, for being ruthless and dangerous. Now, I'm letting a woman get under my skin, a woman I wanted dead not too long ago.

"Ahh!" I roar, slamming my fist into the brick wall of the car garage over and over until my knuckle busts and a spray of blood covers the wall.

"What the fuck are you doing?" A shrill voice spins me on my feet. Adanna's eyes are wide and full of concern as she takes me in, glancing down at my busted knuckles. "Niko, what the fuck is going on?" she gasps but the words don't compute. I lunge forwards, grasping her face between my hands, they engulf her tiny features and plunge my tongue into her mouth, pulling her flush against my body and holding her firmly in place.

She resists at first before I feel her body relax against me and her mouth eagerly accepts mine. Small whimpers pass between our lips as her tongue dances with mine and her hands slowly come up to my own. My sweet little temptress, like a siren you have called to me throughout the years, and now here I am, ready and willing to fall at your feet, but knowing you deserve better than a murderous villain like me.

I pull away, leaving her gasping for breath with a disappointed scowl. She quickly looks around to check nobody was watching then smacks my chest. "What the fuck are you doing, Nikolai?" she snaps, her previous concern completely forgotten and replaced by frustration and confusion.

"Don't call me that." I grit.

Her brows knit together as she gapes at me. "What?"

"Don't call me Nikolai. You call me Niko, not Nikolai."

Her eyes widen before she rolls them. "Alright you psycho. Where are we going?"

I huff a small laugh at the use of her new name for me, she really has no idea. "Get in the car." I direct, getting into the driver's side of her car. "It's a good job you own more than one vehicle" I state, driving us down the long driveway off the property.

"We're going to speak with Ivan. I need to set up a meeting with Anderson." I say matter of factly as we drive through the city of London, the traffic makes the journey twice as long as it should be and I already feel frustrated at the majority of other drivers.

"What do you mean, you need to set up a meeting? Are you being serious?" Adanna gapes at me.

"Yes, I'm serious. It's the best option we have at the moment…"

"No. No, we'll keep following him. We'll get a clear shot soon enough."

If I didn't know better, I'd say she was concerned about my safety. I quite like the thought of that. "There is no other way, Adanna. I want this finished. He'll be spooked after last night so he'll choose somewhere secluded but close enough to his business facility that he feels safe to escape if anything goes wrong. He'll also be heavily guarded, but I will make sure you get your clear shot." I nod, agreeing with the plan the more I say it aloud.

"I guess you've got this all figured out then. Huh?" Adanna huffs.

"Don't be sour, Printsessa, it doesn't suit that pretty face of yours."

Almost an hour later and a multitude of incompetent drivers trying to make their way through endless traffic, we finally sit down with Ivan in the restaurant of his hotel. It's too early for the lunch time rush so we're mainly undisturbed, tucked into the back corner where only the waitstaff come to take our orders and bring us a single round of coffee.

The last time Adanna saw Ivan, he was holding her against her will, but I'm ultimately surprised at how well she's composed herself while we go over the plan to take down Samuel.

What I can't quite shake though, is the way Ivan keeps his eyes on her, even long after she's finished speaking. It's subtle and any other person would brush it off as informality, some remaining anger maybe towards her killing Dimitri and Vladimir. But the way his eyes travel her body with a look I can't quite put my finger on, sends a deep and unnerving warning through my system.

"How do you know he won't suspect you?" Adanna says before taking a sip of her coffee.

I shrug nonchalantly. "He has no reason too, we've been in business for years with Vladimir at the helm. I'll simply tell him I want to reintroduce myself as boss and to go over figures. He'll understand as a man of business."

"A man of business. These are children's lives youre talking about!" Adanna whisper-hisses across the table.

"Which is why this needs to fucking work, Adanna. You're either with us or you're not. But if you're not…"

"I'll set it up," Ivan interjects, silencing us both. "I'll reach out, tell him you want to talk about new figures, that we want to double the intake and that you're in the country on a personal trip." His eyes lock onto Adanna and I notice as she shifts in her chair. "I'll let you know as soon as I have the details."

"Ivan." I snap, feeling the overwhelming desire to stab his eyes through his skull when he finally turns his attention back to me. "Adanna, leave the table. Wait for me back in the car." I order, throwing the keys over without taking my eyes from Ivan as she silently stands and leaves us. "Yest lee chto-to, chto vy khotite skazat?" *Is there anything you want to say?* I ask, narrowing my eyes at Ivan, searching for any hint to what's going through his mind. Something isn't sitting right, and when it comes to Adanna my senses are now on high alert.

Ivan shakes his head and laughs. "The trachnul eye, nay thick lee?" *You fucked her, didn't you?* He goads.

"Dolvolno!" *That's enough!* I growl, slamming my fist onto the table before lunging for his collar. I bunch his shirt, dragging him to his feet. "Not another word out of your fucking mouth. Do you hear me? I don't want to fucking hear it. And if she is ever in your presence again, you keep your fucking eyes to yourself unless you want me to mince them in your skull." I shove his body back against his chair. "Do your fucking job and set up the meeting with Samuel. I'll be expecting your call." I walk through the restaurant, ignoring the behind-hand-whispers from the staff who try to shrink into the shadows, desperate to make themselves as invisible as possible.

CHAPTER TWENTY-SIX
Nikolai

I received the call as I finished my run around the grounds of Adanna's home.

"Got it." I nod, walking the last few yards before I make it back to the house as he informs me that Samuel Anderson has agreed to meet.

"Do smerti, Ubiytsa." *Until death, Killer.* he replies before hanging up, his tone is a little more clipped than usual, raising the hairs on the back of my neck but I shake it off, putting it down to my outburst in the restaurant yesterday.

It took the rest of the day for me to finally let my anger go but I can't fully ignore the wretched feeling in my gut, it's gnawing at me like a festering wound, infecting me with poison. Is it these new feelings I'm experiencing for Adanna? Is that what's making me second guess everything and everyone? I've never had somebody in my life that I needed to look out for, or that

I wanted too. Everybody always looked out for themselves at the compound for fear of punishment or torture, and even when I was subjected to keeping Vladimir alive, it was only ever for my own reasons. But this, this is unfamiliar territory and it makes my fingers twitch with uncertainty. Adanna is bound to me now, whether she agrees to it or not. I would happily lay my life on the line for her and after this meeting tonight, I'll be taking her home with me. Alexander can go fuck himself.

    I make my way back to my room to shower and change, going through the motions of strapping my knives across my body. It's a ritual I perform every morning, I perfected over the years and then became reliant on it, strapping on my armour to survive another day. If this plan works, I shouldn't need them, Adanna will have a clear shot and we'll both walk away happy with the result. Samuel Anderson will be dead, Adanna will be mine and we'll be able to shut down The Facility, saving the lives of thousands.

    I find Adanna sitting with Narcissa having a hushed conversation at the dining table. Before entering the room, I decide to stand back and observe them. My view is obscured slightly by Narcissa and I'm too far away to hear what they're saying but I can tell by her body language that the conversation is slightly heated. I narrow in on Adanna's face which seems otherwise unbothered, but I note the disappointment that saddens her eyes. She has been conditioned to show pride in every aspect of her life, only when she's around those she's comfortable with does she show her vulnerability, and even then it's fleeting. Her act has been perfected but I see straight through it. Adanna schools her features before standing and turning, catching me watching. Shit. She freezes for a moment and Narcissa follows her gaze before she squeezes Adanna's hand and leaves the room, narrowing her eyes at me as she passes.

"How much did you hear?" she asks as I pinch her chin between my fingers forcing her to face me.

"I'm not here to spy on your private conversations, Printsessa. I know everything I need to know already." I state, taking in her sudden intake of breath. I graze my thumb over her bottom lip, wanting nothing more than to devour her mouth but with my meeting with Samuel now set in stone we need to make a move. "I meet with Samuel in two hours, get what you need, I'll be by the car." Adanna pulls back, furrowing her brow before her eyes fully take in my appearance.

"You don't have to do this. I can go alone, I can take him out without you even being there…"

"Adanna, this isn't up for discussion. Get your things, we leave in five." I snarl, practically forcing her through the door.

Adanna strides to the car, kitted out in an all black tight outfit with a thin leather jacket thrown over her shoulders. I swear she purposely shimmies her ass straight past my crotch to get into the car behind me.

"Where are we going?" She asks, a smug smile pulling up her lips and a playful glint in her eye. She knows how fucking hot she looks right now, a killer, ready to assassinate and fuck it makes my cock twitch painfully against my pants.

"It's not far, just over an hour but I want to scope it out beforehand to put you in the best possible position to take your shot." I grab her chin between my fingers, squeezing gently to focus her attention. "We only get one chance at this, Printsessa. Make sure you don't miss."

Adanna scoffs and pulls away. "I never miss, well, you know what I mean." she adds, resting back into her seat as I start the car.

I pull the car in between a large metal shipping container and an industrial waste unit, ordering Adanna to stay put while I quickly scout the area. If Samuel is already here, I won't risk him spotting Adanna if we walk in completely off guard.

"Stay here and stay out of sight, I'll be back in five." I snap, leaving her in the car before she has a chance to object.

The warehouse looks more like an old packing facility used for loading smaller holdalls into the back of the freights. But this particular one doesn't look like it's been used in a few years, making it the perfect location. There's nobody else here yet, and a quick look at my watch tells me we have a good twenty minutes headstart. I make my way through the building, light on my feet and eyes scanning every inch of my surroundings. I need to know the best access and egress should anything go wrong. The ground floor is pretty much empty, save a few leftover shipping crates and a large pile of broken pallets in the corner. There's the main door to the front of the building and one that leads to a small kitchen area to the back of the large communal work space. The upper floor consists of a large mezzanine floor, wrapping around the entire perimeter. Adanna will be better positioned up there, out of the way, it will give her a better view and keep her out of sight. It no longer looks like the lighting works up there, shrouding the upper level in darkness that we can use to our advantage.

"I'll be up there." Adanna's voice startles me, forcing me to draw my knife at the sudden intrusion. I spin quickly, bringing the blade to her cheek, and her eyes widen with shock. "Niko," she gasps before I even register that it's only her.

"Fuck Adanna, I told you to stay in the fucking car!" I snap, sheathing my blade before pulling her into my chest. "I could have fucking killed you!" I whisper, gently stroking my thumb over the whisper of a mark where my blade had kissed her skin.

"I don't believe that. I know you wouldn't hurt me, not intentionally." Adanna's voice is barely above a whisper, and her throat bobs with an uncertain swallow.

My hand threads through her hair, pulling her head back at an uncomfortable angle, baring her neck to me as I drag my teeth from her collar bone up to her jaw, nipping painfully at her skin.

"The thought of hurting you makes my cock solid, Printsessa. Is that what you want to hear?" I grab her hand and thrust it against my rock hard erection, groaning as she grasps my length through my cargos. "I would hurt you so bad, Printsessa and not feel a fucking whisper of regret." Adanna's body shivers against me. She wants me to destroy her, her body begs for it as I pull her impossibly closer against me until I feel my own blades digging into my body. The distant sound of crunching gravel punctures the air and immediately I'm on high alert. Fuck.

"Get up the stairs now and stay out of fucking sight. Remember, don't miss." I order, pushing her away from me towards the steel staircase that leads up to the second floor.

As soon as she slinks through the darkness, a convoy of vehicles pull up outside the warehouse. I didn't expect him to bring so many considering he likes to be inconspicuous but the incident at the docs, he obviously isn't taking any chances. It doesn't change my plans though, the man will die today with or without his entourage, it doesn't phase me. I have all I need, hidden in the shadows.

It's been at least five years since I've seen Samuel, but other than a few more grey hairs and a little more weight pressing against his belt, he hasn't changed. He looks like any regular British politician, pompous and arrogant and he has the bullshit talk to allow you to think the sun shines out of his ass. But what lies on the surface is a facade to hide the depth of his sick obsession for money and power.

"Ahh, Nikolai, it's been too long," Samuel voices, walking through the empty warehouse with a shadow of seven extra men. "My deepest condolences on the loss of your father. He was a dear friend and a trusted client of mine." Samuel pulls me into a hug that I refuse to reciprocate. Pulling away from him before he releases his hold.

"Thank you, Samuel."

"I hear you never did catch the one who did it," he smiles, cocking his head to the side, regarding my response. I made sure that word was spread around that Vladimir's killer was taken care of after taking Adanna to The Manor, so whatever the fuck he thinks he knows he had better spit it out before I make him.

"I'm not sure where you're getting your information, Samuel, but I can assure you, it was taken care of." I state, noticing the way his eyes flare with something that resembles excitement.

"I see, I see… so what have you dragged me all the way out of town for dear boy? Don't keep me waiting. I have an evening dinner to get to in an hour with the members of parliament."

Is he fucking kidding me? "I wanted to discuss the next load of *kittens*." I grit.

"And this couldn't be done over the phone, boy?"

"I want to double Vladimir's original order. I have no specifics, just that they get to me alive. We had to put a bullet through one from the last batch because they fell ill during transport." My mind wanders up to the second floor but I keep my eyes locked onto Samuel. Adanna is the best at what she does, if she hasn't taken the shot yet, it's because she's still waiting for the opportune moment.

"Once they leave my port, they are none of my concern. Vladimir was well aware of that…"

"Well Vladimir is no longer here. I am, and if it happens again, Samuel, I will be posting them back to you, first class. Try and explain that to your fancy fucking parliament friends because I sure as shit would bet that they'd skin you alive."

Samuel's nostrils flare with anger as his fists shake into tight balls at his side. "You're crossing a line, Sidorova." he retorts, and as if they've been given a silent signal from their boss, all seven men widen their stances and tighten the hold on their guns. "You wouldn't be so quick to threaten me if somebody you loved was at the receiving end of that threat now, would you, Niko?" *Adanna.* This was a fucking set up. I can hear my heart racing against my chest and pumping the blood straight to my ears as he smirks. "Come on out little princess, or your boyfriend here will be the one with a bullet through his skull and you will find yourself on the inside of one of my shipping containers." Samuel turns slowly, shouting out to the darkness on the floor above. I pray to anyone that will fucking listen that Adanna stays where she is, but as her frame slowly emerges from behind a large unit of metal racking, her eyes immediately catch mine and my stomach drops at her stupidity. "Ahh, there she is. Miss Adanna Sinclair, how nice of you to join us." Samuel sings, prancing over to the staircase where he meets Adanna coming down and immediately disables her, throwing her gun aside and locking her arm behind her back. "Isn't she a pretty little thing? I can see why you are so taken with her, Niko. She would earn me a pretty penny on the black market that's for sure. A member of the Sinclair Legacy available for purchase, and Alexander's pride and joy, no less." Adanna's eyes haven't left mine but I can see the panic rise when he mentions her father. None of this makes any sense, how the fuck does he know who she is or that she was even here?

"Let her go, Samuel." I bark, drawing the attention of the seven other men as they raise their guns, aiming them at my head.

"Now, now, gentlemen. There's no need for such measures. Mr Sidorova here won't make any sudden or stupid movements, will you, my boy? Not as we take this little prize here out from under your hands." Samuel trails his hand up Adanna's stomach and grasps her neck making her gasp. That's all I need to push me over the edge, my body hums with the need to draw blood. How fucking dare he touch what belongs to me.

"Get your fucking hands off of her, now!" I snarl, flexing my fingers around the knife at my hip. Adanna tracks my movements and in a split second she brings her foot up, thrusting it back into Samuel's knee, snapping it backwards. His scream pierces the air as he hits the floor, flailing at the protruding bone. The rest of the group look shocked before they begin shooting, but I've already moved. With a blade in each hand I take down the first two men, landing to the hilt straight between their eyes. My peripheral vision catches Adanna as she dodges bullets, flying through the group like an angel of death dressed all in black, nimble and quick as she slams the barrel of the gun up as her target shoots. She grabs the gun, her strength catching him off guard as she slams the butt into his nose before she spins it gracefully through the air, catches it and puts a bullet through his skull, blowing blood and brain matter across the floor before she moves onto her next target.

    Three down and four to go. I glide between two oncoming men, their guns forgotten, it appears they've chosen to attempt to fist fight instead. With a fresh blade in each hand I raise my arms, slicing their necks with precision and force, coating their bodies with blood as they choke, clutching their throats at a last desperate attempt to save themselves.

    To my left, Adanna disarms a large bald guy who is easily twice her size, but he has no chance against her as he attempts to grab her, she snaps his wrist forcing him to the ground by kicking out his knee. The fucker screams out in pain before she eventually puts him out of his misery, taking a widened stance behind him as she grabs his head and snaps his neck with a loud grunt as she kicks his body to the ground. It's a fucking turn on watching her work, so much so that its hard to ignore the pulsing sensation throbbing through my cock.

    "NIKO!" Adanna screams, bringing me out of my fantasy. I spin, facing the last of the men as he runs at me. I yield my knife, holding it waist high as his body barrels into mine. He grunts loudly as the blade pierces his body, immediately coating my hand in blood as I twist and thrust it deeper until his body finally sags against me. I shove him to the floor watching the life finally drain from his eyes. I stare at the body, this is going to need a serious clean up. "Niko." Something is wrong. Adanna's voice shakes as she calls to me, snapping my head round, my breath catches in my throat as I watch Samuel thrust Adanna's gun into her temple. His eyes are wild, crazy almost but I can see that he's fighting to stand up straight on his one good leg while his other hangs at an inhuman angle with the bone protruding behind his knee.

    I take a steady step forward. "I will blow her fucking head off if you come any closer!" Samuel spits, his voice is slurred, intoxicated by pain and blood loss. His complexion is greying the longer he stands, with a sheen of sweat beading across his hairline.

    "Let her go, Samuel. It's over. You're fucking ruined. This was all on me, not her…just let her go." I take another steady step closer, my eyes catch Adanna's hand as she brings it to her hip, the glint of a knife flashing beneath her jacket.

    My entire body shakes with rage and a burning desire to bathe in Samuel's blood. At the fact that he thinks it's ok to touch what does not belong to him. "You don't get to do this to me. I'm the…I'm the fucking dealer. I run this god damn city." Samuel's words are becoming more slurred as he thrusts the gun harder into Adanna's face, forcing her head to the side and I all but lose my shit.

    "No Samuel. You don't get to threaten what's mine!" I roar, letting the final string of my humanity snap as my entire body moves on impulse, rushing them both and pushing Adanna's body to the side. Samuel cries out as his already broken leg twists painfully as I drive my knee into the fraying tissue. "Nobody touches what belongs to me!" I growl.

Adanna extends her arm to me, offering over the knife I fucked her with. Her eyes sparkle with a deep hunger as she licks her bottom lip and nods towards Samuel's body. A silent wave passes between us, thrumming through my body, straight to my cock. There's something deliciously poetic about using the blade that's been deep inside of her pussy to take the life of the man who just tried to kill her. I take the blade, flipping it between my fingers before shunting it underneath his chin with a single swoop, taking great pleasure in the blood that spurts across his face, neck and chest as he slowly chokes to death on the thick almost-black liquid. "She is mine!" I grunt, keeping my hand in place with my fingers tight around the handle as I twist my wrist, letting the familiar sound of blade grinding bone fill my ears, pulling me into a sick state of euphoria that I have come to enjoy. I pull the blade out, the blood oozing from the wound, then stab it through his neck. "Mine!" I stab him again, my hands are now coated in his thick red blood but as I bring the knife back for another hit, Adanna's voice calls to me, stopping me just before I puncture his skin.

"Niko," Adanna's hand rests against my shoulder, gently prying me from the darkness that's threatening to drag me under. I tighten my fingers around the knife until my hand begins to shake and the bloody mess of Samuel's body starts to blur. "Look at me, Nikolai." Adanna orders, her voice louder, full of need and desperation. Her bloodied hands cup my face, pulling me to look at her, forcing me to drop the knife. "He's dead. I'm alright. Just look at me." she whispers, pulling my body towards her across the floor. Our eyes meet, her dark browns to my icey blues and my world combusts. My heart ricochets in my chest and my ears ring with silent screams as I take in her dishevelled body, flustered and covered with the blood of several men.

"Printsessa..." Is all I manage before I thrust my blood covered hands into her hair, pulling her to me. I force my tongue between her lips, swallowing down her whimper as our bodies clash together. Her hands rip frantically at my clothes, desperate to find the release she's craving. Her fingers fumble with my zipper before wrapping around my solid cock, pulling it free from my cargos.

Adanna moves with a desperate need, pushing my body up as she lowers her mouth to my cock, swiping her tongue against the bead of precum that's glistening at the tip. I hiss out at the connection, baring my teeth as her gentle lick suddenly turns ravenous and she sucks me between her lips all the way to the base. My cock hits the back of her throat as she swallows me down, glancing up at me through her long thick lashes. What a fucking sight. The woman that's taunted my life for the last several years, eager and willing to choke on my dick. "That's it, Printsessa... Fuck you look so good swallowing my cock like that." I praise, wrapping my fist into her hair and holding tightly, taking control. "That's it, take my cock like a good little slut." I groan, thrusting my hips forward taking full control of her movements as I push further into her throat. Adanna's eyes water as I fuck her mouth without reprieve. Her mascara leaves black tracks down her cheeks that I swipe at with my thumb, leaving smears of Samuel's blood across her face. "You look so beautiful when I make you cry, Printsessa. Especially covered in their blood." Adanna hums around me, sending a delicious wave through to my balls and fuck if it doesn't make me cry out in pleasure as I bottom out, holding Adanna's head in place as I choke her tight throat on the thick girth of my cock. I hold her steady until her pupils blow out, wide with fear as she attempts to swallow around me, desperate for air. "So, so beautiful." I repeat before releasing her body. "But now I want to hear how beautiful you scream for me." Adanna gasps loudly, choking on the air I grant her before forcing her to turn around. "Tell me who owns you, Printsessa. I want to hear you scream my name while my cock fills your greedy little pussy." I flatten my hand to Adanna's back, pushing her onto all fours as she gasps, the concrete floor harsh against her palms.

    I waste no time ripping her tight black leggings and lace panties over her ass, baring her delicious, dripping wet cunt to me. Adanna lowers her chest to the floor, opening herself further, stealing the breath from my lungs at the way her body submits so willinging. "Fuck Printsessa."

    How can I resist? I dip forwards, flattening my tongue against her cunt, savouring her intoxicating flavour and the sultry whimpers that rise from her mouth as I drag my tongue through her slit, all the way up to her taut little hole that I'm still yet to breach. If I didn't need this to be brutal and quick I'd do it now, but for that, I need to luxuriate in it, take my time to stretch her open, to tease her and take her fully in each hole until she's begging me to stop. But now? Now I need to allow the primal need that's ripping through my humanity to take over.

"Niko, oh my God." Adanna moans as I push my tongue against the tight ring of muscle before dragging my attention back down to feast on her weeping cunt.

"That's right sweetheart, I am your fucking God."

Digging my fingers into the flesh of her ass I spread her wide, fucking her with my tongue, and sucking her clit between my teeth. It takes only seconds for her tense body to snap as I suck her most sensitive spot into my mouth, swirling my tongue across the bud, for her to give into everything I can give to her, and for her sweet orgasm to flood my tongue as she cries out with a delectable curse on her lips. I drink her down, swallowing every last drop. I thrust my tongue deep into her gushing hole once more before kissing up the back of her thighs all the way up her back to her shoulder where I embed my teeth into her skin as I sink my solid cock between her swollen pussy lips. The heat swallows me as I slide in, balls deep into her core, feeling whole once again with our bodies connected.

"Now scream for me, Printsessa. Tell me who you belong to." I demand, pulling back and thrusting my hips forward with a brutal force, shifting her knees across the floor.

"You." Adanna gasps, pushing her fingers into the solid ground trying desperately to anchor herself as I release my inner demon and fuck her hard, deep and fast, like a man possessed.

"Louder, Adanna. Who do you fucking belong to?!" I snarl, connecting my palm to the round flesh of her ass with a resounding snap.

"You, Niko. I belong to you." Adanna cries, grinding her hips back against me as my pelvis connects with her ass with echoing slaps of our skin. I hook my fingers tightly into her hips with a promise of bruises as I use her to gain leverage. Leaning slightly back, I lose myself in the sight of her pink pussy lips swallowing my cock as I slow my movements, pulling all the way out and smirking at Adanna's groan from the sudden lack of contact.

"I could watch your pretty pussy take me all day, Printsessa. Do you know that?" I whisper, slowly pushing myself back in, watching as her tight hole stretches out across my thick, veiny cock. "Such a beautiful sight."

"Niko. Please, I need you to fuck me, now." Adanna chokes as she glances back at me over her shoulder, her desperation clear and dripping between her thighs.

I dig my fingers tighter and pull her back, impaling her on my dick. Adanna cries out, and I push her further into the floor again as I bury myself inside of her, letting every single thread of anger come to the surface, fucking it from my system.

I didn't think it would be possible to get harder than I already am but the noises coming from Adanna's mouth have my cock throbbing as I fuck her into the ground. I bring my thumb to my mouth and suck before spitting directly onto her ass hole. I tease her gently, spreading my saliva before pushing my thumb into the tight hole, instantly feeling her clench around me.

"That's it sweetheart…Good girl." I praise, twisting my thumb before I slowly start to fuck her tightest hole with my hand, gradually matching the brutal rhythm of my hips.

"God, Niko, the pressure…I'm going to…" Adanna gasps, arching her back and pushing her ass back onto my cock. "Fuck..I'm coming." Her walls clench around me, gripping me like a vice as her body tightens and tremors beneath me, but I don't stop. Sweat covers my body, sticking my shirt to my chest as I drive forwards and fuck her through her orgasm, drawing out every single moan and whimper until her body sags.

"One more time, tell me who you belong to, Adanna. I want to hear you scream my name as I fill you with my cum." I grunt, feeling the treacherous tingle at the base of my cock. I would fuck her here all night if my cock would allow it. In every position, on every surface, tainting her body in the blood of the deceased. But as her body already begins to tremble with another impending orgasm, I feel my own release spreading through my veins like a wildfire.

I circle my thumb, stretching her from the inside as my thrusts become rapid and the building in the base of my cock suddenly erupts.

"You Niko, only you." Adanna screams, arching her body as she explodes around my cock once again, her tightening holes pulling me right alongside her. I roar out my orgasm as my cock twitches deep inside of her core, filling her cunt with my seed. I've never wanted my own children. All of the darkness I've experienced in my life made me never want to bring another innocent into the praying clutches of the devil, but the thought of Adanna's stomach swollen with my child sends a dangerously exhilarating wave of need through to my soul.

    I collapse against her back, wrapping my arm under her body to keep her off the ground. Our heavy pants are the only sound through the empty warehouse as we slowly come down from the high.

    "I need to call Narcissa." Adanna sighs, finally pushing herself from her floor as she pulls her clothes back in place and I do the same.

    I glance around at the bodies that litter the floor, feeling nothing but sweet justice as I eventually rake my eyes back over Adanna. Her face and clothes are covered with blood and dirt and she's got that just fucked look about her that makes me chest swell with pride, until the gravity of the situation finally settles and the fuck-lust blur clears from my head. She almost died again today because of me, and it was a pretty fucking close call. I watch her intently as she walks away to call her sister to arrange for a clean up crew, but I can't ignore the festering at the back of my mind. She deserves more than this, than me. A psychotic murder who would kill any man that dared look at her. She deserves somebody who doesn't have the blood of a child on his hands. Fuck. FUCK.

"Niko?" Adanna's brows draw together as she ends her phone call. "What's wrong?"

She asks me that too much. There's so much wrong right now. I turn away, unable to look at her, because the more I look the more I feel myself unable to be without her, to know that now the job is done, her father will order me out and Adanna will choose to get as far away from me as possible. "We should get out of here." I state, collecting each of my knives that are embedded into the bodies of Samuel's men.

Adanna's reply is quiet but audible as I replace my last blade into the sheath on my chest. "Narcissa already has a team on the way to sort the bodies. My father will want an update. He's already waiting for us back at the house." I nod, leaving her staring after me as I make my way back to the car, hating myself for the cold shoulder I'm giving her.

Not a word passed between us on the drive home but now as we sit opposite each other in Alexander's office, still dirty and covered in sweat, blood and coated in the remains of each other's cum, there is a thick and penetrable tension that suffocates the room.

The door to the room bursts open, making Adanna jump as Alexander storms into the room heading straight for me. I barely have time to react before his hands are at my throat and I'm being dragged to my feet with his fingers crushing my windpipe.

"Daddy let him go! What's going on?" Adanna jumps to her feet, pulling at her father's shoulders as his face darkens with a recognisable desire to kill.

"I warned you, Mr Sidorova, to keep your hands away from my daughter."

Adanna pulls Alexander's arms as the outer edge of my vision draws in and I feel myself losing consciousness. "Let him go! Just fucking let him go!" Adanna screams, shoving his body and prying his hands from my throat. My throat burns as I finally suck in a breath and my head swims as I shake through the darkened vision and fall against Adanna who struggles to keep my weight upright. "What the fuck is going on!?" Adanna demands, her voice is firm but I can feel the rapid beat of her heart as I will my body to regain composure.

"This…this is what's going on." Alexander growls, walking around the desk to his laptop, tapping on a few keys and spinning it round to face us.

I open my eyes as Adanna's body freezes against mine as the snippet of CCTV begins playing on the screen.

I watch Adanna bent over on the ground, ass in the air as I fuck her hard and fast, holding her hips while I thrust my cock inside her. *"Louder, Adanna. Who do you fucking belong to?!"* My voice demands as I slap my palm to the round flesh of her ass with a loud snap before she cries out her reply.

"You, Niko. I belong to you."

Adanna slams the laptop closed, staring at it for a moment before turning to her father.

"Where…where did you?...How did you?" Her voice comes out broken and fuck I would be lying if I said it didn't hurt me as her fingers loosened around my arms as she tries to draw herself away from me.

"It doesn't matter who sent it. Do you remember our deal? You stay away from my daughter and I keep your secret." His question is aimed at me but the burning rage through my body at whoever the fuck sent this video makes words difficult to possess.

Adanna turns to me, confusion pinching her brows together as she searches my eyes. "What secret? What's going on Niko? What's he talking about?"

"Do you want to tell her or shall I, Ubiytsa?" *Killer.* Alexander's eyes are black as he dares me to do what he knows I won't. I could never tell her. She would never want to see me again, and as that realisation hits him, with my resounding silence his lips part with an evil smirk. "You need to leave, Adanna. Now!" Alexander snaps, keeping his eyes tight on mine. He's going to kill me for breaking my promise, and Adanna knows it.

"Stop it. Stop. I won't let you hurt him!" Adanna pleads, standing in front of me with her arms reaching back to either side of my body. "I don't care what he's done, but I will not let you do this. Please, Father." Her willingness to protect me breaks my heart at the truth that I know would kill her. If she knew, she would be the one to draw my final breath herself but I can't bring myself to tell her to stop.

Alexander opens his mouth to reply but Adanna cuts him off. "If you do this I will never forgive you. I will never be able to look at you as the father I know and love." Her words are desperate as she pleads for my life, a loyalty I don't deserve. "Please, Daddy."

Alexander's eyes twitch as he regards her, surely struggling with his own inner turmoil as he goes against everything he knows in order not to lose his daughter.

"You have twenty four hours to leave the country. If I ever catch a whisper of you visiting England again, I won't hesitate to kill you. Do you understand?" Alexander says through tightly gritted teeth. The fact that he's letting me live obviously causes him a great deal of distress as his body practically vibrates with anger. As he gives into Adanna's pleas her body practically deflates with relief until she turns to face me with tears pooling her eyes and a look of defeat turning down her features. "You need to go," she whispers, gently pushing my chest as she closes her eyes.

No no no, I attempt to protest. She can't do this. "Adanna…"

"Please, Niko. Just leave," she chokes. A single tear tracks down her cheek and it takes every single bit of restraint I have not to swipe at it with my thumb. Instead, I tighten my fists, clench my teeth and leave. I leave her behind and every single piece of my fractured, fucked-up soul with her.

CHAPTER TWENTY-SEVEN
Adanna

I clench my fists as I watch Nikolai leave and a single tear falls down my cheek. I refuse to give into the agony and the realisation that this is the last time I will see him. There's nothing more I want than to chase after him. But I can't. I can't bring my feet to follow him. As the door slams behind me I feel a gentle hand on my shoulder. "Adanna, I know you're upset. But he's not a good man. He isn't worthy of you, my pride and joy." My father says softly in a bad attempt at comforting me, and I shrug him off. How could the man who has protected me for most of my life be the reason for so much pain. All I can feel is rage and loss at those words, pride and joy. It churns my stomach. I have done everything this man has asked of me, more so than the rest of my siblings and I have never once raised my voice about it. I have always been so proud of myself for being number one, daddy's little girl. Hell, I worked myself to the bone for that title, but Nikolai has changed me. He's brought out a side of me I didn't even know existed. He's made me realise that I am more than just my sin and that is something I can never go back from. I love my father, but he has fractured my heart after I only just realised it could love somebody else.

I wipe away the tears as they burn my eyes. I don't want him to see me cry. "I'm not upset, Father. I'm heart broken." I choke as I move to the door.

"The things he has done are not admirable, Adanna."

I can't hold my tongue at that remark and turn to face him, "The things I've done are not admirable, Father, but I've done them at your request. I've taken pride in every trigger I have pulled. Everybody I have mutilated and tortured was because I knew it was what was expected of me. I am what you made me! My only request for you now is that you don't hurt him, can you do that for me?" I spit out at him looking straight into his eyes. His face scrunches like I've just thrown a knife at his chest but he nods, so I take my leave before I say something I might regret.

As I rush down the corridor, I pass Niamh and Lyssa. They look concerned as they take in my appearance and Niamh immediately tries to grab my arm but I pull away, shaking my head, trying to stop the tears from falling once more. I can't do this. I just need to get out of here.

"Adanna, what happened!?" Niamh shouts after me as I break into a run. I know she's worried but I can't face the sympathetic looks I'll get if I let them in. She tries to follow, only to be stopped by Lyssa tugging her back. "Leave her, she needs some time to herself."

Rushing out of the house, I jump on my motorbike and hightail it out. I feel like I'm drowning, trapped underwater, unable to breath, unable to feel anything but the pain ripping my heart from my chest. I'm sinking further and further every second and I don't know how to stop it. I don't know how to control it. Tears sting my eyes as I arrive at the one place that has always made me feel better, always made me lose myself. The shooting range.

I make my way into the building, walking straight over to Emily. I ignore the way she frowns at the sight of my red, blotchy face and bloodied clothes. "Same as usual, Emily. I don't want to be disturbed," I snap. She flinches, not used to me using such a harsh tone and he hands me the keys along with my protective eyewear and ear defenders without a word.

I head to my usual booth and pick up the first gun I see and load it. I don't bother with the eye protection or ear defenders, I just shoot the target over and over. Reloading once I'm empty and starting again. Watching as the wood separates and breaks into a million pieces, mirroring how my heart feels. Memories of Nikolai and me here rush my mind, his touch as he held me close, teaching me to throw his blades. How he would hold me in bed after ravaging my body until I fell asleep. His words ring on repeat in my mind, asking me who I belong to. Him, it's always going to be him. I choke on a sob that rips through my throat as I continue my assault on the target in front of me. I'll never feel his touch again, or hear his low whispers in my ear, or get lost in those eyes that make everything else melt away. The tears and frustration continue to wreck me as I let out a scream and fall to the floor. I wish I didn't feel this way. Wish I could take the pain away and inflict it on someone else. How could I let him get this close to me? How could I allow myself to be so weak? I'm completely lost in my grief that I don't notice that someone has entered the room until they speak.

"Come on, Ada. Get up. Let's get a drink." Gulliver's voice echoes around me causing me to flinch. I look up to him, seeing the same look I have in my eyes staring straight back. His heart is permanently in searing pain. Broken. I now know why he buries his sorrows at the bottom of a bottle with every chance he gets. It's how he copes with the pain. He's felt this way since he was a teenager. Since Father ordered her to leave him. I don't feel shame or embarrassment as he helps me from the floor, just a sense of understanding.

Gulliver guides me out of the range, keeping his hands tight around my waist to keep me on my feet. It feels like a blur as we make it outside and he walks us over to his limo. "What about my bike?" I ask as he opens the door for me and I slide inside, sinking into the leather couch that fills the back of the vehicle.

"Don't worry, Lyssa said she would take care of it." He assures me, pulling me in for a hug as he slides in next to me and the driver pulls away from the range. "It will be okay, Adanna. You learn to live with the pain. If I can get through it, you can. You are the strongest person I know," he mumbles softly into my hair. We don't always see eye to eye, but in these rare moments, I know our bond is unbreakable. We'll always have eachothers backs.

"How did you know where I would be?" I sniff, wiping away my tears.

"Well, apart from the fact that this is where you always are, Lyssa and Niamh called me in a frantic panic after seeing you storm out of the house. Not to mention Father is stomping around like a baby elephant at home. And for once it's not because of me." he smirks and I can't help but smile. If I never get to feel Nikolai again, at least I know I will always have this, my family and their love. It feels bitter sweet, and my smile fades as quickly as it came.

The limo stops and as I look out of the tinted glass windows I notice we're outside of a pub. It looks busy. I anxiously glance down at my clothes. I'm still wearing the clothes I wore when we took out Samuel and I have blood and dirt caked on me.

"No one cares what you're wearing here. It's why I am with you, not Niamh. She wouldn't set foot in this dive bar, even dressed up. Regulars, mourners and general scum drink here. We'll fit right in." He smiles as he squeezes my hand. I huff a small laugh. He's right, she'd hate it here.

As we enter the pub, I notice that most people are already drunk and none of them look our way. Gulliver pulls me along to the bar and we take a stool each while he grabs the attention of the barman and orders us a round of tequila shots and tells the barman

to keep them coming until Gulliver suggests we move to another pub. "If you want to go I won't stop you Gulliver, but I'm a grown woman and I want to stay." I protest.
He shakes his head and mumbles under his breath as he stumbles away from me.

The more I drink, the worse I slur but the easier it feels to deal with the pain. The bartender looks at me like he's about to cut me off so I tell him that if he does, I'll kill him, but he just shakes his head and walks off to serve another customer. I giggle to myself as I realise I threatened him in Russian. No wonder he ignored me. Fuck. Nikolai enters my mind and all of the ways that he made me feel. Okay, I've had enough, I need to leave but as I stand, my feet don't get the message and I tumble to the floor. I assume Gulliver decided to stay as I feel hands begin to pull me back up, but as the hands become rougher my vision begins to fade and very quickly, everything turns black.

Someone needs to turn the volume down. That's the first thought in my head as I come to. I quickly realise that there's no music at all, it's the blood thumping in my head from a disgusting amount of alcohol that's causing the pain. I try to reach out to my bedside table for my water but my arms won't move no matter how hard I try. My eyes snap open and slowly, as my vision begins to clear, I take in my surroundings. This is not my room. Where the fuck am I? I try to move and it quickly dawns on me that I'm tied to a chair. I snap my head from left to right taking in the dark room until I lower my gaze. Oh no. I'm wearing a dress that I sure as shit do not own and I have no shoes on. Panic floods my system as my heart pounds in my chest and I try to piece together how I got here. I remember drinking with Gulliver but nothing after that. I was black out drunk. Nikolai, he left. My father made him leave. All of it comes rushing back, hitting me hard with the horrible shock of reality and I feel the cracks breaking apart in my heart once more. I look around the room again trying to force the feelings away. It's mostly dark, with only a few ceiling lights working. It doesn't look like there's much in here. I can feel cool air tingling over my skin, like an air con unit is close by or a vent to whatever is outside. A small sparkle across my thigh catches my attention and I look down again to see what caused it, quickly realising that it's not just any dress. This is a fucking wedding dress! Why the fuck am I wearing a wedding dress? I panic and my stomach flips as I swallow down the vomit threatening to come up.

    I test the ropes securing me to the chair but they don't budge. The more I pull, the tighter they become. Not an amateur then, good to know I guess. A thought enters my mind, a twisted kind of hope. "Nikolai?" I shout, holding my breath and praying for him to appear, but he doesn't. I'm met with nothing but a loud and eerie silence. Frustration builds, rivalling my headache. How could I be so stupid? "Is there anybody here?" I shout, and suddenly a figure steps out of the shadows. "Niko? Niko, what the fuck?" I shout as the figure steps closer. The shadows concealing his face fall away the closer he gets and I realise that it isn't Niko. "Who are you? What do you want?" I demand.

His face is still partially covered in shadows but I don't ignore the smirk on his face as he replies. "I'm not your precious Niko, printsessa." He sneers, his Russian accent thick and dangerous.

"Then who are you? Because I've got to tell you, I'm hungover as fuck and I don't have the time or patience for this." I reply. And I really don't. I want my fucking bed, some water and some painkillers.

I close my eyes as my headache throbs and am shocked as a sharp slap pierces my cheek.

"You don't remember me, do you?" the man spits out at me and I waste no time in spitting the blood from my lip into his face.

"Suka!" *Bitch!* he hisses at me.

"Well, you're obviously not that memorable" I smirk.

That pisses him off. He lunges at me, grasping me by the throat and cutting off my air. "You don't even remember your dear Nikolai though do you? Not really anyway. You have no idea who he is or things he has done." He laughs.

The blood drains from my face as I pale at the reminder of my father's warning about Niko. So what if he has a past, we all have a past. But what does this guy have to gain from bringing it up? Sure, Nikolai was hell bent on killing me when we first met. He hated me. Has this all been a lie? Was this just his plan from the beginning? Fuck me and then gut me.

The man releases my neck, leaving me gasping as he brings his face into full view. "Shall I tell you his secrets, Adanna?" Ivan taunts me. I try to turn my face away from him, just to process the situation because this is too much for me right now. My head and heart aren't functioning to the best of their ability and everytime he speaks of Niko my chest tightens. "Don't turn away from me." Ivan snaps and tightens his grip on my throat again. I struggle as he crushes my windpipe and my head starts to swim. My eyes follow his movements as he reaches into a sheath, bringing out a knife. I can't even scream with the force of his hand on my throat but the way he grins lets me know exactly what he's going to do before he does it. Ivan stabs his knife into my thigh with a hard and deliberate force, releasing my throat at the same time. The rush of pain mixed with the sudden rush of oxygen causes my head to swim and I scream at the agonising burn that winds across my leg. The blood has already begun to seep out around the blade but he doesn't remove it, no. Instead Ivan leans in close to my face, swiping his tongue across my cheek as he grabs the blade, twisting it against my thigh. The scream that rips through me can't possibly be mine. Painful and desperate for it to go away. I have never let myself make that kind of noise and I want nothing more than to tell him to stop, but my pride won't let me give him the satisfaction.

"So, tell me" I bark, gritting my teeth through the pain splintering my body. "Is he in on this? Was this his plan all along?"

Ivan throws his head back with an unnerving laugh "His plan? Stupid girl. This is *my* plan." He spits at me before he brings his fist to my temple, and everything goes back to black.

CHAPTER TWENTY-EIGHT
Nikolai

"The vyglyadish uzhasno. Ya duman, chto my zdes dla togo, chtoby otprazdnovat." *You look fucking terrible. I thought we were here to celebrate.* Ivan shouts over the thumping base of the club. "You killed him didn't you? What's the problem?"

Honestly, I could list thousands of problems right now but my biggest one is what the fuck just happened? How did Alexander get hold of that footage? I didn't even know there was power to the dilapidated building, let alone a camera…it's all too convenient.

I nurse my drink, swirling the transparent liquid around the glass. The only people who knew about the meeting were Samuel and his team, who are all dead, myself and Ivan. Would Samuel have a backup in case things turned sour? Even if he did, how would they know to send the footage of Adanna and I fucking to Alexander? And surely Ivan wouldn't…would he?

I watch him carefully from the corner of my eye. Should I be suspicious of the only true friend I've had in my life? I can't put my fucking finger on it, but something doesn't add up. My gut has been screaming at me for days but I keep ignoring it.

"Who else did you tell about the meeting with Anderson?" I ask, twisting on my bar stool to face him.

"Nobody else. What's the problem? You've had a sour fucking face since you walked in here. I thought you'd be pleased you got the job done." Ivan states, creasing his brow at me in confusion.

"Somebody else knew we were there."

"What do you mean?"

"I mean, somebody else knew we were there, Ivan. And as far as I'm aware, you were the only other person to know about it. You're the one that set the fucking thing up!" I snarl, losing my temper at the situation that's out of my control. The damage has been done. Adanna pushed me out of her father's office like I was nothing and I was given a death sentence if I refused to leave the country within the next twenty-four hours.

"You think I would do that to you, Ubiytsa?" Ivan asks, slapping his hand onto my shoulder. I don't know what to fucking think. Something has been off with him since we left England, something I haven't been able to nail down.

"I need a fucking piss." I snap, shrugging his hand from my shoulder as I get up and make my way to the bathroom. Why am I even here? I should be back at that fucking house trying to get her to leave with me. To see sense, to see what we are together. I don't think I'll survive the journey home without her by my side, and that's a revelation that scares the shit out of me. The way Adanna has snaked her way inside of my body and twisted her viper grip around the withered cords of my heart leaves me breathless. But fuck I would be lying if I said I didn't enjoy the way my name fell from her lips as her pussy strangled my cock. Fuck...Fuck! I need to get out of here.

I make my way back to Ivan, throwing the rest of my drink back before he slides me over another.

"Just take it you prick, you look like you need it," he says, raising an eyebrow as he holds up his glass between us. "Do smerti," he smirks as I tap my glass to his with a clink and we both throw our heads back as the burning liquid hits our throats. "I'm going to take a piss then we can get out of here. I'll book us the next flight back and we can leave this awful fucking country." Ivan chuckles, smashing his glass on to the bar before I watch him walk away.

I swear somebody has turned the heating up in the last few minutes because the need to strip my body and plunge into a frozen bath of water is overwhelming. My skin feels as if it's bubbling beneath my clothes as I roll my head back and shake out my arms. Surely it's not that hot. I glance around the dimly lit club, nobody else seems to be overheating. I blink my eyes a few times as the strobe lights blur my vision, making my head swim with the effects. What the fuck is happening to me?

I hold my hands out in front of my face but I can't count the fingers on each hand. They're just two flesh coloured shapes that appear to be crackling. Crackling? Skin doesn't crackle. I shake my head, the blurriness becoming progressively worse as my breathing becomes rapid. My heart pounds against my chest so hard I think it may break free of its boney restraint. What the fuck is happening? Did somebody turn the lights off? My body shudders as a stiffening coldness creeps over me and a thick blanket of darkness shrouds my body.

A distant voice penetrates my ears through the darkness. "I'll take good care of her, don't worry." and then there's nothing.

A violent jerk shocks me into consciousness. "What the fuck is going on?" I groan, bringing my hand to my head to assess the damage. "Did I hit my head? Where am I?" I ask, forcing my eyes open to see the fast moving traffic that flies past the window. How did I get here?

"You've been drugged, you need to drink this and take these." A familiar voice orders as a small hand shoves a bottle of water into my face followed by a couple of pills.

"What are they?" I ask, already chuggin on the bottle.

"They'll make you sick. But don't get it in my car or I'll make you wish I left you there."

"Why didn't you? Wait…How do you know I was drugged? How do you know where I was? You never leave the house." I swallow the pills, the dryness of my throat makes me want to retch already as they slowly make their way down.

"Adanna asked me to keep an eye on you while you were here. I was watching you at the club. You went to the toilet and your friend tipped something into your drink. I left straight away." She says, her words rushed, eyes on the road and her knuckles blanching white as she grips the steering wheel to death.

"Ivan." I say, more to myself than to Narcissa, the youngest Sinclair. "Where's Adanna?" I demand, looking in the back seat for her. That fucking backstabbing piece of shit better not have laid a fucker finger on my woman.

"I…I can't get hold of her. Her tracker…it cut out while I was on my way to get you and…" Narcissa is unable to complete her sentence, her bottom lip trembling as she desperately tries to keep her tears at bay while she drives.

My stomach twists at the thought of Adanna being in trouble. I thought I could trust Ivan. He's been my best friend for years, we've been through so much together, seen the dark depravities of Vladimir Sidorova and somehow lived to tell the tale. He was all I had at some of the darkest moments in my life but I can't now ignore the change in him since Adanna killed Vladimir. The way he speaks of her, the way he looks at her…somethings wrong, every single cell in my body feels it. Like it's on fire with the need to protect. I need to find her, I need to save her, because if I don't, I won't have a life worth coming back to.

Before I can stop it, my body seizes with a painful retch as I throw my head between my legs and puke my guts up.

"For fuck sake." I hear Narcissa curse as she opens the window to let fresh air into the car and I puke again and again until whatever Ivan slipped into my drink is frothing against the black car mat of Narcissa's car, sloshing around with each bump and turn she takes.

"Where are we going? Do you have a plan at least?" I groan, swiping my hand across my mouth.

"Home. My father can help. He needs to know Adanna is missing. He'll…he'll know what to do."

"He'll kill me."

"Do you want to get her back?" Narcissa snaps.

"That isn't even a fucking question. There is no other aim here. But if he tries to kill me…you'll never get her back. Ivan will make sure of it." I say, swallowing the dry tightness in my throat. I don't think there's anything left in me to bring up, but the thought of her coming to harm because of me causes a cold sweat to break out over my body, shocking me with sudden and uncontrollable shudders. What the fuck did he slip me?

I must fall unconscious again as the next sudden jolt of the car wakes me to find we're back at the Sinclair mansion. Narcissa punches me in the arm ordering me to wake up. "Get up, Nikolai. Wake the fuck up." She grunts, shoving me into the passenger door.

If the situation was different, I would break this little one's wrist for daring to shove me, and under any other circumstances, I think she'd be too scared to touch me.

"I need to get to my laptop, you find Father and tell him what happened. He'll be in his office, I'll meet you there." Narcissa shouts as she runs into the house.

I take the stairs to Alexander's office three at a time, blinking rapidly as they wobble and blur beneath my feet. I don't bother knocking, I don't have the fucking time for that. I kick the door, slamming it against the wall as I enter.

"I thought I gave you a clear warning, boy. I may have promised my daughter not to harm you but if you come into my house and kick down my office…"

"Shut the fuck up!" I roar, cutting off his bullshit threats as he lunges for me from behind his desk. "Adanna is missing!" I snap, shoving his chest with both hands and pinning him into the large wooden bookcase behind him.

"What…what do you mean, missing?" Alexander's mouth gapes as he takes in my expression and in all of two seconds he knows I'm not fucking joking. "I swear if you have anything to do with this…"

"Yeah, you'll kill me. I get it. Save it, alright? All I care about right now is saving your daughter."

"Get out of my fucking sight you child murdering piece of shit." Alexander spits in my face, headbutting my nose so hard I not only hear the crack but I feel it spread across my cheekbones with a burning fire. Blood streams into my mouth as I stumble backwards, spitting onto the pristine cream carpets and pinching the bridge of my nose to slow the bleeding.

"What the fuck is going on?" Alexander and I both turn our attention to the doorway where Narcissa stands open-mouthed with her laptop in her hands, staring back and forth between us. "Told you he'd be happy to see me." I scoff, tipping my head forward before I brace myself, snapping my nose back into a normal position with a loud crack and a grunt.

"Where is Adanna?" Alexander shouts, aiming his anger at his daughter. "How the fuck did you let this happen? You were supposed to be watching over her, Narcissa. You let your weakness overshadow you and look at what's happened. Your fucking sister is missing!"

Narcissa flinches at his words, it's clear she's already beating herself up, her eyes are red and there's no doubt she's putting herself through hell about her choice to come and save me rather than follow her sister like she should have done. If she had just left me in that club, she would have been able to see what happened and we would have a better idea on where Ivan had taken Adanna.

Narcissa's eyes flick to mine for a brief moment before she inhales and walks into the room, placing her laptop onto her father's desk, completely ignoring his intense stare burning through the back of her skull. "The tracker on her phone was turned off approximately two hours ago."

"Two hours Narcissa. Why am I only just being informed of this now?" Alexander interrupts and once again Narcissa's eyes quickly flick to mine. She doesn't want to tell him.

"She was helping me. Ivan spiked my drink and Narcissa came to help me. Ivan is the one who has Adanna." I state. Even the words coming from my mouth make me want to put my fist through somebody's skull. How fucking dare he take what belongs to me.

Alexander stares at me for a beat, the silence becoming somewhat deafening through the small but crowded room before he finally speaks. "You need to leave before I put a bullet through your skull."

Narcissa gasps. "Father…"

"I am not leaving until Adanna is safe."

"I will stop at nothing to get my daughter back home and safe, and if that means I need to put a bullet between your fucking eyes, Mr Sidorova then believe me, I will not hesitate."

"If I thought it would get Adanna back safely, I would put a bullet between my own eyes but you don't know Ivan like I do." I snap

"It appears you don't know him at all." Alexander throws at me, busying himself as he slips his gun into the waistband of his trousers. "I will sacrifice myself for Adanna's safe return."

I scoff loudly, licking the blood from my lips before narrowing my eyes at Alexander. "She will never forgive me if I let you do that. I'll find her, Alexander. I have nothing left to lose. Without her I am nothing. My life means nothing. There is no reason for me to live without Adanna, and if she chooses to still push me away after I've brought her home to you, then so be it. I will do as she asks, I will leave the country and your family will never hear from me again. As long as she is alive. But know this, Alexander..." I take a step forward, getting into his personal space and making my intentions specifically clear. "If you don't let me leave right now, her blood will be on your hands and so help me God, I will bring down a fire on you so fucking fierce, that it will have you pissing yourself in order to put out. I will skin the flesh from your bones and force you to fucking eat it before I eventually take your last dying breath. There will be no pain you could think of great enough to come close to what I will put you through."

Narcissa stares at me with her eyes wide with horror, her fingers hovering over the keys of her laptop, her bottom lip trembling with the threat of crying while she waits for her fathers reply but I can't wait any fucking longer, we're running out of time.

"Narcissa, if you have Ivan's number can you track his whereabouts?"

Narcissa blinks a few times as if I've just pulled her out of a daydream and then she nods. "Of course, as long as he still has his mobile switched on," she says quietly, trying to look anywhere but directly at me now.

"Right. Let's go. Now!" I snap. Narcissa is through the door in a split second, her laptop tucked under her arm. Alexander watches me with his lips flattened into a grim line but he stays quiet, for once. "I will find her Alexander, and I will bring her home. I promise." I say, with a reignited need for revenge coiling my insides as I think of all of the pain I'm about to inflict on my best friend for daring to take the woman I love.

CHAPTER TWENTY-NINE
Adanna

The excruciating pain in my leg wakes me as I feel the blade being pulled from my thigh. I hiss as I open my eyes to see Ivan stood in front of me with a salacious grin on his face. The only difference from the last time I woke up in this damn place is that there seems to be some netting covering my face and my hair has been swept back. Fuck, he's put me in a veil. This guy is a psychopath, first a wedding dress and now a veil. I squint through the material, watching closely to what Ivan is doing. He has the knife that's covered in my blood in his hand, twisting it between his fingers, flicking small red droplets onto the hem of my dress.

"I know you're awake, Adanna. I felt you flinch as I ripped the knife from your flesh, the sound of your agony sounded so sweet." I refuse to respond. Searching the room once more, trying to see if there is a way out. The only door I can see is at the other end of the warehouse. I guess one way in and one way out. "There, all nice and clean for our game." Ivan mutters to the blade as though it's his friend. I glare at him, of all the people Nikolai would make friends with, it had to be a covert sociopath.

"What game are you going to play?" I ask.

"Ahh, do you want to know the rules, my blushing bride?" He sings and the words and they send a shudder through my body, his bride? This fucker is deluded if he thinks I'll marry him.

"Bride? No thanks, Ivan, I prefer the single life. More variety and let's face it, your cock for the rest of my life just doesn't do it for me." I taunt, enjoying the way he grimaces at my words.

"You don't have a choice my dear, our guest will be arriving soon to help you comply, but I think we should start the game without him. Get you a little warmed up, don't you think?" Ivan turns and grins at me, his previous knife now replaced with what looks like a very sharp boning knife in his hands. Fuck. I am going to die and a fucking bastard called Ivan is going to do it. I at least thought my end would come from a more publicised killer.

I gulp as he approaches me. Ivan runs the tip of the boning knife along my face, and I stay still as he continues down my neck and shoulder, stopping just above my ribs. I try to control my breathing, not letting him see how much I'm panicking but at this point I already know he's lost it. I know that no matter what I do, he's going to hurt me. It's pointless for me to try to move away, I'm stuck and when he chooses to stab me, I'll have no choice but to endure it. Narcissa will know that I'm missing, and she'll have already alerted Father by now and they'll be on their way to find me. As for Nikolai, I hope he's far away from here and safe but I can't shake the doubt in my mind that Nikolai knows Ivan is doing this. Was this his plan all along?

"You really are so very pretty. But you were pretty as a child too, I remember that. If Alexander hadn't taken you, you would have most likely ended up as one of Vladimir's whores. Living purely to service him and the rest of his men." He muses as he pushes the sharp tip of the blade to my skin, not quite piercing it but still causing me to wince.

"How do you know what I looked like as a child, Ivan?" I ask.

"You really don't recognise me? Or your precious Nikolai? I thought you were smart Adanna, I thought you looked at the details. Nikolai really can't be as memorable as all the women he's fucked, say he is." Ivan smirks. He's trying to hit a nerve, to make me move and pierce myself on the knife digging into my ribs. But then it clicks, unless Ivan was one of the other children at The Facility. I frown, but then would that mean Nikolai was one too? Who the fuck are these people? Is this what Father was trying to warn me about? I think back over every conversation Niko and I have had, scouring for information. Vladimir took him under his wing the day I left, right? "You were there with the girl in my bunker. Fuck. Nikolai was the older boy with us. His eyes. How could I have forgotten his eyes? How did we not know he was Vladmir's son? Why was he in that room with us!" I all but shout at him. I don't understand any of this and I'm not sure if it's due to the blood loss or the fact that I've been unconscious and I may have a bleed on the brain, but something just isn't making sense.

Ivan laughs and pushes the knife into my skin again, making me jolt. I glance down as I hiss out. He's only nicked the flesh, but blood still oozes into the fabric of my dress, staining it a vibrant red. He holds the boning knife still, ready to do it again.

"See, this game we're going to play, the rules are quite simple. Everytime you get a detail wrong, I will inflict some pain on you. How much depends on how wrong you are. You are correct about myself, Nikolai and dear Jane, who you met by the way in Russia. You had a little mishap and ended up leaving her wounded, if I recall, when she brought you some food. We were all in that rotten hole together" He cackles and I frown, remembering how she had hissed at me in Russian as though I was filth. "But you are not totally correct, Nikolai is not Vladimir's son, well not by blood. He had to earn that title. Do you want to know how Adanna? How much pain are you willing to receive to earn that truth?" he sneers at me, ripping my head back by my hair. The pain burns across my scalp but I swallow it down, not giving him the satisfaction.

I grit my teeth, staring straight into his eyes. "I don't care how Niko became his son, I want to know why he would want that? Who would want that?"

"Are you sure? It's a very interesting story. I can't tell you the why without the how. Are you ready to hear how the precious Nikolai gained his name Ubiytsa? I know you're not stupid. You know what that word means" Ivan grins a wide toothy smile. I know exactly what it means, killer. We are all killers in this industry but I have a feeling the name has another meaning behind it. My need to know gets the better of me and I nod, waiting for Ivan to continue. I'm not sure I'll ever be ready to hear whatever Niko didn't want to tell me himself. What my father had hidden from me. Ivan smiles down at me before he begins, the tip of his knife just grazing against my skin.

    "Well, you must know that you started a chain of events in The Facility when you abandoned us. Vladimir wasn't happy with how things went down. Rumours spread that he was scared of the Sinclair brothers and at that time, most people were. But Vladimir wanted to show the world that he wasn't. He decided to create a game of sorts. The person, or children as we were, were to impress him with ruthlessness and skill and would secure a place by his side and no longer live in that fucking place as a slave. As I'm sure you already know, Nikolai is the most ruthless and skilled man many of us know. We all knew he would excel. Until the day Vladimir gave him a choice. Kill one of us or let one of us succeed him. I guess he's very much like you in a way, and guess what? His *pride* didn't let him do what he should have done. He turned without a blink of an eye and shot Polina between the eyes. No one, not one of us saw it coming. He showed us all that day how ruthless he truly was and how he didn't care for any life but his own. Polina was seven-years-old. Her scream as he pulled the trigger echoed through the hall, and we all looked at him differently after that. Vladimir crowned him with his new name, Ubiytsa. We all did." Ivan smiles at me, awaiting my response, expecting me to be disgusted with what he's telling me, but I think all of my emotions have finally run dry.

"But why did he do it?" I ask. I'm disgusted, sure, but if I'd been in his position can I honestly say I would have done it any differently? Maybe, maybe not. "I do wish at this point he had chosen to shoot you. Small error on his part." I taunt. And as soon as the words slip from my mouth, Ivan digs the blade into my side, making me hiss in pain.

"He might have been ruthless but I was cunning and smart. I waited my time and earned my own recognition. I didn't have to kill an innocent child to get what I wanted. And I still won't Adanna, as we both know, you are anything but innocent so when I eventually decide to take your life, know that it will be justified."

"So you do plan to kill me?" I choke out, the pain intensifying to excruciating levels as Ivan slowly forces his knife all the way to the handle just under my ribs. I know I am going to bleed out if he doesn't do something quick.

"Not if you comply, maybe I'll get to fuck your pussy before the night is out. I want to see what finally made the great Ubiytsa turn his back on his family." He whispers as his hand strokes up my thigh and under my dress until he paws at my pussy. Thank god he left my underwear on. I squirm as I try to close my legs, trying to stop him from forcing his fingers inside of me. Ivan laughs "Like that would stop me," he spits into my face, forcing my legs apart with his fingers digging into my skin.

 Oh fuck, oh fuck. Think. I need to think. I scrunch my eyes shut tight until I snap. "I thought I was to be your bride? Don't we have to wait until the wedding night?" I say, hoping it's enough to stop him from raping me, for now at least.

 Ivan freezes, his eyes narrowing in on mine and I almost pass out again from the length that I hold my breath waiting for him to reply. "I suppose you are right, I need to see where our guest is. You're such a good girl for reminding me, my future bride. Maybe this won't be so bad after all." Ivan whispers in my ear before I feel the sting of something sharp in my neck. My vision blurs as I feel his hands grope at my flesh before he moves away from me and then darkness swallows me whole once again.

 "Wakey wakey, Adanna." I hear as a sharp pain radiates across my cheek. But the sting that I feel on my face is nothing compared to the agonising pain in my side, reminding me of the possibly fatal wound Ivan has already inflicted. I push away the thoughts that spiral as I realise I may die here. In this dark and dirty room with nobody knowing where to find my body. Opening my eyes, I see him there, smiling like it's the best day of his fucking life and it churns my stomach. What a psycho. "Why so happy?" I ask groggily.

 "It's our wedding day my sweet bride!" He all but skips as he moves away from me.

I feel sick, whatever he injected me with is making the room spin. It's like I'm drunk. I close my eyes to make it stop but it only makes it worse. "What…have you…What have you done to me?" I slur, trying not to puke over myself

"I told you I would make you more compliant, no more struggling, and look! Fuck, open your eyes, you stupid bitch." Ivan hisses, his tone getting irritated as he digs his fingers into my face. I force my eyes open, immediately noticing a strange man in the distance. "Here's the priest, he's come to marry us, my love." Ivan beams. Oh fuck he really is doing this.

"Where are my bridesmaids?" I ask sarcastically, because what the fuck else can I do? I don't see a way out of this now. Ivan laughs and I think he thinks I'm being serious.

"We don't need anyone but us love, and then I will be a Sinclair and have all the power and wealth I have worked so fucking hard for. Remember though, my darling bride, we are still playing our little game. I don't want to get too stabby on our wedding day, you have already ruined your dress" he smiles like it's a normal thing to say before forcing his lips to mine and shoving his tongue into my mouth. I bite down on his tongue causing him to rip away from my body and before I can prepare myself Ivan punches me in the face, snapping my head to the side and stealing the breath from my lungs. "You will regret that" he snaps and turns toward the priest who looks like he's going to piss himself.

"Like fuck am I doing this willingly." I hiss. My vision is blurred and there's a whistling in my ears that I didn't think was there before but I don't miss the speed at which Ivan moves as he cracks his fist into my face again, snapping my nose with the force. My head feels as if it's going to explode as it hangs forward and I watch the blood cover the front of my body. I hadn't realised how much blood I'd already lost from the stab wounds at my side but my dress is no longer white with the blood that saturates it.

 I raise my head, preparing to hit Ivan with another witty remark when an explosion rattles the building. The force of the blast knocks my chair to the ground and chaos erupts around me and I see a dark figure approaching.

 "Niko, is that you?" I laugh in my delirious state.

 "Adanna, shit. Are you alright? Can you hear me?" he asks. His soft and gentle hands whisper over my body and I know that I'll be ok.

 "Hi Ubiytsa." I smile at him. My knight in tight black armour has come to save me, I just hope he's not too late.

CHAPTER THIRTY
Nikolai

Explosions are not my style, too loud, too destructive, but Narcissa said it was the best and only way in. As soon as she located Ivan's phone to a factory site outside the city, we were on our way, my knives resting heavy against my chest with the thrumming need to sink into flesh. Narcissa hacked into the old CCTV system that covered the building and was able to go back to earlier that day and watched Ivan set a tripwire across the only door into the room where he was holding Adanna.

"He'll know you're coming, but he won't know that we know the door is rigged." Narcissa states as her fingers work furiously over her keyboard.

"Can you see her?" My grip is dangerously tight against the steering wheel.

"Yes, she's alive, but she's hurt. The images aren't great but she's got blood on her dress."

I grind my teeth, pushing the accelerator harder as I close the distance on the GPS.

"Do you have a plan?" Narcissa's voice is quiet. I know she's scared for her sister, and I would never admit it out loud, but the feeling is mutual.

I haven't been able to shake the desperate need to spill blood, it's been festering since I woke up in Narcissa's car only hours ago. If I don't release it soon, I'm afraid I'll be drawn too far into the darkness to ever see the light of day again. "Yes. I find Ivan and I kill him."

Narcissa gulps audibly as she continues typing away, the loud tapping grating on every single one of my nerves. "I'm sending the address to the others, they need to know what's happening. I've already had seventeen messages from Father. I'll tell him he needs to get the doctor ready."

"Doctor?...Exactly how hurt is she, Narcissa?" I snap, barely keeping myself together.

She ignores my question. "Here, pull in here. The entrance is behind this silo to the right. Remember, he'll know you're coming as soon as you trigger the bomb so he'll probably be hiding. The room Adanna is being held in is the second on the left. Put this in your ear, it's one way so I won't hear you if you speak back but I can be your eyes in the sky."

Eyes in the sky, did she really just say that? She obviously watches far too many spy movies while she hides in her bedroom. Her love for her sister is the only reason she's here with me now. "Yeah, yeah I got it...I've done raids before. This will be a piece of cake, and his heart will be the fucking cherry on top." I smirk as her face pales while I place the small device in my ear and get out of the car to save the woman I love.

My eyes immediately find the tripwire that sits about six inches from the floor and covers the width of the door.
"You need to trigger the bomb. Ivan has set the explosive on the other side of the door. He'll think you've been caught in the blast." Narcissa's voice filters through the small device nestled in my ear. I nod my head knowing she can see every movement I make. I look around for something to throw at the line. I need to be close enough to trigger it but out of the blast radius. I pray to God that if by some serious stroke of bad fucking luck I do get injured, that she has her own plan to get her sister the fuck out of here alive. I spot a length of pipe laying against a wall. Perfect! "Wait!" Narcissa snaps just as I'm about to roll the pipe and I curse under my breath. If this device was two-way she would be getting a fucking earful. "There's somebody else in the room with them…He…He looks like a priest?" What the fuck is a priest doing in there? She's obviously as confused as I am but I can't wait any longer. I desperately need to get inside. I roll the pipe along the ground with enough force to hit the line and run as fast as I can in the opposite direction. The blast is huge, bigger than I anticipated and I fly through the air and land with a hard thump. "Niko, are you ok? How much fucking explosive did he use? Niko. Niko. Can you hear me? Fuck!"

"I'm here," is all I can grunt out as I pull myself up and brush the debris from my clothes. I know she can't hear me but I'm hoping my movements are enough to get her to stop shouting.

"Thank fuck for that! I was seconds away from calling Dad. Now, go get our girl."

As I make my way through the blast zone, I can't help but wonder if Ivan got his calculations wrong. Maths never was his strong point. This was far too much C4 to take out a single man. I shake my head and unsheath my blades. As I reach the room that Narcissa said he was holding Adanna in, I realise just how wrong Ivan got it. The blast radius was much larger and half the room has been blasted away. My eyes narrow in on Adanna immediately, tied to a chair that's been knocked over in the blast but as Ivan stares wide eyed and panic stricken, a grin cracks my face. I'm going to enjoy taking this out on him and he knows it but he isn't my priority right now.

"Shit! Adanna! Are you alright? Can you hear me?" I panic as I realise the state of her. Her pale skin is a fucked up patchwork of blood, bruises and open wounds, even her nose looks broken with dried and fresh blood coating her chin and neck. And…is she wearing a fucking wedding dress? It's hard to reign in my anger but I have to get her out of here. Ivan can wait. Even if I spend the rest of my days tracking him down, I will ensure he pays for every single bit of pain he has caused her.

Adanna lifts her head and smiles at me but her eyes are completely unfocused and her words are slurred. "Hi Ubiytsa."

"I think she's been drugged." I hear Narcissa whisper through my ear and I immediately snap back.

"Yeah, no fucking shit Sherlock."

"Holmes and Watson…Whatson…What son?" Adanna mumbles as her head lols back.

"Fuck, Printsessa. I'm going to get you out of here, it's ok." I assure her as I cut the ties that bind her to the chair and frantically trace my hands across her body to work out where the blood is coming from.

"Do you like my dress, Ubiytsa? I'm getting married." Adanna sighs with a smile as I hook my arms under her legs and around her back to lift her from the floor.

"Stop calling me that." I snap, "And the only man that will be marrying you is me, Adanna, and it won't be while you're bleeding and barely conscious."

I quickly glance around the room. The corners are dark and my view is only made worse by the dust that still lingers in the air. He's still here, that door was the only way in and out of this room so I know Ivan is still in here and I can't help but hesitate for a fraction of a second as I push back the urge to kill him. A movement to my left immediately draws my attention, it's the priest. He's been knocked over in the blast and unfortunately he'll survive his minor injuries. But I'll make sure that Narcissa finds out who he is so I can make him repent.

"Get fucking moving, Nikolai!" Narcissa shouts through the ear piece. For such a timid woman, she really is bossy.

I make it five feet to the door as a hot white pain pierces my shoulder blade. I falter, my feet scuffing beneath me as I grit my teeth, biting back the pain. "He's behind you! Turn around! Now!" Narcissa screams. I turn quickly, cursing Adanna for her lack of consciousness as I face Ivan.

His face and clothes are covered in dirt from the blast but he seems otherwise unharmed as he stands partly shrouded in shadows, toying with a blade. "You won't leave here with her."

"You won't be leaving at all." I growl, subconsciously tightening my arms around Adanna, hissing at the radiating pain across my shoulder. "What the fuck, Ivan?"

"This is *my* revenge, Ubiytsa. This is where *my* story starts." Ivan bellows, giving me a split second to react as he pulls his arm back and lets the knife fly towards us.

I crouch quickly, the blade missing my head by centimetres as Ivan throws his head back with a sardonic laugh and Narcissa shouts through my ear. I stand Adanna up and hold her to my chest as I reach back to feel for the knife embedded in my back. Fuck, this is going to hurt. Grasping tight and clenching my jaw, I rip the blade free, pushing past the pain and sending it straight back to Ivan. I don't wait to see if it hits because from the scream that rips from his throat, I know I got him good. I pick Adanna up and run towards the priest who is standing, staring open mouthed at Ivan, clutching his rosary beads to his chest. Adanna is my priority but this is now a necessity to ensure her safety. The blood pumping through my veins is toxic with the need to make him pay for what he's done. More so than my want to kill Vladimir ever was. Ivan has touched what doesn't belong to him. He made her bleed, he attempted to marry her. He has touched the woman I love, and for that he will die.

I lie Adanna up against the wall, her eyes fluttering open as she rests her head back and her face lifts into an almost drunken smile. "Hi," she sighs. I press my lips into her forehead, and a warm rush shudders through my body. I have never felt this way about anyone, let alone a woman before. It's confusing, intoxicating and frustrates the fuck out of me, but it feels right. I have never felt this overwhelming need to throw my life down and sacrifice everything I have for another human being. Sure, I would've died for my men, but for her, for the woman with hair as black as my heart, a body that bends to my every touch and that tastes like the sweetest sin against my lips, I would succumb to a life of endless torture to ensure her safety.

Stroking my thumb across her cheek, I whisper gently against her hair. "You're safe now, Printsessa." Before pushing away from her and grabbing the priest by his collar, pulling his face within inches of my own. "You leave her side, I will torture you in ways that the darkest of monsters in your dreams could conjure. No God will recognise you when you enter the afterlife and you will spend the rest of eternity suffering in the pits of hell." I shove his body back against the wall, taking the knife from my thigh and tearing his vestment. "Apply pressure to her wounds." I snap, shoving the fabric into his hands and forcing him to his knees beside Adanna who looks as if she might throw up.

"Yes sir, yes sir…please, just please don't…don't kill me," the priest stutters as he presses the cloth onto Adanna's wounds and she winces.

Ivans rattled voice forces me back into the room. The blade caught his shoulder. A few inches to the left and I'd have hit his carotid. "I won't let you take this from me, Sidorova. I deserve everything you've ever been given." The look in his eyes is wild, almost feral as he spits his words at me. His face is covered in sweat, his hair sticking to his forehead. He looks nothing like the man I know.

"She doesn't belong to you, Ivan." I snarl, fingering the blade at my hip, ready to attack in an instant. Narcissa has fallen quiet in my ear, and if I know anything about her and the love she has for her sister, she's already on her way to the building to help get Adanna out.

"Oh, that's right…She belongs to you, doesn't she? She screams so sweetly bent over for you…Tell me, boss, did her father like to see his pride and joy being railed by a child killer?" Ivan smirks. "I bet I could make her scream louder."

I remove my blade, my vision tunnelling in on my target. Our bodies collide with a loud thump as I tackle him. I swing my arm, slicing across his stomach before a heavy weight cracks across my jaw. I pull back, blinking my vision straight before landing a quick jab to Ivan's chest, knocking the air from his lungs as he sputters, stumbling backwards. "We went through hell together. You were supposed to be my friend, Ivan. My brother." I growl, the intense anger coursing through me burns in my veins, pumping my body with toxic emotions.

Ivan lets out a low cackle, spitting out a blob of bloodied saliva as he presses his hands to the cut along his stomach. "No. *I* went through fucking hell, Nikolai. Do you know what I had to endure to even get a second look from Vladimir? The things he made me do. The people he made me kill?"

"You weren't the only one who had to kill!" I snap, watching his moves carefully as he paces.

"You were never made to experience the shit he put me through. You may have been his chosen one, and in the fucked up version of that delusional world he lived in, the one he called his son. But it was me who was forced to do the shit nobody else would. When you were getting your cock sucked by all of his whores, I was the one cutting the heads off of those who were late on payments. I was his fucking attack dog. He treated me like shit. And your precious fucking Dimitri was no different." Ivan sneers. His body looks as if it's turning a sickly shade of grey due to the blood loss but he's not giving up yet.

"They were never good men, Ivan, you knew that when we were just children and woke up in that fucking room with no food and we were forced to build guns until our fingers bled!"

"You don't deserve her!" Ivan screams, yanking his hair in a frustrated manner. "You don't fucking deserve to be with her."

I know I don't deserve to be with Adanna, not after all of the terrible things I've ever done but that doesn't make the words sting any less, forcing the truth out into the open.

I open my mouth to reply, the betrayal at what he's done overrides everything I think I know about loyalty, but a small cry of pain and whispered protests. "No, you can't move her!" Gains both of our attention. Narcissa has come to help Adanna, but the priest is refusing to let her.

Ivan's wildly crazed eyes widen as he watches Narcissa hook Adanna's arm around her shoulders and she attempts to lift her from the floor. He immediately screams at them, rushing forward in a desperate attempt to intervene.

I move quickly, slamming his body into the wall, holding my blade into his throat, pressing the tip into his Adam's apple. "I think it's about time I taught you what happens when you touch what doesn't belong to you." I smirk. Ivan's throat bobs as he swallows nervously, the edge of my knife nicking the skin and causing him to wince. "What's wrong, Ivan? Not a fan of other people making you bleed?" I taunt and I bring my other fist to his face, cracking his nose against my knuckles at the same time as stabbing my knife into his thigh.

Ivan screams out in pain, buckling over to press on the deep bleeding wound. "The grebany ubludoc."

You fucking bastard, he cries, staring at me with blood stained teeth and a grimace on his face.

"I haven't even started yet," I growl, fisting my hand into his hair and yanking his head down to connect with my knee. I slam into his face before shoving him onto the floor, forcing him down to his knees, I move him, like a puppet master guiding its toys across the stage. "Where did you touch her?" I demand, wrenching his head back at an awkward angle so he can see my face.

Ivan hisses out in pain and his hands grab tightly around my wrist, but beneath the pain a sick smile twists his face. His teeth are smeared red with his blood as he smirks at me. "Are you worried I've replaced your touch with mine?"

The thought of his hands over Adanna's body makes me shudder. A shockwave of coiled up anger wraps itself around my insides, spiralling up my spinal cord and burying itself into my brain, darkening my vision. "She is mine!" I roar as I tighten my grip on him, making him cry out. I bring my knife to his throat again. "Any last words, *friend*?" I hiss, applying pressure to the blade, the blood already trickling from his neck.

"I'm glad I took the opportunity to enjoy all that she had to offer. Her unconscious body holds no secrets, Ubiytsa, I can see why you don't want to share her." Ivan sneers.

The coiling tension suddenly snaps and like a vicious bolt of lightning cracking across the sky, I strike. "Do smerti." *Until death,* I spit, pulling my blade up before slamming it into his throat. His eyes pop as the knife pierces his skin and I see the panic set in as his screams of pain turn to gargled slurs while he struggles in my hold.

    Blood pools at my feet as I watch the life of my long time friend, my brother in all but blood, drain away in front of me. I feel no remorse as his eyes slowly fade, but a strange sense of relief and regret churning in the pit of my stomach. He deserved to be tortured, to be kept alive for years on end with little food and barely any water so I could take away a piece of him, bit by bit until there was nothing left of his body to keep him alive. But my anger took hold, he taunted me with Adanna and the things he had done and as if my body was reacting before my brain could catch up, his blood was already coating my hand.

    "Nikolai, we need to get out of here, She's losing too much blood!" a panicked Narcissa screams at me, immediately dragging me from my downward spiral. Ivan's body hits the floor with a thud as I rip my knife free of his throat, slathered in his blood. I wipe it clean against my thigh before slipping it into its sheath and rush back to where the priest and Narcissa are trying to get Adanna on her feet.

    "Move!" I snap, scooping Adanna into a bridal hold against my chest, her small whimper is the only thing that lets me know she's still conscious, but barely. The irony is not lost on me that she is in a wedding dress as I carry her from this hell hole but I would give my right arm to rip it from her body and set it on fire. "Burn this place to the ground, Narcissa!" I shout behind me and I make my way out of the factory, the priest isn't far behind me, staying quiet but keeping pace. He's lucky I don't leave him in there to meet his fucking maker.

"Is that really necessary?" Narcissa shouts back to me. After carefully laying Adanna onto the backseats of the car, I turn and glare at Narcissa. "Fine, fine, I'll get on it," she rolls her eyes as she pulls her phone from her pocket and quickly makes a call to arrange for the building to be demolished, ASAP.

Turning around I realise the priest has fled, something I note that will have to be dealt with at a later date. Maybe I should have killed him after all. "There's a team on the way. This place will be up in flames before we get home." Narcissa states as we both jump in the car. Her behind the wheel and me in the back with Adanna's head resting on my lap. And sure enough, as Narcissa races us back towards the Sinclair residence, a blanket of smoke and flames lights up the skies of London.

"I love you, Niko." Adanna croaks, and I smile, even covered in blood and dirt, she still takes my breath away. Her eyes flicker closed and I grab her chin between my fingers, pinching it slightly to keep her with me. "Stay with me, Printsessa. You're mine now. You can't get away from me that easily." I whisper. "Just hold on a bit longer, there's a doctor waiting."

The End.

EPILOGUE
12 MONTHS LATER
Nikolai

I watch, completely mesmerised by the sight of my thick cock sinking deep between the slick folds of Adanna's pussy, stretching her out to fit me. "Fuck, Printsessa, your pussy looks so good when it swallows my cock." I pull all the way out to slowly slide straight back in and the warmness of her core wraps around me, sending a jolt straight into my balls. "Do you know what makes it even better?" I ask, leaning over her body and sinking my teeth into her neck, sucking on the skin until she hisses out at me. "Finally fucking you as my wife."

Adanna whimpers softly in my ear, hooking her heels into my ass, pulling me deeper between her legs. "Yes, Niko."

"Who am I?" I ask, ripping the front of her wedding dress down to expose her ample breasts, thrusting into her.

"My husband," Adanna gasps as I take her left nipple between my teeth and tug harshly on the sensitive bud.

"That's right, and who do you belong to?" I switch my attention to the right, tugging with my teeth before circling my tongue around her nipple again.

"You, Niko. I belong to you." Adanna cries, meeting me thrust for thrust with her back arched up from the table.

I couldn't wait to get her into bed, our wedding celebration was still in full swing down the hall but the moment I had the chance to whisk her away, I took it. Pulling her into the first empty room I found and laying her onto the first surface available. I fumbled with the netted layers of her ivory gown like a teenage boy getting his dick wet for the first time as she made quick work of my belt, freeing my solid erection before opening her legs for me, showcasing her glistening cunt. I was ravenous and desperate and had been hard as a fucking rock from the moment she stepped foot down the aisle. But seeing her baring herself to me as my wife made my cock throb with an insatiable need to be inside her. One that couldn't be ignored.

A year ago, almost to the day, my whole world came crashing down on me in a violent and catastrophic torrent of destruction. Adanna's life slipped away right before my eyes and there was nothing I could do to stop it. She lost too much blood and I was rendered helpless. Completely helpless while the woman I loved fell unconscious and I was unable to bring her back. I can still hear Narcissa screaming at me and her father screaming at the doctor to save her as I stood watching the scene unravel before me, her blood stained my skin as if it were burned onto me, reminding me of the life that was being taken. In the days that followed, I refused to leave Adanna's side. For eight days she lay unconscious, but alive thanks to several blood transfusions, and I vowed every single day that I would one day make her my wife.

"Niko, I'm going to come!" Adanna gasps, as she arches into me further. Her tits bounce with each brutal thrust and I can't stop myself from sucking on them once again. I hook my arms under her ass, lifting her for a better angle, hitting that tender spot deep inside her walls.

"That's it, come on your husband's cock. Show me how much of a good girl you are." I order before spitting onto her swollen cunt. I tilt my hips, fucking her fast and deep, and take her weight with one arm, bringing my other to her clit, adding that friction I know she craves with my fingers. I can play her body like a finely tuned guitar, knowing exactly which strings to pull. I apply a little more pressure and just like that, Adanna cries out as her body begins to shudder.

"Yes. Yes. Oh Yes." she sings as her thighs tighten around me and her pussy clamps around my cock, sucking me in balls deep. I pull back and slam forward, scraping the legs of the table across the floor with the force and Adanna screams as she gushes around me, completely coating my thighs with her cum. "Fuck, Niko!" she gasps, rocking her hips against my cock.

"I love you, Wife," I growl, feeling the feral snake of ecstasy winding its way up my spine.

"I love you, Husband," Adanna chokes. My hips hammer into her, the pleasure building like a fire before it erupts and I come so hard that I buckle forward, collapsing onto her chest as my vision blurs. My cock throbs as I fill Adanna's cunt with my cum and I ground myself, nestling my face snugly between her tits with the sound of her rapidly beating heart beneath my ear as we ride out the high. Alive, she is alive, and she is all mine.

It took everything I had to leave the country and fly back home to Russia after Adanna was finally given the all clear. I was all too aware of what I was leaving behind, but I knew I had a job to do, and I'd already made every excuse I could not to face my responsibilities. Alexander also came close to strangling the life out of me more than once, so I knew I had to give him time to come to terms with the fact that I had proposed to Adanna, and she had said yes, accepting her mothers ring as a promise of new beginnings.

With the help of Narcissa and Odette we were able to shut down Vladimir's facility and return the children to their families, ensuring those whose families had been killed were put into the correct organisations to help rehome them with new and loving parents. Bogdan suffered a slow and painful death for all of the innocent lives he had taken and his body was left to rot under the rubble of The Facility after Maksim and Aleksei burnt the entire building down.

I held a meeting on my first night home and to Jane's horror, I gave news of Ivan's treachery, and there I informed the entire compound that we would no longer be associated with the same means of income that Vladimir had dragged us into. Going forward, our guns were to be made by our own hands, we would transport, stock and sell, and anybody who objected, would be granted a bullet to the head.

I knew I would never be able to bring Adanna back home, it would be too dangerous and I would never risk her life for my own selfish need ever again. But I also knew that I was tied to these people who now looked to me for a way forward. Maksim and Aleksei stepped into their new roles and grew into strong leaders at my side, allowing me my time to travel between worlds, between the two opposites of my life I now seemed to be living. For now, it works and although it's not ideal, we have learnt to deal with it. We never really know what tomorrow will bring, but for now, we live to fight another day.

What's next?

So now that Adanna and Nikolai's story is over, we bet you're wondering what the hell happens next. Right? Well buckle up because book two of The Deadly Sins Series is coming soon and Odette has been keeping a secret that could destroy her entire family. And trust us, you're going to want to find out what that is.

We have lots of exciting ideas and projects that we're always working between, so to make sure you don't miss out on event information or new sneak peeks at our WIP, be sure to check out our website and follow us on our Instagram profiles.

About the Authors

S.J Noble

S.J Noble is an adventurer, reader, dreamer, writer, mother and Aries star sign. S.J Noble loves watching horror and crime shows and movies, some of her favourites include Dexter, Saw, The Shining and Luther. She also loves anything fantasy such as Harry Potter, Lord of the Rings, The Hobbit and Star Wars.

S.J Noble lives in England and spends her days working in the local hospital with S.L Wisdom, going to the gym and rounding up her two strong-willed sons. When those activities are not occupying her time she can often be found reading any book with a shocking plot twist and an anti-hero as the main character. Her favourite authors include Thomas Hardy, Bronte sisters, J. Bree and Harlan Coben. She's a slut for the villain but let's face it, if you have gotten this far so are you!

S.L Wisdom

S.L Wisdom is an aspiring new author who lives in England with her husband and daughter. She enjoys reading a wide variety of genres, favouring authors such as Stephen King, M.W Craven and H.D Carlton and always has a soft spot for the bad guys (somebody has to be rooting for them). When she isn't working at her regular job, her downtime is spent listening to anything from AC/DC to Carrie Underwood, frantically going over the manuscript before publishing, baking cookies and cakes with her daughter and drinking tea with an unhealthy amount of biscuits.

Without the constant love, support and words of encouragement from her husband, who endures the bedtime routines and early weekend wake ups so that she can keep on writing until early hours of the morning, she knows that she would never have had the confidence or the time to start this journey, and to be able to publish not just one, but three books, (and counting) and for that, she will forever be grateful to him.

Acknowledgements

First and foremost we'd like to give a big thank you to Heather and Erin, our Beta readers. Thank you for asking, thank you for being involved, thank you for hyping us up on all of the hard work we've put in. We love you both immensely and we appreciate you more than you could know.

Of course a **HUGE** thank you goes to our amazing editor, Ria. You are an angel, a total badass and we're super super grateful to have you alongside us on our book journey. Three books in already, and there's so many more to come. You're an integral part of our team and it's safe to say we couldn't have got this far without you.

Thank you to Francessca at Wingfield Designs for designing such a beautiful front cover for our book series, and always being so patient when we have no idea what we're doing, which is most of the time.

A special thank you to Dina Pietraru, for saving our asses when we realised that google translate Oh pancaked us! IYKYK.

And last but not least, we'd like to thank you, reader. For supporting us in our journey. We love you. .

For more information about both S.J Noble and S.L Wisdoms upcoming releases and signing events please visit the sites listed below:
Website: https://wisdomandnoble.com/
Facebook readers group:
https://www.facebook.com/groups/760611272268230/
Instagram: S.JNoble and S.L_Wisdom

Please check out our amazing editor Ria at Moon and Bloom Editing.
Facebook page:
http://www.facebook.com/moonandbloomediting
Instagram: Moonandbloomediting

Also, if you're on your own publishing journey and in need of a book cover be sure to check out Francessca at Wingfield Designs.
Facebook page:
https://www.facebook.com/groups/wingfielddesigns/
Website: Book Cover Design | Wingfield Designs

Printed in Great Britain
by Amazon